MW01230009

FATE CHALLENGED

Book Two

Tara Lytle

Scribbled Reads

SCRIBBLED READS

Editorial work by Eschler Editing

Published by Scribbled Reads

E-Book ISBN: 9781960319005

Paperback ISBN: 978-1-960319-02-9

Hardcover ISBN: 978-1-960319-04-3

DEDICATION

To those who fight hidden battles with cancer, depression, diabetes and Evans Syndrome. I pray one day you win the war.

ABERRON

PORTS END

JAYDORIA

DRAMERA

FRESTAN

HAYLORE

STRELL

BERUND

ORINDALER

N

W   E

M

KORRUN

CARASMILLE

LAND

THIMBLETON

TRIVAIL FOREST

ABERRON CLIFFS

PRASTIS

LOCHENLOCK

KISTER

SAREN

MANARIA

CAILEN

PENDRA

CALLAN OUTPOST

NEDRA

...... Isabelle's Journey

ABERRON

CARASMILLE

MAJELLA

JAMAYLIN ISLANDS

NISTIER

WEYUT

KASHTINE

DREGAITIA

RAYLORE

ELLA

MACHRA

RAYNORA

HESTAS

SARZE

PROLOGUE

I HUDDLED IN A CORNER of Saren's one-room school, trembling and hugging my knees. Scattered paper and old bread surrounded me. Alone—fresh with fear—I breathed fast. I waited for the schoolteacher to come back with Adel. For a moment, I allowed myself to wish for my parents. Momma's warm lilac-scented hugs. Da's laughter as he spun me in his strong arms. A single tear hit my cheek. *Momma and Da are dead.*

A boy close to my five years of age entered the room. His straw-colored hair swung as he looked about, and his pale blue eyes settled on me. He trotted forward, a small smile on his lips. "Hi, I'm Stefan."

I cowered, afraid he'd find something to throw at me too when I didn't speak.

He kicked some of the garbage away with his boot and sat, not looking offended like the others. "You don't talk, do you?"

I shook my head.

"My da said something bad happened to your folks, that's why you've come here." Stefan eyed me.

I knew that look well. I saw it every day on the faces of Nathan and Adel, my new parents. No, *guardians*, they called themselves. *Momma and Da are dead.*

"Can you talk at all? If you really wanted to?" he asked earnestly.

I nodded.

"You just don't want to, is all." Stefan smiled brightly. "That's all right. I can talk for you and me." He put his hand in his pocket. "Wanna see something?"

I shrugged.

He pulled his hand out and opened it, showing a shiny, sparkling black rock in the middle of his palm. "Pretty, huh?"

I leaned forward to see better and nodded.

Stefan grinned.

I decided I liked his friendly face.

"I got lots of rocks, all colors. Wanna see 'em?"

I nodded and smiled slowly.

"Great." He reached for my hand. I let him take it, beginning a fast friendship.

CHAPTER ONE

"I AM IN LOVE WITH you, Isabelle," Andrew said.

Usually I would reply that I loved him, too, but since he'd chosen to announce this in front of his parents, my brother, his cousin, and Malsin, I paused. We were congregated in the family sitting room. King Brian, Henry, and I played a game of Pilfer. Malsin and Queen Averly, engaged in friendly conversation, sat in soft chairs near the roaring fire. My brother, Joshua, and Andrew had only just arrived.

The strength in Andrew's tone amazed me. "Every day, I fall more in love with you—your smile, the sparkle in your eyes, your tenacity and passion. I cannot bear another second wondering if I will ever have you by my side."

I blinked several times to hold back the tears threatening to overflow and spill down my cheeks. No words ever spoken had sounded so beautiful or rung so deep in my soul. I felt my heart might burst with love, affection, and, most of all, devotion.

Andrew took a deep breath and asked, "Isabelle Elaine Mirran, would you please accept a proposal of marriage and do me the honor of becoming my wife?"

My eyes widened. I looked to my brother and guardian, Joshua, and Andrew's father, King Brian. Joshua had been against my relationship with the prince from the start. Was he seriously letting Andrew propose? Did King Brian think I was suitable enough for his son? Joshua shrugged and King Brian smiled. I took it that they'd given in—at least my brother had. I did not know King Brian well enough to discern his true feelings on the matter.

Past them, Malsin and Queen Averly smiled, and Henry, Andrew's cousin, grinned. I saw no ill feelings anywhere.

Saying yes to Andrew meant I would eventually become queen, a position I'd never wanted. I despised attention. And yet, my chest burned with my love for Andrew. The thought of giving him up sent a thrill of fear through my veins. Losing him scared me more than being queen. So even if he did come with an unwanted job and an abundance of scrutiny, I could not survive without him.

As I opened my mouth to accept his proposal, the door opened. A soldier stood panting, his hands on his knees as he fought for breath.

"Dregaitia—" he choked out, still gasping heavily from his apparent flat-out run to notify King Brian. "The Dregans are attacking."

Queen Averly and Henry gasped. Joshua and Malsin frowned deeply.

King Brian said with exasperation, "Oh, great."

The tender moment between Andrew and me shattered. A shiver went down my spine as the room plunged into ice. So much for our nice quiet night in the royals' personal family sitting room.

I resented the soldier delivering the news, but he couldn't have known that Andrew had been proposing. An offer of marriage seemed inconsequential compared to another country attacking ours. Yet I wished things had unfolded differently.

Everyone's eyes darted between Andrew and me and the soldier. I smiled ruefully at Andrew. "Shall we wait?"

He shook his head. "I won't be able to concentrate on anything else without your answer."

I leaned forward and stopped a breath away from his face. "I love you. My answer is yes."

"Thank the Gods." His blue eyes danced. Closing the distance, he pressed his lips quickly to mine and then stood behind my chair to face the soldier.

Joshua, Malsin, and Andrew's family smiled and offered congratulations. My family now, I supposed. It was hard to imagine King Brian as family when his law sentenced me to death so recently. I saw him as king, not a father-in-law.

"Thank you," Andrew and I said.

King Brian studied the two of us. Seeming satisfied that we were ready to focus our attention on the new threat, he turned to the soldier. The man appeared a tad uncomfortable to have interrupted us.

"Where?" King Brian asked.

The soldier spoke in a rush. "They've overtaken Prastis."

"No!" I cried, my voice strangulated. *Saren's sister town.* The small fishing community was only a four-hour walk from Saren. Nathan often traveled there for business, twice a month for two days. I knew those people almost as well as I knew the residents of Saren.

Eyes flicked to me for a moment with varying degrees of curiosity. Andrew rested his hands on my shoulders and squeezed.

King Brian demanded answers from the soldier. "What else do you know?"

"Nothing else, Highness," The soldier said. "We're gathering information from a messenger at the Thimbleton outpost as we speak."

"Did the messenger come from Prastis?" King Brian asked.

"No, he came from Saren, Highness," the soldier responded.

Stefan. He was the best messenger they had. Dread filled my entire being. I clutched my stomach with unease.

King Brian rose. "I expect a full report by the time I reach my study. You're dismissed."

The soldier bowed and ran out of the room.

King Brian said to Andrew and me, "I suggest we wait to announce your engagement to Aberronians until we have a handle on the Dregans."

I saw no reason to object. Andrew apparently didn't either, because we said "Fine" together.

"Isabelle, walk with me," King Brian ordered.

I jumped out of my seat to follow as he exited the sitting room. Nerves gripped me at being singled out. I didn't want to be a disappointment to him, especially since Andrew and I were now to be married. Andrew and the rest of our family trailed close behind us.

"Tell me what you know about Prastis."

I jogged to keep up with the king's long strides. "It's a small fishing community on the coast, no more than five hundred people. Saren regularly trades crops for their fish."

"How far is Prastis from Saren?" King Brian asked.

"Four hours on foot in good weather," I answered. "The whole area is made up of simple folk, not fighters, and no mages."

"Easy targets for Dregaitia," King Brian growled.

My stomach churned.

Dregaitia was a large country separated from Aberron by a body of water known as the Sea Traveler's Channel or the channel for short. Prastis was situated in the narrowest part of the channel. On a clear day, you could see Dregaitia from their harbor. They had kept their lands closed to Aberron for hundreds of years. I knew nothing of their customs. I had read stories of their ruthlessness in battle when they tried to conquer Aberron three hundred years ago and failed. I read they kept no prisoners of war. They would strike down men, women, and children who got in their way with no qualms.

We arrived at the king's study, where he conducted most of his business. A sandy-haired, blue-eyed soldier stood in front of the doors. We stepped inside and took seats at the long table. The soldier remained standing.

King Brian addressed him. "James."

He bowed. "Highness, the Thimbleton outpost has reported that a messenger arrived carrying the seals of the orate judges of Saren and Prastis. The Dregans have attacked Prastis and sent the residents fleeing to Saren. The Dregans claim an Aberronian ship attacked and destroyed one of their ports on the channel last night. They are seeking retaliation."

A new man entered the room and bowed quickly. "Highness, the Barras outpost is under siege from the Dregans. They say they are grossly outnumbered, and men are dropping like flies. They don't think they can hold it."

"Above Prastis is the Barras outpost," King Brian said mostly to himself.

"Aberron Cliffs services the Barras outpost," I said from memory. "They raise livestock and trade with Saren for crops and Prastis for fish."

"Retreat," King Brian said firmly. "Have the men at the Barras outpost gather as many as they can and move to Saren to await further instructions."

"Yes, Highness." The man hightailed out of the room.

King Brian returned his gaze to James. "Gather more information. Which Dregan port did the ship attack? Did anyone else see it? I need numbers on the Dregans. Who is leading them?"

James nodded and left to seek out answers.

"This is ludicrous," Joshua said. "No sane Aberronian would attack Dregaitia."

"Was magic used to get the information to us quickly?" I asked.

Andrew spoke. "Yes. Blue magic on gold can communicate over long distances." He gestured to the locket he wore.

"Joshua, how soon can you get the First and Second Waves ready?" King Brian asked.

"Eight hours," Joshua said with confidence.

There was a rap on the door and another soldier entered, clutching a note. "Highness, this just came for you. I'm told it's urgent." He handed the paper to King Brian. "I am to wait outside for your response." He left.

King Brian opened the note. His eyes darted across the page and then widened.

"What is it, dear?" Queen Averly asked.

King Brian folded the note but kept it clutched in his hand. "It's Braidus. He is aware of the Dregan attack and wants to meet. He says he lived in Dregaitia and was a member of the king's inner court. He is asking to be reinstated as a citizen and desires to help in our fight against them."

I stiffened, then discovered everyone else had too.

"He wants a pardon?" Andrew asked, his face masked into something unreadable. It reminded me of the way he looked when Braidus told me to end our courtship.

"Yes," King Brian said.

"No," Joshua and I said simultaneously.

Braidus freed, after killing my parents? After kidnapping me and Henry? My stomach rolled at the thought.

"No." I rose from my seat.

Joshua also stood, and both of us paced on opposite sides of the table, arms folded across our chests. This had to be a trick. Maybe Braidus was in league with the Dregans, especially if he once lived there with access to their king.

King Brian sighed and rubbed his temples, clearly deeply troubled. Queen Averly placed a hand on his back and rubbed. I felt a pang in my heart at the predicament of the king, but then memories of my recent kidnapping and near execution flashed through my mind and my anger at Braidus rose to the surface.

King Brian attempted a smile but faltered. "What should I do?" he asked his wife.

"I think you should meet with Braidus. He is your son," she said softly.

"How are we to reconcile when I can't ignore his murderous acts? He must pay for his crimes, and you know his penalty would be death," he said to her with grief.

Braidus deserved to die for his crimes.

"He is all I have of Hannah, Averly. I swore an oath to his mother that I would protect him, and I've failed." Tears glistened in his eyes. His face crumpled in pain. "I cannot sentence him again."

What? He murdered my parents! Did their deaths count for nothing?

"Then don't," Queen Averly said simply. "Leave it up to the Gods."

King Brian stiffened. "A Trial by Fire?"

She nodded, her lips in a thin line. "If the Gods see fit to spare him, then pardon Braidus. If they don't, then they will carry out the judgment. Meet with Braidus and give him the option. Let him decide."

King Brian took a breath and exhaled slowly. Then he nodded with what appeared to be grim determination. His shoulders straightened. "Agreed."

I buried my face in my hands. Stress rose exponentially until I found it hard to breathe. I didn't know what a Trial by Fire was or how King Brian could get the Gods to judge Braidus, but I understood the pardon part well enough. I didn't want to accept it. I couldn't. I had little doubt that with Braidus free, I'd see a whole lot more of him than I wanted. How could I face him again and not want to kill him?

King Brian cast his eyes on Joshua and me. "If the Gods deem Braidus worthy, then he will be pardoned. Little is known to me about the Dregans. If my son truly did live in Dregaitia, his knowledge will be indispensable in our efforts to resolve our conflict. You don't have to agree with my judgment, but my decision is final. There will be consequences if either of you decide to go against this."

Joshua frowned, but his eyes held resignation. "You are my king and a father to me. I'll follow your guidance till the end of time."

Andrew stood and pulled me into his arms. My cheek pressed into his cotton shirt, sending a wave of calm through me.

I took a breath and said words I thought I'd never hear myself say to King Brian: "I might need help to keep me in check, but I'll adhere to your wishes just the same as Joshua. You're my king and soon-to-be family as well."

King Brian eyed me with what appeared to be admiration. It surprised me. "You shall have it. I appreciate your willingness and honesty."

"You're welcome," I said softly.

"He kidnapped me too, you know," Henry said grudgingly.

"And?" King Brian raised an eyebrow.

Henry sighed. "Yes, I'll be good."

"You'd better," King Brian said severely.

"You'll be all right." Andrew led me back to my seat but kept our hands entwined. He leaned in close and whispered, "I'll keep you safe, love."

My heart warmed. I loved Andrew's ability to make me feel protected in a sea of worry. I admit I had questioned our relationship when Braidus held me captive, but Andrew's actions now reminded me why I could not lose him. He anchored me.

King Brian rose and procured a piece of paper and a pen. He scribbled a few lines.

Needing to take my thoughts away from murdering Braidus, I contemplated my engagement to Andrew. I felt a mix of trepidation and joy at the thought of becoming his wife: scared because he was the crown prince and I wasn't thrilled to become royalty; happy because I loved Andrew more than anything. I couldn't wait to spend the rest of my life with him.

King Brian folded the paper and stamped it with a seal. He walked to the door, handed it to the waiting soldier, and then returned to his seat.

Queen Averly rose. "This will be a long night of strategic planning and preparations to ready the soldiers for war. The sooner we get the Dregans out, the better. I will instruct the kitchens to make refreshments. We must keep our strength."

"We cannot afford a minute of sleep." King Brian sighed.

Malsin spoke. "I have a solution in my room that will help. I started working on it after Isabelle's incident with the chains. I wanted something that would keep me awake and sustained for an extended period should I have a patient who needs round-the-clock care again. Fortunately, I made a big batch of it, though not intentionally." He looked to King Brian. "Would you like to try it?"

"Yes, I would," King Brian said.

Malsin followed Queen Averly out.

King Brian retrieved the magical map Haldren had given him, the one that allowed people to see a city as it stood. Just as he unfurled it, James entered.

He bowed. "Highness, an Aberronian merchant ship called the Wind Rogue has just docked at the Elan outpost with news of the attack on the Dregan port—"

King Brian cut him off. "I want the name."

James read from a piece of paper. "The Dreskenar port."

I recognized it. "That's the narrowest part of the channel. On a clear day, you can see the Dreskenar port from Prastis."

"Thank you, Isabelle," King Brian said.

James continued, using his notes for reference. "Two Nistier ships also witnessed the attack. The captain of the Wind Rogue says his sister ship, the Night Crusader, captained by his cousin, was armed with supplies for the Callan outpost. The Night Crusader suddenly veered into the Dregan's half of the channel and set the Dreskenar port ablaze with bombs thrown from their ship. The Dregans destroyed them with bombs of their own. There are no expected survivors. We are unsure whether any Dregans perished. The captain says he and the captains of the two Nistier ships immediately turned around and headed for their home port."

An older man in the crisp white-and-black clothing of a noble entered the room and bowed. "Highness, the Nistierans have just learned of the attack and are demanding answers. They are threatening to end all alliances with us if we have deliberately chosen to start a war with Dregaitia."

Queen Averly appeared and took her place by her husband's side.

King Brian spoke. "Tell the Nistierans we haven't sanctioned an attack on Dregaitia, that this is under investigation."

Multiple maids came in with trays of food and an assortment of drinks.

The older nobleman bowed and left.

The maids set the food at the end of the long table and rushed out with alarmed faces.

Meanwhile, King Brian spoke to James. "I want to speak with the captain of the Wind Rogue. Now."

"Of course." James hurried out.

Malsin and James nearly collided at the door. Malsin poured steaming tea into cups. He unscrewed the cap on a silver flask and poured a green liquid into each drink. "Better take it with tea; I haven't perfected the taste yet." He handed them out. "I haven't detected any side effects yet, but I would recommend getting real sleep as soon as an opportunity arises."

As we sipped on the tea, I noticed my body gradually becoming more alert. My eyes gained a sharper focus as energy poured into my veins.

James returned with a gold locket glowing blue and handed it to King Brian. "This is King Brian Sorren of Aberron speaking. Is this the captain of the Wind Rogue?"

A gravelly voice floated out of the locket. "This is Mark Stimms, captain of the Wind Rogue at your service, Highness."

"I'm told you witnessed a ship attack a Dregan port," King Brian said.

I found myself holding my breath. The room thickened with tension.

"Yes, Highness," Mark said. "My cousin's ship, the Night Crusader. My cousin Brett and I are—were—business partners. We deliver supplies to the outposts and various docks. Highness, I trusted Brett with my life. He had a family, a wife and three little girls he adored. I can't believe he willingly attacked the Dregans."

"But you saw the Night Crusader launch an assault on the Dreskenar port?" King Brian asked.

"Yes. Even in the dark, I knew it was one of our ships," Mark said with rueful conviction.

"Did you notice anything suspicious about the crew before they shipped off?" King Brian asked.

"No," Mark answered.

"I appreciate your insight, and I'm sorry for your loss. Please remain at the Elan outpost in case I have further need of you. That is all." King Brian returned the locket to James, who then vacated the room.

Joshua set his teacup on the saucer. "This doesn't sit well with me. A single merchant ship attacking a Dregan military port? It's a suicide mission. No sane crew would do it. I'm not apt to believe all of them went crazy at once."

"Agreed," King Brian said.

"The Night Crusader attacked at night, right?" Henry asked rhetorically. "What if a crew in smaller boats, rowboats, or something not easily seen in the dark commandeered the vessel? They could've held the crew hostage and assumed their positions, then used the ship and their military supplies for the Callan outpost to attack the Dreskenar port."

"And kill themselves?" Joshua asked dryly.

"Not necessarily." Henry leaned back. "They could've had a yellow mage to camouflage them as they jumped into their escape boats. With the ship and original crew destroyed, there's no one to pin it on but the men who died."

"You think we've been played." King Brian didn't seem to disbelieve the validity of the suggestion.

"I think Dregaitia, or *someone*, was looking for an excuse to start a war for their own enjoyment or profit," Henry answered energetically. "Our natural resources, like our hot springs and fertile growing lands, are the envy of the surrounding kingdoms. Land-wise, we have everything we need to viably sustain ourselves."

A soldier entered and announced the arrival of Braidus.

My stomach clenched. *This is it.*

"Send him in," King Brian said.

CHAPTER TWO

RAIDUS ENTERED CARRYING TWO familiar tan bags: they held the gold I had stolen from the treasury. His long, blond-streaked hair fell in waves around his shoulders and cascaded down his chest. He seemed no worse for wear in a starched, white, open-necked shirt. I saw no weapons on his belt. His hazel eyes did a quick sweep of the room, his expression impassive. Walking forward, he chose the seat at the very end of the table and set the two bags down, jingling the coins inside.

"Father, these belong to you." With a flick of his hand, he used air to push the two bags down the table, stopping them just before they hit the map. "It should count up accordingly."

"Braidus," King Brian said, his tone even as his eyes surveyed his son. "Your appearance has changed greatly, but I wonder about your heart."

"I'm not the angry boy you once knew," Braidus answered, his tone smooth. "I have no wish to harm anyone, *especially* you."

"Your recent actions concerning Isabelle and Henry prove otherwise," King Brian said flatly.

Braidus spoke quickly but firmly. "I did not orchestrate that. I merely acted a part to pay off a debt to a higher power."

Eyebrows rose, including my own.

"I would be more than happy to discuss it with you away from Isabelle's listening ears." Braidus's eyes flicked to mine and held them for a second before returning to his father's.

"Henry, take Isabelle and find George Haskender," King Brian ordered. "Tell him to start preparations for the First and Second Waves. Come back when you're done."

With a glum expression, Henry rose. "As you command."

I scowled, angry that they wanted to discuss me without my presence.

Andrew kissed the top of my head. "Sorry, love." He released my hand.

My ire toward Braidus and King Brian got the best of me. I muttered a stream of curses on my way out that caused Braidus to chuckle as he watched me leave.

"I'm disappointed Uncle Brian kicked us out," Henry said as we walked down the hall with me following because I had no idea where to go.

"Disappointed doesn't even begin to cover what I'm feeling right now. Gods forbid, I should be in there." I balled my hands and fought the urge to smash something.

Henry nodded. "Who do you think this higher power is that Braidus worked for?"

I shrugged. "No clue. A higher power could be anyone Braidus considers better off than him. A noble with a sizable fortune or a foreign king, maybe."

"True," he conceded.

"Ugh. Too much is happening at once," I complained.

Henry laughed as we rounded a corner. "Indeed. I'm talking to the newly engaged Isabelle Mirran, future queen of Aberron."

I grimaced. "I'm pretending that part doesn't exist." I hardly knew anything about what a queen did. I hoped it was something I could manage, because I'd sacrificed my wishes against taking this role in favor of marrying Andrew.

"What happened to the second thoughts you were having about Andrew when we were captured?" Henry asked. "Are you still angry he kept Braidus a secret from you?"

"I've let it go," I said. "I love Andrew too much to let this one omission break us. I mean, Braidus was banished. I assume he thought they'd never cross paths again and we wouldn't be affected by him."

Henry nodded. "I think you're right. Braidus was never talked of when we were growing up. They erased him out of everything."

"So who is this guy we're supposed to find?"

"George Haskender is the previous commander." Henry scratched his chin. "He lost a leg in an explosion gone wrong, but the soldiers still respect him. He has rooms on the other side of the castle and spends his days training recruits."

"I see," I said.

Henry stopped a guard marching the other way. "Hey, have you seen George?"

The soldier shook his head. Henry continued asking every soldier we met with no luck until we stopped at a door at the end of a hall. A gold plate on it read George Haskender. Henry knocked. A thump followed by a heavy boot fall alerted us that someone approached.

The door opened, revealing a well-built man with short graying hair.

"Henry," George acknowledged. He looked at me curiously.

"Isabelle Mirran, Joshua's sister," I supplied.

"Ah." He gave me a smile.

"Have you heard about the Dregans yet?" Henry asked.

"Yes," George said.

"Commander Mirran is tied up with Uncle Brian, who asked me to tell you to start the preparations for the First and Second Waves," Henry said gravely.

"May the Gods bless us." George sighed. "All right, I'm on it."

"Thanks, George," Henry said with gratitude.

We turned around and quickened our pace back to the study.

Henry knocked on the door before we entered. "You guys had better be done with your secret talk."

"We're done," King Brian said.

"George is starting the preparations," Henry said.

"Good," King Brian said. "We'll be leaving for the temple for the Trial by Fire right after I get a look at this map."

I couldn't stop the scowl from forming on my face as I resumed my seat next to Andrew. He took my hand, threading his fingers through mine, with an unreadable expression. I glanced at Braidus to find the corners of his lips curved up. I stiffened. Braidus chuckled. I hated that he affected me so much.

King Brian returned his attention to the map of Aberron that Haldren had given him. He placed the pane of glass over Saren. I took a sharp intake of breath as my home came to life. Little houses surrounded by fields. Shop Street lined with businesses. I spotted Mr. Traver's post office, Jensten's butcher shop, and Agatha's bakery.

King Brian touched the butcher shop, and the map transformed until we appeared to stand on Shop Street. Like before, a glowing blue dot appeared on the corner for King Brian to change it back to the regular view. A second dot appeared alongside it in a darker shade of blue.

"This is new," he murmured.

He pressed the darker blue dot and the map transformed again. Drawn in an architectural style, thin lines in black ink showed the whole layout of the tunnels and rooms underneath the town.

"Isabelle, what is this?" King Brian asked.

"Saren's secret, our haven." I saw little reason to hide it since he could see it on the map. "Occasionally, tornadoes rip through our area, so we constructed a series of tunnels and rooms to protect us. Every building is connected to them through the root cellars and some fields as well, so no matter where you're working, if a storm approaches, you only have to run a short distance to get to safety. Everything used to be held up with wooden supports, but Nathan enforced it with metal. We keep it well maintained."

"Impressive," Andrew murmured.

I pointed to the larger squares. "These areas are for us to group to wait out the storm." I moved my finger to hover over the adjacent smaller squares. "These are supply rooms. They are stocked with everything we'd need to survive in an emergency, including a month's supply of rations and water that are routinely switched and used to keep fresh."

"How wide are these tunnels?" Joshua asked.

"Some only two people can walk comfortably side by side; others can fit up to five people abreast," I answered.

"It can hold all the Saren people?" King Brian asked.

"Yes, with some room to spare," I said. "We figured our sister town Prastis might need it too. We've always come to each other for aid."

"What about the air?" Malsin asked.

"We have ventilation shafts," I answered. "For heat, we have lamps and stoves with pipes going above ground for cooking."

"An underground city," Joshua said with interest. "We could use this."

"The Dregans would not expect it," Braidus said. "You could fool them into thinking your numbers are lesser. It would also keep many men out of the cold."

"Agreed. We will set up Saren as our main base of operations," King Brian said. He grabbed a locket out of a drawer and pressed it until it glowed blue.

James entered. "At your command, Highness."

"I want to talk to someone at the Thimbleton outpost," King Brian said. "Bring me their locket." James left. Meanwhile, King Brian asked Malsin to go to the Healers Guild to recruit. "We'll need as many healers as they can spare."

Malsin nodded. "I'll let them know."

James returned a couple of minutes later. I assumed they kept the lockets stored nearby.

King Brian held the glowing blue locket, introduced himself, and then asked, "To whom am I speaking?"

A man's voice floated out of the locket. "This is Kyle Minslow, overseer of the Thimbleton outpost, Highness."

King Brian listed off a series of orders. "I need a rider sent to Saren—immediately. Tell the orate judge I want all of the residents evacuated to Thimbleton. House them at the outpost."

"Yes, Highness," Kyle said.

"Prepare for the First and Second Waves' arrival tomorrow," King Brian said. "I will be with them. We will stay for a meal and a short rest for our horses, then be on our way. That is all." He handed the locket back to James and rose, his expression resigned. "To the temple, then."

Malsin took off for the Healers Guild. The royal family along with my brother and I, got into an exceptionally large carriage. Horses' hooves pounded against the cobblestone. Silence fell. The air had a strained quality to it, as if we led ourselves to our deaths that very moment. Andrew wrapped his arm around my shoulder and pulled me into him. I leaned my head on his chest and stared listlessly, not wanting to focus on anyone or anything, least of all Braidus.

The carriage jarred to a halt. Joshua, closest to the door, opened it and hopped out, followed by the rest of us. Large torches lit the front steps leading to the expansive, white-marbled temple. Small groups of men and women sat on the steps under the flaming lights. Their worn faces and tattered layered clothing gave me the belief they lived on the streets. It saddened me to see anyone in such a harsh predicament. Simultaneously, I felt grateful to have a warm home in the castle.

"It's the king!" One of the men on the steps shouted in disbelief.

"The king," others marveled. Some bowed.

I squirmed inwardly at the attention on us, then reminded myself I'd better get used to it if I were going to marry Andrew. The royals transformed their faces with charming smiles, save for Braidus, who wore an apathetic expression. It made me wonder what roamed through his thoughts, whether he felt disconnected from the royal family. I knew Andrew had the ability to act well, having seen him unleash this artistry on people previously. However, it still caught me off guard to see him put on his most winning smile when, just a minute ago, his stress was palpable. I doubted I'd ever gain this ability. I hoped it wouldn't matter too much when I became royalty.

We started to make our way inside the temple. King Brian and Queen Averly took the lead.

A disheveled woman sprang up and ran in front of the doors, blocking our entrance. Her eyes landed on King Brian with a crazed glint. "Your illegitimate child laws cost me everything! I had a home and food, and then the law was decreed and I was tossed out like trash and left to give myself up to men to survive."

Many of us grimaced, including King Brian.

"I'm sorry to hear that," he said.

"Undo the law!" the woman demanded.

"I cannot until the current threat of war has passed," King Brian answered, his tone cordial. "If you'll please excuse us, we have business inside to attend to."

The woman moved enough to let King Brian and Queen Averly pass her. Braidus lurched, shoving himself between the woman and his father. King Brian stumbled into Queen Averly, who let out a squeak of surprise. Braidus gasped, his face contorted in pain. The angry woman retreated in earnest, revealing a dagger protruding out of Braidus's lower left ribs.

Gods forbid.

Joshua jumped on the attacker, pinning her arms behind her back while she shrieked, "Kill the king to save illegitimates!"

Braidus faltered.

King Brian swiveled to catch his son. "Braidus!"

Confusion welled within me as I worried about his well-being. How could I be concerned about the man who had killed my parents?

Andrew and Henry darted past me to help King Brian carry Braidus into the temple.

Joshua spoke, shouting to be heard over the deranged woman's cries. "Isabelle, help me."

I hurried over. "What do you need?"

"I need to get to my lockets under my shirt. I can use them to get some patrol guards over here to take care of this woman. See if you can reach them," he said.

I pulled on a gold chain under his shirt, revealing a string of lockets.

"Third one from the right. Press on it until it starts to glow."

Once the locket was glowing blue, I held it up to Joshua's mouth, and he ordered a contingent of patrol guards to the temple.

The king and his family had disappeared. I couldn't hear them either with the temple doors closed.

I waited for the guards with my brother. The murderous woman squirmed and writhed against his hold. Any pity I'd had for her vanished after she tried to kill the king. She shouted obscenities about King Brian until her voice went hoarse. The other people previously on the steps had scattered, perhaps fearing they would be implicated in this woman's wrongdoing.

I replayed the moment Braidus had selflessly put himself in harm's way to save his father. The woman had tried to kill the king for the same reasons Braidus had twelve years ago. Could this event have been planned to make him look heroic?

The patrol guards finally arrived and took hold of the woman. Joshua let out a sigh of relief as they hauled her into a jailer's carriage. I read unease on his face as he gave a brief explanation of what had happened. He sent them off.

We walked inside the temple together. I studied the medium-sized entry hall. A table rested in the middle with a wooden box on top for collecting donations.

Braidus sat on a bench against the wall with his father and Andrew on either side of him. Henry, Queen Averly, and a temple priest hovered nearby. The knife had been taken from the wound and cast aside on the floor. Blood coated the blade. Braidus appeared pale but whole. Andrew and Queen Averly had healed him in time.

Joshua spoke to King Brian. "The woman is in custody and off to Carasmille Prison."

King Brian nodded, his expression tight. "Good. We'll stay here a few minutes longer for Braidus to regain his strength."

While I waited for Braidus, my eyes fell upon the largest painting I'd ever seen on the other side of the room. I walked over to it, passing the table with the donation box. I craned my neck to take in the picture. It was painted as a continuous image showing a series of events. The first showed a young, golden-haired man with his hand out. Something in his palm glowed white. The scene then morphed into a backdrop of a night sky with a white seed flying through the air, followed by a white sapling levitating in the sky with the Mark of the Gods on its trunk. Next, I saw a globe with a map of Aberron on it. It ended with the tree again, now fully grown with multicolored leaves, and the golden-haired man standing beside it with his hand on the trunk.

A marker resided underneath the painting. I read the words carved into the metal:

A spark of light in our Creator's palm

A seed thrown across the cavernous sky

A sapling sprouts the birth of our world

Under the care of our Creator

The tree grows mighty and bright

Its roots infuse life into our earth's core

Its leaves unfurl magical wealth

Mankind prospers

The temple priest joined me. "Pretty, isn't it? King Aberron painted it and wrote the words accompanying it as a gift when our temple's construction was completed."

"Wow." I raised my eyebrows in surprise. Not only had King Aberron taken a disarrayed land and made it into the country we knew today, but he also wrote my prophecy and painted extremely well. The man had numerous talents. "What does it mean?"

"It is the retelling of the birth of our world." The priest pointed to the man. "Our Creator grew our earth with this tree. All that you see in the world is connected to it."

Across the hall, I heard Braidus say, "I am ready."

"You're sure?" King Brian asked, concern in his expression. Regardless of their history, King Brian's love for his son was clear to see.

"Yes." Braidus rose, prompting Andrew and King Brian to stand as well.

"This way." The priest gestured for us to follow him down a bare hallway on his left.

The hallway ended at a large black door with the Mark of the Gods painted in white over the door. It sent a shiver down my spine. My stomach lurched with anxiety in response to what I didn't know.

The priest turned his back on the door and faced us. "Enter, state your purpose, and wait. If more than thirty minutes have passed and no God has appeared, then the Gods do not deem the cause worthy, and you are out of luck. I offer you well wishes, your majesties." He pulled the handle and stepped back, allowing us passage.

Several torches in brackets along the windowless walls lit on their own at our arrival. My eyes were immediately drawn to the five marble thrones resting on a dais, four at equal height and one raised above the others. The dark gray stone underneath our feet was inlaid with the Mark of the Gods. Two angled log benches resided at the back of the room on either side of the door we had entered.

Braidus turned to his father. "Should their judgment result in my death, then it is just. Know that I hold no animosity toward you."

King Brian opened his arms and hugged Braidus. "You are my son and always will be. I hold you in my heart forever."

Everyone but Braidus sat on the benches with rigid postures. I couldn't relax a smidgen; the others didn't appear able to either.

Braidus moved until he stood in the middle of the swirl of the Mark of the Gods. He faced the empty thrones and spoke. "I am Braidus Alexander Sorren, firstborn son of King Brian of Aberron. I seek a trial with the Gods. May they act as my judge for the crimes I have committed."

A minute passed, then two. Suddenly, a flash of bright light blinded me. I shielded my eyes from the glare.

A man's deep voice cut through the air. "Your request has been heard and granted."

My breath caught in my throat. I brought my hand down. Five people—the Gods—now occupied the thrones in front of me. Two men on one side and two women on the other. I held back a gasp when I caught sight of Haldren sitting on the throne raised above the other four Gods and Goddesses.

In person, he appeared exactly as I saw him in my dreams: he had straight black hair that fell to his shoulders, a sharply angled face, a goatee, and a tall, thin frame with long, nimble fingers clasped together. His very real presence riveted my attention. I found it nearly impossible to take my eyes off him.

Haldren's cold blue eyes briefly met mine. He smirked. I flushed and forced myself to look away. For a few seconds, I stared at the dark stone underneath my feet until I had the courage to look up. Then I focused on the other Gods and Goddesses in the room.

I stared at the two Goddesses. One had a devastatingly beautiful appearance with a light, creamy complexion; full, perfect red lips; dazzling purple eyes; and long wavy blonde hair. The other was equally elegant with long black braids adorned with flowers and dark-toned skin. She wore a dazzling green dress with white roses sewn into the bodice. I assumed her to be Nachura and the blonde Goddess to be Amora.

I flicked my gaze over to the two Gods sitting side by side; Zadek and Tomas, I figured, but I didn't know who was who. Their appearances were drastically different but equally striking. One favored black attire, a leather jerkin, breeches, knee-high boots, and leather cuffs on his muscled arms. He reminded me of a tall, huge soldier. Zadek, I decided, the God of men and war.

The blond man beside him was wearing a deep-blue, billowy shirt and tan breeches with brown boots to his knees. Tomas, the God of intellect and negotiations. His attention briefly turned to me. He subtly nodded, as if he had been following my train of thought. I quickly vowed to think carefully around the Gods.

All of them suddenly stared at me with amusement. This did not go unnoticed by those sitting beside me. I shrugged at their quizzical expressions.

Tomas spoke. "May it be said, Braidus Sorren, that our judgment in this trial will be final. Once we start, there will be no turning back."

"I am aware," Braidus said.

Tomas nodded. "Then let us begin."

All of the Gods rose and surrounded Braidus. He sank to his knees while they placed their hands on his head. I took a breath and held it. A white light enveloped the circle. It became too bright for me. I looked at Andrew, who in turn stared at his frozen father.

Something about the way King Brian stared ahead with a carefully masked expression, fingers holding on to Queen Averly with an iron grip, softened my heart. I found myself torn between needing Braidus to pay for his crimes and wanting him to survive for his father's sake.

I glanced at Joshua, who also had his eyes trained on King Brian with a worried expression.

No doubt Joshua faced the same struggle I did, a hunger for retribution tempered by a desire to see King Brian happy with a reformed firstborn son. As Nathan had become a second father to me, King Brian had become so to Joshua.

With one hand in Andrew's, I reached over and grabbed my brother's. He seemed startled at first and then smiled slowly and squeezed.

The light around the Gods started to diminish. They removed their hands from Braidus and stepped backward until we could see him.

A sheen of sweat coated his ashen face, and his chest rose and fell in gasps as he fought for breath. He swayed on his knees as though he had trouble staying upright.

"Now you pay for your crimes," Zadek said.

My chest tightened, as did Andrew's and Joshua's hands around mine. King Brian gasped.

White fire engulfed Braidus. He cried out and fell to the floor, convulsing as the flames ate him alive. I buried my face in Andrew's chest, unable to watch. Braidus's screams twisted my insides to the point I feared I might expel them.

On it went, until I lost track of time. Braidus's cries continued to pierce my soul. Despite believing that he deserved his judgment, I could barely stand his torture. I wanted it to stop. The Gods showed no remorse. I wondered why Braidus hadn't died yet as he thrashed in the flames. I fought the urge to jump up and tell the Gods to stop. Andrew and Joshua kept me grounded.

The Gods raised their hands and the flames vanished. Braidus appeared unconscious but whole, with no burns on his clothes or skin. The Gods returned to their thrones.

King Brian stood. "May I go to him?"

Haldren consented. "You may."

King Brian strode to Braidus. He knelt on the ground and gently placed a hand on his son's shoulder. Haldren flicked his hand and Braidus woke. The king helped Braidus rise and put his arm around him for support.

Zadek spoke to Braidus. "We have seen the very depths of your soul and judged therein. Through our Trial by Fire, you have paid for any crimes committed during your banishment. As the God of men, I now deem you worthy to keep your life."

Tomas spoke. "As the God of intellect and negotiations, I deem you worthy to keep your life."

"As the Goddess of women, I deem you worthy to keep your life," Amora spoke with a soft lilting smile veering on the edge of seduction. It caught me off guard.

"As the Goddess of nature, I also deem you worthy to keep your life," Nachura said, clasping her hands together.

At last, Haldren spoke. "The judgment has been made. Braidus, you are free to live in harmony with Aberron."

Braidus said, "Thank you."

King Brian faced Braidus. "Based on the ruling of the Gods, I hereby pardon and reinstate you as a full citizen—a prince—of Aberron." He reached into his pocket and pulled out a gold locket bearing the king's crest. "I have carried this on me to remind me of you since the day I banished you. I am happy to return this to its rightful owner." He placed the necklace over Braidus's head, allowing it to rest around his throat.

Braidus broke out into a genuine smile that mirrored King Brian's. "Thank you." With his father's support, he sat on the edge of a bench.

I released the breath I'd been holding. *Prince Braidus Alexander Sorren is free.*

Haldren rested his attention on me. "Isabelle, please come forth."

Joshua and Andrew gripped my hands so tightly that I had to bite my lip to keep from gasping in pain. With a seemingly conscious effort on both their parts, they eventually let go and allowed me to stand. We knew better than to refuse Haldren.

As I moved to where Braidus had stood, over the swirl in the Mark of the Gods, Haldren rose and greeted me.

He smiled. "It is time we met in person."

I matched his smile. "I agree." *It'd be even better if he told me what my importance to him is.*

Haldren chuckled, seemingly at my thoughts, and said, "The others would like to meet you."

He stepped back. The other Gods and Goddesses glided to me. Tomas reached me first. A jolt of energy ran through me as he took my hand.

He grinned. "You have a great intellect. Feel free to think of me the next time you play Pilfer. I have a feeling your odds may go up." He winked.

His exuberance was infectious; I couldn't help but reciprocate. "I will."

He returned to his throne, letting Zadek step forward. Energy rippled across to me when our hands touched.

His dark-brown eyes surveyed me with a half-smile. "You are a woman after my own heart. I admire your passion for defensive knowledge. It will serve you well in the weeks ahead."

"I pray that you will protect us as we battle the Dregans," I said.

He nodded. "The Dregans have come well prepared. This will not be an easy fight." He resumed his position on his throne.

"The farmers will never believe I met you," I said to Nachura as she stepped forward and took my hand, giving me a now-expected spark.

Nachura laughed, rich and dark. "They will if you tell them that Mr. Layder's fervent prayers to me before he sows his seeds are the reason his crops turn out best."

"Oh." Everyone considered Mr. Layder to have the worst possible spot in Saren for farming, and yet every season he seemed to pull ahead of the farmers with near-perfect growing conditions. No one understood it and often accused him of using magic, which he adamantly denied.

"I am glad to have met you." Nachura smiled warmly and stepped away.

Amora then took my hand, from which I received yet another small shock. She smiled. "It is good to meet you, Isabelle Mirran. Your heart tells me you're well acquainted with love." She paused, her expression searching. "You worry for your adoptive parents and an ardent suitor you left in Saren."

Stefan. I grimaced. "Yes."

"A postboy no longer. Stefan Ashter is Saren's orate judge," Tomas said from his seat. "He is a good fit."

"What?" I gasped in surprise, my gaze momentarily fixed on Tomas. "How did that happen?"

"I won't spoil the story," he said cryptically.

Of course. Gods and their blasted love of secrets.

I refocused on Amora and her purple eyes that held an unfathomable depth of hidden knowledge.

Her lips curved wickedly as she assessed me. "I see you also have room to let a third man into your heart. I am anxious to see whom you choose."

"Third man?" *What in the Gods is she talking about?* Out of the corner of my eye, I caught Haldren wiggling his fingers.

I had forgotten he wanted me to consider Braidus as a suitor for who knows what reason. He'd probably asked Amora to help him convince me. But it would never happen. I refused to consider Braidus—even if he had just been pardoned by the Gods and his father. There would never be a third man.

"I've already chosen," I said, thinking of my engagement to Andrew.

Amora chuckled lightly, like the tinkling of soft bells. "Oh, I am not so certain." She let go and stepped back.

I faced Haldren once more. He grasped my left hand. My birthmark, shaped like the Mark of the Gods, shimmered and then glowed brightly.

A sudden burst of adrenaline raced through my veins as though I had activated my magic. But I hadn't. I raised an eyebrow in question. What had he done?

Haldren smirked. "Do not be alarmed. I have merely given you a gift. I'm curious to see how you use it." He let go. "Until we meet again, Isabelle Mirran."

Zadek spoke. "The Dregans are setting up base at the Barras outpost. You will reach Saren before they venture out."

King Brian bowed. "Thank you."

The Gods raised their hands in farewell and, with a blinding white light, vanished.

I blinked back the spots in my eyes as Henry came up beside me. "You've got a lot of explaining to do."

Andrew wore a pained expression. "Why haven't you told me you found love before?"

"You heard that?" I asked, mentally cursing.

"We all heard," Joshua said bluntly.

Everyone had their eyes trained on me. I opened my mouth and closed it. I didn't know what to say. It hurt to think about Stefan, so I tucked him safely in my heart and stored the memories. I'd put off telling Andrew because I knew it would cause us both pain. My life took one crazy turn after the next. It seemed like a better idea to leave the past untouched. Now I could see how wrong I had been.

"Are you—" Andrew ran a hand through his hair. His voice choked with emotion. "Are you still in love with him?"

I tried to explain. "Andrew, I—my love for Stefan is different. It's based on years of friendship, and—"

He inhaled as though I had punched him in the gut. "You don't deny it."

Gods forbid. "Please, let me explain."

"No," Andrew said sharply.

I flinched as though he'd slapped me. He'd never used that tone of voice with me before.

"I've heard enough for now." Andrew left the room in angry strides.

Pain lashed through my heart. My feet barely found purchase. The others filed out of the room, disapproval etched in the lines of their faces. Henry stopped in the doorway and waited for me to follow. I stumbled forward, tears clouding my vision. He turned around and continued after the others.

I halted on the front steps of the temple as the carriage came into view. Anxiety tore at my insides. My throat closed up. I could not get inside that cage and face Andrew. Joshua gave me a pointed stare as he waited for me.

"No," I choked.

I ran.

CHAPTER THREE

THE STREETS OF CARASMILLE were dark, icy, and unforgiving. I raced down the sidewalk, darting around stationary objects and the few people braving the night. Tears clouded my vision. The cold air sliced my lungs. My sides ached from the sudden exertion. I kept going anyway.

I turned down a dark alley to avoid people and collect myself. My feet slid out from under me as I stepped on a patch of ice. I fell hard on my right hand and knee. My wrist snapped, and I cried out. A searing, white-hot pain shot up my arm. A warm sticky liquid trickled from my skinned knee down my leg.

A side door opened to reveal a roaring establishment. I could hear dishes clinking, a lively tune, and bawdy laughter. A large, scruffy man stepped out. Our eyes met and held for a fraction of a second. Recognition flared. *Gods forbid.*

"You," the archer growled. He reached into his pocket.

I scrambled to stand, fighting to think coherently through the pain. In one stride, he grabbed hold of my arm and jerked me upright. He plunged a glowing white crossbow bolt into my right breast. I gasped at the violation.

"You cost me everything." The man pushed me against the wall, holding me there with his body.

He reeked of sweat. The bolt sunk deeper. I sucked in a ragged breath. He reached for an arrow from the quiver resting on his back and brought it to my throat. The tip pierced my flesh. I hardly felt it.

I tried to access my magic since I had no other weapons on me. Boomer whined and scratched at the door inside his cage. *Locked.* My fear intensified.

"Magic," I rasped.

The archer grinned. His face was close enough for our noses to touch, and I could smell the alcohol on his breath. I tried not to gag. I should've gotten into that stupid carriage. I mentally cursed my foolishness.

"How lucky is it that I buy a bolt to stop magic off an Abominator in the pub and find you moments later? It's as if the Gods have granted my revenge."

How did he know I had magic?

He must've seen the question in my eyes because he said, "I heard all about your power from the guards in Carasmille Prison when you were arrested. I escaped to find you." He dug the arrow deeper into my neck. "And finish the job."

Oh Gods, I thought, heart pounding in terror. With satisfaction in his eyes, the archer put pressure on the wooden arrow shaft, slowly digging his way to cut through my throat so I would suffer more. I struggled against his huge frame.

Braidus materialized. He grabbed the archer by the shoulders and pulled him off me. The man dropped the arrow as Braidus began pummeling him with his fists. Regaining his bearings, the archer brought his hands up to fight back. He swung wide at Braidus, who ducked and delivered an uppercut blow to the other man's jaw. He flew backward, crashing onto the icy cobblestones. With a flick of his hand, Braidus restrained the archer with a full-body blue shield. My attacker wiggled uselessly.

Braidus towered over him. "You should've stayed in prison where I left you."

The archer let out incoherent muffled cries through the shield. I slid to the ground, clutching my broken wrist to my chest. I didn't bother with the crossbow bolt protruding against my collarbone.

Braidus created a blue orb of light and crouched in front of me, his eyes assessing the damage. He reached under his shirt and pulled out the locket his father had returned to him.

Once it started glowing blue, Braidus spoke into it. "Father." His eyes never left mine.

"Braidus?" King Brian's voice floated out of the locket.

"I require a healer and guards in the alleyway behind The Musing Bard," Braidus said. "Isabelle ran straight into trouble."

My brother cursed loudly in the background. "I knew this would happen!"

"Joshua, go," King Brian said. "Andrew, I need you here. Braidus, remind Isabelle to use her magic to heal herself in the meantime. I expect a full explanation upon your arrival."

"I have no magic!" I blurted, scared witless. With my head, I gestured to the bolt sticking out of my chest. "It's stopping it."

Had the weapon taken it for good?

The archer's muffled cries seemed to increase as he squirmed futilely. Braidus gave him a disgusted glance.

"Braidus. . .?" King Brian spoke slowly as if he didn't want to hear an answer.

Braidus grimaced. "I won't lie; it's bad. I'll update you when I can."

The locket stopped glowing. Braidus let it drop as he ripped at the hem of my shirt. Taking a piece of the material, he folded it and pressed it against my neck.

I hissed.

"I've got to stop the blood flow."

More blood gushed from my neck than my chest with the bolt acting as a block.

"I know," I said through gritted teeth. I wished the pain would stop. "Thank you," I added as an afterthought. "You saved me."

Braidus smiled wryly. "I'd never let you die."

"Then why—"

He cut me off. "Kidnapping you and forcing you to steal wasn't my idea or desire. I didn't come back to Aberron to become a criminal again. I seek peace with my family."

The archer had somehow managed to wiggle his way to the wall and repeatedly hit it as he fought to break free. The light of the magical orb allowed me to see anger flash briefly in Braidus's eyes.

With a nod in the other man's direction, Braidus explained, "When he returned, believing he had killed you, I delivered him to the Carasmille Prison. I gave those men I hired explicit orders that you were not to be harmed or captured. I merely needed their presence to keep the threat real enough for you to run to Joshua, as my proprietor dictated. They acted on their own when they hurt you." With another nod, Braidus said, "What he did tonight was all on him."

"Who is—" I started to ask about his proprietor.

Braidus shook his head. "If it were up to me, I'd tell you."

"It's not, is it?" I asked.

He frowned. "No."

We sat in silence for some minutes until Joshua and a group of soldiers arrived.

"Gods, Isabelle, barely three days and you've gotten yourself into another scrape," Joshua admonished. "I swear, I've never had to work harder to keep someone alive."

In the background, Braidus removed the shield around the archer and allowed the guards to snatch and haul him into a waiting jailer's carriage. The archer swore loudly and said something about this not being over, but I didn't pay much attention.

A healer crouched beside me and introduced himself as Simon. He put his faintly glowing green hand on me. His brow furrowed. "My magic is not working. I can't see the extent of your injuries."

"It's the bolt," I said.

"Pull it out," Joshua said.

Simon shook his head. "There's no guarantee that will work. I am newly apprenticed and still rely heavily on my magic to ascertain the situation. I suggest we take her to the Healer's Guild for someone of more experience to examine her."

"Malsin," I said. "He's worked on me without using magic before."

Simon nodded. "Malsin is the best healer Aberron has to offer. Let me see if you can be moved." He examined me closer. "It should be fine to transport her if you take it easy," he said to Joshua, "but I'd better come along in case something changes on the way."

Joshua gently picked me up, carried me to the carriage, and set me inside. Braidus and Simon followed, settling opposite us. Joshua rapped on the roof and the carriage moved. The guards took off with the archer. I prayed he'd stay in prison this time. The constant jarring as we traveled through Carasmille exacerbated my injuries. I focused on slow, even breaths to distract myself.

"She has a remarkably high pain tolerance," Simon said, keeping careful watch opposite of me.

"She's been through worse," Joshua answered gruffly.

I could feel his fury radiating like heat beside me. I sunk low in my seat, hating his silent censure but knowing I deserved it.

Braidus contacted his father with the locket. "Has Malsin returned?"

"He's just walked in," King Brian answered. "I'll inform him to see you directly."

"We'll be there in a couple of minutes," Braidus said, then let the necklace drop.

The carriage soon rolled to a stop. Braidus jumped out, followed by Simon, then Joshua. My brother reached in and carefully lifted me. Clutching me to his chest, he hurried up the front steps into the castle. King Brian, Andrew, and Malsin stood in the entrance hall. Their eyes widened as they took in my bloody and battered state.

"Gods forbid, Isabelle!" Malsin wore a severe gaze. "I leave you for a couple of hours and look at the mess you're in!"

"I'm sorry!" I apologized.

"Let's get her to my room," Malsin advised.

"Would you like my assistance?" Simon asked.

"I can manage. Thank you." Malsin dismissed him.

"Isabelle, what happened?" King Brian asked as he walked beside Joshua on our way to the healing room.

"Archer—found me," I spoke through hitched gasps as Joshua jostled me up the stairs. On a smoother surface, I managed to get clearer sentences out. "He heard about my arrest from some guards and escaped from prison to kill me. He took my magic with the bolt."

Braidus said, "He had her pressed against the wall and was slowly carving her throat out with an arrow when I arrived."

The men grimaced.

"What is an Abominator?" I asked.

"The Abominators form a group of non-mages who consider magic an abomination," Joshua explained. "They preach on the street corners trying to convince others to shun magic and mages. It's active discrimination, most likely born out of jealousy, not fear and lack of education like in the rural communities." He set me on a table.

"I've got her now," Malsin told the men.

"Let me stay," Andrew said. To his father, he said, "You've got Joshua and Braidus now to help with the preparations."

"Fine. Update me on Isabelle's condition," King Brian said.

Braidus and Joshua followed him out.

Andrew came to my side. "You attract trouble faster than lightning can strike."

"I don't mean to," I said, watching Malsin cut my shirt off with scissors. He left me in my breast band.

"You never do, Isabelle." Andrew sighed. "I'm sorry."

"Not your fault," I whispered.

Andrew started in. "If I hadn't—"

"Wouldn't have mattered," I told him softly. "The archer was after me the second he discovered I hadn't died."

"Drink this." Malsin tipped a green liquid into my mouth.

I sighed in relief as some of the pain abated.

"I've got to get the bolt out. Andrew, can you hold her steady?"

Andrew sat on the table and pulled me to his chest. He kissed my temple. I sensed he had put our issues aside in light of my wounded state. With a knot forming in my gut, I wondered how long he could hold it off.

"Fair warning Isabelle," Malsin told me. "This is going to hurt."

I gathered nerves of steel. "Do it."

I couldn't stop the cry tearing out of my throat as Malsin began pulling the bolt out. Andrew held me tight and murmured assurances in my ear I barely heard. Once I was free of the blasted thing, which was no longer glowing, Malsin held a cloth to my wound and applied pressure.

He then activated his magic and cursed. "It's still not working on you."

I tried to access mine and found Boomer's cage still locked. Another round of terror crashed over me. "Is it gone for good?"

"I don't know yet," Malsin said. "I'm going to have to heal you the conventional way for now."

Panic seized my insides at the realization that even Malsin didn't know what was happening. I fought to sit still as he worked over me. Each minute ticked by, feeling like an eternity and a second simultaneously. I wished I could snap my fingers and make the pain go away instantaneously.

Henry, Dominic, and Falden walked in wearing soldiers' attire just as Malsin finished patching the wound in my chest.

"Gods, Isabelle!" Henry exclaimed. Dominic and Falden appeared equally aghast.

"Don't start," I told them. "I know it's bad." I shuddered as a cold draft touched my skin.

The men had gotten a brief story of what happened out of Braidus before they arrived, making me grateful I didn't have to explain it again.

Malsin peeled back the bit of ripped shirt on my neck. "You're very lucky your veins were unharmed, or we wouldn't be having this conversation."

I lay down on the table with my chin up. Andrew gently held my head in place. Malsin began stitching up the wound.

While he worked, I learned that Henry had gone to the Sorrenian to ask his mother if he could join King Brian on the journey to Saren. "I'm not eighteen till the last month of spring, so I had to ask." After she agreed, he'd woken up his comrades and they had volunteered to join. "Aliyah's not happy, but I feel it's my duty to protect Aberron as best I can."

Aliyah was the lady Henry was courting.

"Us too," Falden said, gesturing to Dominic and himself. "We're eighteen already, so we didn't need our parents' permission."

"Joining us means your lives will be on the line," Andrew said to the three of them, his expression serious. "Are you sure this is what you want?"

"Yes," they said, their tone firm.

This reminded me that I still needed to ask Joshua if I could come. I couldn't help but find it silly that I was of an age to accept a marriage proposal, but I couldn't make other life choices without asking my guardian first. An engaged woman should be able to govern herself however she sees fit.

Although women were allowed to carry a sword, I doubted I'd see any women accompanying the First and Second Waves. I worried my brother would say no based on that fact.

I won't give him a choice, I thought. I had to go. The Dregans were practically on Saren's doorstep. Nathan and Adel were in danger. I would never be able to live with myself if I didn't do everything in my power to ensure their safety.

Malsin set the needle and thread on a tray beside him. He helped me sit up. "All right, now on to the broken wrist."

A trickle of embarrassment ran through me. This injury was entirely my fault. I let out a few low curses as Malsin wrapped it up.

"We'll put it in a sling after you dress."

Andrew had taken to washing the blood off of my skin with a warm washcloth.

Malsin put a simple patch over my knee and declared me done. "As far as your magic goes . . ." He rubbed his chin, thoughtful.

"I can see Boomer scratching at the door, but I can't open his cage," I told him, aggravated at the loss. I didn't have time for these injuries. How could I help Aberron in this state? Would Joshua even let me go to Saren?

Malsin brightened. "That's good. It means the magic is still there. Perhaps we can treat this like a cold, wait for it to die out, and keep trying to open it in the meantime."

I nodded, glum.

Andrew helped me down.

Malsin put a robe around my shoulders. "I can't use my magic to see you internally, so I'm just going off what I see. Better you rest as much as you can."

Andrew kissed my temple. "I must return to my father; come see us when you're changed."

The boys went with him.

Malsin and I walked to my room. Once there, he had to help me change. My breastband was notoriously difficult with one hand. I wiped off the remaining blood and dressed in sturdy but warm clothes. We left my room to join the royal family.

Malsin asked a steady flow of questions as we walked. "Are you feeling any seepage? Are you dizzy?"

"I'm fine," I assured him. "You did an excellent job patching me up." Yes, I still experienced some pain, but not as much as before. I could handle it. Nothing would stop me from going to Saren.

We entered a large council room. Soldiers moved freely about, some studying papers, others speaking into lockets. It was a racket of activity. My family and friends surrounded a paper-strewn table with a large map of Aberron in the middle.

Ignoring the curious gazes of the soldiers, I approached Joshua and lightly touched his arm to get his attention.

He turned to face me. "How are you feeling?"

King Brian's gaze shifted to me as he waited to hear my answer.

"Better." I forced a smile. Knowing I didn't have a moment to lose, I pleaded, "Will you let me go with you to Saren? My home and family are there. I couldn't bear it if you forced me to stay here."

Joshua rubbed his bearded chin and surveyed me. I knew I was a sight with bandages and my arm in a sling, but I prayed he saw the determination in my eyes. I'd find a way whether he said yes or no, but I figured gaining his consent was a better option. I hoped he could also see the warrior in me. I had great fencing skills and extensive magic that would surely be a benefit when it came back.

"I'm not your sole guardian anymore. Andrew now has a claim on you too. It changes when you become engaged. You have to answer to him and me. If Andrew says no, there's nothing I can do."

My eyes widened. "Seriously?"

King Brian spoke. "A woman is under the care of a guardian until she is twenty. A man, eighteen. The legal marrying age is seventeen for a woman, and eighteen for a man. If a woman becomes engaged before she is twenty, then the betrothed man must share the guardianship responsibilities until they are married, and then he becomes her sole guardian. Andrew asked you to marry him tonight, and you agreed. No one has expressed a desire to end it."

"Oh." I sort of wished I had known that beforehand. Then again, I doubted it would have mattered to me when I had originally said yes.

My eyes found Andrew, noting the anger and hurt in the planes of his face. I assumed he felt this way because I had kept Stefan a secret. I dropped my gaze, shrinking in guilt. Had I broken us for good?

"I have a lot of feelings right now about what I heard in the temple, but I don't want to end our engagement," he said. "I still wish to announce it when the time is proper."

My head snapped up with surprise. I saw the hard determination in the set of his lips.

He sighed and raked a hand through his hair. "Even if I did say no, Isabelle would circumvent me. I know her well enough now to see that coming."

"True," most of the men said.

"I say she goes," Andrew said to my brother. "We could use her skills and knowledge of the area. Especially when her magic comes back."

"Agreed," Joshua said. To me, he added, "I want you in my sight or Andrew's at all times."

I smiled, relieved I wouldn't have to fight anyone on this. "I can do that."

Joshua scrutinized me. "We're going to have a hard time finding armor to fit you. Even our smallest attire will swallow you up."

Abruptly, a sphere of thick white smoke appeared and surrounded me. I gasped, caught off guard.

A man's cool voice whispered in my ear. *"This will fit you perfectly."* Zadek.

In a blink of an eye, my clothes disappeared. I didn't have time to be embarrassed over my nakedness when new clothes of warm, soft cotton, dyed black, covered me, not harming the injuries. My boots were switched out for a pair made of something sturdier but equally comfortable. Then armor made of shiny black metal and leather materialized over my new attire. A large insignia of the Mark of the Gods engraved in gold rested over the sculpted breastplate. Additionally, a sturdy weapons belt with three small pouches, two silver daggers, and my personal sword appeared. I stumbled under the weight.

He chuckled. *"A little lighter, perhaps."*

Some of the heaviness lifted, enabling me to stand upright with ease. "Better, thank you."

"May it be useful," Zadek said as the ball of white smoke disappeared.

Silence ensued. My friends and family surrounded me. Past them, every soldier had frozen in place and gaped. *Great.* I discovered my previous clothes had been folded and set on the crowded table.

"Problem solved," I said, "courtesy of our gracious God, Zadek." I received mixed reactions of surprise and petrifaction.

King Brian pursed his lips. "Joshua, instruct the soldiers to be gathered at the south training field by dawn. I want to address them before we leave."

Joshua inclined his head. "As you wish."

"Your injuries?" Malsin asked.

I frowned. "Still present."

He picked up the sling. "Let's put this on just to remind you not to use your right arm until it's healed."

I grimaced. *My sword hand.* I hoped it would heal quickly so that I could see to Nathan and Adel's safety.

Malsin procured a chair for me. "I don't want to see you on your feet for too long."

"All right." I sat and listened to the men plan.

King Brian asked Malsin, "How did the recruiting go at the healers' guild?"

Malsin scowled. "I demanded every healer they could spare, just like you asked, and they tried to give me a quarter of what I knew they had available. Winter is our busy season, and some healers don't like putting in the grunt work for fixing colds and viruses. They'll be stretched thin, but it will be nothing unmanageable."

"Good," King Brian said. He moved on to discuss supply wagons. "Increase the amount of food. There's no telling how long we'll be gone."

Braidus said, "Do not expect a quick resolution with the Dregans. They do not idly invade."

King Brian readily took to Braidus's suggestions as they planned. Andrew and Joshua also listened to him as if every word counted. I noticed an energy in Braidus as he gave his input for everything from weapons and horses to bedrolls and tents. This new *free* Braidus was not the cold-hearted usurper who'd held me captive. Half of me was intrigued and the other half was wary of this change. I doubted I'd ever fully understand him. Then again, I supposed it didn't matter as long as we both worked toward the same goal of getting the Dregans out of Aberron. I'd even work directly with Braidus if it meant Aberron's safety. My issue against him for murdering my parents did not outweigh the needs of Aberronians caught in the Dregans' path.

Haldren whispered in my ear. "Your memories of your parents' deaths do not paint the full picture. A higher being with power like unto myself manipulated Braidus like a puppet on strings. He was a victim chosen to take the blame for someone else's misdeeds and therefore cannot be held accountable for your parents' deaths. He had no control over what happened."

What?

There was a bright flash, and Haldren appeared beside me. I jumped at his sudden presence and started to tumble out of my chair. He caught me by the shoulder and righted me. All conversation stopped.

Haldren spoke to King Brian. "I require some time with Isabelle. Continue your planning, and I will return her to you before you depart." He waved his hand and we vanished.

I stumbled as we arrived in my living quarters. I blinked, and then my vision opened to a bright blue sky and a field of wheat. *What in the Gods?*

"I've moved your body to a safe location and taken your mind here," Haldren explained. He conjured two boulder chairs and gestured for me to sit. "It's time for you to see the truth about Braidus and your parents' murders."

He took my hand and the wheat field dissolved.

We stood in a ballroom surrounded by elaborately dressed nobles and merchants. Music played in the background, nearly overcome by incessant chatter. In front of me stood a younger version of Braidus, his golden hair cut short, with no beard or scar above his right eye. I guessed him to be sixteen. A group of boys similar in age had him cornered.

A dark-haired boy with a prominently curved nose sneered, marring what could have been an attractive face into something ugly and sinister. I had the strangest urge to slap him if only to wipe away the disdain.

"Prince Braidus," the boy said, "the insignificant bastard of our king. Shouldn't you be wiping the floors with the rest of your kind?"

The other boys guffawed. My stomach tightened.

"This is the past, Isabelle," Haldren reminded me. "You can't change it."

"But they're so mean," I said, appalled.

"They're not the only ones. Some servants too." He waved his hand, and suddenly we stood in a dimly lit hallway.

A large man dressed in servants' attire with a light-blue king's crest patch on his upper shoulder pushed a young Braidus against the wall. "I lost everything because of you. My whole inheritance," the man snarled. "You're gonna pay for it." He raised his hand to strike.

Haldren dissolved the scene before I could see Braidus get hurt. We landed in the castle study.

Braidus sat on his father's right-hand side. Papers covered the table. Reports and ledgers, I thought.

"I am your firstborn. The right should fall upon me," Braidus said heatedly, in what had probably been quite a long argument between the two of them.

"Enough!" King Brian roared. "Andrew will become king. My decision is final."

Braidus stood. Papers lifted off the table, flying in a yellow haze of wind as he left the room.

Haldren next showed me a meeting between Braidus and a group of ragtag men in a moonlit courtyard. One of the men stood out to me as familiar. With a second of focus, I placed him in my memory.

"The insurgent." I pointed at him.

He didn't have scratches or dirt on his clothes now, but I recognized his sea-green eyes and fiery hair. He had a noble quality about him, a short, groomed beard and straight nose, slightly thin lips. This was the man who spoke to my parents before they died. The one who promised Braidus's return to power.

Haldren's eyes glittered. "Pay attention to him." His lips curled in displeasure. I had the stark impression he did not like this man.

Scenes of Braidus and the insurgent conversing alone came fast—too fast for me to catch what they said. Braidus appeared to be seeking guidance from this man.

The scene changed. Braidus and an adorable little Andrew, no older than seven, sat together in a window seat. Wooden toys were scattered across the floor: blocks, a horse, and knights. An empty rocking chair sat near a low fire. A nursery. My breath caught in my throat at seeing Braidus completely at ease. He ruffled Andrew's hair and chuckled as his brother ducked his head, attempting to tame his wild locks. Their brotherly bond, strong and filled with love, permeated the room, reaching my heart.

Andrew challenged his brother. "I don't want to be king. You're the oldest. Take it from me."

Braidus smiled pleasantly at Andrew and sighed. "I wish I could."

Andrew's expression brightened. "Maybe if you wouldn't fight so much with Father, we could make it happen."

"Maybe," Braidus agreed, but I didn't think he meant it.

"Promise you'll try—for me?" Andrew asked, his eyes shining bright with hope.

Braidus nodded. "I promise."

Haldren waved his hand, dissolving the picture into a new one. The insurgent and Braidus conversed. Braidus shook his head no, his expression stressed. The insurgent put his hand on Braidus's shoulder. A brief silver glow swathed him.

Haldren explained, "This is where he took control of Braidus." The insurgent handed Braidus a knife and they parted ways.

The scene changed. The insurgent spoke to a lone guard in an empty hallway.

Haldren spoke over them. "This is how your parents found out. He's revealing what he's about to make Braidus do."

I didn't understand.

"Just watch," he said before I could ask more questions.

The guard sprinted down the hall to my parents, catching them as they exited a large office dressed for a ball. Sudden grief surfaced in me. Haldren put his hand on my shoulder, calming me.

"Information is passed along," Haldren said.

We watched the guard speak to my parents, fear in his expression. We then followed my parents as they raced to avert the ensuing crisis.

"Do you think it's true?" Mother asked with a stricken expression. Her green sparkling dress swished with every step.

"Gods forbid. I hope not, but we'd best check it out," Father said. "Keep your magic open; Braidus may be cloaked."

"Mother had yellow magic," I whispered.

A memory flashed of my mother as she lay dying on the forest floor. She turned her head, staring straight up at the oval window in the playhouse, as though she could see me through the illusion. I shivered at her expression of regret and love, now bright and fresh in my mind. Perhaps she really had seen me pounding on the window as she took her last breath.

We followed my parents to the throne room. Two guards blocked the door.

"These men were hired by the insurgent to help Braidus," Haldren explained.

"Can't go in there," one man said. "King Brian doesn't want to be disturbed."

With a flick of her hand, Mother lifted them off the ground and threw them into a wall, knocking them unconscious.

Fierce.

Haldren chuckled. "Very."

They burst into the room, surprising Braidus, who quickly threw the dagger that he had been aiming at his father.

"Braidus and the dagger were concealed," Haldren said. "King Brian had no idea his son was in the room."

"No, Braidus!" Mother screamed.

With yellow magic, she stopped the dagger a fingertip away from King Brian's heart. It fell into his lap, now visible for everyone to see. She raced to Braidus, my father right behind her. Yellow ribbons swirled out of Mother's hands and wrapped around Braidus, revealing him. Father grabbed Braidus, pinning his arms behind his back. Braidus struggled to break free.

The color drained out of King Brian's face as he stared at his son. He rose. The dagger fell from his lap and landed with a thud on the floor. "You tried to kill me."

"I'm sorry I failed," Braidus snarled.

I flinched at the hatred in his tone.

King Brian jerked to a stop, his expression crestfallen. A minute of silence passed before he straightened to his full height.

"Prince Braidus Alexander Sorren, I hereby strip you of your title and citizenship. You are banished from Aberron. If you return, you will be executed." He took Braidus's gold locket with the king's crest off his neck and held it.

He didn't ask questions, give Braidus a chance to redeem himself, or say goodbye. Turning on his magic, King Brian wrapped a blue shield around himself and exited the room.

His actions caught me off guard. When I was arrested for robbing the royal treasury, King Brian stressed to Court Magistrate Philsby the importance of gaining all the facts before sentencing. I saw less softness in him in this vision than I had just a short time ago.

Haldren waved his hand, showing me a new scene. Andrew as a young boy stood in front of his father.

"Where is Braidus?" Andrew asked.

King Brian looked defeated as he placed his large hands on Andrew's shoulders, crouching to meet his son's eyes. "He is banished for attempting to murder me. We must never speak of him again."

Andrew gasped. "No! He promised he wouldn't fight so much with you! He promised!" He pulled on his father's arms. Tears fell down his cheeks. "Don't banish him."

King Brian shook his head. "I'm sorry."

"I'm going with him." Andrew sprinted for the door.

King Brian chased after his son. He caught him at the threshold and hoisted him into his arms. "No, Andrew. You're not going anywhere. Your brother's punishment is his alone."

Andrew fought against his father's hold. "You made him do it. Why couldn't you just make him crown prince? He's older! The duty should be his. I don't want to be king!"

King Brian spoke softly. "That's not how the law works."

Andrew screamed at the top of his lungs. "I hate you!"

Another hand wave. Braidus and his men fought against the soldiers leading them out of Aberron. The next scene showed my parents arriving at our home in Korrun. Braidus's men waited behind large lilac bushes. They ambushed Mother and Father as they dismounted.

"Those ropes they're tying them with are laced with an enchantress plant, provided by the insurgent," Haldren said. "Your parents could not use magic to fight back."

I watched the men drag my parents into the forest where they would be killed. Braidus followed behind.

I stepped closer and searched Braidus's face. "His eyes are glassed over like he's drunk."

"That's the magical hold on him," Haldren explained. "You start to see the effects the longer a person is under."

Braidus's fogged eyes unnerved me. He leaned against a tree as his men surrounded my parents. The insurgent stepped forward, announcing Braidus's return to power. Braidus's smile seemed stretched too thin as he listened, then nodded his approval. The insurgent signaled the men.

I kept my focus on Braidus. I'd seen my parents die countless times in my dreams. I didn't need to see it again. His gaze was unfocused, and sweat perspired on his brow. His skin had a slight greenish tinge. I imagined he had a fever. I didn't enjoy seeing him suffer.

Braidus and the insurgent remained while the other men retreated into the forest. I expected them to talk, but they didn't. Instead, the insurgent flicked his fingers, sending a magical silver ribbon that penetrated Braidus. He didn't seem to notice the magic coming at him, seeping into his chest. My heart went out to him as I saw him imprisoned within his mind and body. With a nod of satisfaction, the insurgent then strode after the others, disappearing out of view. I gasped as Braidus's sickly pallor vanished. Groaning, he rubbed his face. He shook his head as if to wake himself up, then looked around with confusion.

"It's like he doesn't know where he is," I said.

"He doesn't," Haldren answered.

Braidus's hazel eyes landed on my fallen parents. He sucked in a breath, recognition flaring. He moved to them with concern and checked to see if they still lived. He rubbed the back of his neck, visibly upset. Were those tears in his eyes? Then Braidus ran.

I shielded my eyes against two blinding flashes. The insurgent appeared, clean and dressed elaborately, not how I'd seen him moments ago. A past version of Haldren also arrived. The present Haldren muted the sound, but I could see that the man and God argued from their hand gestures and expressions. At length, Haldren and the insurgent vanished.

Suddenly we stood in the wheat field again. Haldren released my hand. I looked to him for clarification.

He picked up a piece of wheat and twiddled it between his fingers. "Braidus was unhappy with his lot. He expressed a desire or thought that called the insurgent's attention to Braidus."

"He's not really an insurgent," I said. "He has God powers."

"Correct. He is known as a Fate over Fates. A ruler over the Realm of Souls and the living."

Realm of Souls. Where our souls go after we die. *Where my parents are.*

"Yes." Haldren dropped the wheat. "We've been feuding for centuries. No, I won't tell you why yet, but suffice it to say, the Fate saw an opportunity to hurt me and took it. I cared deeply for your mother." He paused; his expression saddened. "Braidus was exploited. His hatred for his unfortunate situation as an illegitimate child blinded him into listening as the Fate persuaded him to kill his father. The Fate almost had Braidus convinced, but in the end, he couldn't do it. Braidus's love for his father ran deeper than his anger. The Fate then took control of Braidus and set up the show you saw. The Fate never intended for Braidus to succeed in killing his father; he wanted to alert your parents to stop him. The Fate's entire purpose was to sacrifice Braidus in the murder of your parents to get back at me."

My mind whirled as I fit the pieces together. "The whole thing was an elaborate setup to get back at you?"

"Yes," Haldren said quietly.

I shook my head. How cruel to everyone involved. How utterly despicable. I felt sickened.

Haldren said, "Unfortunately, the Fate concealed himself well, and I did not detect anything amiss until it was too late."

"But why did the Fate go through all the trouble of using Braidus?" I asked.

Haldren frowned as he waved his hand flippantly. "He enjoys chaos and making his kills appear natural or within reason. He finds no enjoyment in quick kills. Braidus proved to be a reliable diversion."

"Does Braidus know this?" I asked.

"No. His memories are ill-defined at best concerning the incident. He believes himself responsible, as the Fate intended," Haldren said solemnly, clasping his hands together.

Gods forbid. I needed to tell Braidus.

"And King Brian, so that trust may be instilled once more," Haldren said. "Braidus's knowledge of Dregaitia is extensive. You need him if you want Aberron to survive." He raised a warning finger. "Be careful how you share this information. Do not speak or think the word *Fate* more than what's necessary. It would be unwise to attract his attention."

"Of course." I saw an unease in Haldren that alarmed me. "Are you scared of this Fate?"

Haldren rubbed his chin. "Scared? No. Cautious? Yes. He is my superior in the hierarchy of Gods. His power makes mine look paltry in comparison. Until we meet again, Isabelle Mirran." Haldren waved.

CHAPTER FOUR

THREW MY HAND OUT for balance as I landed in the council room.

Joshua stood in front of me with a relieved expression. He wore his armor with the Mirran crest engraved on his breastplate. "About time. I was getting worried. The others couldn't wait any longer and went ahead to the training field. Are you all right? You look pale."

I looked about, seeing that we were the only two in the room. All the running soldiers and royals had disappeared. Light shone through the windows. Dawn had come.

"I'm fine," I said.

"Let's go, then. We're going to be late to King Brian's address." He turned on his heel.

I put my hand on his arm as I hurried after him. "I have to tell you what Haldren told me about Braidus."

Joshua stopped, giving me his full attention. "I'm listening."

I explained everything Haldren had revealed to me about Braidus and the murder of our parents. The words tumbled out with my eagerness to get this off my chest.

Joshua tipped his head back, seeming as struck by the news as I was. "Gods forbid."

I explained, "Haldren said Braidus's memories of this event are not clear, but he believes he is to blame as we did—just the way the higher being wanted."

Joshua's expression turned thoughtful. "So this is why he survived the Trial by Fire."

I nodded. "Yes, I think so. We have to tell Braidus—"

"And King Brian and Andrew. We must hurry to the stables, get our horses, and then ride to the training field to meet them." Joshua started walking again in quick strides.

I practically jogged to keep up. I winced as the fast movement jostled my broken wrist and exacerbated my other injuries.

Joshua noticed me struggling and slowed down. "Sorry."

"It's all right. I can manage." I wasn't going to let a little pain stop me from going to Saren.

We arrived at the stables.

I opened Nisha's stall. "Ready for a trip?"

He rocked his head. *"Yes."*

A hostler saddled Nisha for me since I couldn't, and I had a bit of trouble trying to mount Nisha one-handed.

My brother saw and lifted me into the saddle. "You'll be all right?"

"Yes," I told him with the most conviction I could muster.

We rode to a snow-covered training field five minutes away from the castle. A cacophony of noise assaulted my ears: whinnying horses, stomping hooves under the crunch of ice, and men's chatter. A sea of soldiers mounted on horses had their backs turned to us. The sun glinted off their shiny metal armor. I squinted against the glare.

Joshua called over his shoulder at me. "Stay with me!"

Nisha picked up speed until we rode beside my brother around the block of uniformed soldiers to reach the front. A ripple of intrigue went through the men as they saw me.

"Who's the girl?" I heard. "Look at her armor. She wears the Mark of the Gods."

"She's injured," they noted. "Why are we taking a wounded girl with us?"

I followed Joshua's lead, staring ahead and tuning them out as best I could. Questions were to be expected. It didn't mean I had to listen or answer them. Malsin, Dominic, and Falden had chosen to stand on the front line. The commanders faced the soldiers. I noticed the royals' armor all had the king's crest engraved in the breastplates, distinguishing them from everyone else.

King Brian rode forward, putting himself between us and the block of men. "Soldiers of Aberron!" He amplified his voice with magic so that every person could hear him clearly. "The Dregans have invaded Aberron. Our citizens, our brothers and sisters, are in trouble. I have gathered you to answer their call for aid. We will ride straight for the Thimbleton outpost and rest for a short while before moving on. We will spend the night in the Trivail forest. Our end destination is Saren, a small farming community. There we will set up our main base of operations to deal with the Dregans. Expect to move quickly."

I appreciated King Brian's call for urgency. The sooner we got to Saren, the better.

King Brian continued, "I hope to resolve this conflict peacefully through talk, but I warn you we may end up in a war. I will not willingly send you into battle where I would not go myself. Long has it been the tradition of Aberronian kings to fight alongside their men, just as my forebearer King Aberron did when he forged our kingdom. I plan to be with you every step of the way."

Admiration rose within me at King Brian's willingness to involve himself. As king, he didn't have to. A tradition wasn't the law. I was happy for the opportunity to call him family with my ensuing marriage to Andrew.

King Brian held out his hand, gesturing to Braidus. "Beside me, you may see a familiar but new face. My firstborn son Braidus Alexander Sorren has returned to us with the blessing from the Gods. He has been fully pardoned of past crimes and reinstated as a prince of Aberron. I want you to treat him with the respect his station is owed. Braidus's knowledge of Dregaitia is extensive and will be integral in our dealings with them. He is to join his brother, Crown Prince Andrew Brian Jason Sorren, and my commander, Joshua Mirran, in leading you. Please adhere to their counsel in addition to mine."

"Yes, my king!" the soldiers shouted.

King Brian drew his sword. "Now let's march to protect our people. For Aberron!"

We drew our swords. "For Aberron!"

Taking the lead, the king turned his horse and headed to the street. The sound of many hooves hitting cobblestones jarred me. We filed through a side entrance in the curtain wall that met Capitol Road. The path was wide enough for five horses to ride abreast. Andrew and Joshua gestured for me to ride between them. They followed through on their word that I was to be within sight of one or the other at all times. I appreciated the feeling of protection they gave me. Braidus and King Brian rode on Andrew's left.

The wind had a bite and cut into any exposed skin. Travelers approaching or departing Carasmille, whether on foot, horseback, or wagon, hurried to the side and waited for us to pass.

I turned my head to view Andrew, King Brian, and Braidus. I shouted to be heard over the horses and wind. "I need to tell you what I learned from Haldren. It's about Braidus."

Andrew's and King Brian's gazes sharpened. Braidus leaned forward on his mount to see me better. I saw genuine interest in the depth of his eyes.

"I was wrong. You didn't try to murder your father or kill my parents," I said.

"What?" Braidus dropped the reins.

King Brian quickly swooped down to catch them and handed them back.

I began with what Haldren had showed me about Braidus's past, including the quarrels he'd had with his father about becoming king and the discrimination he'd faced as an illegitimate child. "I was aghast at people's behavior toward you. It was awful."

Braidus smiled bitterly. "All illegitimates are born taking the blame for the actions of their parents and treated poorly by their families and society."

King Brian grimaced. I read pain and guilt in his eyes.

I spoke firmly. "No one should ever be treated so horribly for an action that isn't their own."

Everyone spoke his agreement.

I continued by saying, "Haldren showed me a series of meetings you had with a man I recognized from my own memories. I've always called him the insurgent, but he's really a Fate over Fates. Haldren said we should avoid calling attention to him, so I'm going to refer to him as a higher being."

Braidus said, "I knew him by his last name only. Akaray."

I went on to explain Braidus's objection to murdering his father and the higher being taking control of him and supplying him with the dagger.

"I harbored much anger for my father's refusal to reverse the illegitimacy laws. I was tired of being spit on by society and wanted to see my life improved. Despite the many arguments I had with my father, I loved him deeply. He often made me feel valued and seen when others didn't." He looked at his father. "I didn't want to lose you. I was appalled by my actions." His expression showed as much.

Tears trickled down King Brian's cheeks.

I related that I'd seen the higher being help Braidus escape the guards who were escorting him out of Aberron and what had then ensued with the murder of my parents.

"I remember saying no to Akaray when it came down to killing my father, and then my memories became unfocused," said Braidus. "Occasionally flashes appear in my mind of participating in something, like running with a knife in my hand, but it's shrouded in fog." His eyes flicked between me and my brother. "My next sharpest memory is discovering your parents' fallen forms in the forest in Korrun. I was horrified." His brow furrowed as he tried to remember. "I ran and caught up with some other men. They were in a jovial mood, clutching bags of coins—payment Akaray had given them from me for helping me kill your parents. I learned from them the full scope of my misdeeds. After that, I sprinted straight out of Aberron and drifted for many years. I have never seen Akaray or the other men involved since."

King Brian asked, "Did you know the insurgent helping you was a higher being?"

Braidus shook his head. "No. Akaray purported himself as a fellow illegitimate who had become a man of means in the Aberronian underground market. He said he wished to see a change in the monarchy to help other illegitimates like ourselves. I believed him."

His words fell right in line with what Haldren had revealed. "You became a victim in a feud between the higher being and Haldren. The higher being read your unhappiness as an illegitimate prince and exploited you for his own schemes to hurt Haldren—who greatly cared for my mother."

Braidus nodded, his expression contemplative as he digested the new information Haldren had provided me.

"I admit I questioned the Gods' ruling of you during the Trial by Fire. I could not understand why they deemed you worthy, but now I have a better understanding." I took a deep breath, feeling like now was a good time to turn over a new leaf. I wanted to put this whole sorry mess behind me so I could focus on the Dregan invasion. "Braidus, I do not blame you anymore."

He squeezed his eyes shut. Abruptly, he set his hazel eyes upon me, his mouth stretching into a wide grin. "Thank you, Isabelle. You've given me a gift I'll treasure always."

Joshua spoke. "I don't wish to hold on to old grievances either, especially when we need to work well together to get the Dregans out of Aberron. Consider us reconciled as well."

"Thank you," Braidus said with gratitude in his tone.

King Brian said with a bright smile, "It is good to be redeemed."

Talk became minimal for a while. A cold breeze swept through the landscape, keeping us chilled. Malsin's pain-relieving medicines started to wear off, making me feel every bounce on Nisha more acutely. I focused on slow, even breaths to block out the pain as much as I could.

I asked Joshua, "How much further to Thimbleton?"

"Not far." He gave me a concerned glance. "You managing all right?"

"I'm just a little tired, is all," I said, not wanting to tell him how awful I truly felt.

But Joshua read between the lines, for I heard a promise in his voice. "We'll be there soon."

Andrew spoke to me. "What say you to finding a priest in Thimbleton to marry us while the horses and soldiers rest? I think it'd be fitting since we first declared our love to each other there." He grinned.

I smiled widely. "Yes, it would. I'd love to marry you there or anywhere. On a high mountain peak or on a sailing ship on the sea."

"In front of the whole Aberronian Court in the throne room?" Andrew asked.

I wrinkled my nose at the thought of all that attention.

He laughed. He knew how much I abhorred being in the public eye.

Yet I still found myself saying, "Anywhere."

I read desire in his eyes and heard the determination in his voice. "I'm finding a priest in Thimbleton."

King Brian spoke. "No, you're not. Every crown prince and princess since the reign of King Aberron has been married by the High Priest. I won't allow you to break tradition. You can marry Isabelle when we get back to Carasmille."

Andrew argued. "But we don't know how long this is going to take. It might be months!"

I smiled. He acted like we couldn't wait for another second—not that I objected. Seeing him advocate for us and show his affection for me made me love him all the more.

King Brian didn't yield. "My decision is final."

"Another reason why I don't care to be crown prince." Andrew leaned forward in his saddle to speak to his brother. "Braidus, do you have any ideas for the quickest way to get the Dregans out of Aberron?"

Braidus smiled at his brother and then sobered. "Mages. Commoner Dregans are not inherently magical. Most of them fear magic and will run from a mage—much like the commoners here in Aberron. I expect our mages to be our greatest asset in the days ahead."

I lamented, "Oh, if only I hadn't run last night. The archer wouldn't have caught me, and I'd still have my magic."

Andrew spoke encouragingly. "You'll get it back. I refuse to believe you won't."

Joshua said, "Abominators aren't smart enough to take away a mage's power for good. Whatever the archer stabbed you with will wear off soon enough."

"I hope so," I said. "I mean to be a help, not a hindrance."

Soon enough, Thimbleton came into view. Four soldiers on horses met us on Capitol Road. Unease lurched in my stomach. Joshua had not said to expect anyone. Then again, I had missed the bulk of the planning when Haldren was speaking to me about Braidus. I hoped the soldiers weren't there to deliver bad news. We needed all the good luck we could get.

One of the men advanced and bowed his head, addressing King Brian. "Highness. We have food and supplies prepared for the First and Second Waves at the Thimbleton outpost."

"Excellent," King Brian said.

The four soldiers' gazes flicked curiously to me.

"Eyes on your king, soldiers," Joshua ordered.

They quickly turned their complete attention to King Brian. My brother and Andrew scowled at them.

We followed the four soldiers to the Thimbleton outpost, taking a side route to avoid going through the main city. I found it ironic that the first time I had visited this city I was injured by the archer's arrows, and now, months later, I was here with another set of injuries bestowed by the archer. I hoped this wouldn't become a habit.

We stopped at a sizable training field surrounded by large stone buildings. Troughs were scattered around the field, some filled with water and others holding hay for the horses. Soldiers dismounted and led their horses to the troughs.

A man shouted, "Food's in here!" He made waving motions in front of one building. Soldiers made their way to it.

I attempted to lead Nisha to a trough, but he reared his head. *"I'm not sharing."*

"Come on, Nisha, we might be headed straight for battle. Adjustments have to be made." I pulled on the reins. "Please don't fight me on this." I needed him to be well sustained so we could be a help to Aberron. I also worried the men wouldn't take me seriously if I couldn't manage my horse. I wanted to show that I could be a good soldier.

Nisha snorted and pawed the ground. He tossed his head angrily.

I dropped the reins. "Fine, do what you see best." I couldn't control a horse with the mind of a human. It was foolish of me to try.

Joshua said, "Let's eat."

Nodding, I followed him and a line of men to the dining hall. I hoped to find a place to sit and not move for a while.

We entered the largest dining hall I'd ever seen—triple the size of the Sorrenian. The chatter bouncing off the walls and buzzing in my ears reminded me of the school, except louder—and manly. Soldiers crowded numerous tables, gulping down bowls of stew, tearing into bread, and drinking through pitchers of water. I bet the whole city of Thimbleton had cooked to accommodate us.

Henry waved at us from a table on the left. "Hey, over here!"

Questions about me started up again as Joshua and I made our way to Henry.

"Who's the lady? Does anybody know?" soldiers asked each other as we passed.

"Same hair color and eyes as the commander. Maybe he has a sister," was a common response.

"What do you think happened to her?" another asked, eying the sling and the bandages on my neck.

"Perhaps she got into a fight. She looks tenacious; like a feisty kitten," one man drawled. He made his fingers appear like claws and pawed the air with a meow.

Feisty kitten. Really?

The other men within hearing distance laughed raucously. Irritation bloomed in me at the reminder that men never took women seriously.

My brother stopped.

The laughter died as abruptly as it started. A flicker of uncertainty passed over the men's features. Soldiers scrambled out of the way as Joshua climbed onto a table, pushing bowls away with his boot.

"Come up here, Isabelle." With a single hand, he grasped mine and lifted me onto the table.

"Soldiers!" Joshua roared, his voice amplified with magic.

All noise ceased.

Joshua put a hand on my shoulder. "Allow me to introduce my little sister and Crown Prince Andrew's betrothed, Lady Isabelle Mirran. She will be joining us while we deal with the Dregans." He deepened his voice to a menacing growl. "If any of you lustful men so much as look at her, I will flay you alive—slowly."

Andrew suddenly appeared and stepped on the bench beside the table-top we were on, elevating himself above the men. He shouted, his voice amplified, "I won't be so generous. Treat Lady Isabelle like a queen, for that is our future."

The silence thickened.

Joshua asked, "Understood?"

"Yes, Commander!" the soldiers shouted.

"Good." His tone lightened. "Now eat and rest up. Mages, check your levels and recharge if necessary. We'll be leaving in two hours." He jumped down.

Andrew hopped off the bench. He gathered me in his arms, lifting me off the table. Holding me flush against him, he kissed me thoroughly before setting me on my feet. "It's been too long since I kissed you."

My cheeks flushed in response to all of the eyes on us. I focused on Andrew's blazing blue eyes instead to tune them out and gave him a saucy grin. "Mm, I agree."

Desire flared brightly in his eyes. He cursed. "We should be married already."

I laughed. "Soon, I hope."

Conversation didn't resume until we sat, I between Andrew and Henry, and Joshua beside King Brian. Malsin, Henry, Dominic, and Falden also shared our table. I pulled a bowl over to me.

"You handled that well," King Brian said approvingly to my brother and Andrew.

"Thank you," Andrew said.

Joshua nodded, but I caught a hint of a smile around his spoon.

Henry slopped some stew into my bowl. "It's better than it looks; don't worry."

"The bread's not bad either," Falden said, tearing into it.

"I don't envy the washing team after we leave," Dominic said in between bites.

"Aw, Dom, I think you'd be perfect for the job," Henry joked. "You can't stand filth."

King Brian rose first, mentioning needing to talk to someone. Braidus and Andrew soon followed. It occurred to me that this would probably be my life, always watching Andrew go to work. How much time would we actually spend together as husband and wife? I decided to take an optimistic approach. A little time is better than none.

Joshua pushed his empty bowl to the center of the table and held a slice of bread. "I need to talk to some of the men. Stay with Henry or Malsin."

Malsin spoke to me. "I want to do another assessment of you, Isabelle."

While the boys went to charge their magic, Malsin inquired about a room he could use to check me over. We found an office just off to the side of the large dining hall. I tried and failed to open my magic. Boomer whined with his head drooped, lying on his belly. I worried it would be months before I could use my magic again. Perhaps I really would be more of a hindrance than a help to Aberron against the Dregans. My magic might come in too late to be of help.

"We'll just keep trying," Malsin said with a hint of pity in his moss-green eyes.

"I finally accept my powers, and now they're gone. At the worst possible time," I complained.

"The magic will come back," he assured me. "I can't believe it won't."

He helped me undress to check over the rest of me, and then he gave me medicine that had no magic in it to ease the pain and speed up the healing. We headed out to join the others.

As I stepped outside, King Brian cantered by on his snow-white war horse. His voice was amplified with magic. "Soldiers! We march for the Trivail forest!"

We rode for another six or eight hours in the cold, first passing fields and then heading into the forest of Trivail. The thick trees acted as a block for the recent snowy weather, and fewer patches of melting snow covered the muddy ground.

Nisha's hooves sunk a bit in the dirt, which annoyed him. *"I hate mud like this."*

"Sorry," I said with sympathy. "I'd fix it if I could."

We stuck to the main road. I didn't recognize the path since I had avoided it when I left Saren hoping to dodge the archer. When it started to darken, mages of all colors created orbs of light to brighten the path, bathing the scenery in red, blue, green, and even yellow light. Every hour or so I tried my magic. Still nothing.

King Brian turned left at a marker. A short distance off the main road, we halted to rest in a campground. *Finally.* I trembled and ached. I needed to lie down.

Before us was a line of open-faced log shacks. They each had a roof, a back wall, and two sides to separate traveling groups. I suspected the structures had been left open so people could keep an eye on their animals while still getting some respite should the weather be bad. Remnants of fires could be seen in the middle of each shack.

Joshua shouted orders, assigning places for the men to rest. Not everyone could fit in the shacks, so tents were raised beside them with a narrow path to walk in between. The ground was wet with fragments of ice and snow. Red mages dried out spots of yellow tufted grass for their tents and fires. They also created walls of heat for the open parts of the shacks. We would sleep warm tonight.

Soldiers ventured out into the forest to gather enough wood for dozens of fires, a meager attempt to push back the dread and fear that lay heavy over the meadow. The sky lit up as Reds went around and started them. With the flames came courage—and a renewed will to keep Aberron free.

As everyone started to settle, King Brian called out to the soldiers. "Rest well, for tomorrow we may face battle."

I said a silent prayer for Saren and for these soldiers. King Brian, Braidus, Joshua, and Andrew moved about the field and spoke with the men. I sat against the back wall of a shack and rested while Malsin and the boys finished setting out bedrolls and boiling water.

I watched the orange flames flicker, casting shadows against the tents. The field hummed with soft chatter. Occasional laughter rang out. There seemed to be strong comradery among the men, an important thing to have when facing potential war.

At last, King Brian and his sons stepped under the cover of our shack. We settled around the fire. Malsin passed around mugs of tea. A bag of jerky and biscuits went from one person to the next.

After eating, we all lay down to rest. Andrew tucked me against him, my back to his chest, taking care to avoid my injuries. Since I'd gotten hurt, he'd been nothing but comforting. I appreciated that he'd put our issue concerning Stefan on hold while we traveled. I wasn't exactly eager to hear his censure again, which is why I didn't bring it up either. However, now I felt like the problem stared me in the face. I couldn't sleep until I had addressed it with my fiancé.

"Andrew?" I whispered.

"Mmm?" He sounded sleepy.

"I need to talk to you about Stefan."

Andrew sighed. "It's late and I'm tired. We can discuss it later."

"But—"

"We still want to marry each other, right?"

"Yes."

"Then we can work it out, tomorrow. We need the rest now while we can get it."

"All right. Tomorrow, then." I didn't want to deny Andrew sleep when he needed it.

Andrew lifted his head and kissed my cheek. "Sleep well, my love."

"You too." I shut my eyes, hoping sleep would come quickly.

As the night sky began to lighten, we resumed our journey to Saren. This time I rode between King Brian and Andrew.

King Brian wanted me next to him in case he had any questions about the area. "The last time I traveled through Saren was on my Walk many, many years ago. I had originally planned to just pass through, maybe stay for a meal, but on my way, I got caught in a hailstorm. I took shelter under a large tree. The wind blew terribly, and I thought for sure the tree would topple. When I ventured out again, I was frozen, soaked to the bone, and I developed a fever. I arrived stumbling and weak and ended up being nursed back to health by a sweet lady named Millie."

I smiled brightly. "Oh, I love Millie. She makes you feel like family instantly." I missed going to the sewing circle with her and Adel. The three of us used to walk together every week to whichever house was hosting.

King Brian's eyebrows rose. "You mean she's still alive?"

"Alive and full of energy when I left a few months ago," I say. "I think it's all those tinctures she makes and drinks. Her knowledge of herbal medicine is legendary. She's saved many lives."

King Brian inclined his head, a smile on his lips. "Indeed."

It took a good five hours before we emerged out of the Trivail forest. Every step closer to home filled me with a sense of dread. What would I be coming back to? Would Saren look the same as when I'd left it, or had it changed? Would there even be a town left if we ended up in battle? I thought of all the things that made Saren great, like the quiet, family-friendly atmosphere, the smell of the peaches and apples come harvest time, and the way the corn swayed in the wind. I thought of the weekly ladies' sewing circle and the farmers' gatherings where the men could talk for a spell. I didn't want to see Saren lose any of its charm.

Late morning, we ran into a large caravan heading in the opposite direction. By then I'd nearly chewed my bottom lip off with worry over Nathan, Adel, Stefan, and Saren in general.

Not stopping, King Brian called out, "How long until we reach Saren?"

"Two hours," Mr. Vander said.

"Thank you." King Brian waved.

As my eyes rested on the travelers, who had pulled off to the side to let us pass, I recognized some of them as townspeople from Saren. They looked at me with surprise. Some I said hello to, like Mrs. Jensten and Agatha.

I spotted Josiah and Ned, two boys who had often tormented me over my sword fighting. Instinctually, I stiffened, expecting their ridicule. They didn't disappoint.

Josiah said, "Isabelle, you done left us to join the army?"

Ned echoed, "Did you abandon all good sense to be a lady?"

A woman could still be a lady and carry a sword. I couldn't resist retorting, "Ask me again after I marry Crown Prince Andrew." I tilted my head in Andrew's direction.

Josiah's eyes bulged. "You're marrying the crown prince?"

Ned shook his head. "No way; she's lying."

Andrew spoke up. "She is not. Isabelle will be my queen."

I appreciated Andrew coming to my defense.

"Safe travels!" I nodded at Ned's and Josiah's dumbfounded faces as we passed them.

"Who were they?" Andrew asked with curiosity in his gaze.

"Josiah and Ned." I rolled my eyes and then sobered. "Thank you for speaking up. I'm sorry for flaunting our relationship at them, but they have been a thorn in my side since I was five and picked up my first sword. It was petty of me, but I wanted to shut them up for good."

"Ah." Andrew smiled, not seeming offended. "I think you did."

As we continued, we saw more caravans. I searched for Nathan and Adel among the people but did not see them. I did catch sight of the real Boomer with a young family. A young boy cuddled against him in the back of a wagon. It brought a small smile to my face. A forever stray dog had finally been adopted.

Some people called out with well wishes or prayers. "May the Gods protect you!"

"And you!" King Brian would answer with a wave.

Most stared silently.

Anxiety crept up like a fast-rolling fog. I rode leaning so far forward that a sudden stop would have sent me flying over Nisha's head.

"Hang in there, Isabelle," King Brian said, eying me with a hint of concern.

My hand trembled as I gripped the reins. "Trying to."

As the familiar sights, sounds, and smells of Saren came into view, I breathed a sigh of relief. The Dregans hadn't arrived yet, just like Zadek had predicted. We had made it. Nathan, Adel, and Stefan were still safe. *Thank the Gods.*

CHAPTER FIVE

I POINTED TO MR. LAYDER'S grassy fields on the edge of town, bordering the plains. "This would be a good place to stop."

King Brian surveyed the lands with a keen eye. "Agreed." He led the soldiers into the fields and halted before listing off a series of commands to some high-ranked soldiers. Then he turned to me. "All right Isabelle, lead the way to the orate judge."

I turned Nisha around, spurring him into a canter, and raced to Shop Street with my family behind me. The street held the only row of businesses in Saren. If I didn't see Stefan there, I'd find someone who knew his location.

Halfway down the muddy, dirt-compacted road, I pulled Nisha up short. My breath caught in my throat. There was Stefan lifting a wooden crate into the back of a wagon, turned away from me.

"You're good to go." He waved to a family I didn't recognize.

"Stefan!" I shouted.

He turned around and looked up. His eyes widened in surprise, and then he broke into a smile so bright that it rivaled the sun. "Iz!"

I jumped off Nisha and sprinted to him as he raced to me. We crashed into each other, the impact nearly knocking us off our feet. We dug our boots into the dirt as we swayed and hugged fiercely. All pain from my injuries had been forgotten.

I blinked back tears. "Gods, I've missed you!"

Stefan laughed as he lifted me off the ground, squeezing me tight as if afraid to let me go. "Is it really you, Iz? Don't tell me this is a dream."

"No need to suffocate me," I squeaked. "I'm real. I'm here."

He loosened his hold. "I can't believe it."

We broke apart and held each other at arm's length, grinning recklessly. We took a moment to survey each other. I noted Stefan had gained muscle. *Has he taken up sword fighting?* His blond hair fell in his eyes, and a smattering of light freckles continued to dust his cheeks and nose. His smile still dazzled—my ray of sunshine. I detected a gravity in his pale-blue eyes that I'd never seen before. Had he suffered or experienced hardships during my absence?

I grabbed his hand. "Come, meet my family." It seemed easier to call the eight men I interacted with "family" than to explain each person individually.

I swiveled around to see them staring at me with acerbic expressions. Andrew wore an intense stare as his eyes darted between the two of us.

Gods forbid. In retrospect, I should have been more careful in my greeting with Stefan. Unfortunately, my happiness at seeing my best friend had overruled rational thought. I needed to work harder on using my head first over my heart.

"Your *family*?" Stefan's mouth curled around the word as though he had trouble believing it. "They seem angry at you."

I rolled my eyes, deciding to play it off as I pulled him along. I'd fix things when I could. "I'm a troublemaker."

Stefan laughed and bumped shoulders with me. "You've never been anything else. Look at the state of you!"

I grinned, loving his ability to lift my soul. "True."

King Brian dismounted and handed his reins to Braidus.

"Allow me to introduce King Brian Sorren of Aberron," I said.

"*The* king?" Stefan whispered with surprise.

"The very one." I also quickly pointed out my brother, Braidus, and Andrew. "They also command the army we brought with us." As orate judge, Stefan needed to know who was in charge.

"Got it," Stefan said.

King Brian appraised Stefan with an expression that would easily make a brave soldier intimidated and a weak man soil his pants. "You are the current orate judge of Saren."

Stefan exuded confidence. "I am, Highness."

"I hereby declare Saren to be under my charge while we are in a state of war," King Brian said. "As the orate judge, you have the option to stay during our fight or evacuate with the last of the residents. I expect you to have all citizens on their way to Thimbleton within three hours."

"All remaining are expected to depart within the next hour," Stefan said.

"Where are the soldiers from the Barras outpost?" King Brian asked.

"They've stationed themselves on the other side of town, in Millie's barn. She's been tending all the injured." Stefan grimaced. "The healer posted at the Barras outpost died during the Dregan's initial attack."

"I want to see them immediately," King Brian ordered.

"Of course," Stefan readily agreed. "I'll show you the way."

King Brian mounted.

I cast my eyes about Shop Street, noting the businesses and the familiarity I felt. It was so good to be home. I vowed to myself that I would do everything I could to protect my town.

Stefan untied a chestnut mare from a post and swung up. Nisha trotted forward and lowered himself so I could hop on.

I rubbed his neck. "Thank you, Nisha."

"Welcome."

Stefan admired Nisha. "Wow, your horse is magnificent!"

Nisha proudly tossed his head and whinnied. He loved it when people admired him.

I grinned. "He's pretty remarkable, huh?"

Stefan nodded as he met my eyes. "Definitely."

Andrew ran a hand through his hair, his expression stressed.

Nisha sprung forward, choosing to ride next to Stefan as he checked out his mare. *"Pretty."*

"Whoa, Nisha." I pulled on the reins, trying to redirect him to ride next to Andrew.

Nisha flat out refused once he understood my intentions. *"No, I want to walk with this mare."*

Out of the corner of my eye, I saw Joshua putting a hand on Andrew as if he meant to stop him from jumping out of the saddle. I bit back a groan. Nisha's choice was making things worse for me with Andrew. I tried to catch Andrew's eye to explain but he had his gaze trained on Stefan and wouldn't look my way. Just great.

Stefan surveyed me again. "You look hollow, Iz—inside and out. What's happened to you? Who's been mistreating you? Has your *family* learned how to take care of you? I should have written instructions when you left."

"I'm fine," I said, fighting another eye roll.

He snorted. "You're thinner than I've ever seen you. You're wearing a sling, and there are bandages on your neck. You're not fine."

I shrugged, then winced as it put pressure on my injury at my collarbone. "First chance we get, we need to talk. There are some things I have to tell you about me that won't be easy to hear."

"You're a powerful mage," Stefan guessed. "No, wait, the most powerful mage alive."

My mouth popped open. "Not at this exact moment, but how'd you know?"

He leveled with me. "Come on, Iz; you wear the Mark of the Gods. It never mattered that Nathan and Adel didn't test you. We all knew you had magic in you somewhere. It doesn't change anything."

"But—" I started to object.

"No protests." He mockingly covered an ear and then dropped his hand. "Really, Iz. Have you been worrying that I'd hate you because you have magic?"

Among other things. I frowned. "My powers are closer to that of a God than a regular mage."

Stefan appeared impressed. "Really? That's awesome." He laughed at my sour expression. "The Gods should have chosen someone else to bestow their Mark on. You don't appreciate it."

I smiled. "I didn't until now." *Now that my power is inaccessible.*

"Don't knock your power," he said. "I'm sure it will come in handy with the Dregans."

"Yes," I agreed. "That's why I'm here." I needed to be a force for good to save Saren and the people I loved in it.

About eighty soldiers hung about the tiny stone house that belonged to Millie, a widow who always exuded energy despite her old age. Stefan and I dismounted, prompting my family to do the same.

Stefan waved at a barrel-chested, red-haired soldier approaching with Millie. "That's Tom. He oversaw the Barras outpost, and that's Millie, Saren's best herbalist."

"Thank you. I'll take it from here," King Brian said.

Millie checked out King Brian from head to toe. "Highness, welcome back to Saren. It's been a long time. How have you fared these many years?"

King Brian smiled with warmth. "Fine, thank you. My wife, Averly, is a trained healer. She keeps me in good health."

Millie grinned. "Ah, a wise marriage decision." Her gaze flicked between Braidus and King Brian as if searching for a resemblance. "Don't tell me this is your little boy?"

Braidus raised his eyebrows faintly. I doubted he'd been called a little boy since he literally was one.

King Brian grinned proudly. "I have three sons now—Braidus, Andrew, and Joshua."

Millie said to Braidus, "When I tended to your father on his Walk when he was ill, I had to fight to keep him in bed. He kept insisting he needed to be done with his blasted Walk so he could get home to you. Oh, he missed you terribly. You're all he could talk about. It's a pleasure to see you in person."

Braidus glanced at his father with surprise. It gave me the impression he'd never thought his father cared that much.

King Brian shrugged, a smile tugging at the corners of his lips.

Braidus then said with warmth to Millie, "Thank you."

She smiled at him and then turned her attention to me. "Isabelle, what trouble have you gotten yourself into now?"

"Now?" Henry laughed at me. "You've found trouble in this little village?"

Dominic and Falden quietly snickered.

I rolled my eyes with a small laugh. "Location has never mattered." Turning back to Millie, I smiled and shrugged. "It's nothing, really."

Millie made a noise as if she didn't believe me, but she let it go. I'd always made light of my problems to minimize dependence on others. I hated relying on others.

Malsin asked, "May I be shown to the injured?"

Millie waved at him. "Follow me."

The two of them walked to the barn.

I turned around to speak to my brother. "Joshua, I'd like to go home, if it's all right. I didn't see Nathan and Adel in the caravans. I'm eager to see them before they evacuate."

Andrew moved to face me, his expression taut. "I know our engagement is new, but try not to forget you need my permission as well, love."

Stefan gasped like he'd been shot. He nearly choked on his words to me. "You're engaged?"

Andrew smiled coldly at Stefan. "She is."

Stefan's pained expression brought tears to my eyes. I hated hurting him. I reached out to him. "Stefan."

"Not now, Iz. I don't think I can bear it." He moved out of my grasp, holding up his hands as if he dared not touch me. Pain sliced my heart. He'd never done that to me before, not in all the years I'd known him. "I need to help with the evacuations." He mounted his mare and raced away, kicking mud in our direction.

I rounded on Andrew, my hand balled into a fist. "*I* was going to tell him!"

Andrew crossed his arms over his chest, his eyes glittering with equal if not more anger. "Oh? Just like you were going to tell *me* about him?"

"Stefan is my friend. *Only.* I planned to formally introduce you," I said coolly.

He snorted in disbelief. "I did not see *friendship*. He is in love with you, just like Amora said. We'll have a celebration when the third man is revealed." His eyes darted to Braidus, standing beside their father. "Or are you keeping *him* a secret too?"

I flinched as though he'd struck me. Tears stinging in my eyes, I walked backward until I ran into Nisha. Without a moment's hesitation, I pulled my hand free of the sling, swung up, and galloped toward home, not caring if I hurt my wrist further. My heart pounded against my rib cage. The wind dried the threatening wetness, leaving my eyes gritty. Revulsion for myself snaked its way through, constricting every fiber of my being. I should've told Andrew about Stefan a long time ago—and there would never be a third man!

Arriving at my house, I led Nisha into the barn and quietly introduced him to Amber, Nathan and Adel's horse. Once he was settled, I sprinted to the back door, letting myself into the kitchen.

Adel, standing in front of the stove, whirled around. "Isabelle!" In two strides she was hugging me.

Nathan ran into the kitchen and pulled us both into one of his massive bear hugs. I melted into them. I didn't realize how much I relied on their love and guidance until I didn't have them close. It made me appreciate this moment all the more.

The kettle whistled, prompting Nathan and Adel to release me.

"What happened to you?" Nathan asked, surveying me.

"You're cold. Let's get you something warm to drink," Adel said, hastily wiping her eyes.

Nathan pulled out a chair at the kitchen table for me to sit on. Adel served us mugs of spiced cider. I brought my adoptive parents up to speed on what had happened in my life since I had left. I rushed through the major points, jumping from one thing to the next. The attack in the woods, meeting Andrew, the Sorrenian, learning I had magic, and getting kidnapped by Braidus.

Adel leaned back. "Whoa, Braidus is back?"

I nodded.

Nathan looked angry. "He was behind everything—the reason you ran?"

"Yes, and also no," I answered. "Braidus did it, but he didn't orchestrate it. He said if it were his choice, he wouldn't have touched me at all. He said he did it to pay off a debt to a higher power—I don't know whom, but King Brian, Andrew, and my brother do. They won't tell me." I couldn't help but scowl.

"Where is Braidus now?" Nathan asked, his eyes darting to his sword hanging by the back door.

I answered, "Here with—"

Nathan pushed against the table as he jumped out of his seat. He snatched his sword.

I inwardly smiled at his protectiveness. He reminded me of a bear, all gruff but full of heart. I lifted my hand. "There's no need for your blade. Braidus has been pardoned for all his crimes by the Gods and King Brian. I admit the pardon disturbed me greatly until Haldren and I spoke. He showed me visions of the past, and I learned Braidus wasn't the true killer of my parents, nor did he try to kill his father, the crime that got him banished in the first place. He was used for taking the blame in a feud between Haldren and a Fate over Fates. I have forgiven him for his involvement in this matter."

Nathan said, "Fine, but that doesn't excuse the fact that he willingly kidnapped you for someone else's purposes." He tied his sword to his belt. "I'm keeping this on me just in case."

I smiled. "By all means do so."

Adel put her hand on her heart. "This is a lot to take in at once."

"It is, sorry," I apologized.

Nathan returned to his seat. "And your present injuries?" He picked up his drink.

I explained about the archer finding me the other night, resulting in my temporary loss of magic and Braidus's rescue.

"Goodness," Adel said.

"Gods, could there be anything else?" Nathan sounded exhausted for my sake.

"Yes. . ." I squeaked. I had purposely left my engagement to Andrew for last, because I halfway expected them to blow up at me. Both had often been adamant, especially over the last year that I shouldn't become romantically involved with someone at my age. I needed to wait until I was older.

"What?" Nathan prompted, while picking up his cup to take a sip.

Here goes nothing. "I'm sort of engaged to Prince Andrew."

Nathan spluttered through his hot apple cider. Adel patted his back.

"You're *engaged* to Crown Prince Andrew?" He shared a concerned look with Adel I couldn't decipher.

At least they weren't shouting. I grimaced. "I was, at least. I'm not so sure right now."

"What happened, dear?" Adel placed a gentle hand on my arm.

Tears sprang into my eyes again. My lower lip trembled. "Stefan happened."

I couldn't bring myself to say more. I had used the conversation with my parents to avoid the hurt in my heart and had exhausted my energy reserves in the process. I let my head drop to my arms resting on the table. I shivered. Despite the hot cider, my insides hadn't thawed.

Nathan and Adel moved off to the living room. I could hear them speaking, but I couldn't make out their words because of the soft voices they used.

A knock came at the door.

Nathan answered. I couldn't make out who had arrived, but I heard Nathan clearly.

"Yes, she's here," he said angrily.

I strained my ears to catch the other person's voice. Andrew.

"I need to speak with her."

"I don't think that's a good idea," Nathan said firmly. "Better yet, stay away from her, *forever*."

Oh no. I rushed to the front door, glanced briefly at Andrew standing on the threshold, and put a hand on my adoptive father's arm. "Nathan, I love you, but let me handle this, please."

He relented under my hard stare. Muttering crossly, he stomped into the living room and sat in his favorite chair with an angry huff.

Adel went to soothe him. "She's grown up."

"She's still my little girl," he said.

Focusing on Andrew, I stepped outside onto the porch, pulling the door shut behind me. "What are you doing here?" I honestly hadn't expected him to show up, seeing how we had left things at Millie's. Frankly, I didn't mind the space apart, considering our quick tempers.

"We need to talk," Andrew said, stepping backward to lean against a post, arms crossed.

I sighed, tucking a few stray hairs behind my ear. "I made a mistake. I should have told you about Stefan, but I never officially entered into a courtship with him. I would not have said yes to you otherwise."

"Officially." Andrew's mouth twisted around the word.

"We were barely gravitating toward a relationship when I left." I paced as I spoke.

Nathan and Adel watched from the window. I knew they could hear us. Our windows weren't the thickest.

"Stefan has been my best friend since I was five. I care deeply for him, but it's not the same—"

"Have you kissed him?" Andrew asked, his expression hardened with pain.

He deserved the truth. "Yes."

He cringed.

"I know you're angry with me, and you have every right to be, but I can't change the past or how I feel. I never planned to love you. It took me by surprise. I expected to stay in Saren—"

Andrew scowled. "With Stefan."

I shook my head impatiently. "Maybe; I don't know. But I can't go back to Stefan. You set my heart on fire at our first meeting. I have been in love with you ever since. I wanted—want—to share my life with you, not Stefan." I took a breath and exhaled. "As much as I care for him, he doesn't bring out the kinds of feelings in me that you do. If you don't want me, then I'll stay away from love altogether."

Andrew's expression softened. He took my hands in his. "My feelings for you took me by surprise too. I want you, Isabelle, more than anything. As much as this business with Stefan has hurt me, I can't bear the thought of letting you go." He shuddered, seemingly at the notion of leaving me, and cupped my face with his hand.

I leaned into him, craving his touch.

His thumb rubbed softly over my cheek. "I love you, Isabelle."

My heart warmed. "Does this mean we're still engaged?"

A small laugh escaped his lips. "You're not getting away from me. As soon as we get this mess with the Dregans sorted, I'm taking you straight to the high priest."

My smile bordered on a grin. "I look forward to it."

"Me too." Andrew leaned down and kissed me. I melted into him, wanting to assure him that my love resided with him. I couldn't wait to share my life with this man.

We broke apart at the sound of horses' hooves. King Brian and Braidus dismounted and tied their horses to the fence post. I initially felt mild annoyance at the disruption until I remembered Adel and Nathan had probably seen us kissing too. Perhaps it was a good thing we hadn't had time to get too heated. Andrew tucked me against him as the others approached. King Brian and Braidus surveyed us.

"Have you two reconciled?" King Brian asked.

"We have," Andrew said.

"Good." King Brian smiled.

I led everyone inside. "King Brian and Prince Braidus are here," I said to my adoptive parents as we entered the living room.

"Won't you please have a seat?" Adel gestured to the remaining chairs and half end of the couch. "I'll get you some hot spiced cider."

King Brian turned to Nathan and asked, "Are you planning to evacuate?"

"No," Nathan said sharply. "I'm not leaving Isabelle in your care again." He muttered under his breath. I caught the words "abused" and "malnourished."

Adel returned with mugs of hot cider for King Brian, Braidus, and Andrew and also a plate of cookies.

"Adel, the last evacuation group is leaving in thirty minutes." King Brian sipped his cider. "I really think you should go with them. War isn't a place for a gentle woman like you."

"It shouldn't be a place for Isabelle either," Adel said evenly.

"Isabelle is a fighter," Nathan said confidently. "I've trained her well. We talked about it, Adel; don't go back on me now."

Adel wrung her hands, appearing torn. Her eyes darted to mine.

I understood her worry, but I also didn't want my chance to help Aberron against the Dregans to be taken away from me. I could fence just as well as any man, and my magic would be helpful . . . once I got it back. Going with Adel and evacuating with the residents of Saren felt like a waste of my talents.

"Isabelle's mage abilities—when they return—are important for our survival," King Brian said. "We need her."

"I'll take care of her, I promise," Nathan said. "You look after yourself."

Adel sniffed and nodded.

"Come on, I'll escort you." Nathan grabbed her hand.

"I'm coming too," I said.

Millie, the Brunes and Coltrane families, Mr. and Mrs. Bryder, and Mava and Carl had gathered in the center of shop street. Mr. Bryder and Mr. Brunes checked to make sure their luggage was secure in their wagons. Mrs. Bryder muttered quietly to herself as she stared at a list. She grabbed a pencil resting behind her ear to mark something off.

Mrs. Coltrane chased after her little laughing children. "Into the wagon now!"

Mava and Carl eyed me with surprise.

I waved hello to them, then hugged Adel, wishing I had more time with her. I could use her advice when it came to patching things up with Stefan. She always seemed to have the right thing to say to people, and I envied her ability. I had a habit of not giving my words much thought before speaking. Thus, I was more prone to offending others and causing trouble.

"Be safe. I love you," I told Adel.

"Promise me you and Nathan will make it out of this," she said, her brown eyes severe.

"We will. Don't worry," I vowed.

I stepped back, allowing Nathan and Adel to share a goodbye. I walked over to Mava and Carl. "Would you mind keeping an eye on Adel for me, please?"

"Of course," Mava said readily. "Are you going to fight the Dregans?"

My stomach lurched at the thought of war. "I hope it doesn't come to a battle, but I aim to help wherever I can."

"May the Gods bless you," Carl said.

Shortly after, I watched the caravan leave with a tear-streaked Adel, who was riding Amber alongside Carl's wagon. I said a silent prayer to the Gods that they would be protected.

I turned to my family. "Is that everyone?"

"The orate judge has opted to stay," King Brian said.

"No!" I shouted, panic-stricken. "Where is he?"

Everyone was silent.

"Where is he?" I asked again with more force.

"He's in the tunnels advising Joshua," Braidus finally answered.

"I'll see you at home, all right?" I told Nisha.

He whickered. *"I will be there."*

I ran inside the nearest building, Agatha's bakery. The men hitched their mounts to a post and followed.

"Isabelle, stop," Nathan said.

"Stefan can't stay." I yanked on the door handle leading to the stairs. "He's not a soldier."

"I beg to differ," Nathan disagreed. "That boy's a natural. After you left, he started training with me. He took to a sword like a fish to water. He didn't want anyone to get a jump on him again."

"It doesn't matter. He can't be here."

I flew into the cellar and through the door leading to the tunnels. Lanterns had been hung at interval spaces lighting the path. Soldiers sat across from each other, conversing, playing cards, and sharpening knives. I balled my hand into a fist and walked past the soldiers, who were staring at me with gaping expressions. I headed to the three large rooms, simply named First, Second, and Third. Stefan had to be in one of them. I would tell him he had to go. I needed him safe too.

"You're wasting your time," Nathan said behind me. "He's not going to listen to you."

"I'll find out for myself."

I turned the corner and entered the first room. I scanned the soldiers, searching for a face I recognized, but I didn't see anyone. I exited quickly and continued until I reached the second room.

There. I caught sight of the rest of my family, Joshua, Stefan, Malsin, and the boys—leaning over a map of Aberron. I paused for a moment, noticing how focused Joshua seemed to be on Stefan as he pointed things out on the map. Stefan knew this area better than anyone else. It was smart of Joshua to consult him.

I marched over during a pause in their speech. "Stefan."

He met my eyes and attempted a smile but didn't quite manage it. "Hey, Iz."

"Why didn't you evacuate with your family?" I asked.

"I'm needed here." He stuck his hands in his pockets. "They don't know this area like I do."

"You're not a soldier," I said, meaning to speak softly, but my voice carried. The room stilled, or maybe it had a while ago. A quick glance in every direction showed that the soldiers watched me with rapt attention.

"I'm not a postboy, either," Stefan shot back. "Don't try to protect me, Iz. I'm not the prince you're engaged to."

I closed the distance between us, stopping when my boots nearly touched his. I held my hand out in front of me and begged. "Please."

He raised an eyebrow. "Give me a reason to go."

"Your parents, your sisters; I'm sure they're worried sick about you," I said quickly.

He shook his head. "They fully support me in my decision to stay. Try again."

I sighed and rubbed my temple as I stared at the ground. My stomach twisted in knots. "I couldn't bear it if you got hurt or—or killed."

He spoke mockingly but I heard the pain behind it. "Why? Because you love me?"

I forced the air out of my lungs and took another breath as I locked eyes with him. "Yes."

His eyes widened and his lips parted as if he couldn't believe what I'd just admitted. A soft smile slowly crept up his face.

"I've loved you forever," I continued. "You're my best friend. Please."

Stefan frowned as he pulled his hands out of his pockets. "I'm past the best friend stage, Iz, and you've known it for a while. You just never wanted to face it."

I swallowed, hating that I agreed. I knew he had feelings for me, but I didn't want to ruin our friendship, especially when what I had felt for him was nowhere near as strong as what I suspected he felt for me. I loved Stefan with all my heart, but not romantically. Being with Andrew had shown me the difference in my feelings.

I asked, "Is there nothing I can say that will convince you to go?"

He appraised me and then spoke slowly, drawing out the sounds. "There is one thing."

I grabbed his hand. "What?"

"You love me, right?" he asked.

"Yes!" I said, exasperated.

Stefan squeezed my fingers and spoke with conviction. "Then choose me."

I let go and stumbled backward. My eyes darted to Andrew. He'd stiffened to petrified wood, his expression taut.

"You can't want me," I said. "I'm not the same girl who ran out of here. I have magic, and—"

My voice quit working as Stefan stepped forward, undeterred. "I know, but I don't love you any less. Choose me and I'll go. It's the only way."

"I. . ." I choked on the words. "Gods forbid, I can't." I hated myself for hurting Stefan, but I needed to be true to my feelings. Andrew was the one for me.

Stefan stepped back until he hit the table. "Then I'm staying."

I sucked in a sharp breath at his fierce expression. His desires could be read plainly on his face. He wanted to stay to protect Saren just as much as I did, maybe more. As orate judge, he probably had more of a right to be here than I did.

I blinked back moisture and swallowed. "All right then." Words fought through a sludge of emotion. I feared our friendship was finished. "I'm sorry I interrupted. It won't happen again."

In a daze, I turned to go. Andrew stepped forward as if to come to me. I didn't want his comfort, not here in front of Stefan.

Nathan blocked him. "Give her a minute." I saw a future fight on my hands with Nathan's overprotectiveness against Andrew's determination, but at the moment I appreciated he knew me well enough to give me what I needed.

"Fine." Andrew relented under Nathan's hard stare.

As I continued to the exit, Nathan caught up with me. "I told you not to be thinking of romance," he scolded as we passed soldiers, actively transfixed on me. "You've got enough going on already. You shouldn't have thrown your heart out there as well."

I sniffed. "I couldn't help it."

He sighed. "Of course you couldn't. You're all heart and nothing else."

CHAPTER SIX

SAT ON THE COUCH, one arm wrapped around my torso. I struggled to hold myself together and keep a clear head. Pain radiated everywhere as I thought of my broken friendship with Stefan. I wouldn't return to the tunnels unless explicitly ordered. In retrospect, I realized confronting Stefan had caused a scene. I had halted progress on our situation with the Dregans because of my romantic troubles. My shame doubled. *I came to help save Aberron, not impede it.* I scoffed inwardly at this desire. Stefan was now their top consultant on Saren and the surrounding areas. He deserved it as orate judge. I was a shattered mess, with a broken wrist, stitches, no magic, and no job. How could I assist Aberron if I couldn't even save myself?

A knock came at the cellar door. Nathan answered, his fingers curling, probably ready to punch Andrew or Stefan on my behalf. I didn't think he approved of their interest in me. I had half-expected him to send me to my room like a misbehaving child when we arrived back home.

"Relax." Malsin held up his hands. "I'm Ian Malsin, Isabelle's healer and teacher."

Nathan stepped aside, muttering something about barricading the doors. He left the room. I heard the back kitchen door open and close.

Malsin sat beside me and surveyed me with a healer's gaze. I wondered if my outsides looked as bad as my insides felt.

He reached into his bag and handed me a pink vial. "This is an emotion suppressant. It has magical properties, so it might not work until your magic is back, but I want you to keep it. If your emotions become too much to handle, drink it."

"Thanks," I said quietly, slipping it into a pouch on my belt.

"Your neck is bleeding," Malsin observed. "You probably tore your stitches."

We moved into the kitchen so Malsin could lay out his supplies on the table. He helped me take off my armor. "You're safe to leave that off for a bit. There has been no report of the Dregans leaving the Barras outpost. Their ships are still coming in with supplies."

Nathan returned with a basket of eggs. Adel being gone reminded me that I needed to step up and prepare meals for my family while we were here. Keeping the men fed so they could focus on the Dregan threat seemed like a good way to help. I could also do laundry and other menial but necessary chores. Already, the afternoon waned to evening. I realized that I should get started on something to eat. I didn't know when the men would have the time for a meal, but I could certainly keep things warm in the oven for them. Completing tasks like this would be easiest for me if the men all slept here with Nathan and me. It would also make me feel safer and less worried to have them all close.

I asked Nathan to invite all nine members of my family to stay at our house and share in our meals. "Those men are my family, and they deserve a warm place to rest their heads and hot food to eat. We have the space and provisions."

Nathan and Adel had originally planned to have a large family, but their wish did not come to fruition, and the six-bedroom house reflected that. Oftentimes, our house was used by Saren residents who asked if they could put up family who had come to visit. Adel loved chatting with new people and enjoyed playing hostess, which is partly why I became as good of a cook as Adel. We frequently prepared meals for more than just ourselves and always tried to make something enjoyable.

"Fine, but Prince Andrew gets the room with the squeaky door," Nathan replied.

"You still haven't fixed it?" I wondered, remembering Adel asking him months ago to do something about it. She used the closets in that room to hold all her sewing supplies and was often in and out.

"I've been meaning to, but now I'm glad I haven't." He wore a devious smile.

No doubt he wanted to hear Andrew if he tried to sneak into my room in the middle of the night so he could threaten him with his sword.

"Andrew is a gentleman. You have nothing to worry about. If it makes you feel better, go ahead and assign rooms to your liking."

"I will." Nathan strode to the cellar door.

Malsin had just pulled back the layer of bandages near my collarbone when Nathan returned with everyone except Stefan, whom I had also invited. My heart sank. Our friendship was over.

I could hear some of the men settle in the living room. Henry bounded into the kitchen, Dominic and Falden on his heels. They grimaced at the sight of me as they took seats around the table.

Andrew leaned against the doorway, liquid, blazing blue eyes catching mine with sympathy. I held my tongue, stiffening as Malsin applied a salve and complained that I overexerted myself.

"You have no care for your health."

"Sorry," I apologized.

"Try your magic again," Malsin said as he finished patching me up.

I pictured Boomer locked in his cage and pulled the handle. Excitement raced through me when it budged a little. I managed to open it a crack. Boomer stuck his tongue out and lapped my face with a whine. *I'm trying.* Gritting my teeth, I pulled as hard as I could. The door opened a finger length. I tried to access a color. Green, blue, and yellow didn't work. I managed a dull red glow, and a candle flame appeared in my palm.

"It's the best I can do. The other colors aren't working at all."

Malsin grinned. "There's hope for you yet." He activated his magic and managed to lessen the injury to my chest. "We'll have to do this in increments, but you're beginning to respond to my magic now."

Andrew approached as I stood. Gently, he cupped my cheeks, leaned down and kissed me sweetly. When he pulled back, I eyed him questioningly.

"Thank you for staying true to us and our engagement," Andrew said, his voice resonating gratitude. "I'm sure it wasn't easy to turn Stefan down and I'm sorry to see you hurt from a breaking friendship. I'm here whenever you need."

My heart melted at his consideration for me. I wrapped my good arm around his waist and hugged him tight. He felt so good, I wanted to stay in this embrace forever. "You're exactly what I need. I love you, Andrew."

Andrew's smile reached his blazing blue eyes. He pressed a tender kiss to my forehead. "I love you too, Isabelle, more than words can say."

King Brian called for Andrew from the living room. With mutual heavy sighs, we stepped away from each other.

I started on dinner. I had potatoes boiling in our biggest pot and two whole chickens roasting when all the men joined together at the long table in the dining room connected to the kitchen. Falden helped me wherever he could. I tucked the dough into an oiled bowl and left it to rise by the stove.

When I returned to the potatoes, Stefan entered the kitchen. My heart breathed a sigh of relief. He'd come.

He approached with a sorrowful expression. He didn't ask to talk but launched into whatever he wanted to say, knowing I'd listen even if I didn't respond.

"I've made a mess of our friendship." He spoke quietly to not draw the attention of others. "I shouldn't have made you choose like that. That night at Mava's wedding, I had planned to ask you if we could court." He shook his head, seeming to mentally berate himself. "I had it all planned, and then that guy wouldn't take his eyes off you, and, well, you know the rest."

I frowned. All too well . . .

Stefan took a breath and met my eyes, his expression pleading. "Tell me what to do, Iz, because I can't—I can't imagine ever loving someone as much as I love you."

Gods, I couldn't answer that.

Stefan carried the pot to the sink and drained the water out of the potatoes. I suspected he was giving me time to think. Falden melted back to the table, seeing as Stefan had started helping. I mouthed a thank you to Falden, embarrassment trickling through me at what he'd just heard.

He smiled in return. "No problem, Isabelle."

Stefan plunged onward, still keeping his voice soft. "It wouldn't be so hard if you didn't love me, but I know you do. Maybe not the same way you love *him*."

He tilted his head in the direction of the table where Andrew sat, conversing with Braidus. I noticed Andrew had turned slightly to watch us while listening to Braidus.

"I see it as plain as I see the emerald in your eyes," Stefan said. "You. Love. Me."

"Yes," I agreed while I sliced butter and put it in the pot.

"So what makes *him* better? Is it because he's a prince?" he asked.

"No!" I dropped the mashing tool. It clanged on the counter. "You know me probably better than anyone else here except Nathan. I don't want to be queen."

Eyes shot up in my direction, making me mentally curse. I hadn't meant to be loud.

Stefan picked up the masher and handed it to me. "Then what happened? How could you—" He stopped suddenly, then restarted. "Iz, *he* is the epitome of everything you're against. You hate attention and power. You'll suffer more at his side than you would at mine. He can't even take care of you properly. You shouldn't be so beaten up and malnourished. You're worse off than you've ever been."

"That wasn't Andrew's fault," I said, gesturing to my injuries. "I ran into trouble all on my own."

"Well, anyone with a lick of knowledge about you knows you shouldn't be left on your own for very long," he shot back.

"Andrew knows that," I said. "He's saved my life on more than one occasion."

Stefan spoke grudgingly. "You'll lose what's left of your happiness, I know it."

I leveled with him. "When I have all my magic, I am literally the most powerful mage alive, aside from the Gods. I'm going to spend the rest of my life looking over my shoulder, never fully settling for fear of being used for my power. It's happened once before; I have to assume it could happen again. Regardless of whom I choose to spend my life with, happiness will be hard to come by."

"You'll be a bigger target in the capital city." Stefan grabbed my hand. "Come on, Iz, you never wanted to leave Saren. You love its simplicity. Carasmille isn't you, and neither is loving a prince."

I pulled free and set the potatoes aside. I checked the chicken and started making gravy. "I know it's crazy, but I can't help myself. I love Andrew like no other."

"Mind control, maybe?" Stefan said wryly.

A soft, unexpected chuckle escaped my lips.

"I know you hate it when people say it, but you're gorgeous, smart, passionate, kind. Gods, I fell in love with you the moment I saw you when we were five. I knew men would be interested in you when you left, but I hoped you'd be—"

I interrupted, not wanting to hear the rest of that sentence. "You did?"

He shrugged. "Every boy in Saren knows you're the prettiest."

I wondered when the room had gone quiet as I opened the oven door and Stefan took the chicken out to make room for the rolls. Andrew's eyes were riveted on me. So much for a private conversation.

"I would have gladly stayed in Saren if I had that choice, but I didn't, and then I met Andrew, and—Gods forbid, I can't explain it—I just felt drawn to him. I tried to fight the attraction, swear on the Gods I did, but it was like being thrown into a fire. He consumed me."

Stefan scowled. A minute or two of silence passed while I awkwardly shaped the dough into rolls and put them in a pan. I shoved them into the oven, grateful I could do it one-handed.

"I just don't understand, Iz," he finally said. "You're giving up so much that defines you."

Malsin spoke. "Maybe Isabelle and Andrew have the makings of an Amora bond. That would explain her sudden, all-consuming, fiery love for him."

There were raised eyebrows and murmured musings at the possibility among those who understood the term.

"A what?" Stefan and I asked, turning around at the same time.

Malsin explained, "An Amora bond is a connection between two mages, male and female, of procreation age. They are sometimes called "mage mates." Their magic literally binds their hearts together, linking them as a single unit so that they will have children to carry on the magic. A self-preservation sort of thing."

The idea of having children didn't scare me. I'd always seen myself having a family in my future. I knew Andrew would make a great father too. He was attentive, gentle, and firm when the situation called for it. All good qualities for a parent. Still . . .

"No one thought this was relevant to tell me?" I asked, unable to hide the irritation in my voice.

"Slystream waits till the end of the year to teach us about it," Henry said. "We haven't had that lesson yet."

"I thought it more prudent that you understand how to control your newfound magic before we delved into this," Malsin said. "It's not often someone finds their mage mate anyway. I've been around tons of mages and never found mine."

Andrew shrugged when my gaze landed on him. "I honestly didn't give it any thought. I never anticipated searching for a bond when it came time for me to find a wife. I didn't think it mattered too much."

Should it matter?

King Brian said, "It's not a common practice to search one out anymore. Thus, the odds of finding your mage mate are slim. Many settle for someone else."

Malsin responded, "Probably due to the downsides. One of them is that the mages *do not* get to choose who their mage mate is. Another is that the bond is unbreakable. Hence the name "Amora bond," for it is thought that only the Gods have the power to change it. Some even think Amora assigns bonds based on whom she believes would be compatible nature-wise, but I don't know if it's true or not."

"I shared an Amora bond with Hannah, Braidus's mother." King Brian's expression turned distant. "There are no words strong enough to describe its magnificence. Our magic somehow knew that we were meant to be soul mates. I cherish the memories."

The mood in the room turned solemn. Braidus especially looked sad. I couldn't imagine how King Brian must have felt when he lost Hannah. It made me unsure to imagine Andrew and I bonded in such a way. We were preparing for war with the Dregans. If I were in a bond with Andrew and lost him in battle, would I survive, like King Brian did? I didn't know.

"Unexpectedly discovering a mage mate has been known to break up marriages," Joshua added. "And not everyone stays with their mate either. Some people go on to marry someone else."

Stefan perked up at this.

"Actions would have to be truly catastrophic for someone to forsake their bond," King Brian said.

Falden, Nathan, and Stefan helped me set the food on the table.

As dinner commenced, Malsin continued the conversation. "I think it's worth seeing if you are Andrew's mage mate. It might explain why you feel so strongly for him."

Andrew's blazing blue eyes met mine and held them. "It's no secret that as crown prince I've been around hundreds of girls vying for my attention. In seconds, you had me captivated, and in fewer than five days, I fell completely and irrevocably in love with you. Perhaps it is worth it to find out."

Our relationship did come about awfully fast. If we were mage mates, maybe it would convince Stefan that Andrew and I were truly meant to be together. I needed Stefan to give up on me as a lover. I could not offer him what he deserved. With this in mind, I believed this mage mate business was worth checking out. "All right. How can we do it?"

"We'll have to wait until Isabelle can get full access to at least one of her colors," Malsin said.

For the rest of our meal, I worked on activating my magic. I tugged on the door until I could fully access red. None of the other colors worked for me yet since I couldn't get the cage open all the way. Everyone seemed pleased by the progress.

After dinner we moved into the living room, bringing a few chairs from the dining room so everyone could be seated. Now that I had red magic available, we planned to test for the Amora bond. I sat on a wooden chair in the middle of the living room in full view.

King Brian spoke. His eyes surveyed everyone before resting on me. "To be clear, if your mage mate is in the room, you will be linked together for eternity. It is not a decision to be made lightly."

"Does anybody think it's *not* Andrew?" I asked.

"If it's not Andrew, then you probably don't have a mage mate," Henry said. "You haven't shown the slightest romantic interest in any other mage. I think that's a requirement."

I heard agreement ring about the room.

Another thought occurred to me. "If the Gods assign bonds, what if Amora has paired me with Braidus? Haldren did express a wish for me to consider Braidus as a suitor." It pained me to bring this up, especially since I had no interest in Braidus as anything more than my future brother-in-law, but I couldn't ignore that the Gods liked to meddle with me.

Braidus looked startled. "What?"

This was obviously news to him. "Has Haldren not suggested the same to you?" I asked.

He shook his head. "No. This is the first I've heard of this." He wore a deeply troubled expression.

My brow furrowed. "Huh." Why would Haldren tell me to consider Braidus but not ask the same of him regarding me? I looked at Andrew, who also wore a concerned expression. "Do we take the risk or not?"

Andrew ran a hand through his hair and sighed. "If we don't, we're always going to wonder, and that might drive me insane. I'd rather get the truth."

"Me too." Something in my gut urged me to find out. It was stronger than the potential risk of being bonded to someone other than Andrew. "All right. Let's do it."

Malsin grabbed my hand. I let my mind go blank, allowing him to connect his magic with mine and direct it.

My heart pulsed. The rhythmic thump of my heartbeat grew louder until I heard nothing else. Originating from my heart, going through my attire, a nautical rope appeared. It nearly stole my vision with its brilliancy. Threads of ruby intertwined silver as it wrapped itself around my chest in a soft caress. Frozen, I waited for a strong emotion to hit me, but nothing came. Perhaps because I hadn't connected with anyone yet?

Malsin spoke in awed tones. "I've never seen a bond this strong before. This is triple the normal size."

"When has Isabelle ever been the standard?" Dominic said rhetorically, causing others to chuckle. He turned to Henry. "I'll bet you a sundal something unexpected happens."

"Deal," Henry said.

"If your mage mate is in the room, your rope will naturally seek him out," Malsin explained. "His will connect with yours to create an unbreakable bond."

On cue, the two ends of the cord shot forth, going opposite directions. A blazing silvery light speckled with ruby, sapphire, and gold blasted the room. Blinded, the men shouted indiscernibly. I fell out of my chair, startled by the surge of adrenaline to my heart, like I'd been zapped with a lightning bolt.

The light dimmed. Dumbfounded silence permeated the room. I looked up to see the rope going in two different directions. One end wrapped around Andrew, joining a silver rope with threads of sapphire. The other coiled around Braidus, linking to a silver and gold line. The cords interweaved as they came closer to me, creating a thick braid of silver, gold, sapphire, and ruby. It circled my chest twice, ending and beginning with my heart. It effectively tied *me* to the princes.

Sitting on opposite sides of the room, Braidus and Andrew stared at each other with mirrored shocked expressions. Stefan's face fell and he put his hand on his forehead as if he didn't want to look anymore, but couldn't stop himself.

Suddenly frantic to get the rope off, I gripped it, relieved it was as tangible as a real cord. As I tried to pull it off, a sharp pain pricked my heart. Braidus and Andrew gasped. Undeterred, I blasted at it with a series of mini fireballs. The pain increased. I refused to let it intimidate me.

Braidus and Andrew gripped their chests. "That hurts, Isabelle!" they cried.

The rope remained whole. I pulled a dagger off my belt.

"Oh no you don't!" Andrew dropped to the ground and wrestled the knife out of my hand.

"I don't want it!" I shrieked. "Get it off!"

I pulled on the rope, digging my nails into the fibers as though I were piercing my fleshy heart. My knife slid under the couch as Andrew struggled to pry my hand off. Braidus joined the fray. Together they restrained me.

"It's unbreakable," Braidus reminded me. "You're only causing us pain."

I spoke vehemently. "No, I'm not going to be tied to two men. It needs to go. *Now.*"

"There's nothing we can do," Andrew said gently.

"I refuse to believe that." *Amora, if you make the bonds, undo this!* I shouted mentally.

There was a spark of blinding white light and Amora appeared. She flashed pearly white teeth at me. "Congratulations; you've discovered the third man."

I glared.

She sighed. Her lips pinched. "Contrary to popular belief, I do not assign mage mates. This is not of my doing." She studied the cord wrapped around the three of us. "Your bond is too strong, even for me. I cannot break it."

My heart plummeted into despair. "We're really stuck?"

"You are bonded to Princes Braidus and Andrew Sorren for eternity." Amora's eyes gleamed with delight. "Do keep up the romantic drama with your three lovers. It has certainly kept me entertained." Laughing, she vanished before I could retort.

Dominic held out his hand. Henry grudgingly reached into his pocket and paid him a sundal.

Gods forbid, I'm bound. I clamped my eyes shut as the room swayed. Nausea rolled into my stomach. Braidus and Andrew let go of me, seeming to sense my defeat. I shut off my magic, praying I'd never have to see the bond again. The rope vanished, but my heart felt funny, as if it lay just under the surface, pulsing like its own entity.

"We should talk about this," Andrew said after a couple of minutes of silence.

My eyes snapped open. "There's nothing to talk about. It was a mistake. I shouldn't have agreed to do this." I rose and left the room, anxious to get away—process.

"Let her go; she needs a minute alone," Nathan said.

"Someone should warn Isabelle she's going to experience some changes," Malsin said, guilt in his tone. "There's no on-and-off switch with the bond, not like her regular magic. We should've discussed that beforehand."

I paused in the hallway to catch my breath and decide where I wanted to go.

Andrew spoke with confusion. "Yes, you should have, but I really didn't think Isabelle could be bonded. Did you?"

"No," King Brian, Joshua, Braidus, and Nathan said.

Overwhelmed, I stumbled to a kitchen chair and sat, resting my face in my hand. *How in the Gods could this have happened?*

I took my frustrations out on the kitchen, cleaning every nook and cranny. I mercilessly scrubbed everything in sight, muttering a stream of curses as I worked. *Inexplicably tied to Braidus too.* No wonder Haldren had done his best to redeem Braidus in my eyes and suggested I consider him a suitor. He'd probably peered into my heart like Amora had and known we could be bonded too. *Ugh, why did I decide to go with my gut?* I wished Malsin had never brought up the bond and that I'd never learned of it. Had the magic made me fall in love with Andrew? Would it make me love Braidus too?

My stress levels rose exponentially.

Andrew came up behind me. Deftly he snatched the towel and set it on the counter. "The kitchen is clean."

"I'm sorry," I whispered with tears in my eyes. "I'm so sorry."

Andrew turned me around and wrapped me in a hug. He kissed the top of my head. "I know."

I clung to him, pressing my cheek to his chest. I breathed in his cinnamon woodsy cologne. *Home.* His exuded calm transferred to me, healing my fiery veins with cool water. Exhaustion seeped into my bones. I closed my eyes.

Andrew removed my weapons belt. I heard it being set on the counter. He lifted me into his arms, cradling me like a child. "Come on, let's get you into bed."

Barely awake, I subconsciously snuggled against him as he carried me up the stairs behind Nathan, who led the way. Andrew set me on my bed.

"I'll take over," Nathan said.

Andrew pressed a light kiss to my lips. "I love you, Isabelle."

"I love you," I mumbled as I buried my face into the pillow.

Nathan removed my boots and pulled the blanket over me. "Sleep."

CHAPTER SEVEN

HE SUN HAD YET to rise when I woke. Distorted memories of chasing Andrew through the Trivail forest only to be thwarted by Stefan and Braidus darted through my mind. A dream. No, a reality. *Bonded.*

Abruptly fully awake, I slipped out of my room and slinked through the dark and silent house, catching sleeping forms sprawled over couches and chairs. I headed to the bath. While washing and dressing, I worked on opening my magic further. I yanked on the door to Boomer's cage until I got it halfway open. I managed to access yellow and a dim blue along with the red. This meant if our issues with the Dregans turned into a battle, I had the power to work with fire, wind, and water. I could create fireballs, tornadoes, and ice spears. Progress.

While fixing my hair, I shielded my eyes against a sudden bright silver flash. My hairbrush clattered to the floor. My heart stuttered as I gazed upon a man with fiery red-blond hair and sea-green eyes who was suddenly sitting in the chair in the corner. He had a perfect complexion against ornate silver-trimmed black clothes. The insurgent. No, the Fate.

He smiled, radiating power. "Call me Isaac, little mage."

Gods forbid. I fought against the urge to bolt. It was a silly notion to think I could outrun a Fate. No, I needed to stand my ground and respond with a cool head. I willed myself to calm down.

"What brings you here?" I asked slowly, forgoing niceties, as he'd see through them.

His eyes roamed over me as if dissecting my insides. No doubt he could see into the very recesses of my soul. "I grow interested in Haldren's pet project."

"Project?" My voice rose an octave.

Isaac rested his elbows on the arms of the chair and pressed the tips of his fingers together. "Project," he confirmed, his voice ringing with conviction. "I'm surprised at how well you're turning out. For a mere slip of a girl, you're proving to be stubbornly resilient." His lips curved into a hint of a frown.

"Excuse me?" I quirked an eyebrow, needing clarification.

He spoke knowingly. "Haldren is providing life experiences to shape you into whom *he* wants you to be. For example, it was very clever of him to use Braidus to kidnap you and force you to steal in exchange for Henry's life. It revealed so much about your character. Haldren benefited greatly from the discoveries."

My eyes widened. *Haldren is the proprietor?*

Isaac grinned as he read my thoughts. "One and the same."

He waved his hand and a large bead of water hovered in the air. A scene formed inside the bead. Braidus was shackled to a stone wall, barely recognizable underneath bruises and cuts. My stomach lurched. Two exceptionally tall men carrying large syringes with needles moved toward him. A bright flash and Haldren appeared. He grabbed Braidus. Together, they vanished.

With a flick of the Fate's fingers, the water bead disappeared. "Haldren is crafting you into a tool. A momentarily useful product to use and discard." Isaac shrugged dramatically as he revealed the secret.

I fought to get breath into my lungs. "What?"

He chuckled. "It shouldn't come as a surprise. The Gods do not appear to the same mortal for pure enjoyment's sake as often as Haldren does for you. His arrivals at your most dire moments, like that poisonous chains incident, are to instill trust so you'll blindly follow him and carry out his future needs."

I narrowed my eyes. "Why are you telling me this?" *Is it even true?*

"Oh it's true, little mage," he assured me as he leaned back. "Speak with Braidus if you seek additional validation. He will confirm it."

I repeated my question.

"Ruining Haldren's plans amuses me," he said with a satisfied gleam in his eyes. "Enjoy your new reality, *little mage puppet*." With a silver-colored flash, he disappeared.

With trembling hands, I bent and picked up my hairbrush. Haldren was the proprietor? He was behind my kidnapping? Forcing Braidus into it the same way Isaac had forced him to kill my parents? Were all Gods the same? I wanted to ask Braidus if this were true, but I wondered if he even knew for sure. How much of his life had they stolen from him? And why? What did they want with me? A part of me wanted to get back at Haldren for all the trouble he'd caused me. Despite being an exceptionally strong mage, I had no power against a God. It would be foolish to try anything.

I finished pinning my hair and exited the bathroom. The house remained quiet. The men still slept. Good. They needed as much rest as they could get in case we battled today. I appreciated the silence that allowed me to work through my tumbling thoughts. Isaac's voice still rang in my ears: "Little mage puppet." Ugh! I entered the kitchen and got a start on breakfast. Keeping my hands busy was my best line of defense against mental turmoil.

The clock chimed six a.m. when I pulled hot, spiced-apple muffins out of the oven, which would join the mountain of bacon, eggs, potatoes, and oatmeal I'd cooked. I might've overdone it.

King Brian arrived as I poured myself a cup of hot chocolate. He was freshly washed, and a pine-soap scent wafted around him.

"Good morning, Isabelle," he spoke cautiously, as if I might suddenly turn hostile.

I'd better behave today. "Good morning." I forced a smile.

"How are you?" he asked, settling at the head of the table.

I deflected. "Hot chocolate?" I held up an empty mug.

He smiled. "Yes, please."

Pouring some into a cup, I handed it to him. King Brian took a sip.

His eyebrows raised in surprise. "Oh, that's good."

My chest seized with sudden emotion—a deep, raw pain. I gripped the back of a chair with one hand; the other flew to my heart as I gasped for breath. As quickly as it came it eased. *What in the Gods was that?* The bond?

"Isabelle, speak with Malsin as soon as you can," King Brian said. "There's relevant information concerning bonds that should have been explained to you last evening before we performed the check. It was a lapse of judgment on our parts."

I nodded.

My chest pulsed wildly with feelings I struggled to name. The rest of the men trickled into the kitchen within the next ten minutes. Suddenly, the same dark and heavy emotion again slammed into me like a tidal wave, stealing my breath. Braidus and Andrew walked in together, deep in conversation.

"She feels too Gods-forbidden much," Braidus growled.

Andrew grimaced as he rubbed his heart. "I know."

Abruptly ill, I ran out the back door into the snowstorm and vomited. The intensity of the emotion increased. I clutched my chest.

Malsin was at my side almost instantly.

"It's all right, Isabelle." He fished out a pink vial. "Drink this. It'll help."

Desperate for relief, I downed the contents. A quiet calm thankfully muffled the force lying under the surface. Malsin supported me as we went back inside. Falden handed me a warm wet cloth to wipe my mouth. Pity shone strong in almost everyone's eyes.

"Can someone please tell me what in the Gods is happening?" I asked as Malsin helped me into a chair.

Malsin spoke. "As you well know, magic is based on emotions and intent. Amora bonds take that to a new level. The rope literally connects your heart to theirs, allowing you to share emotion, impressions, and, in some cases, magic."

"Share emotion," I repeated. My eyes darted unwillingly to the princes. I groaned. "Oh Gods, no." I buried my face in my hand.

"Probably should've explained this before; alas, nothing can be done about it. Sorry." Malsin spoke gently, regretfully, as if giving a death sentence to his patient. "You now experience Braidus's and Andrew's emotions and they feel yours, all simultaneously—though the princes should not be able to feel the emotions of one another. Unfortunately, there is no turn off valve like for magic."

Dismay plowed through me like a stampede of cows. First Isaac and his news about Haldren and now this.

"Isabelle!" Braidus cursed my name through gritted teeth.

"Tone it down, please," Andrew begged.

Stefan entered the kitchen. He must have gone through the tunnels, for no snow coated him. He assessed the situation in seconds. In two strides, he came to my side.

"Come here, Iz." He pulled me out of the chair and enfolded me in a hug. "You're all right." He rubbed my back. "Whatever it is, you'll be fine."

I didn't think I had it in me to speak, so I hugged him tighter and buried my face into his thick fur jacket. My distress ebbed through his calming presence. I wasn't happy in the slightest about the bond, but I had to face up to my actions and suffer the consequences. I took a deep breath, exhaled, and did it again, forcing myself to adapt.

"That's better," Stefan said approvingly as he felt me relax.

A sharp sting of jealousy that clearly wasn't mine pricked my heart.

I maneuvered out of Stefan's grasp. "Come eat." I tugged him into a chair.

"Have you eaten?" he asked.

"I'm good," I said, settling into my chair again.

"She just threw up breakfast," Dominic explained to Stefan.

"Why?" he asked.

"This Gods-forbidden bond!" I complained. "We get to share each other's emotions, and there's no way to stop it."

Stefan frowned. "That's not good."

Not at all. I spoke to the group. "Is there anything else that should have been explained to me before I agreed to check for a bond?"

Malsin set his cup of hot chocolate down. "Mage mates possessing the same color can share their magic."

Everyone was listening as they ate.

Malsin spoke to the group. "Both princes can now tap into Isabelle's blue. Andrew, her green. Braidus, her yellow, and the same for Isabelle with their colors. They also—obviously—have the ability to look into each other's mage cores at any time. You can check levels on *all* colors. So even if Braidus and Andrew can't use Isabelle's red magic, they'll know when she's low or full. On shared magic, they all can give or take without consent."

"So if Isabelle sees that Braidus is low on yellow sand, she could send him some of hers?" Henry asked.

"Precisely." Malsin sipped his hot chocolate. "You're not so connected that you would die if one of you emptied your core, but you may feel some of their weakness when their levels are low. Why don't you try it out? Look into each other's mage cores."

Braidus had shut his eyes the moment Malsin mentioned sharing cores, causing my heart to twinge as he checked our bond. Abruptly his eyes snapped open and met mine with intensity. A feeling of accusation from Braidus burned in my heart.

"How long were you planning to keep your new color a secret?" he asked.

"What?" I questioned, along with others.

"Andrew, look," Braidus encouraged.

Andrew shut his eyes and went still. Shock rippled through the bond. He opened his eyes, his expression stern. "Why haven't you said anything?"

Irritation flashed through me. "Excuse me—locked magic! I still can't access green, and I can only get a bit of blue. I haven't looked into my core."

A large sphere of my mage core appeared over the kitchen table as Braidus projected it. Inside the sphere, ribbons of color circled five glass balls, filled to the brim.

"Purple?" I said with surprise.

"This is impossible!" Malsin exclaimed. "There are only four colors."

"What does it do?" Falden asked.

"Like I know," I said with exasperation.

This had to have been Haldren's doing. I focused a minute on pulling Boomer's cage door open and barely moved it another crack.

"I can't get to it."

One of Joshua's lockets started glowing. He grabbed it. "Report."

"Commander Mirran," a man's voice floated out of the locket. "The snowstorm has halted movement. We've seen no major activity out of the Barras outpost or from Prastis since it started five hours ago."

"Thank you for the update. Alert me if anything changes. That is all." Joshua tucked his necklace under his shirt.

King Brian spoke. "This will give us time to better prepare our men. Let's descend to the tunnels and meet with the captains and lieutenants in the First and Second Waves to work on some strategy planning. And let's try to contact that blasted Dregaitian king again to see if we can put a stop to this madness before we end up in battle."

Braidus pushed his long hair away from his face. "I highly doubt he will answer."

"Nevertheless, we must try." King Brian turned to me. "Thank you, Isabelle, for a wonderful breakfast."

"You're welcome." I smiled.

The men rose to go down into the tunnels.

I placed a hand on Braidus's arm, stopping him. "Wait."

He paused, his hazel eyes penetrating mine. The other men stopped and listened as well.

"I saw you shackled to a stone wall, bruised and beaten. Men came toward you carrying syringes with needles. Haldren freed you and became your proprietor in exchange for saving your life."

Braidus nodded. "Haldren told you, then."

Henry's blazing blue eyes widened. "Whoa."

"Haldren told me nothing." I dropped my touch.

Worry slammed into my heart. I stumbled and shook from the force of it. Stefan swooped in and held me. Braidus, Andrew, and Joshua cornered us.

"Who did you speak to?" Braidus asked.

There was a bright flash, and Haldren appeared by the stove. Suddenly I felt a simmering betrayal that heated to a rolling boil. Braidus and Andrew inhaled sharply, hands clutching their hearts. I stepped out of Stefan's grasp to face Haldren.

I lifted my chin, gaze pinned on him. "How dare you try to form me to suit yourself."

He calmly moved forward as everyone got out of his way. "Are you really going to believe the Fate who orchestrated the murder of your parents? Isaac thrives on chaos. He stirs up trouble wherever he can."

"I will not be your puppet, nor will I allow you to play me along for your own purposes—whatever they are." Steel coated my tone. "What you did was wrong."

"Everything I've done has been to make you stronger—to survive this world." A bit of his Godly power flared, causing a gold, ethereal glow around him. "I promised Anne that I would watch out for you. This is me keeping my oath."

"Why did you care so much about my mother?" I asked with suspicion.

"Anne was the spitting image of her ancestor, my sister Helen," Haldren explained. "Because of her likeness, I developed a friendship."

That stopped me in my tracks. "We're related?"

I peeked around Haldren to catch Joshua's eye. His surprised expression told me he hadn't known either.

"Yes." Haldren nodded. "I have always kept an eye on my sister's descendants, following births, marriages, and deaths. Occasionally, I gave aid when needed." He looked at me with the air of a man in power. "Isaac neglected to tell you this. He twists information to make you think the worst of someone. He did it with Braidus and his father, and now he seeks to pit you against me for his own enjoyment."

I couldn't deny that Isaac had seemed awfully happy to make me upset with Haldren.

The God placed his long, nimble hand on my shoulder, causing a jolt to go through me. His eyes briefly focused on my brother's. "You and

Joshua are the last living descendants of my family. I have no intention of discarding you. I seek only the best interests of us all."

My hurt lessened with his admission, but I wasn't completely mollified. I wished he would have said something earlier about our being related.

Haldren read my thoughts. "Gods are meant to watch over the world. Showing favoritism is frowned upon." He dropped his hand. "I ask that this information not leave this room."

Everyone murmured his agreement.

"Why did you make Braidus play a villain?" I asked.

"To test your limitations and strengths and to build character," he answered. "You'll never reach your true potential without trials, and you have *so much* potential. It would be a pity to see it go to waste. I'd like to think Anne would be pleased with the woman you're becoming."

Great, a God of trials. I let my mouth run away from me. "Perhaps it's best if you stay away. I think I've had enough from you."

He chuckled. "Come now, Isabelle, my tests have been a benefit. Your inner strength is growing immensely."

Right, I thought with doubt.

"Do not let Isaac poison you with twisted versions of the truth," Haldren said, his tone a warning. "I will take my leave." He vanished with a bright flash.

I took a breath and exhaled slowly. If Haldren wanted to test me so I could reach my full potential because we were family, why wasn't he doing the same for Joshua? Why had I been singled out?

A new thought occurred to me. Perhaps Joshua's test was keeping an eye on me—a master troublemaker. No doubt he had to exert himself to keep me safe.

Stefan took my hand in his and squeezed. His pale blue eyes gently bore into mine. "Are you all right?"

"Fine."

The Gods were my problem to make sense of. I didn't need to worry my friend. Again, I'd made everyone pause in their efforts against the Dregans to deal with my issues. I didn't want to make that a recurring offense. My focus should be on keeping the men fed and sustained to help them have energy and be ready to tackle the problems at hand. Also, I wanted to work on getting the rest of my magic opened so that if we ended up in a battle, I could use it. Braidus said mages were our best defense against the Dregans, and I wanted to be proof of that with my extensive power.

I forced a smile for Stefan. "Go help strategize with the others. I'm going to clean up here and try to get the rest of my magic working."

Malsin spoke to the group. "I'll remain with Isabelle. I want to do another healing session."

"You've got my support whenever you need it." Stefan kissed my cheek, causing my heart to spike hot from jealousy and irritation. I assumed this emotion came from Andrew, though I could not tell his emotions apart from Braidus's yet.

I watched Stefan file out with most of the men and held back a frown. My attempt to convince him to give up on me by checking for an Amora bond obviously hadn't worked. How long would it take for him to accept that Andrew and I were meant to be together?

Andrew stayed a moment longer. He leaned down and kissed me. "Try not to get into any trouble for the few hours I'm gone."

I smiled up at him. "Don't worry. I intend to do what ladies do best: keep house and ensure my family is fed. I don't want to get in the way of the men."

Relief melted the lines of stress on his face, and I felt it along with him. "That's perfect." He pressed another quick kiss to my lips. "I love you, Isabelle."

My heart warmed at his affection. "I love you too."

Andrew strode down the stairs and into the tunnels.

Malsin turned to me with a smile. "You've got enough magic open that I think we might get you all healed in one go."

"Please," I begged.

He chuckled. He took out the stitches first, then placed his hand in mine and closed his eyes. A moan escaped my lips as his magic soothed the hurts I'd deliberately been putting in the back of my mind. Energy flooded through me. I felt the bone in my wrist snap into place. The wound to my chest eased as did the cuts on my neck and the abrasions on my knee.

Malsin opened his eyes with a grin. "All better."

"I love you, Malsin," I blurted.

He laughed and gave me a hug. "I'm quite fond of you too, Isabelle."

With the men in the tunnels with the soldiers, the house felt empty. The snow came down in torrents, restricting me to in-house chores. It had to be one the worst storms Saren had ever seen. Thoughts of Haldren and Isaac filled my mind and ended fruitlessly. I couldn't decide which man was telling the truth. Flickers of emotions from Andrew and Braidus entered my heart at seemingly random times.

I started preparations for the next meal, retrieving a huge slab of beef for a slow roast in the oven. Nathan always kept our cold cellar stocked well. Food preparedness was important to him, he having once been caught in a storm as a child that holed his family up, ill-equipped. "Almost started eating my leather boots," he'd told me with a shudder.

Malsin sat at the dining room table, writing notes in his journal and inspecting a handful of small jars with strong-smelling contents.

I recognized the tinctures as Millie's. "I see you got your hands on some of Millie's remedies."

He grinned, his eyes alight with excitement. "That lady is a treasure. She was kind enough to give me all these bottles to inspect. I am astounded by her knowledge of herbal medicine." He gestured to the jars. "These are amazing!" He grabbed a leather-bound book and held it up to me. "Look, she even gave me her only copy of her personal medicine journal to help injured soldiers. It has recipes and family case histories and everything. I love it."

I matched his grin. "That's wonderful."

Dominic suddenly appeared to fetch Malsin for King Brian, who had some questions.

Malsin eyed me sternly, his hand on the cellar door. "Stay inside and don't get any rash ideas. I'll be back soon."

I held back an eye roll. "It'll be fine."

All morning, I continued to tug on Boomer's cage, determined above all else to get my magic back. I opened as many colors as I could and played around. I produced a small fireball, a palm-sized tornado, and star-shaped ice sculptures I put in the sink to melt.

I jumped on the balls of my feet with excitement when I managed to access green. Immediately, I used it to brighten the house plants.

Henry walked in from the cellar door during my happy dance. He laughed. "You got all your magic back?"

"Not purple yet, but green!" I beamed. "It's progress." I wasn't sure I wanted to touch purple anyway. The fact that no one knew anything about it disturbed me.

"We're going to do some training outside," he said. "I came to get you."

I put on my armor and followed him into the tunnels. I did my best to ignore the stares of the men who again questioned my presence.

"All healed up, it looks like," one man said.

Another spoke. "She's too small to be a warrior, and yet they gave her a sword."

"Must be a good mage like the commander," a dark-haired man replied. "The Gods know we need mages against the Dregans."

I followed Henry into the second room. Soldiers congregated everywhere, making the space feel tight. My family surrounded the table with Haldren's magical map of Aberron on it.

Braidus approached me with a smile. "Congratulations on accessing green. It is good to see your magic returning so quickly."

My eyes widened. "How did you know?" Could my emotions convey thoughts? Did he and Andrew get a picture or sense of what I saw? If I wished for a piece of berry pie, would they know I wanted it?

Braidus said, "The longer we are acquainted, the more impressions I get of you. It's not word-for-word mind reading, but I get a gist of where your thoughts lie based on your desires. You have so much going on in your mind that you probably haven't noticed it yet."

Malsin spoke up. "I don't know if it's true, but I've heard that you can increase impressions and intensify the connection if mage mates show mutual whole-hearted acceptance for their bond while their rope is visible."

"Really?" Braidus's interest caught me off guard.

"It's not happening."

My alarm made him chuckle.

King Brian pulled back from the map. "Let's work out some of this tension."

King Brian and Joshua planned out our training session. A group of five hundred soldiers would come up to the surface. Braidus would teach them what they needed to know and, in turn, they would show what they had learned to a new group, freeing time for Braidus to be on hand for his father.

The first group of soldiers followed behind us as we exited the tunnels through Mr. Layder's house. The snow still hadn't let up and had accumulated to heights I'd never seen before in Saren.

Stepping out, I sunk all the way up to my middle thigh. "How am I supposed to fight in this?"

The men pouring out of the tunnel chuckled. I scowled.

"You're the size of a child." Braidus plucked me out and carried me in his arms, trudging easily through the powder to the open field.

My retort died on my lips as my heart thumped faster and slightly offbeat at our proximity. I willed myself to calm down, not wanting him to sense my discomfort. Though I still had a hard time differentiating Braidus from Andrew with the bond, I had the sense that Braidus felt perfectly at ease while carrying me. It made me wonder how he could be so comfortable when I was not. Didn't he feel any sort of annoyance or frustration to have become tied to me? We were not lovers, barely even friends. It was cruel for us to be bonded.

Braidus set me down in the middle of the field. Again, I sank and threw my hands out to steady myself, eliciting a laugh from the men.

"Use your magic to create a workable space," Braidus said.

"Melt the snow, Isabelle." Falden held out his glowing red hand. The snow vanished as he turned around in a circle creating a space.

"Right." I felt stupid for not thinking of it. Following Falden's actions, I liquefied the snow, giving me ten paces in either direction to work with.

Joshua gave a quick introduction and stated the reason for our assembly. "Braidus will be leading these lessons. He is the only one among us who has any real experience with the Dregans and their king. His instruction will be vital to our survival. Give him your full cooperation. Understood?"

"Yes, Commander!" the soldiers shouted.

Joshua stepped back, allowing Braidus to take his place.

Braidus amplified his voice with magic, allowing it to carry. "It is extremely rare for a Dregan to possess magic. They rely on their mammoth size and brute strength. Treat them like giants. Attack low. Knock them down and go for the quickest kill." He gestured to the blanket of white. "The snow will not hinder them as much as us. The Dregans are used to freezing weather, so their armor consists of thick fur with metal spikes sewn into it. They enjoy impaling their opponent as they crush them." He wrinkled his nose in a way that made me think he'd seen it happen more than once. "Try not to let them get their arms around you."

A host of soldiers grimaced. One outright shuddered.

"Show no mercy, for you will get none in return," Braidus said. "The first son of every family in Dregaitia is delivered to King Cekaiden at the age of five. They immediately start training to become a soldier and never see their families again. At the age of thirty—if they've survived—they can take on a wife. At forty, they leave the king's service to produce an heir to send back. Every Dregan you will see has spent his whole life training to kill. They know of nothing else."

Many soldiers, including myself, paled at this.

Braidus continued as if he were lecturing about the weather. But really, he didn't have a choice; we needed to be prepared. "The Dregans prefer to work in swarms, fifty men to a group with one acting as a leader. That leader chooses their targets. They flock, annihilate, and move on. It is swift and efficient."

I imagined a swarm of bees or grasshoppers. Both could be devastating.

Braidus shifted on his feet, the wind catching his long hair. "We must work in units to combat our foe. If you find yourself alone, you will die. Always keep an eye on the size of your group. If your numbers are lower than twenty-five, join another unit."

It would be a challenge to keep an eye on your unit and simultaneously fight. I hoped we could manage it.

Braidus's voice boomed with intensity. "Do not try to pull anyone to safety. The Dregans will switch focus and center their attack on you, resulting in multiple deaths. Some will deliver non-lethal but crippling injuries. If you're unable to fight and miraculously still alive, play dead. It is your *only* chance of survival. Dregans leave no job unfinished."

I frowned. Thorough killing machines, exactly what we needed to face. I prayed for Aberron to come to a resolution before we ended up in a fight.

Braidus enlisted Joshua's help to separate the mages from the other soldiers. There were only about thirty soldiers out of the five hundred with us who had mage abilities. I found the number disheartening considering they were our best defense. Perhaps there were more numbers in other groups.

"Mages, you are our best advantage," Braidus told them. "Use your magic wisely. Common Dregans naturally fear magic and will only target you if they are in a large enough swarm. A Dregan will never face off against a mage alone." He paused. "Although, when I left Dregaitia, King Cekaiden was putting extreme effort into training his men not to fear magic. It's possible we may get bolder Dregans than I anticipate. If it comes to a fight, there will not be time for a mage to recharge, so keep an eye on your levels, and connect with other mages if you want to do something big."

The mages nodded, their expressions grim.

"Greens will be assigned to stay in the back. Your healing powers are our most valuable asset. Yellows are to use their camouflage ability and work as assassins. Take out any Dregans that appear to be issuing commands. You are the only ones who shouldn't concern yourselves with staying within a unit. Red and Blue mages will be spread out amongst the groups. If possible, every group should have at least one mage. That will better our odds for all concerned. Remember, Dregan soldiers work fast; killing is second nature to them. They will not retreat unless ordered by their present general or king—even if they are losing."

Joshua joined Braidus again and assigned units following Braidus's instructions. The two of them went over several mock scenarios with Braidus acting as a Dregan and using their tactics.

"It's all about speed and efficiency," Braidus said. "They will go for the quick kill and move on. They do not want to get locked in a sword battle. If you appear to be unwinnable, they may retreat to look for a weaker link, then return for you with greater numbers."

Anxiousness curled low in my belly at the skill with which Braidus wielded his sword against my brother. Joshua held his own but some of his moves were jerky, revealing their newness to him as he adapted to combat Braidus. If all Dregans moved with the instinct and calculation that Braidus did, we were in big trouble.

"All right, boys, go practice." King Brian shooed the men in my family away to train with the soldiers. "Isabelle, stay with me, please. I don't want you joining all the men just yet."

I nodded and remained by his side, though my fingers itched to use my sword. It'd been too long since I'd exercised. I caught sight of Stefan fencing with Nathan and was momentarily surprised by his skills. Farmer turned postboy turned orate judge turned soldier. He really had taken to a sword like a fish took to water. Perhaps I didn't need to worry so much about him after all.

I hated standing around while everyone else got to have their blade in their hands. I worried King Brian would keep me away from the fighting altogether. I had just as much of a right as everyone else here to do my part to keep Aberron safe. I took a deep breath and mustered up some courage to say as much to King Brian. "If it comes to a fight, I want to be in the thick of it. I'm a good fighter and my magic is extensive. Let me use it."

King Brian appraised me, his eyes calculative. "I've never seen you fight."

"You've only spent a week in my company," I answered. "I'd be happy to demonstrate."

"All right," he said, "fence with me. If I deem you good enough, I'll put you with me in the middle of the fray."

I quickly agreed.

We moved into position. King Brian wrapped himself in some sort of blue shield with his magic. I briefly recalled Henry coating himself in a similar shield when we were escaping from Braidus during our kidnappings.

I needed to learn this. "How did you do that?"

"Shield making hasn't been taught to you yet?" King Brian asked me with surprise.

I got the impression it must be a basic lesson. "No."

"Well, we must remedy that quickly. Shields made of blue magic are the strongest out of all the four colors. Therefore, they are called Zadek shields, for it is commonly said that only a God has the power to break through them."

A memory sparked within me of my imprisonment after I had robbed the royal treasury. "A soldier covered the cell door with a Zadek shield to prevent me from breaking out. It worked well."

King Brian nodded; his expression pleased. "All mages who are imprisoned will have a Zadek shield over their cell doors since they have an easier chance of escaping compared with a regular person. It is good to know a mage as powerful as you could not break it."

I smiled. "Well, I may be powerful, but I'm woefully inexperienced when it comes to magic. Hence your need to teach me how to make a shield." I hoped King Brian wouldn't see my lack of knowledge as a detriment. I would accept any teaching I could get to improve.

"Right," he said. "Here's how to make one. Think of water as a protection. Imagine the water clinging to you, forming a shield around your body or what you want to protect or block. Letting the magic know the level of threat you feel will determine how strong your shield is."

Activating my magic, I pictured a wall of water and imagined walking through it, letting the water cling to me as a shield. *Protect me.* A weightless, cool, liquid substance like syrup formed and enveloped me. I held my hands up to my face, intrigued and also surprised that I was able to see through it perfectly, even though it protected my eyes.

"It's weak, but you get the idea," King Brian said.

"How do I get rid of it?" I asked.

"Simply tell your magic that you don't need it, that you're safe."

He drew his sword and pointed it at me. Seeing the threat of the pointed blade helped me strengthen my Zadek shield until he deemed it good enough to deflect an attack. "Now show me what you can do."

I felt a surge of anticipation. My eyes darted to the left to see that Braidus, Joshua, and Andrew had quit practicing and come to watch. I realized, despite professing a love of my sword, they'd never actually seen me fence before either. *Here's my chance to prove I'm a warrior.*

The second I slid into place, King Brian sprang. Adrenaline running high, I met his attacks with vigor, blocking and lunging with a fierceness I didn't even know I had in me. Our bodies were dancing, our blades a blur of motion. A laugh escaped my lips as King Brian bent to avoid impalement. He grinned, obviously surprised and pleased by my skill. He intensified our fight, pulling moves I'd never seen before. I jumped, ducked, blocked, and twisted to maintain a defensive position while I searched for an offensive. Midtwist, he struck hard and, despite my best efforts, my sword slipped from my grasp. I struggled to reclaim it, but King Brian's sword swung again and hit me in a killing blow that bounced off my shield. I had lost. Now they'd never let me fight. I removed the shield and turned off my magic.

Through the bond, I felt admiration and . . . lust? I whipped my head around to figure out which brother felt what. Braidus wore a soft smile, but Andrew grinned wolfishly. Not Braidus, then. Thank the Gods.

"You fight well, Isabelle," King Brian said approvingly. "You've earned your place."

My jaw dropped. "But I lost."

"There are not many who can withstand a duel like we just had. I was harder on you than I usually am on my soldiers." He smiled, clapping a hand on my shoulder. "With your magic, I think you'll be a great asset."

Braidus, Joshua, and Andrew approached.

"Nathan's taught her well, don't you think?" King Brian asked his sons.

"She'll do," Braidus said.

I fought against an eye roll because I knew he had been impressed with me.

"Let's work on your offensive and defensive magic," Joshua said to me.

"Great." I smiled

"How about some practice dummies." Andrew created a man's form out of ice, easily a head taller than him. "Did I get the size right?" he asked Braidus.

"Close enough." Braidus lifted his hands and created an ice sculpture beside Andrew's with a few more details, like a spiked coat.

King Brian gestured to the ice soldier Braidus made. "Keep this one for the soldiers to study. Andrew's may be destroyed for defensive training."

"Activate your magic, Isabelle," Joshua said.

I opened the cage, letting Boomer out. My skin lit up like a rainbow as I embraced four colors. All fighting stopped as I caught everyone's attention. The rest of my family joined us. The soldiers approached hesitantly, as if afraid they'd be ordered back.

"Isabelle, stand in the middle," Andrew said.

I moved a few paces, while my family melted to stand with the soldiers now watching. Braidus and Andrew created a series of Dregan ice sculptures to surround me. I shifted my weight restlessly as an eagerness to learn flooded through me. I would gladly accept any teaching to help me become a greater asset to Aberron against the Dregans. Now that I had proved myself well enough with my sword, I wanted to earn their approval with my magic too. I didn't want to give anyone any reason to doubt me.

"Here's where you get to be creative." Andrew grinned.

His and Braidus's excitement came through the bond. I fought against a returning grin.

Braidus gestured to the ice Dregans. "Knock them down using every color available."

"Imagine them as living. Use tactics you would on a real person," Joshua said.

Boomer flashed in front of my eyes, seeking direction. I showed him the ice sculptures and sent a single command. *Destroy.* With a bark, he chose a response from each color. Fireballs shot out of my left hand, ice spears out of my right. The ground rumbled as roots grew, pushing out of the snow to wrap around the ice and tear it down. A yellow tornado lifted one high into the air and dropped it. Ice flew in all directions. Not a single sculpture remained standing.

"Whoo!" Henry, Dominic, and Falden hollered, fists in the air.

Henry jumped with excitement. "That was amazing! Do it again!"

I laughed. My family grinned at me. Shocked smiles appeared on the soldiers' faces.

Hopping over broken pieces of ice, I faced King Brian. "How did I do?"

"You exceeded expectations, Isabelle," King Brian said with a smile.

CHAPTER EIGHT

THE NEXT SEVERAL HOURS passed in a frigid blur. I tugged on Boomer's door, trying to access my purple magic, and got nowhere. It wouldn't budge at all. It frustrated me that I didn't have all my magic back, but I also had much apprehension over a color of magic I knew nothing about. I hoped it would be useful in our plight involving the Dregans.

My family took it upon themselves to train me in battle magic. I learned how to maximize my power to do the most with the littlest amount of magic. My fireballs became smaller but still packed a punch. Though blue was the strongest, I practiced making shields with the other colors. Yellow acted like a tornado; as a weapon came close, it used the wind to redirect. Green shaped itself like thick wrapping vines and shot out a rope to catch what came close. Extremely sharp objects or fireballs could cut through the vines, but they slowed the missiles down enough for me to react before any hit my skin. I loved the red shield that encased me in flames and melted objects.

On fire, I chased Stefan. "Give me a hug; I'll warm you up."

Stefan laughed as he ran. "Not on your life, Iz!"

Pursuing, I turned off red and switched to yellow magic, making myself invisible.

Stefan swiveled around to search for me. "Where'd you go?"

I covered my mouth to hide my snicker. At the last second, I revealed myself and then tackled him from behind. "Got you!"

We fell forward together into the snow, laughing heartily. Stefan shoved snow in my face. I gasped in shock, causing him to laugh harder. We both clutched our sides in merriment. I relished the sort of happiness I'd been missing.

As we stood, I took Stefan's hand. "I'll warm you up."

"Not with fire," he said with warning.

I chuckled. "Of course not." I sent a trickle of heat through our clasped hands to his body, warming him from the inside out.

"Mmm," Stefan moaned. A contented smile graced his face. "That's a real handy trick."

"Great, huh?" I grinned. "I'd better warm up the others."

Stefan reluctantly let me go.

I sidled up to Andrew, who was watching the new set of soldiers learn the fighting tactics needed against the Dregans. I wrapped an arm around his waist and used my magic to heat him.

Andrew sighed and put his arm around me. "Thanks, Isabelle."

"You're welcome," I murmured.

"Stefan makes you happy," he said slowly, not meeting my eyes.

"He does," I agreed. "But my heart is still yours."

"As mine is yours." Andrew pressed a kiss to the top of my head.

I planned to go to Nathan next, but my feet carried me to Braidus. He stood beside his father, shouting directions at the new group of soldiers.

"Are you coming to warm me up too?" Braidus asked, wearing his signature smirk.

"Only if you want it." I shrugged.

"If he doesn't, I do," King Brian said.

I grabbed his hand and sent him heat, earning a delighted smile.

"Thank you, Isabelle."

"You're welcome," I said, happy to be useful.

"I want it too," Braidus said suddenly.

When our hands met, a jolt of lightning sizzled to my bones. Braidus's sudden unsteady breathing, the shock that traveled mutually through the bond, told me he felt it too. Unwilling to study it further—I doubted I could ever truly be comfortable around him—I focused on my task and then let go as politely as possible.

Braidus wore a genuine smile. I found I liked it better than his smirk. It made him more approachable. "Thank you." Affection rippled through the bond.

"You're welcome. Now to Nathan." I hurried away, unsettled at the warmth between us. *Why is Braidus in this bond?*

Right before dinner, Joshua retrieved a case of lockets, allowing King Brian to check with people around Aberron. He started with his spymaster in Carasmille, who had nothing new to report. He then switched lockets to speak with Queen Averly.

"Everyone's scared," she said. "They've started holding vigils in the temples. I'm doing my best to assure the people. The Amora Champions and patrol guards are working overtime. Criminal activity has spiked now that the First and Second Waves are out. Until we have substantial evidence that we didn't start this attack with Dregaitia, the Nistier and Jamaylin ports will be closed to us. They're refusing to ally with 'war starters.' Their words, not mine."

Annoyance shot through me. Of course criminals would take advantage of the situation. They didn't care that Aberron hung on a precipice. As for the other countries' accusations, we were not war starters. How could they give up on King Brian so quickly? He was a great king and profoundly invested in peace—more so than his predecessor, King Jason, had been.

"Figures." King Brian ran a hand through his hair, displeasure written all over him.

"Business is chaotic. Market prices are soaring for imported goods. Brian," Queen Averly sighed. "It's not looking very good for us."

All the men frowned. My chest tightened with Andrew's and Braidus's concern, which magnified my own.

"We'll manage," King Brian said briskly. He quickly updated her on our wellbeing, telling her about the snow and the halted movement from the Dregans. He then added, "Isabelle is taking good care of us." His mouth twitched with a smile as he looked in my direction. "She'd make a fine chef in the castle kitchens."

"Hear, hear!" Henry called, pounding his fist on the table.

I smiled, pleased that they were happy with me. I wanted to be useful wherever I could.

"Oh, that's excellent." Queen Averly sounded relieved. "Promise me, Brian, that you'll do everything in your power to keep our family safe. You all mean everything to me. I'm not strong enough to survive without you."

"Nor am I," King Brian said.

"Make sure the soldiers are getting enough food and rest, too," Queen Averly said. "Don't work them too hard. Did you bring those canisters of sweets?"

"Yes, everyone has a tin of candy from you in their rations."

I admired her big heart and thoughtfulness toward others.

King Brian and Averly said their goodbyes.

I placed a jug of apple cider on the table, finishing off the preparations for dinner. "Let's eat."

The men heartily dug in. Over dinner, Joshua's locket glowed. He picked it up. "This is Commander Mirran speaking."

"Multiple Dregan ships are docking at the Callan outpost," yelled a soldier. "They're pouring out. Gods! There's too many of them!" A loud boom could be heard through the locket.

"They're going to be slaughtered," Braidus said, his voice practical. "We cannot afford to lose our men over a small holding."

"Retreat," King Brian told Joshua. "Send out a notice to all villages in the southeastern province to evacuate to the nearest walled city."

Joshua took the case of lockets and moved into another room to begin relaying instructions. The boys helped me clear the table so King Brian could unfurl Haldren's map of Aberron.

Braidus put his finger on the Barras outpost, near us on the northern side of our province. "They've attacked here and here." He moved his finger down to the Callan outpost. It resided at the base of Aberron, as southward as possible in our province, a two-day ride from Saren, if not more.

"Two points wide apart from each other," Andrew murmured.

"No doubt to conquer the whole southeastern province," Braidus said darkly. "Cekaiden desires additional fertile ground to feed his armies and has eyed this piece of land for far too long. The Dregans will move north from the Callan outpost and inland from the Barras outpost, killing and driving our people out until they have it fortified with Dregan soldiers in every direction."

The thought made my stomach twist unpleasantly. "We can't let them. The southeastern province is almost entirely made up of farmers and ranchers. Sixty percent of Aberron's food comes from this area. All of Aberron would starve."

King Brian spoke firmly. "We're not going to let them take it, not while I am king."

"We'll need to split up the First and Second Waves and choose a spot down south to meet them," Andrew said.

"What terrain advantages do we have in this province?" King Brian asked.

"There aren't many," Stefan said.

We hovered over the map for what seemed like hours, planning and weighing the pros and cons of different battle tactics. Though I had little to contribute, it felt good to be involved. My eyes darted to the window. The men's voices faded into the background of my mind. The snow continued to fall. It would make it very hard for villagers to get to safety. I focused on the map again, seeing the names of the little communities much like Saren. I followed the roads leading from the villages to the nearest fortified cities. The southeastern province had two to speak of: Lokenloch, by Stone Lake, and Pendra, by Grass Lake.

"How is the weather holding by the Callan outpost?" I asked the group.

"The storm has not reached them yet, but they see it," Joshua replied.

I pointed to a spot on the map a little below Saren. Three small towns were grouped there—Kister, Manaria, and Cailen. They would need to travel to Pendra, which would take roughly eight hours on a good day.

"What about this area?"

"Likely snowing there," Stefan said. "The wind has been moving in a southern direction."

"We need Reds to help along the path," I said. "Otherwise, we could doom people to freeze to death. There're hardly any mages in that province—they are too feared—but we need all the help we can get. I suggest we send out a wide notice to attract any in the southern province who may be willing to help with evacuations. Even a few would be better than none." I tapped my finger on the map. "Pendra is one of our largest cities. They may have some they can send."

"Good thinking, Isabelle," King Brian said. "I'll send out an order."

"People are going to balk at the sight of a mage," Stefan told me.

"They either accept our help or face more hardship and possible death," I said bluntly. "Their choice."

"Most Aberronians are sensible enough to accept magic in a life-or-death situation," Nathan said. "I don't think the mages will run into too much trouble."

Joshua rattled off numbers concerning our soldiers, weapons, and food supplies. Information spewed out of him like a bubbling spring. Braidus and Andrew had ready action plans to counter-attack anything the Dregans threw at us. Stefan pointed out the best travel routes to get us to the places we needed to go.

"Make sure you get an equal amount of green mages for each Wave," Malsin said. "It won't do anyone any good to have them all in the First Wave and none in the Second or vice versa."

Henry, Dominic, and Falden listened with rapt attention, no doubt absorbing every detail. This was a great opportunity to get firsthand experience in leadership. My shoulders felt heavy with the weight of all the decisions being made. The bond I shared with the princes tightened with stress as the night went on. I felt for King Brian, who had to be the one to ultimately approve or reject the proposals. Aberron was at stake. What was decided here would affect many lives.

My desire to be of help to Aberron steadily increased to a fervor. I tugged on Boomer's cage, anxious now to get to the purple magic and have all my power available to me. It moved a crack but no more. Near silent curses left my lips toward the archer who had hindered me. While I had great fencing skills, I knew my magic would be even more instrumental.

The clock struck midnight. King Brian rubbed at his temples, as if he fought a headache. Activating my green magic, I reached over and touched his arm, easing his aches and pains.

He smiled at me, his eyes shining with gratitude. "Thank you, Isabelle." He focused on our family. "Let's get some sleep while we can. We'll move into position tomorrow and hope the weather gets better."

We broke apart. I climbed up the stairs to my room with Nathan behind me.

Before I went inside, he pulled me into a one-armed hug and kissed the top of my head. "Sleep well, daughter."

I smiled up at him. "You too."

He attempted a smile and failed. "It's hard without Adel."

I nodded. "I miss her too." Adel was the embodiment of peace and comfort. She never failed to make me feel seen, whole, and loved. I wouldn't be the person I am without her.

"We'll be reunited again as soon as the Dregans are out of Aberron." A real smile graced Nathan's lips. "I'm sure of it."

I appreciated his optimism. "Me too."

I watched him walk down the hall to his room in slow, measured steps before I entered mine and shut the door behind me. I climbed into bed, wishing beyond hope that Aberron would see peace again.

I dreamed of my mage core. Smoky ribbons of red, yellow, green, blue, and purple swirled around. I lifted my hand, casually touching the ribbons, allowing them to seep into my skin. My eyes followed a bright purple ribbon as it danced across the room. I wondered what power it held. Turning, I stopped short and let out a surprised gasp. A man with bright blue robes stood before me. I stilled as his cerulean eyes roved over me. A soft smile graced his lips.

I jolted awake to darkness. My heart raced, my body on fire. I scrambled out of bed in a prickling, pain-induced stupor and fell hard on the floor.

"Ouch!" I rolled onto my back, hitting a table with force. A vase shattered on my head. "Ah!"

Thirty seconds later, my door flew open. Family members piled into my room, bringing with them light from magical orbs. I squinted against the brightness. Braidus used his magic to lift the pieces of glass into the air. He placed them in my washing bowl.

Malsin put a hand on me.

I shot to my feet, skin now blazing. Even a feather touch hurt.

"Don't touch me!" I bit back a cry.

Andrew and Braidus clutched their hearts, wincing with me.

I began to glow a shimmering gold, as though I had collided with stardust. The brilliancy near blinded me. The men gasped. Fear shot through my veins. *What in the Gods is happening?*

Abruptly, it stopped. I sat on my bed, gasping for breath.

Haldren appeared with a flash of bright light. "That went better than expected." He grinned.

Of course he had to be behind it.

"That hurt!" I growled.

"You're fine," he said, seeming unconcerned. "Better than fine, actually."

"What have you done?" I demanded.

Haldren wore an affronted expression. "No need to be so angry. I've given you another gift. Your magic is now extended. It's needed against the Dregans."

"Extended?" I repeated, my brows furrowing. "So, I could heal three people on the verge of death and still have magic to spare; is that what you're saying?"

"You could heal twenty deathly ill people and not even lower your levels to the halfway mark," he answered, smug.

"Oh."

Perhaps I should be grateful. I could do so much more to help Aberron now. But all I felt was suspicion. *Why is Haldren doing this to me?* What had I done to deserve his attention? Couldn't the Gods ensure Aberron had a fighting chance against the Dregans without using me as their tool?

"And the purple magic?"

I detected a bit of exasperation in Haldren's tone. "I told you already; it's a gift to satisfy my curiosity."

"What does it do?" I asked.

He grinned wickedly. "I'm not telling."

I groaned. "Do I have to recharge it?"

"Yes."

"How?"

Haldren shrugged. "With any precious metal—gold, silver, copper, platinum."

My mouth popped open. "Those are not easy to acquire."

Haldren closed his palm, then opened it, revealing a lump of gold. "Use this." He dropped it into my palm.

My hand wavered with the weight.

"The metal will become smaller the more you use it to recharge until it becomes nothing. You will then need to search for a new source. Enjoy your new powers, Isabelle." He disappeared with a roguish grin.

I stuck the lump of gold into my pocket.

My heart tugged as Braidus delved into our bond. A minute later he said, "All colors have gold flecks interspersed."

He projected my core to show everyone the new changes. Gold, smoky ribbons joined the other colors swirling around five glass spheres. I felt a flicker of unease from my mage mates. Braidus made my mage core disappear.

I pictured Boomer. The cage door swung all the way open with barely a tug. He jumped out, tail wagging, barking excitedly.

"I've got all my magic back!"

"That's good," King Brian said with a tight smile.

The clock struck five. I felt bad for waking everyone up so early when we hadn't had much time to sleep. Still, no one seemed inclined to return to slumber, so we retreated to the kitchen to get a start on the day with mugs of spiced apple cider. Before I started making breakfast, I went around and gave everyone (save Stefan, who wasn't there) a boost of energy with my green magic. Immediately, I noticed that the green glow emanating from my skin now sparkled with gold as well due to the changes Haldren had made.

Braidus's eyes danced when I got to him, the last one of the group. "Thank you, Isabelle."

The bond between us heightened with warmth. I froze, staring into Braidus's face. He made no effort to hide that he had some romantic feelings for me. It had a different flavor and tone than what I felt from Andrew. It was softer—less flame and intensity, more ember and tendrils of smoke. Trying to make sense of it, I soaked up the heat, letting it wrap around my heart and settle. It was so different from the feeling I got from Andrew that I didn't know what to think.

Braidus smiled, and I felt that he was pleased. It jolted me into the awareness that I had accepted his affection when I had meant only to understand it. He thought I liked it. Did I? It struck me that I couldn't unequivocally say no.

Gods forbid.

My body spiked with adrenaline. Panic clawed at my insides, twisting and scraping. I made a break for the back door. My movements were jerky as I wrenched it open and leaped out into the dark. I couldn't breathe. I sprinted as fast as my legs could manage. My lungs burned from the cold and lack of oxygen, but I couldn't stop. Not until I had put considerable distance between me and Braidus.

Black spots swam in my vision. I collapsed in front of the maple tree by the creek—my favorite spot in all of Saren—with no knowledge of how I'd made it there so fast. My tightened throat eased up, allowing me to take in air. My lungs rattled with stilted breaths. I couldn't feel my face or my hands. The snow seeped through my shirt and pants, soaking me to the bone.

There was something fundamentally wrong with me. I was wholeheartedly in love with Andrew. I wanted to marry him. How in the Gods could I have liked Braidus's affection for me? It was wrong on every level imaginable. I was a Gods-forbidden traitor. Andrew would surely call off our engagement now. No doubt he had felt me accepting Braidus—albeit unintentionally at first. He wouldn't want to marry a cheater. I dug my stiff fingers into my hair. I hated this bond something fierce.

Footsteps crunched in the snow an hour or so later. People approached. I looked up to see Stefan, Andrew, and Malsin. I wasn't surprised Stefan knew where to find me. I was a little shocked that he had led Andrew with him, in addition to Malsin.

My heart rate picked up speed as the men stopped in front of me. No doubt Andrew would have a host of censuring words that would end with "I don't want to marry you." I wished Braidus had never shown me his feelings. I didn't need this complication.

Stefan dropped to his knees beside me. "Gods, Iz, you're an icicle. You know better than to run out in this weather."

I did, but fear didn't always let me think rationally. Getting away from Braidus took precedence.

Malsin crouched on the other side of me and put his hand on my arm. "We need to get her warmed up. Isabelle, turn on your red magic before you get hypothermia."

"She's still panicking." Andrew bent and scooped me up into his arms. "Relax, Isabelle. I'm not giving you up. I know you still want to be with me, just as much I want to be with you." Turning, he started walking back in the direction he'd come.

Malsin and Stefan followed.

Words tumbled from my chattering lips. "Braidus, he showed me—"

Andrew nodded, his expression even. "I know. You've captured his heart as well."

"I'm sorry," I apologized. "I swear I didn't mean to encourage him. I was just trying to understand. Malsin—" I flicked my eyes in his direction. "There has to be a way to get rid of this bond, please. I don't want to feel this." I didn't want to be affected by two men.

He shook his head. "You heard Amora. There's nothing we can do. You're going to have to work this out with the princes." His tone softened. "A reminder: Amora bonds are meant to be romantic. Your hearts are bound together with constant emotion shared. You can't place too much blame on Braidus for developing feelings for you."

"No, I suppose not," I reluctantly agreed.

I couldn't control Braidus. He had a right to his emotions just as I did. However, what scared me so badly that I had run out of the house was how *I* responded to Braidus. A part of me had *liked* experiencing the heat he emitted. It challenged the trust I had in myself, and that knifed me. I lived with the mentality that I should depend on myself first. If I couldn't do that, then what good was I? What good would I be to help in our efforts against the Dregans?

We reached the house. I petitioned Andrew to set me down. Switching on my magic, I used red to warm myself up. My clothes steamed as I dried them.

Malsin put his hand on me. He let go after a few seconds. "Much better."

The four of us walked through the back door and into the kitchen. Everyone, save for Nathan, had left. I felt relief to not have to come face-to-face with Braidus so soon, although I couldn't avoid him forever. We were still bonded, and since I still wanted to be of assistance with Aberron's efforts against the Dregans, I had to work with him.

My priorities had gotten switched again with my romance troubles taking the lead. If I couldn't control myself then I would lose any standing I had with the men. King Brian would take back his promise to let me fight—should we end up in battle.

"I need to be on hand for my father." Andrew kissed my cheek, then strode for the cellar door.

"I have to go over the routes again." Stefan put his hand on my shoulder. "Don't beat yourself up so much, Iz." He followed Andrew to the tunnels.

"I'm to remain here with you." Malsin sat at the table beside Nathan.

Nathan gave me his best fatherly stern expression.

I cringed. "I'm really sorry for running."

He crossed his arms. "You're always sorry. When are you going to learn that running is not the answer?"

"I don't know." I sat across from him at the table. "I panicked."

Nathan pushed a plate of food and a glass of milk at me. "That's understandable, considering your circumstances, but we're in a war with Dregaitia. Saren is crawling with soldiers. I'm not apt to believe every single one of them has good intentions." He gestured at me. "Especially when it comes to a beautiful woman. It's not safe to run around Saren like it used to be."

"I completely agree," Malsin said.

I fiddled with the fork in my hand. "You're right. I didn't think."

"Eat," Nathan encouraged.

I shoveled a bite of cold eggs into my mouth. Switching on my magic, I waved my hand over my food, heating it again. The second bite tasted much better than the first.

"What are you going to do when something like this happens again?" Nathan asked me. "Your life is one surprise after the next. What do we need to do to help you stand your ground?"

Malsin's mouth twitched with a teasing smile. "Tie a rope to her and someone else. Joshua or one of the boys would be a good choice since they don't pull on her romantically."

I rolled my eyes. "Great option."

Malsin chuckled.

Nathan rested his elbows on the table. "King Brian is talking about having the princes lead the Second Wave down south to engage with the Dregans. I think separating you from them would do you some good."

My heart lurched at the idea of being separated from Andrew. "No, I don't want that. I'll behave, I promise."

Nathan eyed me skeptically.

I'd always been a runner when things got tough for me emotionally. Nathan and Adel had a hard time holding me down the first year I lived with them. I ran all over Saren, hiding in all sorts of places, from cornfields and haystacks to barn lofts and overturned crates in the cellar. They spent countless hours searching for me—and this was made worse by the fact that I didn't utter a single word that whole year.

It got better when Nathan put a sword in my hand. I didn't feel the need to run as much, and I gained confidence in speaking. Still, the urge to escape had never fully been squashed out. Luckily, I was a creature of habit, and once I discovered the maple tree by the creek, I could be counted on to run to it. I doubted Nathan would've batted an eye to see me go to the tree had we not been in a war with soldiers stationed everywhere. But the fact was, we weren't living in peaceful times. I needed to be more sensible, and if I didn't convey my stability to Nathan I'd never be let out of the house again.

I took a breath, concluding that I needed to be real with Nathan and Malsin. "I'm honestly not trying to be a troublemaker. I care about earning everyone's trust so that I can help in our fight against the Dregans. This place means the world to me. I don't want to see it overrun with Dregan soldiers. Haldren has given me a crazy amount of magic to work with for who knows what reason." I lifted my hands and dropped them. "It's important to me that I put it to good use."

Nathan and Malsin nodded.

I stared at the wood of the table. "I ran out of the house today, not so much because of Braidus, but because of me. I felt interest in response to Braidus's feelings for me. It scared me so much that I had to get away."

"You're bonded," Malsin said, his tone soft but matter-of-fact. "It's natural to have feelings for your mage mate."

I spoke with insistence. "But I am engaged to Andrew. He is the one I want to marry. Showing even the slightest inclination for Braidus makes me a cheater and untrustworthy to Andrew. That's the last thing I want. I'm on thin ice already because of Stefan. I can't let Braidus affect me, or I'll lose Andrew entirely."

Malsin leaned back in his chair. "You're only seventeen—just barely into marriageable age. Perhaps it would be best if you took a step back from Andrew—take off the pressure of an engagement. You might find you're better suited to Braidus—"

"Absolutely not!"

While Braidus had many redeeming qualities, he did not compare to Andrew. He was my anchor. I needed him to survive.

"You're bonded to both," Nathan said. "Now's not the time to be hardheaded."

I gripped the edge of the table. "I'm not being hardheaded. I know for a fact that I can't lose Andrew. I've agreed to accept the worst job possible—queen—to be his wife. I wouldn't make that sacrifice for just anybody."

Malsin shook his head. "You're the only woman in Aberron who would consider being queen a disadvantage."

CHAPTER NINE

DOMINIC ENTERED THE KITCHEN from the cellar door. "Sorry to interrupt, but King Brian wants to see Isabelle—something about testing her purple magic."

I took one last bite of eggs, then rose from the table and descended into the tunnels behind Dominic. Nathan and Malsin followed us. Soldiers actively stared at me as I passed them in the tunnels. I fought against the urge to shudder at the attention.

One soldier spoke to another. "Did you see the little lady training yesterday?"

"No, but I heard about it. Four colors of magic! She's got to be the most powerful mage alive—and most of us thought she was just a pretty face."

The first one said, "Crazy, right? It's no wonder Prince Andrew wants to marry her. Just think of all the power she'll bring to the monarchy."

I mentally frowned at the thought of a calculated union. Marriages should be meant for love.

A third soldier entered the conversation. "She's good with a blade too. I watched her fencing with the king. She nearly bested him."

"The king?" the other two soldiers sounded incredulous.

A fourth soldier said, "It's a good thing she's on our side. She'll be able to inflict so much damage on the Dregans."

All the men made a noise of agreement.

I smiled at that. It felt good to be seen as a benefit in our efforts against the Dregans.

I entered the second room. Soldiers moved about and conversed with each other as if each were on a mission. I suspected a good portion of the men in this room had a leadership position. My family hung about the large table in the middle of the room, appearing deep in planning mode. A flow of soldiers approached Joshua and Andrew, received instruction from one or the other of them, then left to carry it out. Braidus spotted me coming first. He walked to me in quick strides. I couldn't help but tense as he stopped in front of me.

He spoke with sincerity. "Forgive me for frightening you this morning. That was not my intention."

"I'd rather we just forget about it, if that's all right," I said quietly.

He kept his expression neutral. "If that is what you wish."

"It is." I could not tell what Braidus thought concerning my response. He guarded his emotions, ensuring I felt next to nothing from him. It unsettled me that I could not discern him easily, but I didn't see anything I could do about it. Maybe this was a good thing for now. He couldn't influence me if I didn't experience his emotions.

Braidus moved to the side, allowing me to pass him. I meandered my way around soldiers to reach King Brian.

Stopping in front of him, I said, "I'm told you sent for me?"

He nodded. "Yes, I want to see what your purple magic is."

"Here? What if it's not safe?" I asked. "I don't want to hurt anyone."

"She has a point," Malsin said, standing on my left.

King Brian called out to the First Wave soldiers. "We're conducting an experiment. Please back up to the walls."

The soldiers crammed themselves against the walls, leaving an open space for me. Silence fell.

"Thank you." King Brian smiled at his men, then turned his attention back on me. "There. Now try it."

"All right. I'll ask what it can do." I stepped into the open space. "Malsin, you'd better be ready in case this magic is dangerous and I hurt someone."

"I'll be ready," he said, using his healer's gaze.

I squirmed uncomfortably at all the curious eyes on me. *Get it together, Isabelle.* I shook out my hands and danced on my feet, gearing myself up for the task. Boomer flashed to the forefront of my mind as I focused on my magic. He barked excitedly when I let him out and called on the purple magic. The soldiers gasped in shock. I brought my hands up to my face, intrigued by the soft purple glow flecked with gold.

Show me what you can do.

Voices filled my mind until I couldn't see straight. I dropped. The chatter was so great, it came out in a stream of babble. I rolled on the ground in agony, my fingernails digging into my scalp. Screams tore out of my throat. Multiple hands pressed on me, but I couldn't concentrate.

Suddenly I found myself staring into Andrew's face, his hands cupping my cheeks. His voice rose above the others, though I did not see his mouth move. *"Shut it off."*

I gritted my teeth and pushed back the gibberish, fighting to hear myself through it. *Stop!* I yelled at Boomer.

The noise vanished. My mind cleared but throbbed mercilessly. I dragged Boomer back to his cage and shut the magic off. Gasping, I sat up and rubbed my temples.

Malsin used his green magic to find the source of my discomfort. He cringed. My headache lessened as he let go.

"Her head feels like the whole army trampled on it," Malsin said.

"It did," I said. "Unless everybody started shouting at once, I think purple magic lets me read minds." I couldn't think of another explanation for how Andrew spoke to me without moving his mouth.

My family wore stricken expressions. Soldier chatter picked up again, outside of my mind this time, but I didn't pay enough attention to make out any conversations.

"Try it again," King Brian ordered. "This time be more specific. Ask to read one person's mind only."

"Read mine," Henry volunteered. "I've got nothing to hide."

Activating the purple magic again, I focused on Boomer. *Tell me what Henry is thinking.*

I felt Henry's thoughts trickle in like cool water, similar to the way Nisha spoke, but with Henry's tone. With a big grin, Henry repeated the same thought. *"If you can hear me, punch Dominic."*

I made a fist and lightly hit his upper arm. "How about I punch you?"

Henry laughed and thought, *"Oh, come on, it would've been funny."*

I rolled my eyes and told Boomer to quit listening. "It's like talking to Nisha. I heard Henry's thoughts loud and clear."

I caught distinct frowns; no doubt everyone worried about what I could overhear.

"Your horse?" Dominic asked dubiously.

"Remember at the Sorrenian when we wondered why Isabelle kept talking to her horse during class?" Henry asked.

Dominic and Falden nodded.

"We thought she was crazy, but it turns out Nisha *can* talk." At seeing their skeptical expressions, Henry said, "It's true, swear it on the Gods. It's like he has the mind of a human stuck in a horse's body. You hear this foreign voice in your head, and you just know it isn't yours."

"Soldiers, you may move now," King Brian said.

They shuffled about the room but didn't say much, no doubt interested in what was going on.

Braidus spoke. "For the sake of us all, we should know the extent of Isabelle's power. Listening to someone's mind is a breach of privacy I am not fond of." He met my eyes. "Perhaps you have the power to plant thoughts as well, or control us like the Gods do?"

Uneasiness formed on everybody's faces.

I bristled. "I don't want to control anyone or listen to their thoughts."

Fear and anger emanated from Braidus. I didn't fault him for it considering the Gods had abused him and stolen much of his life.

"I don't trust you," Braidus said, his hazel eyes intense. "You may be a bad liar, but you're good at keeping things to yourself. Your relationships are proof of that."

I gasped at the verbal slap. With magic still pulsing through my veins, I sent him a thought, unsure whether he would hear me. *You're already in my heart through our bond. I don't need you in my head.*

A surge of pleasure broke through the icy confines of my emotions. Braidus chuckled. "Why, that sounded almost romantic."

My mouth parted in surprise. "You heard me?"

Braidus pushed his hair back, a smirk on his lips. "Loud and clear."

"So you can listen to our thoughts and speak to us mentally." Malsin rubbed his forehead. "How very intriguing, if slightly disturbing."

King Brian spoke. "I agree with Braidus. We need to know if you can control us."

I sighed. "I'll ask."

I closed my eyes and pictured Boomer. *Can I control people?*

Boomer cocked his head and stared.

I tried again. *Make Henry bleat like a sheep.*

Boomer whined. Henry did nothing. I got the distinct impression that I couldn't make anyone do anything.

I turned to Henry. "Did you feel any urge to act like a sheep?"

Henry stared at me incredulously. "You tried to—"

I cut him off. "Just answer the question."

"None," Henry said. "I didn't even hear or think the thought."

"Well, that answers that. I can't control people," I said. "Braidus, if I'm such a bad liar, you'd know it."

"I believe you," he said.

"Thank the Gods," Joshua said, relieved.

"Send me a thought," Stefan prompted, moving to face me. "I want to know how it feels to talk back and forth mentally."

"All right." I took a breath and locked eyes with Stefan. I sent a command to the magic that I only wanted to connect with Stefan. Boomer wagged his tail and barked.

Stefan's thoughts and emotions slammed into me as we connected. His breath hitched as my mind hit him. It was like we were suddenly one person, joined on a deeply intimate, personal level. We couldn't hide anything from each other. If we thought it or felt it, the other would see it. His love for me burned brighter than the hottest flame.

Stefan let his thoughts drift to old memories, long hugs and laughter at the creek under the maple tree. Dancing at Mava and Carl's wedding. The man Braidus had hired chasing us afterward and punching Stefan to the ground. The kiss we shared in the tunnels before he let me go. My promise to come back.

Guilt punched my gut. Stefan sifted through it to discover the extent of my love for him. It was strong and unyielding, though not of the same romantic nature that I felt for Andrew. I never wanted to hurt Stefan, and it killed me that I had.

He smiled. *"Remember the first time we kissed?"*

A memory briefly flashed in my mind with Stefan's help. In the middle of summer, we sat on the embankment of the creek, our feet in the water. We shared a bowl of strawberries and cream. Stefan said something silly. I threw a spoonful of cream at his face. He retaliated. We were quickly covered in a sticky, sweet mess.

I'd waded into the creek to clean up when Stefan said, "Let me help wash that off for you." He pulled me into his arms. "I'll start right here." Then he brought his lips down to mine and kissed me slow and sweet. Shocked, I pushed him into the creek.

"But then you pulled me up and kissed me again," Stefan reminded me, pulling me out of the memory and back to the present.

Yes. I remembered. I had wanted to love Stefan that way even if I didn't feel it with the same ardor he did. He made me happy—almost as much as Andrew. I had hoped I would grow to love him with the romantic passion he deserved.

His pale-blue eyes met mine, and I knew nothing and everything had changed. My heart did not burn in his presence, and time wouldn't change that. I would never be able to love him the way he wanted me to. Emotion threatening to choke me, I stepped forward. Standing on my tiptoes, I kissed his cheek. "I'm sorry," I whispered with regret for causing him pain—for making him see that my affection for him lived through friendship and not romance. I shut off the connection and backed away.

Stefan's hand shot out and grabbed mine. "Don't make this goodbye."

"It's not." My heart wouldn't allow me to let him go completely. I relied on his friendship. "But we can't go back to how it was. No matter how much you want it." I pulled my hand free.

"Maybe you're right, but that doesn't change how I feel. I still want to fight for you until you've said your vows in front of the high priest," Stefan said, shoving his hands in his pockets.

"Isabelle," King Brian addressed me.

I turned around, realizing I'd been so focused on Stefan that I forgot about everything else going on around me. Andrew scowled at Stefan before his gaze flicked to me. I felt his appreciation that I continued to favor him over Stefan.

"Tell me about the telepathy experience you shared with Stefan," King Brian said.

"It's invasive," I answered promptly. "It's like our bodies merged. Not only thoughts but feelings were conveyed. If you think or feel it, the other will too. Emotions-wise it can be intense, and I fear it has the potential to do damage if a person is not careful."

King Brian turned on Stefan. "Would you agree with this assessment?"

"Yes," Stefan answered. "But it's seriously amazing. I wouldn't trade the experience I just had for anything."

I sucked in a breath as surges of emotion flooded my heart through the bond. Jealousy, irritation, curiosity, and something else I couldn't pinpoint. It all jumbled together until I couldn't tell who felt what. I rubbed my heart with a frown, desperately wishing I had a shut-off valve.

King Brian said, "Isabelle, I want to know if you can connect multiple people at once."

"Volunteers?" I asked.

"Me," Braidus offered, surprising me.

I met his hazel eyes, letting Boomer connect him to me. His presence held an intensity I'd never before experienced—like bottled-up lightning—which was ridiculously intriguing but also dangerous.

"Lightning?" Braidus threw back his head and laughed.

His sudden strong amusement startled me. He laughed harder.

I couldn't help but giggle with him. *"It's true!"* Turning away from him, I focused on the others. "Who else?" I asked.

Nathan and Stefan opted not to be involved. I then connected King Brian, the boys, Malsin, Joshua, and Andrew. Each person had his own tone and feeling that distinctly set him apart as a unique individual. My mind thickened with the thoughts and emotions of the others, but then I realized they were experiencing it too. Any random thought one of us had filtered through the group, and we all heard, saw, and felt it—like a collective mind. It was enough to make someone crazy if they didn't watch themselves.

"See if you can read someone's mind while connected to us," King Brian said.

His mind was so sharp and clear. I envied his ability to adapt while remaining calm and smart. He had the intensity Braidus possessed, but it seemed softer, on purpose or not I didn't know. As king he intimidated me, for I often got the impression that he could see into my very soul and judge.

"Isabelle . . ." King Brian gently reminded me of his order, though underneath I felt a flicker of amusement at my assessment of him.

Sorry!

It was difficult to find my voice amid everyone else's. They tried to keep their minds clear, but becoming distracted happened easily. I pictured Boomer, his tail wagging, tongue lolling out in bliss at the amount of magic I used.

"Aww, your dog is so cute," Henry said.

"So fluffy," Falden said with admiration, comparing him to the bloodhounds his family bred.

All right, Boomer, pick a random soldier in this room and let me hear his thoughts. Boomer woofed and danced excitedly. A collective "aww" went through the men.

"I am not going to die fighting the Dregans. Not going to die. Gods forbid, I should have kissed Suzy." The soldier's thoughts streamed in as if we heard him talking face to face.

I shut it off before we heard any more. A person's thoughts should be their own, especially with the emotions that come with the potential of battle. Everyone agreed, and our emotions turned solemn.

"What about using multiple colors while connected?" Andrew asked.

I shrugged. *I can try it.* I pictured Boomer in my mind once more, making sure the magic understood that I wanted to continue my usage of purple while I added red. I lit my hand on fire. The telepathic connections remained in place. I turned off the red magic.

"I want to know distances," King Brian said. *"See if you can contact Averly in Carasmille."*

I took a second to relay the command, and Queen Averly's thoughts filled my mind. *"Assure the people, keep the smile, make Brian proud. Deep breath. Walk in."*

King Brian's love for his wife burned bright through all of us connected. I quit projecting her thoughts.

"Disconnect us, Isabelle. We've learned enough," King Brian said.

With pleasure. I shut off the magic.

We returned to planning mode at the table in the tunnels. I stood by Andrew, his arm around my shoulder, tucking me close against him. Peace and warmth filled me. There was no other place I'd rather be than at his side.

"The Dregans have just been sighted leaving the Callan outpost," Joshua spoke to the group. "They're moving at a steady pace, unhindered by the large quantities of snow we have here."

"How are the evacuations going for the little towns?" Braidus asked.

My brother frowned. "They're not moving fast enough. At the rate the Dregans are going, it's suspected several towns will be overrun."

"And Aberronians slaughtered." Braidus looked at his father. "We need to get the Second Wave down there now."

"Yes, I agree." King Brian looked at his timepiece. "It's nearly ten in the morning. Are our soldiers ready to ship out?"

Joshua nodded. "Yes."

"Excellent." King Brian's gaze darted between Andrew and Braidus. "I want you two to lead the Second Wave as equal partners. Andrew, no pulling rank over your brother should you two come to a disagreement."

Andrew said, "That would be folly. Braidus is the more experienced warrior. You should put him in charge."

Braidus's fondness for his brother came through the bond. I liked seeing the care and friendship between them.

King Brian shook his head, "No, I want you as equals."

"Fine," the princes said.

Where Andrew went, I wanted to go too. I had an innate need to see to his safety as best I could. Taking a breath of courage, I spoke to King Brian. "May I please go with Andrew and Braidus? I believe I will be more useful with them than remaining here."

"It's fine with me," Andrew said, showing enthusiasm for it through the bond.

King Brian turned to Braidus with a raised eyebrow.

Braidus said, "We'll be stationed outdoors. It would be good for us if Isabelle could use her magic to create a large, heated dome to keep us warm. We can't have our soldiers freezing to death before we face the Dregans."

"Exactly," I said. "I have more magic than I know what to do with. Let me help!"

King Brian nodded slowly. "I see no reason to object, but I'll leave the answer up to your guardians." His gaze landed on Joshua and Nathan.

Neither of them was convinced.

"You'll get into trouble," Joshua said.

"I get into trouble anywhere I go," I retorted.

Nathan crossed his arms. "You'll get distracted by the princes, making you more liable to make mistakes."

I spoke in a resolute tone. "We're bonded. I'll have just as much of an opportunity to be distracted here as I would with them. There's no shut-off valve for the shared emotion."

Andrew said, "Isabelle is determined. She will circumvent you if you say no."

Nathan cursed and threw up his hands. "All right, go."

"So be it," Joshua agreed, though he still showed great reluctance.

Yes! I hugged them one after the other. "Thank you. You won't regret it, I promise."

"I doubt that," Nathan said.

Joshua vigorously nodded.

Their concern made me want to prove myself all the more. I would do my absolute best to not give them a reason to worry about me.

It was determined that I, Andrew, Braidus, Stefan—acting as a guide to the location he had helped pick—and Malsin would accompany the Second Wave.

"I go where Isabelle goes," Malsin said simply.

King Brian, Joshua, the boys, and Nathan would remain in Saren.

Joshua assembled all the men in leadership positions in the Second Wave for King Brian to address them.

To start, King Brian said, "Please relay what I say to each of your units."

"Yes, my king," the men said.

King Brian nodded in approval. "The Dregans are running freely in the south. I have hereby ordered the Second Wave to travel down to meet them. Your purpose is to drive them out of Aberron and protect our towns and cities. Expect to engage in battle."

Many soldiers put their hands on the pommels of their swords. One man had a fierce expression as if ready to fight right then and there.

King Brian gestured to his sons. "Andrew and Braidus are to command. They are equal partners in this venture, so look to them both for instruction. Joining them will be Saren's orate judge, Stefan Ashter. He will be acting as your guide. His knowledge of this province is extensive and very much needed. Please treat him with respect."

"Yes, my king," the men chorused.

King Brian turned and motioned for me to join him. I stepped forward. He put his hand on my shoulder. "Lady Isabelle's petition to join you has also been granted. Accompanying her will be Ian Malsin, her personal healer. He is to act as her guardian during this venture. I'm sure you're all well aware by now that Lady Isabelle has been blessed with an abundance of magic." His voice turned stern. "Protect her at all costs. She is Aberron's greatest weapon."

Internally, I recoiled at King Brian calling me a weapon. I didn't want to be thought of as an object and feared. Yet the Gods had turned me into an incredibly powerful mage, and I did want to use every bit of magic I had to save Aberron from Dregaitia—even if that included doing some damage. Technically, that made me a weapon—but not a bad person, not something to be scared of. I wanted to be seen as useful, protective, and kind.

"Understood?" King Brian asked.

"Yes, my king!" the men shouted.

King Brian let go of my shoulder. "I wish to offer my heartfelt thanks for your willingness to serve and protect Aberron. May the Gods watch over you and keep you safe. That is all."

Joshua stepped forward. "Gather your men and be ready to march out in ten minutes."

"Yes, Commander!" The soldiers left.

Malsin, the princes, and I returned to the house to pack our belongings. We tried to be quick about it since the Second Wave was shipping out in just a few minutes. Wanting some of the comforts of home, I stuck a jar of Saren's best apple cider mix into my bag.

Nathan appeared and handed me a package of peppermint sticks. "For the road."

I hugged him. "Thank you." I added the sweets to my bag.

The boys and King Brian came up from the tunnels.

I said my goodbyes to them. "Please look after yourselves."

"We'll be all right," Henry said confidently.

"Yeah, don't worry about us." Dominic grinned. "Go out there and be spectacular."

"It's going to get mighty boring without Isabelle," Falden said, making everyone chortle.

I smiled brightly. "That's a good thing."

"Check in with us often," King Brian said to me, Malsin, and his sons.

"Will do," Andrew said.

The four of us went to the barn and led our horses out of the stables. Joshua came over just as I was about to mount Nisha.

"The only reason I'm letting you go is that I know those men love you enough to sacrifice themselves before letting hurt befall you." He jerked his thumb in Stefan, Andrew, and Braidus's direction. "I expect you to handle yourself with the decorum of a trained soldier. No distractions."

"I just want to save Aberron from Dregaitia. That's it," I told him frankly. "I have no intention of causing problems with my romance troubles."

"Good," Joshua said. "I expect you to check in with me frequently. Don't make me regret my choice."

"I won't," I said firmly.

He smiled and pulled me in for a crushing bear hug. "I love you, little sister."

My eyes misted. Joshua was rarely affectionate.

"I love you too, brother."

He stepped back. "You're causing all sorts of problems with my soldiers." Seeing my raised eyebrow, he explained, "Word's spread fast that you're heading out. The First Wave is jealous that the Second Wave gets you. You've made a big impression."

I swung up on Nisha. "With my magic or romance problems?"

"Both," Joshua chuckled. We waved a final goodbye.

The princes, Stefan, Malsin, and I rode to Mr. Layder's fields, where blocks of uniformed soldiers waited. The snow had let up to a light flurry. I wondered if this meant the end of the storm or if it was just a respite. We rode around the men, making our way to the head of the line. Andrew and Braidus turned their mounts around to face the men.

Andrew magnified his voice with magic and spoke. "Is everyone ready to fight for Aberron?"

"Yes!" the soldiers roared.

Andrew and Braidus unsheathed their swords and raised them high into the air. Together, they shouted, "Let's march!"

CHAPTER TEN

HE PRINCES SPURRED THEIR horses into a canter, taking the lead on our journey.

Nisha trotted toward Stefan and his horse. *"I want to run next to this pretty mare."*

I laughed and patted Nisha's neck. "As you wish."

Stefan raised his eyebrows as Nisha sidled up to him for the ride. "You're riding next to me?"

I nodded. "Nisha is fond of your mare. Says she's pretty."

Stefan grinned. "Lady is a pretty girl. I rescued her from a horse breeder from Nedra. She was supposed to be sold to some noble in Thimbleton, but she got sick along their travels. The breeder thought for sure she was going to die, so I got her for practically nothing. I took the mare to Millie, and she nursed her back to health with one of her herb concoctions. It's been great. She's really well trained."

"That's awesome," I told him. "You've always had the best luck."

Stefan smiled wryly. "Not all the time, but occasionally."

Malsin, who rode on the other side of me, spoke to Stefan. "Where are we planning to stop for the night?"

"I'm hoping we'll be able to make it to or close to Nachura's Meadow," Stefan said. "It's far enough away from the last reported sighting of the Dregans that I don't think they will happen upon us while we sleep."

"How close will we be to the Dregans there?" I asked.

"Depends on which direction the Dregans choose to go when morning hits," Stefan said. "Could be a few hours away or more."

Braidus spoke over his shoulder at us. He and Andrew rode just barely ahead of us and were able to hear my conversations with Stefan and Malsin. "Expect to get your sword bloody by tomorrow. I don't believe there'll be any negotiating between us."

"I take it they're a fight first, then ask questions sort of people?" I asked.

Braidus said, "It's all fight until someone's dead. Never questions."

I frowned. That was awful. We had to get them out of Aberron as fast as possible.

We rode for many hours, mostly in silence, through plains and small forests. Stefan used his postboy memory to find us shortcuts.

"You get better tips the quicker you deliver the post," he said. "Naturally, we work out the best paths."

Occasionally something stopped our progression, such as a fallen tree or too much snow piled up. For objects like broken branches and whatnot, I used yellow to lift and toss them on the side. For the large amounts of ice, I used red to torch it.

As afternoon began to fade, I struck up another conversation with Stefan. "How'd you become orate judge?"

He smiled wryly. "I wondered when you'd ask. Mr. Travers took ill a month or so after you left. Mrs. Coltrane and Millie did all they could, but he didn't make it. He left everything to me, post shop and all. I started going through his things and, lo and behold, ten decent-sized chests of gold sundals appeared in a locked closet in his room."

"You're kidding!" I said, shocked.

Stefan shook his head. "Not in the slightest."

"But the man argued over two pristals for bread," I said, trying to make sense of it.

"I know; crazy, right?" he said. "Anyway, I decided to use some of the money to help others who were struggling a bit. People started coming to me for advice and business deals. Then Wilson, our previous orate judge, decided he'd rather be closer to his daughter and moved to Thimbleton. Names were put forth for a new judge, and I was elected."

"Where do you think Travers got all that money?" I asked. "Being the postmaster doesn't make much money."

"Not a clue," Stefan said. "I searched every nook and cranny for some sort of answer and came up empty."

"How much farther to go?" Andrew asked Stefan. "The horses will need a rest."

Stefan stood in the stirrups, eyes squinting into the distance. We currently rode in a forest, where snow-covered fir trees encompassed us. Mages had begun creating light orbs so we could see.

"Half an hour," he said. "Nachura's Meadow is just around the bend."

"The shortcuts have saved us a good three, four hours," Braidus observed. "This is excellent."

"This'll give our men more time to rest before we engage the Dregans," Andrew said.

"The main roads go around the forest," Stefan said, "because most people prefer the open plains over the woods where it's easier for ruffians to hide. But I don't think we need to worry about them. They won't want to be massacred by the Dregans and have probably evacuated to pilfer in the walled cities."

"Let's hope so," Malsin said.

True to Stefan's word, we reached Nachura's Meadow a half hour later. It had a bit of a downward slope, but it was easily the size of a cornfield and, I assumed, relatively grassy under the blanket of white.

Braidus set his hazel eyes upon me. "Care to make it livable?"

"Certainly." I hopped off Nisha and sunk all the way to my stomach in the snow. Cursing, I threw my hands out to stop myself from tumbling face-first.

This elicited a snicker from the men.

I let out a huff of frustration. A plan formed in my mind as I activated my yellow magic. I used air to shoot me into the sky. First things first: I needed to get rid of the snow to make it possible for soldiers to set up their tents, have fires, and stay warm.

Maintaining yellow, I added red. Boomer flashed in front of my eyes, seeking direction. I focused on the large patch of snow underneath me. *Melt it.* Heat shot from my hands as a thin layer of red haze descended, creating a blanket over the land. The ice rapidly diminished, leaving patches of brown grass in its wake. When all remnants of winter vanished, I increased the heat. *Dry it.*

Dropping to the ground, I crouched, placing a hand on the dry earth. I switched to green, revitalizing the grass until it shined a vibrant spring emerald and felt soft to the touch. I hoped it would be comfortable for us to sleep on. I created a red dome of heat over the area to keep it warm and dry for a continued amount of time. Finished, I walked on air, taking measured steps to Nisha.

Andrew turned his mount around to face the soldiers. He stood in the stirrups and magnified his voice with magic. "Soldiers! Welcome to your camp!"

The men cheered.

They made short work of setting up. Soon fires and tiny two-person tents dotted the meadow. My family's tent was decidedly the biggest with two rooms for us to share. All were insistent that I be kept within their sights. Even though I felt like I had heard this multiple times, I did have a tendency to run, so I let them say it again.

"Propriety doesn't mean much in war. It is unthinkable to let you have a tent to yourself as the only female surrounded by four thousand men," Braidus said as we settled in the tent.

"Fine," I readily agreed. Truthfully, I felt comforted knowing I'd have them all close.

He smiled, no doubt reading the bond. "Good."

Andrew spoke. "Isabelle, you're not to go anywhere without one of us." He gestured to himself, Braidus, Stefan, and Malsin. "That includes finding a latrine."

"No running, Iz," Stefan said sternly.

Again, I agreed. "I'm not here to put up a fight. Believe it or not, I can avoid trouble sometimes."

The men chuckled.

"'Sometimes' being the key word there," Malsin said.

"I'm going to check in with Joshua." I moved to a corner of the tent, sat, and activated my purple magic. Linking my mind with his, I assured him of our well-being.

"Some strange explosions are happening around the Barras outpost. Be on the watch," he said.

"Will do." I ended the connection and relayed the information to the others.

Braidus said, "Cekaiden enjoys black-powder bombs with special insides. Bits and pieces of metal or poisons."

He tucked his long hair behind his ear. The firelight glinted off his tresses, making them appear more golden and silky than usual. *Is it as soft as it looks?* What would he do to keep it away from his face during battle? Braid it like I'd do with my hair? That seemed a bit womanly though.

"Isabelle," Andrew spoke my name in reprimanding tones.

I jerked, snapping out of my imaginings. Andrew eyed me with exasperation. Stefan appeared unhappy at me too. Malsin wore a passive expression though his eyes were large and alert. Braidus grinned, soaking up my attention like a cat sunbathing in the sun. I flushed. Gods, could I be any more stupid? What possessed me to start thinking more about him anyway?

Braidus addressed me, his tone gentle. "There is nothing wrong with finding your mage mate attractive."

I shook my head. Self-revulsion smothered my heart for the way I had started to consider Braidus. I wanted Andrew as my husband. Why had I given myself a single thought about Braidus? Fear snaked through my revulsion. *I'm going to lose Andrew for good if I can't control myself.*

I scooted away from the others and lay down to sleep. I shut my eyes, hoping oblivion would claim me fast. A few minutes of silence passed. I had almost fallen asleep when Braidus spoke.

"She is being unreasonably hard on herself," he said with displeasure.

"How long have you wanted her?" Andrew asked his brother quietly.

"Since I first laid my eyes on her at the Sorrenian months ago," he admitted with a sigh. "On her first day, she sat at an empty table in the dining hall with such a forsaken expression that my heart went out to her. I often sat across from her during meals—invisible—when she had no one to turn to. I had planned to keep my feelings to myself—"

"But then the bond happened," Andrew supplied.

"Yes," Braidus agreed. "I know her love for you currently shines the brightest, but this direct access to her heart has also shown that her feelings for me are steadily changing."

"Yes, I've seen it too," Andrew said.

"I wish for Isabelle to know that I favor her so that I may be seen as an option," Braidus said, his tone soft but persistent. "If she continues to desire you more, I will not stand in your way, but I feel I deserve a chance to be noticed before you two are married."

"I understand," Andrew said.

Stefan spoke in a commiserating tone. "What a sorry lot we are, all pining after the same woman and hating each other for it."

Quiet chuckles escaped the men.

Malsin said, "It's not doing Isabelle any favors."

The men murmured in agreement.

Then Andrew said, "What are we to do about it when none of us is willing to give her up?"

I spoke, not wanting to hear any more "Forget about me and go to sleep." Switching on my magic, I put myself under.

The following morning, I woke to Braidus speaking to his father through a locket. Malsin, Stefan, and Andrew were already awake and listening with rapt attention.

"The Dregans are not far behind," King Brian said. "You've got a limited window."

Braidus tucked his locket underneath his shirt.

"What's going on?" I asked.

"The Dregans that we planned to engage with have split up into raiding parties and are scattering themselves all over the province," Andrew said.

"This makes it harder for us to combat them. Also, a bridge on the way to Pendra has collapsed. Families are trapped and the Dregans are heading in their direction."

"Let me go," I urged. "I can build a temporary bridge with my magic to get them across."

The men looked at each other. I could almost see their minds weighing it over.

"Come on, I'm your best asset. Use me."

"All right," Braidus said with the other three nodding.

"Let's send six contingents of fifty," Braidus said. "We'll get the Aberronians across, then dismantle Isabelle's bridge. Let's not make it easy for the intruders."

"Sounds good to me." Andrew turned to Stefan. "How far is the bridge from here again?"

"Three-and-a-half hours if we ride fast," Stefan said. "Isabelle, we're going to need your help to make a clear path along the way."

"You've got it," I said.

We departed within twenty minutes. Three hundred soldiers trailed behind me, the princes, Stefan, and Malsin. Huge flakes cascaded down as the snow increased again. I tilted my face upward and stuck out my tongue to moisten my mouth after eating the jerky that had been passed around. Warmth flickered in my heart. Out of the corner of my eye, I caught Andrew, Stefan, and Braidus watching me with soft smiles of fascination. I quickly drew back. *Don't encourage them all, Isabelle*, I scolded myself.

I cleared debris from fallen trees and torched several areas with an absurd amount of snow. We rode for what felt like forever before we came upon the broken bridge. The white, foaming water rushed ferociously under it. The bridge went out a few paces on either side of the bank before it dropped off to nothing. The middle was gone.

A group of men stood still on the other side of the small river. Catching sight of us, they waved frantically. The rushing water drowned out their cries for help. In the distance, I could see wagons surrounded by a grove of trees. The smoke plumes were small and struggling against the falling snow. The camp appeared motionless, everyone probably hiding from the elements.

Braidus turned to us. "I'm going to fly over there and assess the situation. Isabelle, get started on patching the bridge."

"On it," I said.

We all dismounted. The soldiers stood by their mounts behind us, quietly whispering. Andrew, Malsin, Stefan, and I stood at the edge of the broken bridge. I activated my magic, letting all colors shine. Boomer woofed, seeking direction. I pictured a path to bring me to the other side. *As strong as you can make it,* I told him with as much determination as I could muster. A blue clear substance began forming along the jagged edges and crept over the river to join the other side.

Boomer danced when he finished, tail swishing excitedly.

I smiled. "Let me go first. I can fly if it breaks."

Andrew darted a boot forward and put a good amount of weight down. "I think it'll hold, but if you insist."

My feet found purchase easily with the first few steps. It felt solid. I walked to the middle of the bridge and jumped up and down. Nothing happened.

"That's not going to do much. You're as light as a new lamb!" Stefan called.

"Fine, come over!" I waved at them.

The three of them approached.

"I think it's good," Andrew said.

"It's excellent." Malsin smiled approvingly.

Braidus joined us on the bridge and surveyed my efforts with a grin. We learned from him that some people needed medical attention. I went with Malsin to the camp. About three hundred people, give or take, gathered around wagons and small fires. Fear and exhaustion were visible on numerous faces. Small children chased each other, oblivious to the tension. Several babies wailed. My heart ached for their suffering.

Malsin spoke to the group. "I am Ian Malsin, a healer under King Brian's command. Beside me is Lady Isabelle Mirran, also a healer in her own right.

If you would please lead us to your sick or injured, we would be glad to offer our assistance."

"I fixed the bridge," I added. "It is safe to go across."

People sprang into action, dismantling the camp. A motherly, middle-aged lady named Margaret led Malsin and me to the sick. She explained that a particularly nasty cold had swept through the people a few days ago, leaving many frail and feverous with breathing difficulties. It had killed an older woman yesterday.

"We've run out of our tinctures, and the illness shows no sign of letting up."

Malsin spoke to me. "Normally we just try to ease the symptoms and let the sickness run its course to build up immunity. If it's too hardy of a virus, we'll put a shield around it to stop it from moving until it dies out. I want to make sure you'll have enough magic should the Dregans come upon us."

"Sounds good," I answered.

The sick, at least fifty, were huddled together, lying in the back of wagons or in makeshift tents, a little farther apart from the healthy. They stared at Malsin and me and our magical glow with blatant fear.

"We don't want no magic," a man said, breathing heavily and clutching his chest.

"No magic," other people echoed.

Malsin spoke firmly, his moss-green eyes severe. "Reject us and you will die. There's no question about it."

"Quit being fools!" Margaret admonished with fire in her eyes. "We won't have time to take care of you when the Dregans come here to kill us."

The people were cowed. I bit my cheek to hide my smile. I liked Margaret and her no-nonsense attitude.

Yet fear still shone strongly in everybody's eyes. I understood that apprehension, having experienced it myself. I wanted to put the people at ease as best I could. "I'm from Saren. I grew up terrified of magic. Not too long ago, I was attacked and shot with two arrows. I refused to see a healer, despite being in a life-or-death situation, because I was convinced they were more harm than good."

Many people nodded at this as if they believed that too.

"Only a few months ago, I learned I had magic flowing through my veins." I put my hand on my chest. "I thought I had been given a curse of the worst kind. I believed everybody in Saren—my family and friends—was going to hate me. I was wrong. My family and friends don't hate me at all, and what I thought was a curse has turned into a blessing. My magic saves lives; it doesn't destroy them. I promise you will not be harmed by me or Malsin." I held my hand out to them. "Who's willing to take a chance on us?"

"Me." An older man lifted his hand.

His willingness prompted others to voice their agreement. Malsin and I joined our power together and began working on the man who had first volunteered. I cringed as I felt the man's aches, pains, and fever. He had so much phlegm that I wondered how he managed to breathe at all.

Malsin shuddered. "This is a nasty one. Let's ease the symptoms and shield the virus until it dies out. We need to save as much of your magic as we can in case we need it against the Dregans."

"All right," I said.

With that plan in mind, we worked on one person after another.

"You sure I ain't gonna die from your magic?" A ten-year-old boy asked Malsin and me when we finished healing him.

I flashed a bright smile. "No. I use magic to heal myself when I get hurt or sick, and I'm living great."

The boy grinned. "Thanks, lady! I feel better." He took off to join his family.

When we were a little over halfway through healing all the sick, a man ran into camp and shouted hysterically. "The Dregans are here!"

Screaming people started running around their wagons, scrambling to pick up the pace. Some of the sick were trying to get up, no doubt thinking it better not to wait to be healed.

"Let's hurry this up," Malsin said.

Margaret stood on top of a wagon and yelled, "Quiet!"

The noise level dropped considerably.

"We must have order if we're to make it. No sense acting like headless chickens." She began shouting commands to the villagers, keeping them organized so they could be quick to depart.

Her voice faded to the back of my mind as I concentrated on my healing duties, mending one after another with Malsin.

I jumped at the blast heard in the distance. *Gods forbid.*

"Focus on our present task, Isabelle," Malsin urged as we placed our hands on a teenage girl.

I bolted to my feet after we helped the last person—a middle-aged man. Finally. Switching on my purple magic, I connected with Braidus. I hoped he wouldn't mind the intrusion, but I needed information and the next set of instructions. *"What's going on?"*

"A raiding party," he replied. Through his eyes, I could see about two hundred Dregans advancing on horses.

"Gods forbid. What do you want me to do?"

"Get the people across as fast as you can. We'll try to hold them off."

"Will do. Stay safe."

"You too," Braidus answered.

I felt his concern for me through the bond as I ended the connection and turned to Malsin. "No time to lose. We've got to get the people across."

I ran to the bridge, Malsin beside me. The camp had entirely dissolved and was venturing over the river with some tears and wails.

I didn't dare look to see the soldiers assembling to engage the Dregans. I worried it would distract me from ensuring the villagers got across the bridge.

"Come on, you blockhead!" A man tugged on the halter of a braying mule adamantly refusing to set foot on the bridge.

"We don't have time for this." I switched to yellow magic and approached the man. "I'll get him across."

The man eyed me with disbelief but stepped away. I raised my hands and lifted his entire wagon and mule into the air. The animal brayed and kicked as I flew him over the water and set him on the other side. The man ran after his property. I held the mule in place until the man had him controlled. I dropped my hands. *Problem solved.*

The line started going again, but it wasn't as fast as I wanted. More animals balked over my magical bridge. Behind me, I heard agonized screams and clashing metal. Impressions of swords slicing through flesh had me shuddering. My heart tugged as Andrew and Braidus accessed my powers. I needed to be out there, helping.

Impatient, I shouted at everybody to climb into their wagons. "Hold tight!" In one fell swoop, I carried the remaining twenty across.

"Mama, we're flying!" a girl cried with glee.

I set them down and magnified my voice. "Go as far as you can. Don't stop!"

Nisha nudged my shoulder. I swung up into his saddle. Malsin had already mounted his brown gelding. I sent a mental message to Andrew, Braidus, and Stefan. *People are across. Coming to help.* I turned off the purple magic.

I unsheathed my blade. "Let's save Aberron!"

Nisha reared, whinnied, and took off at a full gallop to the battle. *Ready to fight.* I wrapped a shield around me and Nisha, as well as Malsin and his mount beside us. My stomach lurched as the Dregans came into sight. They were just as menacing as Braidus had described: tall and heavily muscled, wearing fur coats with metal spikes embedded over their chests. I grimaced as I watched one try to wrap his arms around an Aberronian soldier to impale him. Thankfully, he got away. I searched for Andrew, Braidus, and Stefan amongst the fighting but I could not see them. I would simply have to charge my way in and find them.

Several Aberronians cheered as I entered the fray, which was taking place over a snowy plain. "Lady Isabelle!"

"Watch out for the bombs!" An Aberronian soldier covered in white said. "Kills your magic!"

"On your right!" another soldier yelled.

With one hand wrapped around the reins, I turned halfway in my saddle and blocked a Dregan's blade. Nisha bucked, kicking his back legs out, and hit the Dregan square in his lower stomach and groin. The Dregan fell onto his back, and Nisha trampled him.

"*No one tries to hurt my lady.*" Nisha snorted and stomped on the Dregan once more for good measure.

My eyes darted for a new target, searching for someone to save. I caught sight of Stefan back-to-back with an Aberronian soldier. Five Dregans surrounded them.

"Oh no you don't!" I charged.

I sliced into a Dregan's neck with my sword. Nisha kicked him into his comrade and they both went tumbling into the snow. Stefan and the other soldier finished them off.

"Thanks, Iz!" Stefan shouted to be heard over the battle.

The remaining Dregans ran away, seemingly to search for a target without a mage protecting him. My shield was visible for all to see.

"Stefan, stay put for a second." I put a shield over him.

"Bombs!" he yelled, eyes raised to the sky.

I looked up just as they exploded over Nisha and me. The Dregans cheered in their guttural language. A white powder descended, coating us. I cursed. Triple amounts of dismay choked my heart. I shook my head to clear my eyes. Wait. *My shield is holding.* Boomer woofed and danced outside of his cage. *I still have my magic. Must be Haldren's doing.*

I stood in the stirrups and shouted. "Nice try, you invaders!" I shot into the sky from Nisha's back, wanting to get a better view. Many Dregans roared, eyes set on me. Hope bloomed in my heart from Andrew and Braidus through the bond. I had dual impressions that they wanted to see me do some damage. I wouldn't disappoint. The Dregans had to go. In rapid succession, I lobbed fireballs at them. They fled from me.

Using yellow magic, I snatched the few Dregans locked in sword battles and lifted them into the sky. They screamed and writhed in the air. The second I set them down away from our men, they started running to catch up with their party.

"Let 'em run!" Braidus shouted at our soldiers. "They won't come back until they have bigger numbers."

"Search for wounded!" Andrew ordered.

I returned to Nisha, trying not to see the bodies littering the ground. My stomach churned. I took measured breaths. *Stay calm.* Andrew and Braidus cantered over, blood splattered over the both of them. My heart nearly stopped.

"We're fine," Andrew assured me. "Not our blood."

"Oh, good," I breathed.

"Isabelle, I could use your help over here!" Malsin waved a bloody sword in the air.

I urged Nisha over and dismounted. A white-faced soldier lay on the ground covered in crimson liquid. I put my hands on him and healed, biting back a cry at the extent of his injuries.

"Thank the Gods for you," the soldier choked out.

"Happy to help." I effused charm as much as I could under the circumstances. Someone needed to be strong.

I lost track of how many people I put my hands on, including a few injured Dregans, taken into our care as prisoners of war. My fingers were coated red and losing feeling. A mantra played in my head: "Heal and move on."

I jumped at the touch on my shoulder. Resting on my knees, I looked up into Andrew's blazing blue eyes. I let go of the cured soldier.

"Thank you, Lady Isabelle," he said.

"Not a problem," I said breathlessly.

"That's the last one," Andrew said.

My eyes swept the battlefield. Soldiers guarded a handful of Dregans sitting on the ground, Zadek Shields wrapped around their wrists like handcuffs. The dead had been gathered. Smoke rose into the air as Reds lit them on fire. Malsin, Stefan, Braidus, and some soldiers stood by them, expressions grim.

I rose. Exhaustion seeped into my bones, and I swayed. Andrew stepped toward me to help, but I waved him off.

"I'm fine."

I stumbled to the main group of men. Halfway there, I got a brief sense of the world spinning before my legs gave out. Strong arms caught me. *Andrew.*

I blinked, trying to see his face properly. "Put me down." My command came out feebler than I wanted.

"Not on your life," he said.

Seemingly in seconds, concerned men surrounded me. "Is she all right?" The question rippled through them like a wave.

"Worn out is all," Andrew said, sounding tired himself. "We must get her recharged."

The men scrambled over themselves to help. A Red melted the snow until he got to the ground underneath. Others jabbed at the frozen ground with their swords, turning the soil over. Another created a bowl out of ice and melted water into it. Someone had restarted a fire with the remnants left in the camp. Who knew men could act like fussing mother hens?

I recharged green first, then blue, red, yellow, and, last, purple with the lump of gold Haldren had given me. It had shrunken half a size when I put it back in my pouch on my belt.

"Let's return to camp once Isabelle's rested," Andrew said to Braidus.

"Agreed," he said.

Andrew continued to clutch me protectively. Stefan refused to leave my side. Braidus kept shooting anxious glances my way. Malsin stayed close but silent, using his healer's gaze to assess me. Other soldiers filled in the spaces until I felt we were huddled sheep.

As a bit of my strength returned, I batted away the hovering men. "Enough fretting; I'm fine."

I squirmed out of Andrew's hold and fell onto the ground with a huff. The men wore amused smiles, as if they had expected this. Irritated, I switched on my green magic and gave myself a boost of energy. I could not afford to be weak right now. I switched to yellow and managed to stand. I shot into the sky, landed in Nisha's saddle, and waited for the others to follow suit. When the last soldier crossed the bridge, I dismantled it with a command to Boomer to take it away.

CHAPTER ELEVEN

THE RIDE BACK WAS somber. I removed the shields I'd made. Braidus spoke into his locket, informing his father of the short battle that had occurred. We held six Dregans captive. Twenty-nine of them had perished, and we'd lost thirty-six Aberronians. The deaths weighed heavily on us all.

After getting the horses settled at camp, Stefan slung an arm over my shoulder. "Come on, Iz, let's get you cleaned up."

I looked down, realizing I still had dried blood on my hands. "Right."

Using blue magic, Braidus constructed a bath inside our tent. He filled it with water taken from the moisture in the air. "You'll have to use red to heat it," he told me.

I smiled at his thoughtfulness. "Thank you." As my family filed out to give me privacy, I called out, "I expect all of you to make use of this too."

"Gladly," Malsin replied, "if you keep it heated."

"Yes," the others chorused.

I warmed the water, then peeled off my armor and clothing and stepped into the bath. I snatched the bar of soap Braidus had supplied and scrubbed vigorously. Images of the short battle played in my mind. The clash of metal, the screams, the carnage staining white snow crimson. Dead faces loomed in my head.

Andrew called into the tent. "Isabelle, I think you're clean."

I blinked, forcing the memories back, and discovered I had rubbed my skin raw. Using magic, I created a large bead of water and put my clothes inside it along with the bar of soap. I swished it around, cleaning everything as best I could. Then I heated my clothes until they steamed. I stepped out of the bath and dressed. Then I evaporated my bathwater, refilled it, and heated it.

Running a brush through my long hair, I stepped out of the tent to see Andrew, Braidus, Malsin, and Stefan just outside, sitting around a fire. A pot bubbled in the flames. "It's ready for the next person. If you'll just leave your clothes by the door, I'll wash them."

Braidus rose, offering a warm smile in passing. I took a seat by Malsin and continued my quest to tame my locks, catching Andrew's and Stefan's quiet attention.

The evening passed in an almost normal fashion. While the men rotated through the bath, I washed their clothes and checked in with Joshua, safe in the living room of my home in Saren. Through my memories, I gave him a firsthand account of the battle.

"You did well, little sister," he told me.

My eyes welled with tears. *"But I killed too. I'm a murderer."*

In my previous fights to protect myself, I had always focused on disarming versus killing. I did come close to murdering Braidus when he'd held me captive. Anger over his involvement in the deaths of my parents had clouded my judgment. I was thankful that I never went through with it, for Braidus did not deserve to die.

Killing the Dregans had felt mechanical. I hadn't had time to think about what I was doing. All that mattered was stopping them from getting to the innocent villagers. Now that the battle was over, my actions rushed to the forefront of my mind—along with horror and shame. Lives were meant to be saved, not extinguished.

"No, you were defending," Joshua disagreed. *"You protected yourself from death just as other Aberronian soldiers did. The Dregans started that fight. You made sure they didn't pummel us to nothing. That's all there is to it."*

I sniffed, not quite convinced.

"Get rid of that pain, Isabelle. Don't harbor any guilt over what happened. You did your best. You were good."

Through our link, I felt his love for me and also his anguish that I had been turned into a soldier through battle involvement. He didn't want me to go through this, to experience the trauma that came with war. However, he also had to acknowledge that Aberron needed my magic. Without me in the fight, many more Aberronians would die.

"I was your age when I first killed someone. It was an early Gods Day morning, and I was walking with King Brian through the gardens to the forge to get the handle on my sword looked at. A man popped out of the bushes with a dagger poised to stab the king. The world seemed to slow down, and at that moment, I saw that King Brian didn't have enough time to defend himself. My sword was already in my hand, so I plunged my blade into the man's chest, killing him almost instantly. I had reacted almost entirely without thought. When it hit me that I had killed a man, I retched into the flower beds. When word spread, I was applauded for saving the life of our king, and yet inside I was so horrified, I never wanted to see the light of day."

I related to that feeling.

"King Brian and Queen Averly noticed I struggled, and they took me aside to help me work through my feelings. They took me to a healer and let me talk through everything that was going on in my head—my terror that I would always be seen as a murderer. With the healer and my family's help, I was able to dislodge the negativity running rampant. I had acted in self-defense to protect myself and the king. Killing that man didn't make me an evil person. It didn't make me eager to do it again. In war, you fight to defend yourself and those around you. Killing is often, sadly, inevitable. Just remember that you're only doing it as a means of defense, and you'll get through it."

"I'll remember." Joshua had a healing effect on me. He spoke to my soul. I took a deep breath and exhaled, dislodging my remorse for my actions during the fight. It felt good. One less burden weighing down my heart.

"Thanks, brother."

"You're welcome." His affection for me warmed my heart as I ended our connection.

"Everything all right?" Andrew asked me.

I wiped my eyes. "Everyone is safe."

"Good." Andrew pulled me into him. I rested my head on his chest and wrapped my arms around his waist. He practically hummed with delight, making me feel warm and cherished.

I rode Nisha. Snow fell lightly. The frosty air burned my lungs. Andrew, Braidus, and Stefan stood on top of a hill. They waved and called out to me. Dregans littered the base, blocking my path to them. Upon my approach, the Dregans positioned their swords to act like pikes, bracing themselves for Nisha's impact. Kicking his front hooves out, Nisha bowled into the Dregans. Swords hit my shield, nearly unseating me. I tightened my grip on the reins. A Dregan jumped. Grabbing my shoulder, he pulled me down with him. I fell heavily onto the packed snow, surrounded. Alone.

I woke with a jolt to darkness and sat upright. My head swam with the fast movement. I touched my forehead, willing the dizziness to stop. My breath came fast. My heart thumped heavily against my ribs. Needing air, I rose, stepped over Malsin, and exited the tent.

Braidus sat alone by the fire, staring into the flames, hands clasped and resting on his knees. He turned at my approach. "Are you all right?"

I sat beside him. "Just a nightmare." I shivered as flashes replayed in my mind.

"You're cold." He tucked me into his side.

I opened my mouth to protest, then realized I *was* cold. Through the bond, I sensed nothing more from Braidus than a wish to see me well. I shut my mouth and welcomed his body heat, forgoing the option to warm myself up with my magic. Braidus smiled, pleased.

After a few beats of silence, I said quietly, "Tell me about yourself. I know nothing."

He chuckled. "What would you have me tell you?"

"How do you know so much about the Dregans?" I asked.

"I lived in Dregaitia for some years in King Cekaiden's court." He shifted, getting more comfortable, I assumed. His arm tightened around me. He explained that he'd traveled extensively before settling in Dregaitia, surviving by using yellow magic to ferret out secrets for merchants mostly. "It's a risky business, sometimes very profitable and other times deadly. I am glad to be out of it."

"I'm sure." It was not something I would want to do.

"A Dregaitian noble hired me to discover who was pilfering from his gold stashes. He owed a large sum to Cekaiden and worried he could not pay it. I sorted it out. The noble paid his dues and mentioned my talents to Cekaiden, aware of the king's interest in powerful mages." Braidus threw a couple of sticks onto the fire and poked at it with a long branch, stoking the flames. "Cekaiden keeps track of all mages in Dregaitia and was miffed I had entered undetected. I was brought before him and, after a short interview, given the option to work for him or die."

"Not much of a choice there," I answered, eyes trained on the rising ashes.

Braidus smiled bitterly. "No."

"What next?" I asked.

He shrugged. "I gained Cekaiden's favor and was coerced into marrying his daughter Kiella—"

"Coerced?" I interrupted.

Braidus clarified. "Cekaiden seeks magic for his lineage. The Sorren family has never failed to produce a magical heir. The line of magic since Aberron, and possibly before that, has never been broken. I was a straight shot to his goal."

"I see," I said.

Through the bond, I got an impression of a raven-haired beauty with purple eyes. *Braidus's wife.* Grief touched my heart. I had the sense that something bad had happened to her.

"Kiella changed me from a cold-hearted drifter into a man with stability and purpose. She wasn't insensitive and callous like the rest of her family. She had ambitions to make Dregaitia a better place for their people. She was good." His last words came softly, barely above a whisper. "I didn't deserve Kiella then; nonetheless, I loved her."

"What happened?" I asked quietly. I hurried to add, "You don't have to tell me if you don't want to."

Braidus smiled. His hand absent-mindedly rubbed my arm. "I don't mind." He took a breath and said, "Kiella showed interest in me around her father, but she was also secretly invested in Leeson, Cekaiden's general second. Leeson hated me for taking Kiella from him. It did not matter that I had little choice. I learned after I married that Kiella had started a rebellion with Leeson. They had a small but loyal group of followers attempting to abolish some of the Dregans' barbaric practices, like snatching the first-born son to become a soldier—a killer. Also, the people starve to feed the army. Cekaiden taxes his people to the breaking point."

I frowned. "That's horrible."

Braidus nodded. "Kiella and I eventually grew to love one another but, unhappy with Cekaiden's rule, Kiella refused to have a child with me. She feared her father's influence on a young mind. As the months went by and no announcement was made, Cekaiden became incensed. He had not anticipated a disobedient daughter unwilling to give him a grandson or granddaughter."

"Oh." I didn't quite know what to say to that.

"Kiella was fiercely passionate about saving the lower-class people with her rebellion. I refused to be a part of it, fearing the wrath of her father. We fought often over duty and loyalties." Braidus cleared his throat. "At Winderzin, the Dregans' winter celebration, she was goaded by their general first, Drekaris—who'd heard rumors about her illicit activities—into an argument that caught her father's attention. Kiella then openly denounced the king and his practices. Cekaiden plunged a sword into her heart."

A father had killed his own daughter. Braidus had lost his wife. My heart clenched. I couldn't even begin to imagine that kind of pain. "I'm sorry." I knew it wasn't enough, but I couldn't stay silent.

Braidus continued, his eyes misted with memories of the past. "Kiella's rebellion party disbanded. Some were outed and executed by Drekaris.

Others claimed Kiella blackmailed them, and even went as far as to say I used my magic to bewitch them. I am unsure of what happened to Leeson." Braidus pushed his hair back, tucking locks behind his ear. "Since my marriage failed to produce an heir, Cekaiden tried to force me into a union with his other daughter, Sarkyah—the obedient one. I refused. We argued. He opted to have me turned into a science experiment—slowly slice me open, search for the source of my magic, and inject it into Dregans. I escaped with the aid of Haldren."

Who then used you to kidnap me, I thought, unsure what to think about it all.

Braidus met my eyes with his liquid hazel. "Yes," he agreed.

I hadn't realized I'd thought with enough force for it to be transmitted through the bond.

"And now, I'm free."

"So you are," I answered, becoming aware of my fully comfortable state. When had I wrapped my arms around him? *Gods, what is wrong with me?*

I started to move, hating myself for my inability to maintain distance.

Braidus tensed. "Stay. Please."

I stilled and searched the bond. He didn't resist. I saw no expectations of cultivating a romance. He simply didn't want to be alone, not after the journey to the past I had taken him on. Seeing that it was my fault since I had asked about it, I relaxed against him.

His relief wrapped around my heart. "Thank you," he whispered.

"You're welcome," I whispered back.

We sat in easy silence, both staring into the dwindling flames until sleep beckoned and my eyelids closed.

I woke against something warm and solid, smelling faintly of citrus and wood smoke. I wasn't ready to face the day, so I kept my eyes shut, searching for that elusive oblivion. My hand slowly moved to my chest. I rubbed, trying to rid myself of the thundering pain. In a sleepy haze, I couldn't figure out what I had done to make it hurt so much.

The warm, solid something my cheek was pressed against rumbled. "Andrew, you're hurting her."

"She's hurting me," Andrew replied in a low, viperous tone. "Are you on a kissing basis with her now too?"

My eyes flew open. I lay by the fire curled up against Braidus, his arm snug around me. Andrew, Malsin, and Stefan hovered over us. Malsin had an unreadable expression. Stefan wore a deep frown, his shoulders drooping as if he were disappointed. Andrew seethed, his blazing blue eyes ready to burn me to a crisp.

I nearly fell into the fire as I shot to my feet. The world spun as I scrambled to put distance between me and the men. I clutched my chest as the pain intensified. Tears pricked my eyes. I swiveled on the balls of my feet and entered the tent. I went to the back room and wrapped my arms around my middle, trying to gain some control before I completely lost it.

Outside, an argument brewed. I heard them clearly through the thin walls.

"You're being too harsh with Isabelle," Braidus admonished his brother.

"No," Andrew disagreed. "She is my betrothed! I understand you feel you have a right to her because of the bond, and I have tried to come to terms with your wish, but do you have any idea how difficult it is for me to see her be charmed by you? To feel her heart warming up to you? She says she wants to marry me, but then I find her snug in your arms. It is too much!"

I flinched.

Braidus matched his brother's unforgiving tone. "She had a nightmare and stepped outside during my watch. We talked about my past—no charming was involved. She fell asleep. I kept her warm. Nothing untoward happened."

A new voice, a soldier's, I suspected, called to the two princes. "An avalanche has trapped villagers of Emerstine on their way to Lokenloch. They require assistance. A Dregan raiding party has been spotted nearby."

The men's moods abruptly changed to face the problem at hand. They pushed their displeasure at each other and me under the surface. I stepped out of the tent when the men finished discussing routes and strategies and had everyone ready to go. I marched straight to Nisha. I didn't spare a glance at my family, believing another barbed strike would cripple me. I shouldn't have stepped out of the tent last night.

Nisha snuffled my face. *"You're upset."*

"I'll be fine." I swung up and stared ahead into the trees, trying to perfect a soldier's appearance. *Cool and collected.* Emotion didn't belong on a battlefield.

"Let's march out!" Andrew and Braidus shouted.

Leaving my magical shelter around our camp, I noticed the weather had again reverted to heavy snowfall. We had poor visibility. The levels of snow had increased enough to make it hard for Nisha to trot at a comfortable pace. I switched on my magic. I carved out a path, shooting heat as far as my eyes could see. Several hours passed with me using red nonstop.

Braidus called for a halt as we reached the base of a hill. "Our horses need a rest. Stefan, how much farther?"

"We're getting close," he answered. "Should be—"

"Bombs!" Malsin cried.

A volley of arrows and bombs flew toward us from the top of the hill. I blasted them with a flick of my hand. The white powder exploded above our heads. I switched to yellow and swept it away. Loud yells drifted down. Within seconds, several hundred Dregans raced down the slope, swords drawn. My stomach lurched. They had at least a hundred men more than we did. Andrew turned his mount around to shout instructions at the soldiers behind us.

"Isabelle, keep the bombs away from us." Braidus drew his sword.

"I'll be in the sky." I rose into the air, sword in hand.

A second volley of arrows and bombs flew. I turned my attention to it, ignoring the first sounds of clashing metal and screams. I zoomed through the sky, breaking up bombs, rocks, and arrows. The Dregans launching missiles from the top of the hill roared at me in their guttural language. Keeping an eye on the sky with my peripheral vision, I turned my focus to the ground. I shot fireballs at groups of Dregans engaging the Aberronians.

"Go back to Dregaitia!" I yelled.

Something hard struck the back of my head. I careened, spiraling at the mercy of the wind. My heart flooded with terror before darkness carried me away.

I woke spluttering through a splash of cold water. I tried to lift my throbbing head, and sharp points touched my neck. I gasped. My head fell back with a thud. I blinked rapidly to dispel the water. I lay on a wooden table. My wrists and ankles pinched. I couldn't move my arms or my legs. *Gods forbid.*

Two Dregans stood over me, wearing inscrutable expressions. Panic bloomed as I recognized the men as the ones I saw in the vision Isaac had shown me. They had experimented on Braidus before Haldren saved him. I switched on my magic. The points surrounding my neck began digging into my skin. I shoved Boomer back into his cage. The spikes retracted. Hot liquid trickled down my throat.

One of the Dregans, a middle-aged man with a gnarled face and mud-brown eyes and hair smiled in satisfaction. My insides recoiled. Muddy man barked something at the second Dregan, a considerably younger male with a large red scar running from his left temple down to his chin. Red Scar guy handed a needle to Muddy. With a thick finger, he poked at the crease in my elbow. I sucked in a breath as he jabbed the needle into my vein. Straining my eyes, I could just barely see the syringe fill up with my blood.

Muddy jerked the needle out. He turned his back on me and began fiddling with something on an adjacent table. Red Scar slapped a linen patch over my wound and held pressure, enough to make me worry about crushing bones. Red Scar watched me with unsettling fascination.

I shut my eyes to avoid his gaze and turned my full attention to the bond. Intense worry, regret, and terror plagued me. I received a strong impression of Andrew and Braidus consulting. A bit of relief warmed me to know they lived. I recalled how we had left things in an argument and sorrow punched me. I hated the thought of a squabble being our last memories of each other. My heart tugged, alerting me that the princes checked the bond. I hoped they could gather enough out of my impressions to be of help.

A hand lightly slapped my face. I opened my eyes. Red Scar unstrapped me from the table, while keeping the contraption around my neck. He helped me to a standing position then led me to the other side of the tent. Pulling back a sheet acting as a partition, he gestured to a chamber pot. I wasn't exactly thrilled to use it, but I appreciated that they gave me the option to relieve myself. Thankfully, Red Scar turned his back to me. I hurried as quick as I could. After, he practically dragged me back to the table and strapped me back in.

A few minutes later, Red Scar held a bowl in one hand and a spoon in the other. He spoke a word, but I couldn't understand him. He pressed the spoon to my closed mouth. A warm liquid slopped onto my lips and dribbled down my chin. I inhaled spices, salt, pepper, and thyme. Red Scar barked at me. I subtly shook my head, refusing to eat their food. What if they'd poisoned it? The Dregan set the bowl down and roughly grabbed my jaw. Prying my mouth open with strong fingers, he rammed a spoonful of soup into my mouth.

I choked. The points surrounding my neck gouged my skin as I coughed. Muddy turned around and yelled at Red Scar. Muddy lifted the table while Red Scar grabbed two small wooden crates and placed them under two of the table legs, propping the table with me on it up a bit. I could now see the entirety of the tent.

It had one large open room, near the size of the two-room tent I'd been sharing with family. Three cots were pressed against one wall. Two tables took up the middle space. They were filled with papers, lanterns, a couple of books, and all manner of strange metal instruments. Some I recognized from Malsin's healing rooms, though I did not know their purpose.

Red Scar picked up the soup. Muddy held my jaw, forcing my mouth open while Red Scar fed me. I didn't choke as much. My stomach churned, and I prayed the food wasn't poisoned. I worked hard to stay calm, knowing if I tossed up the food, I'd run the risk of further injury. When the spoon scraped the bottom, Muddy let go and returned to his worktable. Again, his back was turned so I couldn't see. Red Scar left the tent.

Red Scar returned with two Dregan soldiers in tow. Twins. Both were black-haired, black-eyed, and humungous. They eyed me curiously. Muddy injected a dark liquid into each of their arms. Red Scar led them to the cots and made them sit. Red Scar and Muddy held a conversation as they stood over the twins. After a while, they began questioning the two soldiers, who shook their heads and shrugged a lot. Muddy and Red Scar frowned deeply. I suspected plan one for my blood, whatever it was, hadn't worked.

A Dregan stuck his head in and yelled at Muddy and Red Scar. Some sort of argument broke out, but the Dregan looking in seemed insistent. Red Scar and Muddy left, taking a bag of equipment with them. The twins remained on the cots, turning their silent attention to me. Some time passed. I held a staring contest with the twins. After a while, one got up, seeming restless. He walked about the tent, picking up papers and instruments, studying, then returning them. I followed him with my eyes. This earned me a smirk. I had the impression he enjoyed my attention. He came over and began inspecting the cuffs and contraption around my neck. He prodded at me with a long thick finger, then quickly drew his hand back as if not expecting me to be real. I raised an eyebrow. His lips curved in the barest hint of a smile. The soldier on the cot, Twin Two, said something to Twin One. Twin One returned to his seat. Another staring contest commenced.

Red Scar and Muddy stepped into the tent. I saw a brief flash of darkness, alerting me that night had fallen. *How long had I been here?* The two Dregans went over to the twins and began a conversation. From the tones and air of expectation, I suspected an interrogation. The twins shrugged and shook their heads often. I wondered if Red Scar and Muddy had altered their faces to wear permanent frowns.

Not long after, Muddy left. Red Scar turned the lanterns down low. He and the twins settled down on the cots to sleep.

I let out a breath, upset over the turn of events. Through the bond, I had the sense that the princes, and probably the rest of my family, were going out of their minds with my absence. I wracked my brain for a way out. I had limited mobility, and activating my magic triggered the weapon around my neck. I doubted I could convince Red Scar or Muddy to release me.

An hour or so later, Muddy returned. He strode to me, glancing at the sleeping men. He gripped my jaw and poured a foul-tasting liquid down my throat. My eyes closed.

I jolted awake at the cold water dousing my face. Red Scar and Muddy hovered over me. The twins sat up on their cots and watched, riveted. Red Scar picked up a dagger and pressed it to my chest. I inhaled sharply as the tip pierced my skin, reaching for my fleshy heart. Red Scar smiled.

Muddy positioned himself by my arm. He had another needle. "Magic, on."

I then realized the contraption around my neck had been loosened. I didn't feel the spikes brushing against my skin.

"Magic. On." Muddy repeated slower and louder.

Red Scar dug the blade in a little deeper. I bit back a gasp. Not seeing much of an option, I turned on my magic. The sharp points began moving in. Muddy jammed the needle into my vein and began sucking up shimmering blood. When the points reached my neck, Muddy pulled out. I quickly turned off my power. Red Scar removed the blade from my chest.

Muddy went directly over to the twins and injected Twin Two with my shimmering blood. Anticipation hung in the air. Much to my shock, Twin Two began glowing softly with my rainbow colors. The twins dropped their mouths open in surprise. Muddy and Red Scar cheered with fists raised and clapped each other on the back. My stomach dropped. *Not good.*

Muddy barked an order at Twin Two, who then lifted his glowing hands. All colors went off at once. Fireballs shot out of one hand. Yellow wind swirled papers and instruments. Green syrupy vines latched around Twin

One. Purple mist repeated thoughts out loud in Gaitian. Blue ice began coating Twin Two's arm and moved upward.

All four men shouted in panic. Twin Two scrambled to stand and flapped his arms like a bird. Twin One hacked at the vines with a blade. Red Scar whacked at the purple mist with a wooden rod. Muddy ducked as a fireball nearly took off his head. I found the whole thing so comical that a small laugh escaped my lips.

Muddy yelled at Twin Two in a voice that shook the tent. Abruptly Twin Two stilled. The magic retracted. He still glowed, though not as brightly. He and Muddy both looked relieved. Twin One began pleading with Muddy and gesturing to Twin Two. When Red Scar nodded, the twins sat on the cots, and Red Scar and Muddy started preparing the tools they'd used to extract my blood.

I began to worry they'd bleed me dry for their cause. I had to figure out an escape and fast. Perhaps I could blast my way out when they loosened the device to take more magical blood. *Gods, let this work*, I prayed. I couldn't think of a better option.

Muddy and Red Scar stood on my left and right. I pictured Boomer's cage, hands at the ready. They started fiddling with the contraption around my neck. As it loosened, I activated my magic. Boomer burst out of his cage with a bark. I lit myself on fire. Muddy and Red Scar jumped back with shouts. I burned through the cuffs on my wrists and ankles and blasted at the device around my neck until I broke free. Simultaneously, I sent tendrils of green magic at Muddy and Red Scar. They fell in a heap, unconscious. I shut off the flames.

Twin Two lifted his hands while Twin One shouted at him. Twin Two detonated with bright multicolored light. I hit the ground. The tent ripped from its pegs and shot into the sky.

A beat of silence passed. Cool wind touched my skin. I lifted my head to see that the twins were out cold, lying half on top of each other, near Muddy and Red Scar. I saw no glow whatsoever from Twin Two. I hoped that meant he didn't have any more of my magic to use.

The ground beneath me trembled. Gingerly, I rose to my feet. Hundreds of Dregans moved in to surround me, swords drawn. *Time to go.* I spotted my armor near Muddy. With a flick of my hand, I took it with me into the sky, just as the first blade came within swinging distance. The Dregans roared below as I raced into the clouds, hiding myself from their view.

I flew for a while, scanning the grounds below me for Dregans. Once I felt like I had put a considerable distance between us, I dropped down to a wooded area. I ran into the bushes to relieve myself, grateful I had privacy now. After, I healed all the cuts and bruises littering my body and then put on my armor. My heart panged at the realization that I'd lost my sword.

Using purple magic, I connected with my brother. Considering how I'd left things in an argument with the princes, I thought it safer to contact him first.

"Isabelle!" Joshua shouted, making me cringe.

"Keep it down. I'm all right," I told him. I gave him a brief overview of what had happened to me through my memories.

"Gods forbid," my brother cursed, horrified.

Through him, I learned I'd been gone for three days. We'd suffered heavy losses during the battle that had knocked me out. *"Stefan, Malsin, and your mage mates are safe."*

"Thank the Gods." I breathed a sigh of relief.

He updated me on the war. *"Dregan raiding parties are running freely through this province and pilfering through the evacuated towns for anything of value. The princes have been stretched thin, sending contingents from the Second Wave all over the place to control them."*

"That's not good. Have you suffered many losses?"

"No, they're teasing us." Joshua's frustration came clearly through our link. *"As soon as we come into sight, they start launching enchantress bombs to kill our magic, then run. I think they're trying to even the playing field before they try something big. They know they're formidable as long as they're not facing a mage."*

"They're not taking away magic permanently, are they?"

"*No,*" he said with relief. "*It's temporary, and the timing of when you get your powers back depends on how much contact you had with the white powder and how quickly you could get it off. The hardest hit lose their magic for a good two—sometimes three—days, plenty of time for the Dregans to do some damage.*"

"*Definitely. What's the situation for you in Saren?*"

"*The Dregans have started to venture out of the Barras outpost. We drove a horde back yesterday.*" He showed me his memories of engaging the Dregans with a group of soldiers.

Oh Gods. The Dregans had swarmed them like locusts. A handful of Aberronian soldiers had turned tail and run. Fear and despair shone on everyone's faces. Bombs fell, coating people in a white powder. The Dregans cheered in their guttural tongue, their attacks becoming more forceful with every exploding enchantress bomb. Some of the powder had landed on Joshua, and he had lost his magic for almost twenty-four hours. Terror wrapped itself around my heart at how vulnerable my brother had become. Thank the Gods, he had made it out of that fight alive.

Luckily the enchantress bombs didn't work on me. I needed to get back into the fight as quickly as possible. I feared for Aberron if I didn't. My brother did too.

"*I'm on my way to find the Second Wave,*" I told him.

"*Stay safe and alert, little sister.*"

"*I will.*" I shut off the connection.

A bright flash came, and Tomas appeared before me. "The Dregans are furious you escaped. They're ready to lynch those two healers for their incompetence." He grinned boyishly. "Their antics in using your blood to create a mage thoroughly entertained us Gods."

I shivered with unease. How often did the Gods watch me? "Is it possible to make a mage that way?"

He shook his head. "Not a full-fledged one. It's possible to give another person temporary powers, but it's nothing to speak of. The more blood they receive the longer it lasts, but even if you drained a mage dry, it would not last more than an hour."

"Oh." Perhaps someone should inform Muddy and Red Scar of that before they get another victim to experiment on.

Tomas closed and then opened his palm. A compass appeared in it, which he handed to me. "A gift to help guide you quickly to your camp. I've listened to more prayers on your behalf than anything else since you were taken."

My chest warmed at the thoughtfulness of others. "Thank you."

Tomas leaned in and spoke sagely. "Take heed: I have been watching this war closely, weighing the risks and casualties for both sides. I see much superiority among the Dregans. Without your presence in the fight, I fear for Aberron's survival."

My stomach lurched. "I'll take care not to be captured again. Thank you for your gift and words of wisdom."

Tomas waved, a friendly smile on his lips. "Until next time." With a bright flash, he vanished.

I took to the cloudy skies. I moved at a fast pace, following the needle on the compass. Tomas's words about my importance in this war settled like a dead weight on my shoulders. I hated the thought that my presence mattered so much. And yet, I'd do whatever was necessary to ensure Aberron's survival.

As the afternoon waned into a gorgeous sunset, I found my red dome. *Finally.* Stuffing the compass into my pocket, I descended and sent a quick thought to Joshua that I had arrived. I shut off my magic and walked through the wall of heat.

"Lady Isabelle!" Soldiers watching the wall cried out at the sight of me. "It's Lady Isabelle! She's here!"

News of my appearance raced like wildfire. Cheers erupted. I smiled, unnerved by the attention but warmed by the affection. Almost halfway to my tent, I caught sight of Stefan, Andrew, Braidus, and Malsin sprinting to me.

Stefan barreled into me. "I was so worried!"

I dug my feet into the earth to avoid falling over as he pulled me into a tight hug.

Andrew stole me. He crushed me to him. "Gods, you had me so scared."

Andrew's mouth captured mine, not showing any of that earlier ire for my falling asleep next to Braidus. I kissed him back with fervor, loving every moment he consumed me.

Braidus pushed us apart with surprising force. "No—more—please." He gasped for breath, as his hand gripped his chest. "I—can't—take it."

Oops. "Sorry." I willed myself to calm for Braidus's sake. "I'll try to control myself better."

"Thank you." Braidus took my hand in his and squeezed lightly. "Good to see you safe."

Malsin gently extracted me. "Perhaps the healer should have a look."

Soldiers around us chuckled. Some grinned wickedly at me. I flushed, realizing they'd witnessed my passionate embrace with Andrew.

I refocused on Malsin. "I'm all right. I had a little dalliance with the Dregans. I escaped and healed myself."

"You healed yourself," Malsin repeated. "What sort of injuries are we talking about?"

I shrugged. "A few cuts and bruises. Nothing major."

"I want a full assessment." Malsin towed me toward our tent. Soldiers parted to let us through.

When we arrived at the tent, Nisha trotted forward and snuffled my face. *"I missed you."*

"I missed you too, Nisha." I pressed a light kiss on his nose.

My family fussed over me. Malsin and Andrew used their green magic to check me out. Braidus gathered things for a bath. Stefan went to prepare some food. Not accustomed to so much attention, I found it a relief when they all left so I could wash. I counted my blessings that I was alive and well while I scrubbed the dried dirt, grime, and blood off me. Not surprisingly, I had lost the lump of gold for recharging my purple magic. I'd have to acquire a new source.

When I exited the tent, clean and refreshed, I saw Malsin, Braidus, Stefan, and Andrew sitting around a fire. I chose the open seat by Malsin.

"Care to give us a firsthand account of what happened?" he asked. "Joshua mentioned something about you becoming a healer's experiment."

I shrugged. "I replaced Braidus for those two Dregan healers trying to make mages through the use of magical blood."

I received four horrified expressions.

Malsin recovered the quickest. "How much did they take?"

"Two syringes," I answered, using my fingers to show the size.

"What effects did it have?" Malsin asked.

I delved into an explanation of Muddy and Red Scar's attempts to make the twins into mages. The men found my made-up names comical.

Braidus said, "Their real names are Bagoravichtersen and Caizum."

I shook my head. "I'm not even going to try to pronounce those."

Braidus laughed. "Gaitian is by far the most complicated language I've come across."

I smiled. "I believe you."

"Oh, I nearly forgot." Stefan rushed into the tent. He returned carrying my blade.

"My sword!" I gasped, taking it from him.

He smiled. "I found it during the cleanup. Figured you'd want it back."

"Yes, thank you." I smiled brightly. "The Dregans took the gold I was using to charge purple. I'll need a new source."

"We'll find something for you," Braidus replied, not seeming very concerned.

As night fell and we moved to retire, Andrew gently grabbed a hold of my elbow. "Isabelle." I paused and looked up to meet his eyes. "I'm sorry." I tensed as his regret pulsed through me. "While you were captured, all I could think about was that I reacted poorly to discovering you with Braidus. I hurt you, and I'm sorry for it."

I felt his sincerity, but he still harbored an ache because I had been close to Braidus in the first place. Shame twisted my insides for putting that pain there. Andrew could see the truth as well as I could. The more time I spent with Braidus, the more he managed to tug on my heart, taking pieces of it for himself. I wouldn't call it romantic love yet, but Braidus did have a hold on me. The potential was definitely there.

"I should be apologizing, not you," I whispered and stepped into the tent before he could respond.

I went to the back and settled in a corner as far away from everybody as I could get. My whole body ached with physical and emotional exhaustion. I felt my family's gaze on me and read concern in the bond as I shut my eyes.

CHAPTER TWELVE

 WOKE TO DARKNESS AND familiar, prickling pain. I sat up, gritting my teeth to combat it. Not again! Golden light swathed my body. The illumination woke the princes, Stefan, and Malsin. They watched me with trepidation. I let out a slow breath as the golden glow and pain diminished.

Malsin moved over to me and took my hand, his magic activated. He chased away the remnants of my discomfort. Andrew projected my mage core, revealing more gold flecks interspersed among my five colors.

I groaned at Haldren's doing. Didn't I already have enough power? Why did he feel the need to give me more when I didn't want it? Aggravation bit at my insides, mixing with the unease I felt from Braidus and Andrew. When would the Gods stop messing around with me?

Haldren whispered in my ear. *"You need more power against the Dregans if you want to save Aberron. Use it well."*

"Thanks, but also no thanks," I thought back to him.

He chuckled.

I rolled my eyes.

Andrew quit projecting my core.

"Isabelle?" Malsin entreated.

I sighed. "It's fine. Haldren says we need it against the Dregans. Sorry to have woken you all. Please return to sleep." I settled back into the farthest corner away from the men again. Lying down, I curled into a ball and shut my eyes. I wanted to forget the whole thing had ever happened.

I woke snuggled against someone. Anxiety flipped my stomach upside down. I shot to my feet, elbowing whoever held me in the process.

"Ouch!" Andrew complained.

I blinked back the sleep to see Andrew sitting up and rubbing his chest. I stilled with relief that it had been him and not somebody else.

I dropped to my knees before him. "I'm so sorry." I put my hand on his chest and massaged where he had a moment ago.

My brows furrowed. I remembered choosing the farthest corner away from the men. How had I woken up beside Andrew?

Andrew caught my unspoken question. "You were stone cold and shivering through a nightmare. I picked you up to keep you warm."

"Oh. I'm really sorry," I apologized again.

"It's all right, Isabelle," Andrew said. "I know you didn't mean it."

Braidus's locket glowed. He picked it up. "Braidus speaking."

Joshua's voice floated out. "The raiding parties have regrouped. Masses of Dregans have been sighted near Pendra. I need you to get the Second Wave down there. The wall defenses are older than we perceived and will not stand up against their bombs."

Our camp disassembled within the hour. Outside my dome, the sky was overcast with the promise of snow and the wind had a biting edge. It would take hours of cold travel before we reached Pendra, and then we would probably be expected to jump straight into battle. I doubted the Dregans would allow us to warm our fingers first.

A sudden thought occurred to me. I created a large sheet of red heat and let it hover above our men like a blanket. It radiated warmth down to our soldiers, keeping them and their mounts comfortable for travel. It followed us as we moved.

Malsin said, "Excellent thinking."

We stopped on a plain in the early afternoon to give the horses a rest. Rations were opened and shared.

Stefan consulted his map. "We're about two hours away."

Andrew picked up his locket and spoke to his father, giving him an update on our whereabouts.

"The Dregans are lining up outside of Pendra," King Brian said. "I've ordered the women and children to gather in their assembly hall and told any men fifteen and older to be prepared to fight. I hope you can get there before they're fully engaged."

Joshua could be heard in the background. "Keep my sister safe this time."

"We'll do our best," Andrew promised.

We mounted our horses and proceeded south. Anxiousness gnawed at me. Most of the little towns in this province had been ordered to evacuate to either Pendra or Lochenlock. There would be many families in Pendra. The thought of women and children huddling in fear with Dregans breaking down the doors made me ill.

Braidus called out to me. "You're making it hard for me to think. Turn your worry into focus. Think of battle strategies or how you can put your magic to good use. Something other than women and children dying under a Dregan's blade." He paused, then seemed to pluck the question out of my mind. "Yes, they've done it before."

My stomach churned, but I tried to center my thoughts on something useful. I peeked into my mage mates' cores and filled them cram-full with magic, blue for both, green for Andrew, and yellow for Braidus. They hadn't really required much, but I figured they'd need every grain of sand they could get in battle.

Stefan distracted me by regaling me with tales of our childhood adventures until we were both laughing and using one hand to clutch our sides. Andrew, Malsin, and Braidus listened with soft smiles, chuckling occasionally at some of the stupid things we'd done.

"And that time we fell in that old empty well," Stefan said.

"Yes! You tripped over Mousey and took me with you," I answered.

"That old cat was always looking to trip somebody," he agreed. "You kept your face buried in my chest nearly the whole time because of spiders." He seemed to think back on it with fondness.

I shuddered. "There was a tarantula!"

He laughed. "I never saw it."

"It scurried into its lair for reinforcements!" I insisted.

"Sure Iz, k—" Stefan's response stopped short as we crested a hill and came within view of Pendra.

There had to be at least three to four thousand Dregans camped right outside on the snow-covered plains. Small fires dotted the area, but I saw no tents set up. They weren't planning to stay outside.

"It's an entire brigade," Braidus said with dismay.

A trebuchet launched, sending a bomb into the city wall near the top. Pieces of stone exploded. I could easily imagine the screams within Pendra.

"We've got to get down there," I said.

Andrew gestured to my red hazy ribbon above us. "Take the heat away, Isabelle; we'll be exerting enough energy battling to keep warm."

I removed it with a flick of my fingers.

Braidus said to me, "Fly down there and put a shield over the front entrance. Push back any Dregans looking for an opening. We cannot let them get inside."

"What are you going to do?" I asked.

"We're going to shift their attention to us," Braidus replied evenly.

Stefan spoke up before I launched, "Hey, how about a kiss for good luck?"

I leaned forward to kiss his cheek. He turned at the last second and captured my mouth with his. I was so shocked that his lips managed to peruse mine before I gathered my wits and pulled back. "Stefan!"

He grinned, excitement lighting up his pale-blue eyes. "We're about to battle for our lives. I need a good memory to keep me going."

Andrew glared daggers at Stefan. I felt his ire at Stefan's subterfuge. "That better be your last memory of her kiss."

Shaking my head, I put a Zadek's shield on him, Malsin, their mounts, and Nisha. I jumped into the sky, wrapping myself with protection in the process.

Angry yells and shouts sounded below as I flew over the Dregans. Their weapons jabbed the air with indignation.

I don't like you either.

I dodged rocks and bombs as they turned their trebuchets on me.

A bomb exploded eerily close to my face. Shrapnel hit my shield and bounced off.

"That's it." I reversed course.

The Dregans scrambled to form groups beneath me. I searched out their trebuchets, intent on destroying every last one.

A volley of arrows flew straight at me. I stopped short and used yellow to gather them. The arrows slowed until they hovered in a bunch before me. With a flick of my hand, I sent them back. Many Dregans dove for cover with cries of alarm. *That'll teach them.*

Keeping my position, I shot fireballs out of my hands in rapid succession. They zoomed downward, circumnavigating the soldiers to hit the wooden trebuchets. Timber burst into flames. Splinters soared in every direction. The Dregans screamed, some in outrage, others in pain as pieces of lumber made contact.

Yes! Andrew and Braidus's appreciation warmed my heart. I looked at them. They had their swords raised in the air.

"For Aberron!" The Second Wave roared as they cantered to engage the Dregans. I said a silent prayer to the Gods. *Please protect them.* Turning around, I resumed my journey to the wall.

Men ranging from fifteen to in their sixties stood on the wall walk above the portcullis. They held a variety of makeshift weapons, from swords to pitchforks. I hovered just in front of the gate. They gaped and scurried backward, weapons pointed at me.

I flashed a smile, trying not to look menacing. They had nothing to fear from me. I amplified my voice so they could hear me over the noise of the Second Wave and the Dregans. "Do not fear; I come under the direction of King Brian to help protect Pendra against the Dregans. I'm putting a shield over your portcullis to stop them from getting in." Holding my hands outward, I did just that.

A large boom sounded to the right of me. I swiveled just in time to see broken pieces of rock flying close to where the north wall met the west.

Five hundred or so Dregans huddled just out of range of the debris. They cheered loudly.

I sent Braidus and Andrew a quick thought as I zoomed over. *They've broken through. I'm dropping down to fight.*

Double dismay hit me.

Arrows flew into Pendra through the gaping hole easily large enough to let a handful of Dregans in at a time. Three men went down. Aberronian villagers scurried away, terror written all over their faces. I landed near the gaping hole in the inside of the city, just as the first couple of Dregans barreled through. I sprang into action with a mix of sword fighting and magic. I sent out blasts, swirling winds, purple mist, green syrupy vines, and blue ice spears. As best I could, I engaged every Dregan that came through while looking for an opening to put a shield over the hole.

Seeing the cowering villagers, I yelled, "Help me!"

"We're all gonna die!" wailed a man in his thirties, carrying a pitchfork.

"No, you're not," I declared with as much vigor as I possessed, shoving ten Dregans back with a blast of wind and fire. "Line up behind me; I'll put shields on you." I waved, urging them to come away from their huddled group and join me.

Three boys close to my age ran forward. With a flick of my hand, I equipped them with Zadek Shields. "Feel all right?"

"Good," they said.

I turned five arrows around that the Dregans had fired and sent them back through the hole. The Dregans entering ducked.

"Hey, it's all right!" the tallest boy yelled, gesturing for the others to come.

Seeming encouraged, others advanced to assist me. I glanced behind me and lobbed fireballs at the Dregans. They roared and retreated but not far enough for me to have an opening to close the hole with a shield.

"Magic is poison! Mages are a menace to us all," a man inside the wall yelled with venom. He stared at me with open hate. An Abominator. It appeared their reach went beyond Carasmille. "She'll kill us too!" He turned tail and sprinted the other way.

Coward.

"We're gonna die!" the pitchfork guy wailed again.

Chatter picked up amongst the men. I saw indecision on many faces, along with distrust of magic and fear of dying. *I don't have time for this.* The Dregans had begun moving forward again. Boomer flashed in front of my mind, seeking direction. *Magnify my voice.* He barked happily.

"Shut it!" I screamed at the Aberronians.

Total silence. *Thank the Gods.*

"Line up now!"

Two hundred or so farmers formed a group, even the wailing guy. I lifted my hand. *Shield them,* I told Boomer. I visualized my mage core and watched my levels of blue sand drop from practically full to half. I had to be careful how I used blue magic until I could recharge, especially since Andrew and Braidus may have needed to take from my stores to keep their own levels up.

"Oh! It's on me! It's on me!" A white-haired man danced as blue magic began coating him.

I fought against an eye roll. "You'll be safe. Now fight with me!"

I turned around, blade raised, just as a huge group of Dregans charged through with yells. This time, the farmers joined me. They jabbed and whacked at the Dregans relentlessly, encouraged by the stability of my protection. The Dregans growled and shouted at each other and us in their guttural tongue with clear frustration on their faces as they attempted to penetrate my shields. They sliced through wooden shafts on pitchforks, pikes, and spears, disarming the Aberronians with speed and precision. But no matter how many weapons they destroyed; they couldn't break through my blue magic. The Dregans resorted to pushing and shoving.

"We need more weapons!" An Aberronian held up half a rod and then used it to smack a Dregan's shins.

Some Aberronians snatched the weapons on the ground from fallen Dregans. I started making spears out of blue magic and passed them out with yellow.

Dregans surged through the hole like ants racing to a sugar pile. We were hard-pressed to keep them back. They became bolder, herding Aberronians like sheep with their swords.

"There's too many of them!" an Aberronian shouted.

"We're doomed!" pitchfork guy wailed.

"Form a line! Shoulder to shoulder!" I yelled.

The Aberronians rushed to obey. I created a swirling wind and began tossing Dregans over the wall to buy us time.

I ran to the front of the line and put myself in the center. "Weapons out! March with me!"

Step by step, we forced the Dregans back, using ourselves as a human wall with sharp ends.

"It's working!" Aberronians said excitedly.

Arrows and crossbow bolts zoomed.

"Keep your positions!" I ordered. "They can't hurt us!"

The arrows and bolts bounced off our shields and fell to the ground.

We shoved the Dregans right through the hole and followed, putting ourselves outside of the city walls. As the last Aberronian stepped through and moved into place, I covered the broken wall behind us with a shield. The Dregans would never be able to get through now.

"We did it!" I cheered with my comrades.

The Dregans we ousted yelled and shook their weapons at us.

A wiry farmer turned around and started pounding on my shield with his fist. "Put us back!"

"Not happening!" I told him. "You're stuck with me. Now come on, let's get these Dregans out of Aberron! March!"

We advanced on the Dregans, shoulder to shoulder. Ahead of us, I sent ribbons of fire, urging the Dregans to run in the opposite direction. Aberronians stationed on the wall walk shot arrows and threw spears, axes, stones, and even clay pots at the Dregans below them. The Second Wave had fully engaged the Dregans, and blasts of magic, enchantress bombs, and black-powder bombs lit the cloudy sky.

"Stay in formation! We're going in!" I commanded.

"You'll kill us!" Another Aberronian tried to turn around and run.

The man on his left grabbed him and held him in place. "Quit being a coward, Bernard! We're shielded!"

"What if it doesn't last?" Bernard asked.

"It'll hold; I promise," I said.

I took my mini army along the north wall, pushing the Dregans back from the stone fortifications until they joined their main group. Our efforts gathered the attention of the rest of their army. I returned the bombs that came our way, sending streams of fire and swirling winds to block and destroy our enemies. To confuse the Dregans, I let loose a purple mist to loudly project their thoughts.

When members of the Second Wave caught sight of us, they whooped and hollered. "Lady Isabelle!" When I could, I raised my sword in acknowledgment.

I shouted to the Aberronians with me. "Courage, men! Keep Aberron free and our families safe! Show some Aberronian bravery!"

I could hear Andrew and Braidus repeating similar phrases, their voices also magnified.

The farmers and shopkeepers I ordered about loudly complained. "There're too many Dregans!"

"They just keep coming!"

"When is it going to end?"

Pitchfork guy wailed, "We're gonna die from exhaustion!"

"Hold it together! I'll see what I can do." I shot into the sky to get a better vantage point.

My stomach lurched at the amount of carnage happening below me. The Dregans fearlessly charged through the Second Wave, weapons swinging. Boomer flashed in my mind for directions. *Gather the wind and use it to pick Dregans up.* I darted through the air. Yellow ribbons leapt out of my hands, shooting down to wrap around Dregan's torsos and lift. I snatched entire Dregan swarms running to engage. They flailed, shrieking in fear as I carried them upward and left them hovering, wind pressing on their bodies to hold them in place.

Adding to yellow, I created walls of fire and others of thick ice, dividing the Dregans from the Aberronians. I danced around enchantress bombs and black-powder bombs. Shrapnel and arrows constantly bounced off my shield as I worked. My body swelled with adrenaline as I used copious amounts of magic. I'd never felt such exhilaration.

I turned at the sound of Braidus's magnified voice. He hovered just above people's heads, gesturing to me with his red sword as he shouted in Gaitian. Something must have connected, because not long later, the Dregans shouted the same phrase at each other. Those locked in a battle abruptly stopped, turned around, and started running in the opposite direction. *Yes!*

"They're retreating!" Aberronian cheers rent the air.

Braidus spoke. "Let 'em go!"

As the Dregans fled, I grew the ice just behind them to block them from turning around and attacking again. I deposited the Dregans I had captured in the air just over the wall on the ground. They ran like mad.

Andrew's voice rang out. "Search for injured!"

I shouted, "If you find someone hurt, wave your hands; I'll come to you!"

"Over here!" Five or six soldiers jumped and waved.

I raced over and dropped to the ground, putting my hands on a blood-coated, ashen man. Gritting my teeth at the pain, I ordered Boomer to heal.

I fell into a routine: jump into the sky, find someone waving, drop down, fix. Over and over again I placed crimson-stained hands on injured men. Other green mages rushed about to heal as well. Since my magic was limited, I focused on healing Aberronians first. Occasionally, a hurt Dregan was nearby an injured Aberronian, so I healed them both. All Dregans found alive were restrained before I or another green mage mended them. The Dregans I fixed eyed me with venom. I steeled myself not to react to it.

I worked beyond the setting of the sun. Around me, debris from the battle was picked up, the dead gathered and burned.

Finished with the final injury—a sliced leg—I got to my feet, relieved to be done for the day. Seeing double, I swayed and had to throw my hands out for balance.

The soldier I had just healed touched my shoulder. "Are you all right?"

I gave him a wobbly smile. "Just tired." I stepped back. My legs gave out. I landed flat on my backside.

"Lady Isabelle!" Surrounding soldiers rushed to render aid.

I held up my hands. "I'm fine, really."

I shook my head to clear it and gingerly moved to a standing position. I needed to get to the portcullis and remove the shield so Aberronians could get in and out of the city.

With the last reserves of my energy, I jumped into the sky. The world spun. I blinked furiously, zigzagging to my destination. I crashed spectacularly in a rolling heap in front of the portcullis. Catching my breath, I halfway sat up and removed the shield. Access granted. I lay back down and shut my eyes, willing the pounding in my head to stop. We'd saved Pendra. *All is well.*

CHAPTER THIRTEEN

ITH MY EYES STILL closed, I heard incessant chatter buzzing around my head. I covered my ears with my hands and contemplated how to get everyone to shut it so I could sleep.

Andrew picked me up and pressed a kiss on my forehead. "Let's get you recharged."

"Sleep," I complained, touching my pounding temple.

"You'll feel better if you recharge." He carried me back into the battlefield.

Malsin joined us. "I've got everything set up, except for purple. How is she doing?"

"She's not in the mood to cooperate," Andrew said frankly.

"That's normal," Malsin said.

Andrew chuckled. "Indeed."

I cracked one eye open to see that Malsin had created a charging station for me with a fire, a basin of water, and dug-up earth. Braidus and Stefan sat near the fire. Anxious soldiers formed a ring around us.

It took some cajoling to get me to recharge. Exhaustion had seeped into my very soul. I struggled to move and keep my eyes open. I grumbled through the first color and groaned through the second. But as my energy returned and my head cleared, I quieted.

Braidus removed his gold ring off his pointer finger and handed it to me to recharge purple.

"Are you sure?" I didn't want to take something of value to him just to recharge a color. I'd find another way.

"Yes. It is time I let go of the past," Braidus said with surety in his voice. I hesitated, not entirely convinced.

He put his hand over mine. "Use it, please."

"Thank you," I whispered.

The gold band melted to a small ball the size of a pumpkin seed when I finished recharging. I slipped it into my pouch.

"Better?" Malsin asked with a smile when all colors had been strengthened.

I nodded.

"Good. Now can you take off my shield?"

"Mine too," Stefan said.

"And theirs." Braidus pointed to the Aberronian villagers sitting in a group a hundred or so paces away.

"Yes." I removed Stefan's and Malsin's shields.

I stood on wobbly legs. Stefan looped his arm through mine to give me support. Now that death wasn't imminent, I felt some exasperation at him for kissing me. I couldn't give him what he wanted. He needed to give up on me.

We began making our way over to the Aberronians. Malsin, Andrew, and Braidus followed.

The men hurried to stand.

I flashed a smile. "You were all amazing. Thank you for your help against the Dregans. I'm removing your shields now." I waved my hand and the blue syrupy substance coating them vanished.

They held out their hands for inspection with murmurs of relief.

Abruptly the white-haired man dropped to the ground, clutching his chest. "Oh! Oh! I'm dying." He rolled on frozen ground.

Malsin and I rushed forward to help.

We placed our hands on him and then looked at each other, puzzled. Meanwhile, the man moaned in pain. Other than a bit of exhaustion and a few stiff joints, we couldn't seem to find an issue. We removed our hands and sat back.

"What seems to be your problem?" Malsin asked, his eyebrow arched.

"Magic on me—too long," the man huffed. He started rolling and groaning again. "Oh, it's the end. Tell Valene I loved her." He stilled and closed his eyes.

Uneasy mutterings erupted amongst the others. Several started patting themselves down as if checking for injury. Malsin and I rose.

"Oh, come off it," I snapped and prodded the still man with the tip of my boot. "Quit the act. There's not a single thing wrong with you."

He cracked an eye open. "You sure?"

I stared him down. "Positive."

"Oh." He sat up. "False alarm boys, she took it off just in time." He raised a finger. "Another second, mind you, and we all might've been goners."

Malsin burst into laughter, his green eyes centered on me. "To think this is how you used to feel."

My mage mates and Stefan joined him with soft chuckles.

I huffed. "I was an idiot."

Malsin clapped me on the shoulder. "You've come a long way, and I'm proud of you for it."

I smiled, warmed. "Thank you."

"He's not the only one," Stefan said. "Gods, you were amazing out there." He picked me up around the middle and swung me around, making me laugh.

My heart stung. Why did love have to hurt so much? I gently extracted myself. "Sleep now?" I said, so Stefan wouldn't know my reason for pulling away.

He smiled. "I think you've earned it."

I cleared the ice off a section of the plains on the side of Pendra, away from where the main battle had taken place. Then I created my red dome of heat.

"Rest," Andrew called out to the soldiers, his voice magnified. "You've earned it!"

The soldiers cheered and then made their way inside to set up their tents for the night.

A man approached the princes and introduced himself as the orate judge of Pendra. "I wish to offer you our best rooms in the city."

"No thank you," Andrew and Braidus declined before the man could get another word out. I was slightly amazed at how in tune they were with each other.

"Then allow me to offer you a selection of our finest foods." The orate judge motioned for two young maidens to come forth. They presented us with two baskets, one with fruits, cheeses, meats, and bread, the other with bottles of juices and wine.

Andrew and Braidus took the baskets. "Thank you."

"May the Gods protect you." The orate judge and the maidens took their leave.

I turned to the princes. "Why did you decline the rooms?" I hurried to add, "Not that I wanted them; I was just curious why you said no."

"Our place is with our men," Andrew said.

"A commander who lives like a soldier earns more trust from his men," Braidus said.

I admired my mage mates for their thinking.

As I helped with preparations for our own tent, Braidus approached me from behind. "I wanted to commend you. You turned the tide for us against the Dregans. I was amazed when you marched out with your ragtag group, ordering them like a true commander." He grinned.

I felt his pride surge through the bond as he seemingly reflected on the memory. It added strength to his words, confirming to me he hadn't just said it to charm me. My cheeks grew hot at his praise. I doubted he handed out compliments often.

"What did you say to the Dregans to get them to run?"

He smirked. "I made them take a good look at the number of men you had impeded and said their whole army would hang from the skies before our Mage Conqueror claimed defeat."

"Mage Conqueror?" A surprised laugh escaped my lips. It wasn't something I would ever consider myself as. Trouble Attractor sounded more fitting.

Braidus dipped his head, chuckling with me. "I suspect they took it to heart when nothing they had could kill you."

"Hmm," I agreed.

Andrew called out for his brother from the other side of the tent.

"I'm coming," Braidus shouted back. Before leaving, he leaned down and spoke softly in my ear. "Love whomever your heart desires and enjoy it. Don't allow Andrew and me to influence your choices."

"Impossible not to with how much space you both take up in my heart," I answered. Who knew men carried a plethora of emotions?

Delight squeezed me like a warm hug. "Why, that almost sounds like you're starting to love me too."

I rolled my eyes. "You know what I mean."

His warm breath tickled my ear. "Yes, but I'll choose to believe differently. It brings me greater pleasure." He stepped back before I had time to fully process his words.

I shivered and wrapped my arms around myself, suddenly cold. I heard his chuckle as he retreated to the other side of the tent. I bent down to resume tying tent strings to the stake. *Braidus is trouble.* His nonpressuring attitude concerning whom I loved had endeared him further to me. He was becoming good at knowing just how to capture my attention and leave me wanting more. I didn't know what to do about it. I couldn't exactly put space between us when we were both working together to save Aberron from Dregaitia. Plus, we shared a bond, so even if I traveled to the other side of Aberron, I'd never truly escape him or the feelings he brought out in me.

As I settled by the fire, Malsin passed out mugs of tea and the food from the baskets brought to us from the orate judge of Pendra. While eating, I checked in with Joshua and recounted the events of the day.

"At this rate, the Second Wave will want you as their commander," Joshua joked.

"Right," I scoffed. *"You're an amazing commander."*

"I'm proud of you, little sister. Keep up the good work," he said.

Braidus stared into the flames as he spoke to his brother. "Andrew, we need to prepare our men against Cekaiden's retaliation. He will be furious that Isabelle has beat his men again. I expect he's going to start sending some mages to fight us. He doesn't have many under his employ, but the ones he has are extremely formidable." His next words were weighted. "They scare me."

I stiffened as I felt Braidus's apprehension and Andrew's growing concern.

"Why hasn't Cekaiden brought mages out to fight us yet if he has them?" Andrew asked.

I wanted to know that too.

"Mages are a precious resource to him because of his limited numbers, although he seeks to acquire more." Braidus rubbed his beard. "He prefers to keep them close to him and send them out only as a last resort."

"You think he's reached that point?" Andrew asked.

Braidus nodded. "I think we would be foolish not to expect a greater effort from him to stop Isabelle."

I didn't envy the prospect.

"What specifically should we prepare for?" Andrew asked.

Malsin, Stefan, and I leaned in closer to hear.

Braidus straightened. "The possibility of Dregans breaking through our magical shields. Many of our mages rely heavily on their shields to protect them during battle—thus, they put less effort in their combat skills. We need to ensure they can defend themselves well enough without using a shield as a buffer."

"All right," Andrew said. "Let's talk to the men about it tomorrow on our rounds."

My family and I settled down to sleep in our tent. Andrew pulled me against him. After a difficult day of battle, I felt his desire to have me close. I needed him too. His familiarity brought comfort to me, and I knew I could spend the rest of my life sleeping next to him and never tire of it.

"Just don't elbow me in the morning, please."

I laughed softly. "I won't, promise."

I dreamed I stood in an expansive white stone courtyard. Stars glimmered against an inky black sky. The moon hung low and large. I stood on the Mark of the Gods inlaid in the white cobblestone. Looking ahead, I saw a huge tree with opal bark and a canopy of shimmering multicolored leaves the same colors as those found in mage cores: red, green, yellow, blue, and purple. I also saw copper, gold, white, and silver leaves. On the trunk, I spied the Mark of the Gods. It glowed white and pulsed, bright and then dim, reminding me of a beating heart. Recognition flared: King Aberron's painting in the temple in Carasmille.

A golden-haired man in bright blue robes flashed into existence. I held back a gasp. I had seen this man before in another dream when he had appeared in my mage core. He walked to the tree and put his hand on the trunk over the Mark of the Gods. His body was swathed in opal light. This was the Creator in King Aberron's painting. Why had I dreamed of him in my mage core?

The tree shuddered. Opal smoky ribbons shot out of the uppermost branches of the tree and swirled around the air. Some cascaded down to penetrate the man. He laughed, his voice rich and melodic. Though no words were spoken, I had the sense he communicated with the tree.

Curious, I took a step forward. The scene dissolved. I woke to Andrew gently nudging me awake. Disappointment that he had taken me from my dream thrummed strong within me.

Andrew read my feelings through the bond. "I'm sorry, but it's time to go. The Dregans are moving north, and we have to chase them."

For hours we rode north over frozen land, going through forests and plains, passing signs for empty towns. The sky was clear, but low temperatures didn't allow the ice to melt. We stopped to rest in Nachura's Meadow, where we had camped before, in the middle of the forest.

I woke to the sound of Joshua's voice. "My scout says another snowstorm has halted the Dregan brigade. It appears they're staying put for the moment. Take the time to get your soldiers rested up."

"Will do," Braidus said, holding his locket to his face. "Do you still think the Dregans are on course to join with those at the Barras outpost?"

"I can't say for certain, but it's what I'm leaning toward," Joshua said. "Isabelle continues to impede them; it's logical for them to regroup to rethink their strategies."

"I agree," Braidus said.

"How is the weather by you?" Joshua asked.

"Snowing heavily," Braidus said. "We have plans to be on the move when it lets up."

"Good." Joshua said his goodbyes.

Braidus let his locket fall back against his chest.

Stefan shook his head. "The weather we've been having in the southeastern province is crazy. We've never had so many snowstorms one after another."

I nod. "It's unnatural."

Malsin smiled. "Well, I, for one, am going to enjoy the time not battling."

We all heartily agreed with that.

Braidus turned to Andrew. "Let's tell our men they get to rest a little longer."

Andrew nodded. "They'll enjoy that."

The four of us stepped out of the tent. I looked up into the sky. Snow beat upon my red heat dome and melted. It was a blizzard again outside. I inwardly shook my head at the strange weather.

Braidus grabbed Andrew by the hand and lifted him into the air with him until they hovered over the men.

Both of them magnified their voices with magic. "Soldiers!"

The echoing chatter around us ceased.

Braidus spoke. "The current snowstorm has halted the Dregans' movement. We are to remain here until the snow lessens."

"Take this time to rest," Andrew said, "sharpen your battle skills, recharge your magic. Green mages, I ask that a few more of you rotate through the healers' station. If any of you have been putting off a health concern, now is the time to have it assessed. We need you all healthy to help against the Dregans."

I perked up at this. Perhaps I should join the healers' station for a bit today. I had more green magic than I knew what to do with. It could go a long way in helping our soldiers.

"If you have any questions, please speak to your commanding officer within your unit," Braidus said. "That is all."

He descended with Andrew.

The four of us made short work of getting ready for the day. I went with Malsin to the latrines while Andrew and Braidus went to acquire food and talk to some of the men. Stefan stayed behind to stoke up the flames to make tea. We enjoyed a simple breakfast of oatmeal mixed in with applesauce and cinnamon.

As breakfast ended, I spoke to the men. "I'd like to spend some time at the healers' station, if that's all right. See if I can be a help."

"I'll join you." Malsin drained the last of his tea.

"Me too." Andrew rose and took my hand, pulling me up with him.

Braidus and Stefan ended up coming with us as well. I snuggled into Andrew's side, letting him take the lead through the tents to the station. Our mutual delight in having each other close warmed me.

The healers' station was a huge tent. Tables, chairs, and cots made from blue magic dotted the room. I found it an ingenious setup and marveled at the Greens' use of a blue mage to create what they needed.

A handful of soldiers stationed at the tent gave us questioning and uneasy glances. They probably didn't think this was our territory. Perhaps it wasn't the princes', but I didn't see why it couldn't be mine. My abundance of green magic could be incredibly beneficial here.

One of the men stepped forward and inclined his head, acknowledging royalty. "My princes, is there something I can help you with?"

"No," Andrew said. "We're here at Lady Isabelle's request to be an aid to any soldier in need of a healer."

I activated my magic and held up a glowing green and gold hand. "Put me to work, please."

The man's eyes lit up. "Right this way, my lady." He directed me to a soldier sitting in a chair with a hand on his cheek. "The complaint is an ache on the inside of his cheek."

"Thank you," I said to the healer. "Send as many men as you want my way. I have more than enough magic to spare."

"As you wish, my lady." The healer bowed and then took his leave.

Malsin addressed me. "I think it might be best if you and I connect our magic before you start working on patients, so I can help direct you on the healing."

I nodded. "Of course." I wasn't a fully trained healer like Malsin. His wisdom would be just as much needed as my power.

Malsin and I held hands, connecting our magic.

I focused on the soldier in front of me. "Do you mind if we take a look?"

He shook his head and winced. "No, my lady."

I put my hand on his shoulder and cringed as I felt his throbbing. He had a cut on the inside of his cheek, as if he had bitten it and it had become infected. "Ouch. You poor man."

The man chuckled humorlessly. "It hurts a bit."

Malsin shuddered. "This is a nasty one. You should've had a healer look at this days ago."

The man shrugged. "I thought I could manage it."

Malsin made a tsking noise of disapproval. "All you soldiers, trying to act brave. Mark my words, it'll lead you to an early death." He turned to me and said, "Go ahead and mend it."

I directed Boomer to absolve the infection and mend the inside of the man's cheek. After, I gave him a boost of energy to chase away his exhaustion. I doubted the man had been getting much sleep with the amount of pain he was in.

I lifted my hand. "All done."

The man smiled in relief. "That feels much better; thank you."

"Mind if I ask how it happened?" I said, curiosity coloring my tone.

"A Dregan knocked me into the ground during the Pendra battle," he answered. "I accidentally bit my cheek as I went down."

Andrew put his hand on the soldier's shoulder. "Thank you for your service."

Malsin and I worked on all kinds of random ailments for the next four hours. From blisters to headaches, from stomachaches to a mysterious itchy rash. One soldier hobbled in with three broken toes due to a horse stomping on his boot. I found it interesting that many of the men who came in appeared to have waited till the last second to take care of their ailments, as if they could wish them away. They were soldiers, trained to handle pain.

Malsin and I often gave each other frustrated looks after hearing the same thing repeated: "I thought I could handle it."

I understood their mentality, for I often thought the same way. However, when we were in a state of war, I found it stupid that they didn't jump to ensure their good health. Any ailment could become a distraction during battle, making a soldier an easier target for the Dregans.

When a man came in with an infected laceration on his arm that would have surely cost him his life had he not sought treatment, I reached my breaking point. Using purple magic, I connected with my brother. *"Joshua, you need to have a talk with your men about their health."* I let him see through my eyes the man with the infected laceration. *"These men should not be soldiering through stuff like this. We're going to lose good men due to their pride."*

Joshua shuddered with disgust at the ghastly wound. *"Oh Gods."*

"I don't care if it's a simple hangnail, these men need to come into the healers' station," I demanded. *"We can't afford ridiculousness like this."*

"I'll talk to the men," Joshua said. *"You have my word."*

"Thank you." Through his eyes, I saw him open a stable door to get to his horse. *"Where are you off to?"*

"Going on patrol with a few men," he said.

"Stay safe."

"You too."

I ended the connection.

Malsin and I finished healing the injured man and sent him on his way.

I turned to Malsin and said, "Joshua said he's going to talk to his men about going in for healing."

"Good," Malsin said. "Something needs to be said."

"Definitely." I cast my eyes over to my mage mates and Stefan. They had retreated to a corner of the tent to work on war business. Walking over, I repeated the same thing to them that I told Joshua about the soldiers' health. "Too many of your men are trying to act brave when they're just being stupid. I think everyone should be evaluated by a healer when they come back to camp after a day of battles."

Malsin nodded vigorously beside me. "Every man's waiting till the last second to come in, putting strain on green mages to use more of their magic to heal them. Now, obviously, that doesn't matter too much for Isabelle, but she isn't always going to be in here to help. If our camp was suddenly ambushed, the green mages in here aren't going to have much magic to be of assistance. They'll have spent it all working on Gods-forbidden infections that wouldn't have happened if they had been seen earlier."

"We'll see to it," Braidus said.

"It would be good if the men had a refresher on wound care too," Malsin said. "Some of your men aren't changing their bandages often enough."

"Duly noted," Andrew said.

Stefan rose and slung his arm around my shoulder. "How about we get a bite to eat? I bet you're famished after all the work you've been doing."

"I'm a little hungry," I admitted.

Malsin and I recharged our green magic first, and then the five of us left the healers' tent in search of the food supply wagon. We got ourselves some bread stuffed with jerky, cheese, and some sort of tasty reddish-brown sauce. We sat at a table made from blue magic.

While we ate, we watched soldiers train in an adjacent open space. Their fast movements and ease with the blade riveted me.

Stefan nudged my elbow. "Focus on your food before it goes to waste."

"I am eating." I took a large bite to prove it.

He chuckled and held up the last of his meal. "Then tell me why I'm almost finished, and you've barely nibbled yours."

I rolled my eyes. "You've always eaten faster than me."

"Not always," Stefan countered. "Remember when we had that pie-eating contest last summer? You ate that whole berry pie in like four minutes when it took me ten."

Andrew's, Braidus's, and Malsin's eyebrows subtly rose with interest.

I shrugged, a wide smile on my face. "What can I say? I love pie, and last year's berries were extra delicious."

Stefan matched my smile as he nodded. "They were. It was a good year for farming."

I cast my eyes upward, noting the heavy snow still hitting my red heat dome. "Let's hope next year's will be too."

I ate as much as I could and gave the last few bites of my meal to Andrew. Meanwhile, the training soldiers had started some sort of tournament. Two men fenced while soldiers formed a ring around them.

"Come on, Lawson!"

"To your right, Peter!"

A soldier ran around the ring taking bets.

Additional men appeared to watch the fight, diminishing my view. "Mind if we get closer?"

No one objected. Andrew tucked me into his side as we approached the fight. Soldiers shuffled, giving us space to see. The perks of royalty. Unfortunately, we got there right as one soldier disarmed the other. Half the men groaned while the other cheered.

A man ran to the middle and said, "Lawson is the winner!"

We all clapped appreciatively. Lawson bowed dramatically, a wolfish smile on his lips.

Another two men stepped forward to fight. The bets started up again. Braidus and Andrew surprised me by both flipping a sundal into the collection. They chose against each other. Shouts rang out as soldiers encouraged the two men. I clapped for both, much to Andrew's amused dismay.

"Hey," he said teasingly. "Why aren't you rooting for my guy?"

Braidus answered for me. "Because she thinks mine will win, and she doesn't want to hurt your feelings."

Andrew mock gasped. "Is that true?"

I laughed as I shook my head. "No, I'm having more fun cheering for them both."

"Me too," Malsin said with a smile.

"I'm not a betting man either," Stefan said.

I recalled Stefan had an uncle with a bad gambling habit who often moseyed into Saren looking for handouts from Stefan's family when he was down on his luck. Stefan's parents had drilled into their children the curse that gambling was.

Braidus's man ended up winning. I felt his delight and Andrew's disappointment simultaneously through the bond. I rubbed my heart at the strangeness of two strong, entirely different emotions.

Andrew groaned at his brother. "You have an eye for tournaments."

Braidus inclined his head, a smirk on his lips. "I have watched and participated in many."

I looked up at him. "In Dregaitia?"

He nodded. "There and other places. Dregaitian contests are much more ruthless. All their fights involve cheating. The dirtier the better."

I grimaced. It was a wonder anyone survived in that country.

Another two soldiers stepped up to fight. Andrew and Braidus didn't bet this time. Instead, Braidus gave pointers to Andrew on who he thought would win and why.

"A good indicator is their demeanor." Braidus gestured to the burlier man. "See how calm this soldier is with a blade?"

"Perhaps he is calm because he doesn't mind losing," Andrew suggested. "The other man is swifter and lighter on his feet."

"True, but my soldier isn't failing to block," Braidus said. "Look at the frustration starting to form on your lithe soldier. He dances around too much."

Andrew frowned. "Yes, I see it."

It didn't take very long after that for the burly man to win. Braidus grinned at Andrew, earning himself an eye roll.

I put my hand on Andrew's shoulder. "May I suggest you never try to bet against your brother?"

Andrew chuckled. "Indeed, it would only be folly."

Braidus's amusement surged through the bond.

A soldier stepped into the ring to fence, but he didn't have a partner. He approached my group and stopped before me. "Would the lady care to fence?"

Surprise flitted through me. "I?"

He smiled and nodded. "Why not? I hear you are good with a blade but have been unfortunate not to see it in action."

I didn't detect any deviousness in his demeanor—as if he wanted to prove women didn't belong on the battlefield. I read only curiosity in his gaze. My fingers were itching to get some practice in. I looked to my mage mates and Malsin for their permission.

Malsin shrugged. "I don't see the harm."

"Go ahead and show them your worth, Isabelle." Andrew grinned.

"Don't hold back," Braidus said. "These men can take it."

I focused on the soldier. "All right, I'll give it a try. Your name?"

"Timothy," he said.

I smiled. "Nice to meet you."

"Same," he said, his tone welcoming.

The two of us stepped forward to fence. Chatter picked up tenfold. I shuddered internally at the attention on me, and yet my itch to wield my sword outweighed my distaste for becoming a contestant. Multiple men ran around taking bets. More people were choosing to weigh in on this fight than the others. Andrew and Braidus put a handful of sundals into the betting pool. I raised an eyebrow at the larger sum. Both grinned at me. I felt their encouragement for me to succeed through the bond. I appreciated their confidence.

Stefan shouted at me. "Smoke'em, Iz!"

I laughed. "We'll see."

Anticipation hung in the air as Timothy and I unsheathed our blades. I slowed my breathing and narrowed my eyes, focusing only on Timothy and the threat of his sword.

"Don't go easy on me," I said. "I can handle it."

He inclined his head, a small smile on his lips. "As you wish, my lady."

The soldier conducting the tournament raised his hands and then dropped them. "Begin!"

Timothy lunged and I blocked him with a flick of my wrist. His smile grew, seemingly at my quick defense. We tested each other with a few jabs and parries. I could see the years of training in Timothy with every simple thrust and block. I had my work cut out for me, but I loved it. This was an opportunity to learn and become stronger.

"You ready to step it up?" Timothy asked, his eyes alight with anticipation and interest.

"Do your worst." Tightening my fingers on the sword's grip, I moved into an offensive position and sprang, my blade swinging to meet his.

"Yes!" The soldiers watching cheered.

The bond allowed me to experience Braidus's and Andrew's instincts along with mine. Their urges and impressions to move, parry, and thrust unsettled me and warred with my own way of doing things. When Timothy's blade came at me, I second-guessed my timing and didn't get my blade up in time. I twisted out of the way, coming within a hair's breadth of getting impaled through my shoulder.

"Ooh," the watching soldiers said.

Gods forbid. Irritation bloomed within me at my sloppiness. Simultaneously, I felt concern from the princes. I could fence better than this. So could the princes. I quit trying to dismiss the bond and leaned into it instead. New energy filled my bones as I listened to their impressions and instincts, taking their fencing experience and blending it with my own.

Soldier chatter and shouts increased as I moved more fluidly, my weapon an extension of me. Timothy fought harder too, blocking and lunging with ferocity. We ducked, parried, jumped, and twisted our bodies and swords, blurring with our fast movements.

I feinted to the left, then lunged forward and struck my opponent's sword with all the force I had in me. His sword fell to the ground. I pointed my saber at his chest, a warm smile on my lips. Success! He held his hands up, his expression surprised.

I sheathed my sword. My heart pounded with Andrew's and Braidus's pride. It occurred to me that I wouldn't have fought nearly as well as I had without them. Suddenly, my win felt tainted, and a rush of disappointment overtook my joy. I had cheated by leaning into the bond.

The man conducting shouted, "Lady Isabelle is the winner!"

Cheers erupted. I pasted on a small smile, trying not to show my disappointment in myself. I never wanted to fence in a tournament like this again.

Timothy approached and held out his hand. "Your fencing is exceptional. It is an honor to have you with us."

I winced internally as we shook. It certainly didn't feel like an honor after leaning into the bond like I had. "Thank you. You fight well also."

Soldiers looked at me with open admiration and respect as I walked over to my family. A part of me enjoyed seeing it. The rest of me despised myself for liking it.

"Let's return to our tent," Andrew said.

Stefan hugged me on our walk back. "You were awesome!"

"Really great job," Malsin praised me.

I shrugged. "I guess."

I flicked my eyes over to the princes, walking just ahead of me. They spoke to each other in murmurs. My heart tugged as they studied the bond, gleaning impressions of my thoughts.

Stefan picked up on my glum attitude. "Why aren't you happy? You were utterly brilliant. I've never seen you fence so well."

"I've never fenced like I just did before." All due to the Gods-forbidden bond. I hated how much it had affected me during the tournament. I despised the confusion and uncertainty it had introduced into the skill I took the most pride in. My sword was my life. I trusted myself and my instincts with it. The throwing in of the emotions and impressions of two others had rattled me and forced me to heed them.

Would this be my life now? Would every choice I made be influenced by the princes if they were nearby? If so, I was in for a miserable life. I'd never felt so disconnected from my blade and defensive skills before.

Andrew and Braidus turned their attention to me as we entered the tent and sat on our bedrolls.

Braidus tucked his hair behind an ear. "You're being too hard on yourself, Isabelle. The bond is something we're all still trying to get used to."

"We can't help that we influence each other," Andrew said. "Believe me, I get frustrated too when your emotions make me question my way of doing things."

"I'm sorry; I feel like I've missed something," Malsin said, his eyes darting between me and my mage mates.

I rubbed a hand over my forehead. "I cheated when I fenced against Timothy."

"What?" Stefan and Malsin said with disbelief.

"But you didn't use any magic," Stefan said.

"You didn't cheat; you adapted," Braidus said firmly. "I took great pleasure from the experience."

His mouth curved into a warm smile. My chest heated as I felt his excitement at how connected we had become during the fight. Oh Gods, I had encouraged him.

Andrew eyed his brother with exasperation before turning to me. "What happened was unavoidable. Had we switched places, I would have struggled based on what I felt from you through the bond as you watched the fight. Instead of letting the bond cause your defeat, you found a way to work with it. I don't see any shame in overcoming that obstacle."

"Nor do I," Braidus said.

I sighed, not sure I agreed with the princes. Perhaps they were just trying to placate me so they wouldn't have to feel my negative emotions.

"What exactly happened with the bond?" Stefan asked.

"I leaned into it during the fight," I explained. "I was having a hard time separating their emotions from mine. Their instincts to move and block were strong and had me flustered and second-guessing myself." I threw my hands up and dropped them. "I changed tactics and took what I was feeling from the princes and used it in the fight. We became connected somehow. It wasn't just me making those moves, it was them too. We fought together."

Malsin rubbed his chin. "How interesting."

"It wasn't fair to my opponent," I said. "I should've tried harder to block out the bond, not use it like I did. I should go find Timothy and apologize."

"No," all the men said.

I furrowed my brows. "Why?"

"The soldiers need to see you as a formidable threat," Braidus said. "Not only does it strengthen your position among us, but you showed the men what they're in for if one of them tries to make a move on you. It is best that they all continue to believe you are just as strong with a blade as you are with your magic."

"Yes," Andrew, Stefan, and Malsin said.

I shook my head. "King Brian literally told everyone I am your greatest weapon. What man would try something?"

Andrew raked a hand through his hair. "Do you not see the way the men's gazes follow you throughout the camp? You're a Gods-forbidden sun in a pitch-black cave."

I scowled, not liking his bluntness about facts I couldn't dispute. "You know how much I detest attention. I try to ignore the men as best I can."

My mage mates, Stefan, and Malsin all groaned.

"You can't do that, Iz," Stefan said. "Not when you're the only female in a sea of men, not sure if they're going to make it out of this war with their skin on. Any man, including us, would much rather enjoy something pleasurable to cope."

"I understand." I too, had the desire to be closer to Andrew during our efforts against the Dregans. "So you think I should leave this cheating thing alone."

"In a way," Malsin said, "I can agree that you cheated, but I also see Braidus and Andrew's point. The bond will be your constant companion for the rest of your life. You can't help that the princes affect you, nor can they help that you affect them. Had it been a Dregan you fenced off with instead of an Aberronian, you wouldn't have thought twice about using your bond, and you wouldn't have cared even after the fight because all that would've mattered was your survival. You've been nothing but resistant to this bond. The fact that you opened yourself up to work with it shows an improvement, in my eyes, to your overall health."

"I don't know about that," I said. "My distaste for this bond hasn't changed."

"But you're getting used to it enough to apply it," Malsin insisted.

"I suppose so," I agreed.

I still felt bad about the tournament, but the men wouldn't hear any more about it. All of them agreed that I needed to win that fight for morale and protection. It didn't matter how I won it. I got the impression that Andrew and Braidus had perhaps been pushing their emotions on me on purpose to ensure I won. The thought of them doing that bothered me greatly, but I couldn't exactly do anything about it. What was done was done.

CHAPTER FOURTEEN

S EVENING SET IN, I walked hand in hand with Andrew through the camp to the food supply wagons. I pushed my irritation over the bond aside and basked in the time I had to spend with him. Sure, it was only a short trip to acquire dinner, but it was just him and me. I didn't get near enough time like this anymore.

"Let's take a detour." Andrew tugged me in the opposite direction of the food wagons.

He took us outside of the heat dome. I shivered as the snow started to cover us. Switching on my magic, I created a red haze over our heads to keep the snow off and radiate heat down to us.

"Where are we going?" I asked as we got farther away from camp.

"Just over here." Andrew slowed to a stop in front of an exceptionally large walnut tree.

I spied a few walnuts on the ground and some still clinging to the tree. I picked one up and inspected it. I didn't see any blemishes in the shell. "Oh, this is a great find."

Andrew chuckled. "I didn't come out here for the nuts. I didn't even know this was here." He pulled me flush against him.

"Then what did—"

He kissed me. Surprise quickly gave way to passion. *Oh.* I reached up to wrap my arms around his neck as I kissed him back. His presence invaded all my senses. Nothing mattered more to me at that moment than him. My heart burned with our mutual desire for each other.

Abrupt strong annoyance from Braidus snapped me out of my haze. I stepped back and rubbed my heart, cursing his existence in the bond. Andrew's disappointment snaked around Braidus's annoyance and my ire.

"I'm sorry," I said, hating that I had cut our time short.

Andrew sighed, tenderness in his expression. "It's all right, love. There's a lot to work out yet with the bond. I'm happy for the minute we had."

"Me too." I wanted more of it. Lots more. I loved this man with a passion. I couldn't wait to marry and share my life with him.

Andrew grinned, no doubt reading the bond.

I bent to collect some of the walnuts. Andrew constructed a basket out of blue magic to hold them. We set it on the ground between us and threw the nuts into the basket.

Using yellow magic, I rose into the air to get the walnuts in the middle of the tree out of our reach. I plucked a bunch off and let them drop for Andrew to collect.

"I'm going to go a bit higher," I told him.

"All right, but our basket is nearly full," Andrew said.

"Just a few more." I knew these walnuts would be appreciated back at the camp. The wind carried me above the tree. I looked out over the tree-tops and marveled at the beauty of the snow-covered forest. Despite not liking how much the snow hindered us, there was something pretty about trees dressed in icicles and white glittery powder. Movement through the trees in the distance caught my eye.

"Andrew, something is coming toward us." I squinted, trying to get a better look through the falling snow.

"What is it?"

Through a break in a small section of trees, I made out marching humans. Metal glinted off their chests. "Dregans."

"How many?"

The first row of Dregans disappeared back into the trees, but more came after them. They reminded me of ants racing to a piece of dropped food. "More than I can count." I lowered myself back to the ground. "They're going to be upon us in minutes."

Andrew cursed. "Contact Braidus. We've got to warn our men. Come on." He took my hand to run back to camp.

"Wait!" I snatched the basket of walnuts and clutched it to my chest. I wasn't going to leave them to the Dregans, not after all the work we had done to pick them.

Andrew rolled his eyes, but his mouth twitched with a smile. The two of us sprinted toward camp. On the way, I switched to purple magic and melded my mind with Braidus's. He sat by the fire with Malsin and Stefan. I showed him what I'd seen. *"We don't have much time."*

His dismay hit me hard. *"We're not prepared. Our men have been told to rest and relax. Most are not wearing their armor and won't have time to put it on. The Dregans will slaughter many of us."*

My blood ran cold at Braidus's practicality. *"How can we buy ourselves time?"*

Braidus cast his eyes upward at the red dome. *"Can you shield us in?"*

"Yes, I think so." I hadn't touched my blue magic in a while and still had plenty of it to use.

"Then do it," Braidus ordered.

I shut off the purple magic and then said to Andrew, "Braidus says I need to shield everyone in to get us some time to prepare."

"Great idea," Andrew said.

Braidus's voice boomed as we came in sight of the camp. "All soldiers remain inside the heat dome! A shield is being placed over our camp. The Dregans have found us. They will be upon us in minutes!"

Andrew and I ran through the heat dome. Braidus hovered in the air beside our tent. Reaching it, I set the basket on the ground and rose into the air beside him.

I magnified my voice with magic. "Is everyone inside?"

A soldier called from below. "Wait! There are some men running in."

"Hurry up!" A bunch of people called out.

A group of men raced inside, carrying a man with a Dregan arrow embedded in his side. "We need a healer!"

"We can't wait any longer," Braidus said.

"All right." Lifting my hands, I directed Boomer to put a Zadek shield on top of the heat dome. Guttural yells reached my ears as Dregans started appearing through the trees. The blue syrupy substance coated the top of the dome. *Come on.* I urged the magic to go faster. A volley of arrows flew toward our camp. The shield poured down the sides of the heat dome. A flash of panic hit me that the arrows would get through. I redirected them with a gust of air. Aberronians formed a line, their swords at the ready. The Dregans sprinted to engage. The shield hit the ground. Their blades bounced harmlessly off.

I let out a breath of relief. "Done."

"Not a moment too soon," Braidus said, eyeing the masses of Dregans now pounding on the shield with angry shouts.

"You think they'll be able to break through?" I asked.

"It's possible, yes," he said. "Best if we keep our men at the ready."

The two of us descended. Andrew had already begun directing our soldiers to prepare to fight. The camp had become a hive of activity with men sprinting to do what needed to be done.

"Don't worry about disassembling your tents!" Andrew called. "Make sure you have your armor on and a sword in your hand."

"I don't understand." Malsin put a hand to his forehead, his expression confused. "Didn't Joshua say the snow had the Dregans staying put? How did they sneak up on us like this?"

"That's what I want to know," I said. "I'm contacting him." I melded my mind to Joshua's. He sat at my dining room table with the boys, Nathan, and King Brian. Plates of food were in front of them.

"The Dregans are attacking our camp." I showed him the siege we were under. The Dregans had begun to launch bombs at my shield. The white powder of enchantress bombs coated parts of my shield. Thankfully, it still held.

"Gods forbid," Joshua said out loud and mentally.

Through his eyes, I saw King Brian look at him. "What?"

"I'm talking to Isabelle," he said. "The Dregans have found their camp and are attacking them."

"I want to see," he demanded.

I added King Brian to the mind meld. His dismay at what he saw through my eyes hit me square in the chest. Additional rows of our men lined up together, their swords at the ready.

"What is going on?" I asked. *"You told us to take a rest day—that the Dregans were staying put due to the snow."*

"That's what my scout reported," Joshua insisted. He recalled the direct words his scout had said through the locket. *"It's too snowy out there. The Dregans aren't moving anywhere today."*

"Clearly, he lied." The Dregans had probably been on the move all day.

"Or maybe the Dregans found and killed him," King Brian suggested.

"I'm going to find out," Joshua said. *"Contact me again in a few minutes."*

"Stay safe," King Brian said. *"Keep us posted."*

"Will do." I ended the connection and then focused on the princes, Malsin, and Stefan. "Either Joshua's scout lied or the Dregans killed him before he could warn us that they were on the move. Joshua is checking things out."

"So what's our plan?" Stefan gestured to the shield. "It's looking like the Dregans can't break through."

"I don't think we should be so quick to drop the shield and fight," Malsin said. "We'll lose a lot of men quickly. Perhaps they will give up after a while and give us a chance to meet them again on a better playing field."

"Dregans aren't taught to give up," Braidus said. "We'll be stuck like this for days."

"I don't like the idea of trying to fight through these trees," Andrew said. "There are too many places for the Dregans to hide. I suggest we hold our position until a better solution comes to mind."

Braidus shook his head. "I don't think we'll find one. We either drop the shield and fight, or we stay in here and slowly starve to death. It is also possible the Dregans have brought with them something to break Isabelle's shield and they're waiting for the right moment to use it."

Andrew threw a hand up. "We don't even know the extent of their group."

"Perhaps I could fly out and see," I said. "I'll make a small hole on the top of the dome just big enough for me to get through."

"They'll shoot you down," Braidus said.

"Not if I'm shielded," Isabelle said.

"What if Isabelle made herself invisible?" Malsin suggested. "The Dregans can't shoot at what they can't see."

Braidus pushed his hair back from his face. "That would help, but the Dregans are watching every part of this shield. They will notice the hole at the top for her to get out. Once they see that, they'll shoot at the area and hope they hit their target."

"I have to contact Joshua again." It had been a few minutes. I hoped he had answers for me. "Why don't we decide after I speak to him?"

"Fine," the men said.

Switching to purple magic, I melded my mind with Joshua's. *"Find anything out?"*

His fury whooshed through me. I clutched my heart, sucking in a sharp breath. Malsin patted my shoulder, his expression concerned.

"You were right," Joshua said. *"My scout lied. He found an empty pub and holed himself up in there with the rum. He hasn't been watching the Dregans at all. I've sent some men to retrieve him and put him under arrest."*

"What's going to stop him from running?"

"Guilt. I made him believe the Second Wave had all been slaughtered and it was his fault." Joshua had no remorse. *"It's no less than what could've happened if you weren't with them, and it's still possible considering your current situation."*

My stomach twisted at Joshua's actions, and yet I also saw his point. The man needed to know what he did was inexcusable and a serious crime. We would not be in this situation if he had been doing his job.

"What do you think we should do? Braidus wants to drop the shield and fight, and Andrew thinks we should stay under it until they give up or we find a better answer that would save more of our men. He doesn't want to do any forest fighting. We don't have a good idea of what the Dregans' numbers are. I suggested I fly out to see, but Braidus is worried about me getting hurt."

"It's getting dark," Joshua said, seeing twilight descend through my eyes. *"I think you should wait till dawn to do any attacking. You'll have better light."*

"All right. I'll let them know." I ended the connection and then cast my eyes on Andrew and Braidus. I relayed what Joshua had said to me about the scout and our plight with the Dregans.

Andrew cursed. "We need to interview our scouts better before giving them the job."

"Oh, I don't think Joshua's going to let something like this happen again." I shuddered as I recalled his fury.

"So are we agreed to not do any fighting tonight?" Stefan asked.

Andrew and Braidus nodded.

"We must still keep our men at the ready," Braidus said, "in case the Dregans have the means to break Isabelle's shield."

The two of them took off into the throngs of soldiers. I stared at my shield for a moment, watching the Dregans lining it with menacing faces. They had quit pounding and shouting and now reminded me of bears or ravenous wolves biding their time before attacking. My stomach rolled with unease. I hated war and what it did to people. Why did people choose to fight first and talk second? Didn't lives mean something?

My feet carried me over to the shield. Pressing my hands upon it, I looked up into the gaze of a young Dregan soldier. He glared at me, his mouth set in a hard line. I assumed he meant to intimidate me; however, I didn't feel it. Probably because a shield separated us. As we stared at each other, slowly his expression morphed from harsh to curious. He raised an eyebrow, seeming to ask what I was doing. I shrugged. Truthfully, I didn't know. I was the only Aberronian standing this close to the shield. The others hovered some paces behind me, tense due to the potential fight. The Dregan's dark, curling hair ruffled in the wind, and he shivered. With a quick thought to Boomer, I sent red magic through my shield and to the man to warm him up. He jumped, his eyes widening in wonder at me. I smiled softly, doing my best to appear nonthreatening. His shoulders relaxed, and his mouth twitched as he seemingly fought a smile.

"What are you doing?" Braidus joined my side.

"Trying to make friends so we don't have to fight each other." I glanced briefly at him before returning my attention to the Dregan soldier. *Should I introduce myself?* I wondered.

Braidus sighed. "You're wasting your time. These Dregans are not going to be friends with you. They'd rather kill you."

I lifted my chin defiantly. "We don't have to be enemies."

"You're right; we don't." Braidus gestured to the soldier in front of me. "But this soldier has been trained since birth to obey the orders of his king. He will see them carried out regardless of his personal feelings. You could be his sister or wife and he'd murder you in a heartbeat if that's what his king demanded."

I frowned. "You really think they're that heartless?"

He shook his head. "No, not heartless. Faithful. This soldier would mourn the loss and his actions, but his belief that his king had good reasons for it would be stronger than his grief. To him, King Cekaiden is like a God and a cherished father. He instructs, houses, feeds, and looks out for his wellbeing." He gestured to the soldier again with a tilt of his head. "This man knows his king loves him and would not hurt him needlessly. The faith of a Dregan soldier is unparalleled."

"You have seen this faith in action?" I asked.

Braidus nodded. "I have witnessed soldiers turn in their friends and family whom they caught disobeying a law. I saw no qualms if the punishment was death. They seek only Cekaiden's praise."

"Mmm, how unfortunate." This disconcerted me. To have that much power and influence over a people sounded insane. It made me think of my engagement with Andrew. He was going to be king one day, and I would be his queen. Together, we would rule over Aberron and its inhabitants. The thought of so much supremacy left a sour taste in my mouth. I had zero desire to oversee others, much less a country. A part of me resented Andrew for his noble birth.

Braidus put his hand on my shoulder. "Come, let us go back to our tent for the meal Andrew is acquiring."

"Wait." I glanced at the Dregan soldier, who actively watched us with interest. "Will you ask him his name?"

Braidus frowned. "It won't do you any good."

"Please?" I don't know why it mattered so much to me, but it did. Perhaps I just wanted to see some humanity out of a Dregan.

"Fine." Braidus turned to the man and spoke in Gaitian.

The soldier responded. "Danovic."

"Danovic," I repeated, hoping I got the pronunciation right.

He nodded, a small smile on his lips.

I gestured to myself. "Isabelle."

"Iza. . .bell," Danovic spoke slowly, his accent thick.

I smiled. "Yes."

Danovic then spoke in rapid Gaitian, his eyes darting between me and Braidus.

While Braidus responded, he wrapped his arms around my stomach and pulled me flush against him, my back to his chest. I stiffened at the intimacy and the possessiveness I felt from him.

He and Danovic had a short conversation while Braidus held me like his lover. I worried what Andrew would think if he caught us like this. What were the soldiers behind us thinking? And yet, I didn't think I should move out of his grasp, for I suspected Braidus was trying to make a point to Danovic. A small sliver of terror raced through me as I admitted to myself that I liked how he made me feel wanted.

"All right, let's go." Braidus gently tugged me away while keeping me close against him.

I didn't protest and waved goodbye to Danovic. He smiled and responded in kind.

Aberronian soldiers stared at me and Braidus with interest. Great, now they were all going to be talking about us and, no doubt, questioning my loyalty to Andrew.

Once in the midst of our men, Braidus let me go. "Forgive me for being overly familiar."

"Why did you do it?" I asked.

"I'll tell you once we're at our tent with the others," Braidus said.

I didn't see Andrew or Stefan when we arrived. Malsin sat by the fire, getting into the basket of walnuts and shelling them. He handed me a freshly shelled nut.

I popped it into my mouth. "Mmm, delicious."

Malsin chuckled. "Walnuts are a favorite of mine. This basket has been a welcome delight."

Stefan and Andrew appeared with a jug and a basket of rations.

Andrew sat beside me, his eyes darting between me and Braidus. No doubt he'd gotten enough out of me through the bond to know something somewhat personal had happened between me and Braidus. Or perhaps the soldiers' chatter had raced through camp like wildfire.

I spoke before he could utter a word or jump to a conclusion. "It wasn't me. I was only trying to make friends with the Dregans to see if we could stop fighting with each other. Braidus hugged me while talking to Danovic."

Everyone cast their eyes on him.

He tucked his hair behind his ears. "Danovic informed me of their current orders." He scowled. "Cekaiden has told his men to capture Isabelle again. Danovic says if we give her up, they'll leave and fight us another day."

My stomach dropped. Who knew what the Dregans would do with me? Would I become a science experiment again and be mutilated or killed? Andrew wrapped his arm around me, tucking me against him. I appreciated his comfort.

Braidus picked an unshelled walnut from the basket and fiddled with it. "No surprise, Isabelle charmed Danovic. He assured me he would personally escort her to Cekaiden and no harm would be done on their part."

"How did you answer?" Andrew asked.

"In a way he would understand," Braidus said. "In Dregaitia, women are considered property. Their fathers sell their daughters to the highest bidder. Men save up for years to be able to afford a wife."

"The women have no say?" I asked, appalled.

Braidus shook his head. "All women are taught to follow a man's rule. They have no voice of their own. It is another one of the things Kiella fought to change before her execution. She believed all women deserved the right to choose their husbands—that they shouldn't be sold and used like broodmares to increase the army."

"Definitely." I shuddered at the thought of not being able to have a say in whom I married.

"I told Danovic that Isabelle was mine and that our men were ordered to protect my property at all costs," Braidus said.

It surprised me that I didn't take offense to Braidus calling me his. Frustration then bit at my insides that Braidus continued to grow on me—despite my earnest wish to marry Andrew. I also had to acknowledge that due to the bond, Braidus did, in a way, have a claim on me.

Braidus continued, "I was then informed that if the Dregans are unable to capture Isabelle, eliminating all of us will be their next course of action. They are giving us the night to think it through and get their men rested up before they resort to harsher methods to break our shield."

Andrew's grip around me tightened. "I would rather die than give up Isabelle to the Dregans."

"Me too," Stefan, Braidus, and Malsin said.

"If King Cekaiden is interested in me, do you think we could make a deal to get him to end the war?" My life did not matter more than someone else's. If I could end this war, I'd do it in a heartbeat.

"No," Braidus said sharply. His refusal to even entertain the thought swallowed my heart.

I pressed him anyway. "Why not?"

His eyes burned with intensity. His hatred for Cekaiden grew stronger through the bond by the second. "There is no deal you can negotiate that will make you come out the winner. Cekaiden only makes deals that suit him. I've never seen him reach an equal agreement with anyone. He is a king and therefore only caters to himself. Getting him to stop the war in exchange for your life would only make him come up with another way to cripple Aberron. Your 'sacrifice' would be for naught."

Andrew reached up and pushed a lock of my hair away from my eyes. "The best thing you can do for Aberron is to make your stand with us and not give in to any of Dregaitia's demands. Fight and protect us as you have been doing. Your magic is incredibly strong and will see us through this war to victory. The Dregans will learn that they can't get their way here."

"Yes," Braidus, Stefan, and Malsin said.

I sighed and leaned into Andrew. "I'm just so tired of fighting. I don't want to see any more death. I want this constant worry over my family and Aberron to end."

"I think we all feel that way, Iz," Stefan said.

"It will happen," Malsin said, his tone encouraging. "Many good people are working to end this. One way or another we'll see peace."

Andrew cupped my cheek with his hand. His blazing blue eyes bore into mine. "Promise me you won't give yourself up to the Dregans." His need to see me safe pulsed strongly through the bond.

I gently pulled Andrew's hand away from my face and held it. "I can't." It hurt me to say no, but I never made a promise I couldn't keep. I had to do all that I could to save Aberron and my family—and if that included giving myself up for a higher purpose, for peace, or for someone's safety, I would do it.

My heart boiled with the princes' double anger. I had riled Stefan and Malsin too. The four of them shouted over each other at me, making their words indiscernible. I raised my hand. They quieted but openly glared at me.

"I have no plan or desire to give myself up to the Dregans." I spoke calmly, hoping to settle them all. "All I see is them trying to get me out of the way so they can conquer Aberron. My place is here with you all and the Second Wave." I took a breath. "That being said, there are too many scenarios in which I would give myself up to save Aberron or one of you. For example, if a Dregan had a knife to one of your throats, and it was either you or me, I would choose you, every time. Therefore, I can't make a promise I won't keep."

"You can't trust a Dregan when it comes to war," Braidus said, his tone firm. He gestured to his brother. "If a Dregan had a knife to Andrew's throat, the second you gave yourself up, he would still immediately murder Andrew to ensure he couldn't come after them to steal you back. There is no scenario that would result in you saving any of us or Aberron."

"You are certain of this?" I asked.

Braidus didn't hesitate. "I would stake my life on it." His strong conviction consumed the bond. "You cannot, under any circumstances, give in to the Dregans—even if that included seeing one of us die."

"All right, I'll trust you." I had enough sense to realize I needed to put my faith in Braidus on this. He had lived in Dregaitia. He knew the Dregans better than anyone else. I simply had to keep fighting to get the Dregans out of our land and protect my family.

My heart tugged, and Braidus smiled as he sensed my disappearing resistance and my growing assurance in him. "Thank you, Isabelle."

Stefan wiped his forehead with his hand. "Whew, glad we got that out of the way. Now what are we going to do to get out of here unscathed?"

Malsin grabbed the basket of food. "First, we eat, then we strategize."

We ate quietly. Through most of the meal, Andrew wore a soft frown, his eyebrows puckering. His eyes darted frequently between me and Braidus, as if we were a bigger threat than the Dregans standing outside of my shield. I wanted to say something, to assure him that he was whom I wanted, but the silence was too thick to wade through, and I couldn't seem to get the words out of my throat.

As our meal ended, Andrew asked his brother, "Were you able to find out how many Dregan soldiers are here?"

Braidus shook his head. "No. I would wager a guess it's the entire brigade we fought in Pendra since they're here for Isabelle. Common Dregans fear mages, and with Isabelle being as powerful as she is, they wouldn't attempt to take her without many numbers."

Andrew frowned. "Our men won't stand much of a chance if we drop the shield."

Braidus nodded. "We would lose a substantial amount for sure."

"What if I could distract the Dregans?" I suggested. "Get their attention on me and allow you guys to sneak out?"

"Too dangerous," everyone said.

"How confident are we that Isabelle's shield will hold?" Stefan asked.

"The enchantress bombs don't work on her magic," Malsin said. "That's a positive."

"Cekaiden is a master of breaking magic," Braidus said. "He has shattered my strongest shields before with weapons made from his assassin mages. He doesn't need the enchantress plant to break a mage. Danovic sounded too confident to me. I believe they have the means to break Isabelle's shield."

Braidus's news made my stomach slosh sickeningly. We weren't safe, no matter how much I wanted us to be.

"So we have the night," Andrew said. "That is all."

"If we're lucky," Braidus said. "I wouldn't put it past them to attack in the middle of the night when exhaustion is threatening to do us under."

Resting my elbows on my knees, I dug my fingers into my hair. Stress rose exponentially until I found it hard to breathe. There had to be a solution to get ourselves out of here without losing a substantial portion of our men. I stared at the fire, watching the red-orange flames flicker.

"Fire." Perhaps we could use it to get us out.

"What about it?" Andrew asked.

"What if we use fire as a shield and make a path out of here," I suggested. "No sane person would run through it to engage us."

"It is a novel idea," Andrew said, "but our horses would balk. We'd never get them through."

"Arrows and other projectiles would also get through the flames and hit us," Malsin said.

"We have no other option but to fight," Braidus said.

Andrew's blue eyes blazed. "Then let's fight for all our worth and show these Dregans some Aberronian courage."

I raised my hand in a cheer. "For Aberron!"

The men answered my call. "Aberron!"

CHAPTER FIFTEEN

THE SKY LIGHTENED AS dawn fast approached. Surprisingly, the Dregans had kept their word and had not attacked us during the night. We sat on our horses; our camp was disassembled. The men were quiet, the air still with the dread that always comes before a fight. I fiddled with Nisha's reins, my magic open and at the ready. I had made sure to charge all colors of magic during the night. I suspected I'd need every grain I had to get us out of this.

The Dregans on the other side of my shield had also assembled. Unlike us, they were loud and raucous, with many clanging swords together in some sort of salute to battle. I saw no fear on their faces and admitted to myself that I admired their bravery. I wished our men had the same confidence they had.

A Dregan on a dapple-gray horse that easily rivaled Nisha's size put himself front and center. A quiver of multicolored glowing arrows rested on his back and a bow was slung on his shoulder. A Dregan archer with magical arrows. I knew this wouldn't be good. He raised his hand and his men quieted.

His gaze leveled on us. "Give us your woman mage."

Danovic shouted, "Izabel!"

All the Dregans, save for the one on the dapple-gray horse, yelled my name. I cringed at the attention, hating to be the object of their desire. No way did I want to go with them. I'd probably end up on a butchering block. Then Aberron's chance of being conquered would grow greater than it already was.

The Dregan leader gestured to me. "Give us your woman, Izabel, and we will not fight this day."

Andrew stood in his stirrups and twisted to face the Second Wave. He magnified his voice. "What do you think, men? Do we give Lady Isabelle up to save ourselves a day of fighting?"

"No!" The Aberronians shouted with so much force it startled me.

Were they all really that protective over me? Guilt hit me hard that I had elevated to a person of importance. I didn't want anyone to die over me. My life wasn't worth more than someone else's. This was wrong.

Andrew turned back to face the Dregan leader. "The answer is no."

Braidus spoke in Gaitian, his voice firm. I had the impression he repeated what Andrew had said to make sure the Dregans understood that the Aberronians weren't giving me up. The possessiveness I felt from Andrew and Braidus cloaked my heart like a heavy blanket. The word *mine* seared through my brain.

The Dregan leader shrugged. "Then we fight to take her."

In one swift move, he slid his bow down his shoulder to his hand, reached for a magical arrow, notched it, and sent it zooming toward my shield. The arrowhead lodged itself into the blue syrupy substance. My shield cracked like glass and then entirely disintegrated.

Gods forbid.

The Dregans surged forward, their swords swinging.

"Don't let them reach you!" Stefan shouted at me.

"I won't!" I lifted my hands and pushed the Dregans back with a gust of wind.

The first row of Dregans fell back into their comrades, who quickly helped right them. My tactic only halted them for a few seconds before they sprinted again with guttural yells.

"Isabelle, watch out!" Braidus called.

A magical arrow flew straight toward me at an impossible speed. Instinct kicked in, and I threw up a shield. The missile sliced through it as though it wasn't there and pierced through my armor into my upper arm. My body seized and then went cold. I couldn't feel a Gods-forbidden thing. I struggled to think or move my limbs. The arrow had completely immobilized me.

"Isabelle!" Aberronians screamed my name.

The world spun. Hands reached for me but missed. My view became clouded by blades of grass. I had fallen off Nisha. Blasts, clanging metal, and screams pounded on my eardrums. I wanted it to stop, but I couldn't do anything about it. My vision blurred, and I discovered the ability to close my eyes.

When I opened my eyes again, I found myself staring at Danovic's face. The noise of battle had vanished, replaced by the crunching of boots on ice. Daylight shone, and the snowy trees bounced around us. The arrow had been removed from my arm. Danovic sprinted with other Dregans through the forest with me in his arms. I did not know how he'd managed to acquire me after I had fallen off Nisha. How long had I been unconscious? Was the battle over? I still couldn't move my limbs or feel anything. Mentally, I knew I should be panicking. I had no idea how the Second Wave fared or whether the princes, Stefan, and Malsin lived. And yet I didn't have the energy to worry about them or myself—though, surely, the Dregans were taking me to my death.

As if sensing I had awakened, Danovic looked down at me. He grinned with unmistakable affection. I wasn't sure if I should be comforted by that or not. Braidus had made it clear that Dregans weren't to be trusted.

We ran for who knows how long. Danovic's steady breathing and the strength he possessed in carrying me astounded me. He acted as if I weighed nothing. I wondered if the man would ever get tired. He glanced at me often, always with a warm, excited smile, as he jogged. Perhaps he couldn't wait for the praise he would be getting from his king for capturing me.

Eventually, we emerged out of the forest and met up with another Dregan party. This one had horses. Danovic maneuvered me like a puppet on strings as he put me on a brown horse and climbed up behind me. He clutched me tight against him, my back to his chest. I knew I should be embarrassed at the intimacy of this whole ordeal with Danovic; however,

I still couldn't feel anything, and my mind moved slower than molasses. I had barely enough energy to take note of what was happening to me. Had they immobilized me for good?

We rode well past the setting of the sun and into the night. The clouds and snowy ground lit enough of our path for the horses to see. No snowflakes cascaded from the skies. Eventually, we stopped in a copse of trees. Danovic held me in his lap as he sat on a fur blanket by a small fire. Other Dregans crowded around us, keeping close to the flames for warmth. One of them went to touch me, speaking in Gaitian as he did so. Danovic slapped his hand away and rebuked the man in a harsh tone. Many men laughed. I appreciated Danovic for that. I didn't want to be touched and handled by a lot of men, especially since I had no way to fight back.

Rations were passed around. Danovic put a canteen to my lips and had me drink. I hardly had enough muscle movement to swallow. The water mostly slid down my throat of its own accord. Thankfully, I didn't choke.

The men soon lay down to rest. Danovic laid me on my back and hunkered down on his side to see me better. He kept a hand on my wrist and spoke to me in gentle tones. I found it strange to hear Gaitian spoken in a soft manner, and I wished I could understand him. He reached up and put his hand over my eyes, then let go. I got the message. Sleep.

I didn't want to close my eyes. I didn't trust these men, especially the Dregan who had tried to touch me. Danovic put his hand over my eyes once more and spoke in encouraging tones. Reluctantly, I shut my eyes. Perhaps it would be better to not see what became of me.

I woke with dawn on the horizon. Danovic carried me in his arms again as he walked somewhere. I didn't feel any better than yesterday and had no fight in me at all. I hated it. Danovic stopped and spoke to another Dregan. With great effort, I managed to turn my head a little to see what was before us. I discovered a prison cell made from blue magic on a wagon pulled by two large horses. *Just great,* I thought with distaste.

Danovic placed me inside on the floor. When I looked at him, he grinned. I couldn't make sense of it, couldn't decide whether he was happy to see me awake or happy to get rid of me. He gripped my hand and squeezed lightly, then stepped back, allowing another Dregan to shut the door. A third Dregan appeared with a needle. He reached through the bars and jabbed me with it. The world went black.

I came to with my chest pounding with fear, fury, and anxiety. I wasn't numb and immobilized anymore and felt everything acutely, the bond especially. Braidus and Andrew lived. Thank the Gods. I groaned at the aches and pains riddling my body. Everything hurt. I blinked rapidly, trying to clear my eyes and head from the fog of whatever concoction the Dregans had used to knock me out. I was still in the magical prison, and snow lightly fell through the bars onto me. The constant jostling and clatter of wheels indicated the wagon was on the move.

I sat up. Around me, hundreds of Dregans had formed lines. They all wore fierce expressions with their weapons at the ready. I did not see Danovic anywhere. Stomach lurching at the promise of a fight, I scrambled to stand, using the bars to help me up.

We were in a farmer's fields. I spotted a house not too far from us, and my stomach sank as I recognized the stone building with the bright-orange shutters. We were in Saren, and these were Mr. Layder's fields. On the other side of the field, Aberronians were forming into groups. I made out King Brian riding on his white horse. He cantered up and down the front line, his sword in the air, his voice magnified. "Courage, men!"

Gods forbid. I put a hand over my mouth. My home was going to turn into a bloody battlefield.

I switched on my magic and checked my levels. They were all full, save a couple of grains from yellow. Boomer danced, itching to be used. Relief hit me that I had my powers available and the thinking capacity again to use them. I had to get out of this cage at all costs. First things first: I needed my health up to scratch. Using green magic, I chased away all remnants of discomfort and gave myself a boost of energy.

A Dregan riding a dapple-gray horse cantered to the middle of the field. I recognized him as the archer who had captured me. He shouted at the Aberronians. "Surrender this province and we will let you live."

King Brian shouted back, his voice magnified. "Never!"

The Dregan archer raised his hand. The driver of the wagon my prison was on snapped the reins. I lurched and snatched onto the bars, nearly losing my balance as we started moving to the center of the field. As we got closer, I made out Joshua, Nathan, and the boys, Henry, Dominic, and Falden. I didn't see the princes, Stefan, or Malsin. They weren't here with the Second Wave. Turning, I stared at the sea of Dregans. Their numbers doubled ours, making us grossly outnumbered. I silently cried out with dismay. Where was the Second Wave when we needed them? The First Wave was going to be massacred.

The driver halted when I was parallel with the Dregan archer.

The archer gestured to me, his expression triumphant. "We have your woman mage! Your great power is no more. Fight us, and you will all be defeated."

"Isabelle!" the boys yelled, their tones full of concern.

"I'm all right!" I screamed back.

Joshua rode forward to join King Brian. He magnified his voice. "Release my sister and I'll think about letting you live."

The Dregan archer's lip curled. "No. She is Dregaitia's property now."

"Absolutely not!" I cried.

Using red magic, I blasted at the bars holding me captive. The blue magic expanded, transforming the bars into solid see-through walls. A curse escaped my lips. I was now in a box and unable to send my magic outside of my prison. The Dregan archer laughed, no doubt having anticipated this. I hated his cockiness. I'd break out of this, one way or another, and then I'd let him have it.

"Give up now!" the Dregan archer shouted.

"Never!" King Brian declared with a hard edge in his tone.

The archer shrugged. "Then you die." He yelled what sounded like a command in Gaitian.

With a roar, the Dregans sprinted to engage the First Wave. The driver leapt off the wagon and ran to join his comrades, leaving the horses unattended.

I shook with genuine fear for the First Wave and my family accompanying them. "No, no, no, please no."

Frantic, I blasted at the box again. It did nothing. I grabbed my sword, surprisingly still attached to me, and tried to cut through it. Not even a scratch. I sheathed my blade again. Magic made this; it would have to get me out.

I cringed at the first sounds of metal hitting metal. The Dregans were overtaking our men like a tidal wave. A bomb exploded eerily close to the wagon. The horses reared and took off at a canter. I screamed as I was thrown onto the floor. The wagon moved erratically, making sharp turns as the horses avoided the fighting men. I was tossed from side to side.

A fireball hit the wagon and it burst into flames. Oh Gods. Flashes of chains and the fiery hallucinations I'd experienced at the Sorrenian flooded my brain. I whimpered as I recalled how it felt to be burned alive. The wagon suddenly pitched onto its side, and I slammed into the ground. The magical box remained unharmed, while the wagon rapidly turned to ash due to the fire. The horses had broken free. I crawled onto my hands and knees and pressed my hands on the walls. Around me, bodies dropped left and right. Desperation to get out clawed at my insides, making me feel raw and bloody despite not being so.

Suddenly, I heard Braidus's voice, enhanced by magic. "Charge!"

"For Aberron!" Andrew screamed along with a multitude of men.

The Second Wave had joined the fight. My shoulders sagged with relief, despite not being able to see the men.

Joshua rode into view. His hands were outstretched and streaming fire. A group of Aberronians rode with him, cutting down any Dregans running to engage them.

He pulled up short in front of me. "Isabelle!"

"On your left!" I pointed at the Dregan swinging his sword to strike.

Joshua dispatched him with a mini fireball. "We've got to get you out."

"I'm trying!" I said. "Nothing is working. I don't know what to do!"

Above the din of the battle, a guttural chant started up. "Mazika!" Over and over the Dregans shouted, weapons raised if they weren't currently engaged.

Joshua and I shared a look. That didn't sound good.

A glowing bomb exploded in the air. Little multicolored shimmering balls zoomed out and struck nearby mages with shields on. The shields froze and then shattered. Dregans surged, using the momentary weakness to dispatch Aberronians.

"We need that bomb," we said to each other.

Joshua turned around, presumably to figure out how to get one from a Dregan.

Suddenly, Braidus appeared on his horse with Nisha beside him. He held the bomb we needed. Thank the Gods.

I backed up to the other side of the box as he sent the bomb hurtling toward the prison. Hitting the shield, it exploded. Little multicolored shimmering balls zoomed out and struck the box. It cracked, then disintegrated. I was free.

"Yes!" I cheered.

I ran toward Nisha, swung up into the saddle, and wrapped us in Zadek shields. My eyes sought Braidus. "Thank you."

He grinned. "My pleasure."

"What is a Mazika?" I asked.

"The Mazika are King Cekaiden's quartet of assassin mages," Braidus answered, thrusting his weapon into his opponent. "They work as a group to make up four colors. It is their magic that captured you. They have been undefeatable."

Great. I did not want to be stolen by the Dregans again. "You think we'll lose." I redirected an enchantress bomb.

"I won't say," Braidus replied, throwing a shield up against a mace heading for a comrade.

"Well, let's give it all we've got." Joshua projected his voice and announced to the Aberronians: "My sister is free!"

Our men cheered. I read fury on the faces of the nearby Dregans.

I cantered into the fray with Joshua and Braidus. Time to let these Dregans know they couldn't own me. I let all colors loose as arrows flew at me. I blasted them apart with red, then formed a wall of fire as tall as a one-story house and sent it racing down the field, trapping a good portion of Dregans on one side. Our soldiers whooped. The Dregans could go around the flames, but it would buy our warriors a few minutes.

"Isabelle, with me!" King Brian shouted, waving a crimson sword.

I had to shout for Nisha to hear me. "Stay by King Brian. You're in control while I blast."

Nisha whinnied and charged. Aberronian soldiers raced to their king, forming a group with Dregan swarms on their heels. A volley of arrows soared from the Dregans. King Brian threw up a blue shield. The projectiles hit and bounced off.

Charging into a group of Dregans, King Brian wielded his weapon. The enemy fell wherever his blade touched them. His presence renewed the vigor in our surrounding soldiers, and they attacked more forcefully, blocking and thrusting.

King Brian shouted encouragements, amplifying his voice so all could hear. "Protect Aberron! Keep us free!"

I stood in the stirrups, using the wind to hold me in place. It pressed against my back and front. The magic swelled, an intoxicating adrenaline that hummed in my veins. *So good. . .* Noise faded as I centered my gaze on the swarm of Dregans gathering to charge at me. Darkness carved its way into my heart and whispered retaliation against the enemy for attacking my home and thinking they could own me. I gave in to it. *Take them out.*

I killed without batting an eye. Ice spears impaled hearts. Fireballs exploded, sending body parts flying. Green smoke wrapped its way around Dregans like a noxious gas. Yellow smoky ribbons spiraled around their faces, stealing their air. Purple mist drove the Dregans to the ground, wailing as they grabbed their heads.

Those near paused to take in my actions. Approaching Dregans halted with fear. The Aberronians stared slack-jawed at me.

"Falden!" Dominic screamed nearby.

I whipped my head around to see Falden collapse. Dominic quickly obliterated the Dregan Falden had been fighting with using red magic. I cantered to them and jumped off Nisha, dropping into the snow beside Falden.

"My arm!" Falden screamed. His right forearm had been severed just below his elbow. Blood poured and soaked into the snow.

Dominic grabbed Falden's detached arm and threw it at me. "Put it back!"

My fingers slipped on the blood as I grabbed what was left of Falden's arm and shoved the severed part onto it. I drowned out Falden's agonized screams and focused solely on reattaching the limb. The magic latched onto his injury, fusing bone, veins, muscle, and skin.

"Is it working?" Dominic was blasting any Dregans who approached, searching for an easy kill.

"Yes, but it's going to take a while," I said through clenched teeth, suffering through Falden's pain.

"How long?" Dominic asked, throwing a fireball at a Dregan poised to lunge.

"I don't know! I've never done this!" I said, exasperated. "Get others to help keep the Dregans away."

Dominic waved. "Over here!"

Ten soldiers ran over. This didn't scare the Dregans. Dominic and other soldiers fought hard to keep them away.

Falden had stopped screaming, but his face turned ashen. He was dangerously close to passing out.

"Hang in there, Falden; nearly finished." I sent him a burst of energy to make up for the blood loss as the magic finished. "Done." I removed my hands.

Falden sat up and inspected his reattached forearm. He looked up at Dominic, his expression serious. "You sure you gave Isabelle the right arm?"

His eyes went wide. "Gods forbid!"

With Dominic blasting the Dregans left and right, we'd had several severed limbs to choose from around us.

Falden laughed and lifted his reattached right hand. "I doubt a Dregan would be wearing a ring with my family's crest."

"Don't get anything chopped off again." I threw a blue shield over Dominic and Falden and then I hopped back on Nisha, pleased I'd managed to help.

"Good to see you too!" Falden said.

Around us, the Dregans continued to chant. "Mazika! Mazika!"

"Isabelle, over here!" King Brian waved at me, heading to a particularly heavy part of the fighting. I saw Joshua, Braidus, and Henry among this group.

"Watch out!" Henry shouted.

A glowing bomb exploded above our heads. Little multicolored shimmering balls struck us. Our Zadek shields seized and then disintegrated.

The Dregans hollered and whooped. "Mazika! Mazika!"

CHAPTER SIXTEEN

COULD TASTE FEAR IN the air. Aberronian soldiers sprinted from the Dregans, yelling, "They're breaking through our magic!"

Braidus projected his voice. "Avoid the Mazika!"

Dispatching a Dregan, I took a second to look ahead of me. Four Dregans, the Mazika, stood on a wheeled wooden platform, being pulled and directed by oxen and a driver. The platform sported a trebuchet, and the entire vehicle was wrapped in a Zadek shield. Each member of the Mazika glowed brightly with his respective color. I watched as the blue mage created a sphere filled with blue beads. The green mage took it and added his color to the beads, followed by red, then yellow, until each bead shone brilliantly with four colors. The yellow mage then launched the bomb with the trebuchet. It exploded over a group of Aberronians. The tiny beads flew, latching onto those amongst the assembly who had shields and destroying them. The bomb affected every color of magic. As each protection shattered, any Dregans nearby lunged, taking advantage of the momentary weakness to kill as many as they could.

Dregans also ran to and from a small cart nearby the Mazika. From the cart, they retrieved Mazika bombs then ran back into battle. One Dregan had a large pouch strapped around his stomach. He stuffed as many bombs as he could in his pouch before sprinting off to fight. The yellow mage added more bombs to refill the cart.

I had to do something. Despite wanting to dodge the Mazika, I worried we'd never make it if I gave in to my fear of getting captured again or, worse, killed. Aberron relied on us mages to get us through our battles with the Dregans. We couldn't lose any mage.

I shouted to King Brian. "We've got to take the Mazika out!"

"Go!" King Brian said.

Come on. Now was not the time to be a coward. I threw another shield over Nisha, and I then steered him around the fights and cantered toward the Mazika, intent on stopping their operation.

Retreating Aberronians called out to me wearing mixtures of fear, surprise, and support. I saw Danovic riding on a horse, encouraging other Dregans. Our eyes met. He grinned and raised his sword in salute. I did the same. He directed his men to go in the opposite direction. *And Braidus said we couldn't make friends with the Dregans,* I thought. Danovic and I must be an exception.

"Iz!" Stefan rode over with Andrew right behind him. The three of us joined forces to face the Mazika.

"Focus on them," Andrew said. "We'll keep others at bay."

"Right." I nudged Nisha forward.

The Mazika watched me with interest, their lips curled into half smiles, as they continued to create bombs and send them out. Clearly, they anticipated my arrival.

"Any time now, Iz!" Stefan shouted behind me. "Throw some fire at it or something!"

I watched as the Mazika's hands moved, passing the bomb from one person to the next, each adding their color to the beads. They worked together like extensions of one person. If they could merge their colors to create something stronger, so could I.

Boomer flashed in front of my mind for direction. *Combine all colors and blast this shield apart.* With a stern desire, I didn't give Boomer any room to disobey me. It had to work. A stream of multicolored fire shot out of my hands. It hit the shield around the Dregan mages and began melting it to nothing. Shocked anger formed on the Mazika's faces. They jabbered at one another, pausing in their work. Triumph enveloped me. Now that I knew how to break Zadek shields, they could never trap me in one again.

"Yes!" Andrew, Stefan, and other Aberronians shouted behind me.

I wanted to draw the mages' attention away from our men. "Come out and fight!"

With a nod to each other, they stepped off the platform to face me.

I dismounted, not willing to risk Nisha, and drew my sword. I didn't think about the odds—four trained mages against one semitrained girl. Even if I did have an abundance of magic, this could be fatal. *Focus, Isabelle.* . . My heart pounded. Throat dry, I swallowed, lips pressed tight in determination. My fingers tightened on my sword grip, knuckles white, muscles straining. *This is it.*

Green threw a bead, shattering my shield. Red lunged, swinging a flaming sword. I blocked and then ducked, avoiding the ice bolts from Blue. Yellow kicked my chest, sending me flying backward. The air escaped my lungs. I landed on the ground, my head slamming into the icy snow. Blinking back the pain, I rolled, narrowly avoiding Red's blade. It sliced through the earth as easily as if it cut butter.

I scrambled to my feet, sending out a purple mist in the process. It loudly projected the Mazika's thoughts. Using the momentary confusion, I sent out a stream of multicolored fire, breaking the mages' shields.

The Mazika glanced at each other, each wearing half-curled, angry smiles. Yellow vanished. Green shot syrupy vines. I twisted away and blocked a simultaneous attack from Red. Yellow reappeared at my side. He wrapped his arm around my neck and swung a dagger toward my chest. I lit myself on fire. He yelled and jumped back as his clothes ignited. Blue threw a stream of water at Yellow and then at me, dousing the flames.

Green smacked me with a long staff. I stumbled. A foreign weight pressed on my back, like something had latched on. Abruptly, I felt my energy level sinking. I jerked hard while reaching behind myself. My fingers brushed against a rod. I detached it and burned it to ash while giving myself a boost of adrenaline.

Meanwhile, the Mazika lined up and took each other's hands. Blue held his palm out, directing all their power to form a multicolored ice arrow. With a flick of his fingers, he sent it zooming.

Gods forbid. I threw a shield up. It broke through, shattering my shield to nothing and grazing my neck as I dodged. I pressed a hand to my throat and came away with blood. The Mazika members all grinned.

I narrowed my eyes. *Combine colors, rapid-fire,* I told Boomer. He growled. Four mini rainbow fireballs shot out of my hand in quick succession. The Mazika scattered. I struck Blue's thigh. He cried out, cursing in his native tongue. Green ran to place his hand on Blue. Yellow reversed two of my fireballs. I ducked to avoid them.

With a guttural yell, Red surged forward, swinging his flaming blade. I blocked with my own sword while simultaneously coating my steel in ice in hopes to put out his fire. He retreated and sprang again. I slid to the right, parried, then thrust. Our swords locked. Fire melted ice. Steam rose, clouding us.

Yellow materialized beside me, a dagger in each hand. I pushed Red away while dodging Yellow. The larger battle roared in the background as our mage fight plunged on, weapons a blur of motion. Yellow darted around me, appearing and vanishing in a blink of an eye. Sweat covered my brow. Muscles screamed in protest as I moved in ways I'd previously thought inhumanly possible.

A familiar cry pierced my ears. I swiveled. Andrew pulled an arrow out of his upper arm. His body glowed green as he healed himself.

Red struck my chest. The tip of his sword sliced my breastplate from top to bottom. Yellow appeared and carved down the back of my armor. I faltered. My skin stung where the blades had managed to nick through my clothes. My severed breastplate fell to the ground.

I gasped sharply as ice bolts impaled my shoulders. The force knocked me backward. My back struck the icy ground. The bolts went straight through me, reaching for the snow beneath me. The ends fused. Full-blown panic and pain erupted. *I'm pinned.*

The Mazika converged. Dark eyes alight, they approached to finish me off.

Andrew and Stefan ran into my line of sight. Through hazy vision, I watched as they engaged the Mazika. Blurs of magic passed back and forth.

Stefan barreled toward the Dregan mages, sword swinging. Red dropped. Shields appeared and shattered.

Tears pricked my eyes as I scrambled to form a coherent thought to send to Boomer. *Help!* He flashed in front of my mind, whining. *Melt.* The ice disintegrated. *Heal.*

Red jumped to his feet, back in the fight. He thrust his fiery sword into Stefan's lower back. The end of the blade showed through his stomach. With a sickening squelch, Red removed it. Stefan's eyes widened as he crumpled.

"No!" I rolled onto my stomach and pushed myself to my feet. I connected minds with him. *I'm coming!*

"I love you, Iz." Stefan's presence faded.

No. Gods forbid, no. I couldn't feel him. *Stefan!*

"Stefan!" I screamed, reaching his still form.

I placed my hands on him. Boomer snuffled, then turned away. He returned to my injuries. *Stop it!* I shrieked. *Heal Stefan.* Boomer whined, his tail tucked between his legs.

A flash of blue came within a breath of my nose. I looked up to see Andrew battling the Mazika on his own.

Red sidestepped Andrew and came at me. I shoved my hand out. *Kill.* Boomer chose rainbow fire. It streamed out and engulfed the mage. He collapsed, becoming a charred pile of bones. I got to my feet, sending the rainbow blaze out at the three remaining Mazika members. Within seconds, ashes replaced their forms.

Andrew, poised to fight, stared at me wide-eyed. I waved my hand over Andrew. *Shield.* A rainbow-syrupy substance coated him. I made a dome of the same material over Stefan. I would come back soon to make him better.

Using purple magic, I connected Andrew, King Brian, Joshua, and Braidus. *Tell the First and Second Waves to retreat. I'm going to round up the Dregans and shield them in a prison.*

I read their concern in my foolhardy plan. The Dregans were fierce, and all of us struggled. More than likely, I'd end up getting myself killed, and we'd be back to where we had started except without my magic to help. And yet, doubts that we could win by hand-to-hand combat also flowed freely. I let the men feel my vengeance and determination, burning brighter than the hottest flame. Although I felt Andrew's and Braidus's apprehension, I wouldn't allow it to control me. Braidus was the first to put his faith in me and my magic. The others quickly followed suit.

"Do it," King Brian agreed.

I ended the connection.

Andrew hopped on Nisha and called for a retreat. Nearby Aberronians followed him with dismay on their faces. I threw up a short wall of fire, blocking a swarm of Dregans from chasing some of our withdrawing men.

"We can't let the Dregans win!" a dark-haired soldier cried, seeming to want to run back and engage the enemy.

"Yes!" other men nearby agreed.

"We're not!" I declared to the men with hard conviction. "Trust me!"

The dark-haired soldier must have seen something in my face, because he said, "May the Gods be with you." He motioned to other men. "Let's get out of Lady Isabelle's way!"

I ran to help a few other soldiers escape the Dregans.

"I'm not giving up my freedom!" A burly Aberronian soldier growled, jumping back in to attack.

"We can't retreat!" Other soldiers seemed determined to fight as well.

I didn't have time to convince them. With a flick of my hand, I used yellow to snatch a handful of Aberronians into the air. I sent them careening through the air and deposited them next to other gathering soldiers.

I did a quick sweep with my eyes of the battlefield, assuring myself of our men's active withdrawal. King Brian, Joshua, Andrew, and Braidus rode through the First and Second Waves, calling and assisting their men to retreat. *This is it.*

Boomer barked, seeking new direction. *Magnify my voice as loud as you can and lift me.* For the first time ever, I *wanted* attention on myself. I rose above everyone's heads and flew toward the gathering Dregan swarms. They were cheering at our departure. *It's not over yet.* Fire lit my veins.

"Hey! You haven't defeated me. I made it out of your prison and killed your Mazika. Give me a better challenge!" I waved my sword, motioning for Dregans to come at me.

Their cheers died down as their concentration switched to me. The Dregan archer rode in front of his men, shouting what appeared to be instructions. He pointed a red-tinged sword at me.

I dropped to the ground and sheathed my sword. Magic would end this better than my blade could. Hundreds of Dregans charged with battle cries.

"For Aberron!" I ran to meet them.

Boomer growled, teeth bared. *Knock out,* I told him. Streams of rainbow ribbons shot out of my hands. They raced ahead, weaving through the air. Dregans swerved and ducked to avoid them. Not all were lucky. Upon contact, eyes rolled to the back of heads. They dropped like puppets whose strings had been cut.

Some Dregans came within sword-swinging distance. Thrusting my hands out, I pushed them back with a gust of air. They fell into their comrades, knocking them over. They righted themselves with angry shouts.

"Above!" Aberronian soldiers shouted from behind me.

I looked up. A volley of arrows, enchantress bombs, Mazika bombs, and black-powder bombs rained. I sent them high into the clouds and then decimated them with rainbow beads of fire. The Dregans screamed at me in their guttural tongue.

Hands outstretched, I spun in a circle, taking the opportunity to see that most of the First and Second Waves had disengaged and waited out of immediate danger. "You can do better! Challenge me!" I called to the Dregans.

More Dregans joined ranks as the Dregan archer appeared to call for reinforcements. *Good.* I wanted every Dregan's attention on me and off of my family and fellow Aberronians.

An enemy swarm charged, the bulk of their army. Daggers, arrows, and crossbow bolts flew from the front lines. I grunted as I felt the impact of one of their projectiles while I jumped into the air. *Round up.* Smoky streams of rainbow ribbon sailed out from me, going around the Dregans like string wrapping a present. As the two ribbon ends connected, the ribbon expanded, going up and down to form an impenetrable rainbow shield two stories tall. The Dregans roared and pounded on the shield to no avail.

Now gather up the rest. I went after the Dregans I hadn't managed to catch, sending more smoky ribbons out. They sprinted from my magic, yelling in fear. Several whacked futilely at the ribbons with their swords.

I dodged a few arrows and a bomb or two. Small pieces of shrapnel struck me.

With a singular focus, I picked up every running Dregan I saw. With a pulling motion, I hauled them over to the prison and gently dropped them inside with the others. Last, I collected the unconscious Dregans. I placed their still forms just outside the confined and enlarged the shield once more to combine them. *It's done.*

Aberronian cheers thundered. I directed the wind to carry me back to Stefan. My family and the First and Second Waves raced toward me. Seeing Andrew and Nisha still protected by my shields, I flicked my fingers and had Boomer remove them. I touched the ground when the men were about twenty paces away. My strength faltered. I stumbled. Looking down, I discovered a dagger in my hip, an arrow in my lower leg, and multiple embedded pieces of shrapnel in other areas of my body. I frowned. I felt nothing. How did those get there?

I wrapped my fingers around the handle of the dagger and tugged. *Heal,* I told Boomer, as I pulled it out. I bent and yanked out the arrow. *Fix that too.* He woofed softly as he lay on his belly. My magic waned.

I removed the dome around Stefan and pulled his head onto my lap. His eyes were closed, a soft smile on his face as though he dreamed something pleasant.

I pressed my green magic into him. "Come back." I shook him gently. Nothing happened.

Haldren! I begged. *Bring him back.*

Silence.

Malsin and Andrew put their glowing green hands on me.

"You can't be dead. I love you." I clutched him to me. Tears spilled down my cheeks. "Gods, I love you!" I kissed his cold lips.

A corner of my mind noticed Malsin and Andrew working over me, pulling out the shrapnel and healing the rest of my injuries. The soldiers dispersed. They picked up pieces of the battle and burned the dead. I held Stefan protectively the entire time. When Malsin and Andrew finished, other family members took turns at my side, keeping a hand on my shoulder at all times. Even Nisha stood vigil nearby. If they spoke, I heard nothing.

As night fell, the soldiers and my family congregated around me again. I hadn't budged for hours.

Andrew reached for me. "Isabelle, it's time. We've got to move."

I leaned away. "I'm not leaving Stefan."

"He's gone. There's nothing you can do," he said patiently.

"I'm not moving!" I roared.

He reared back, his expression hurt.

"Enough," Joshua said. He and Nathan pried me off Stefan. They dragged me backward as I shrieked. I threw them off me with a gust of air, then scrambled to Stefan. There was a flash of bright light and Haldren appeared. With a wave of his hand, Stefan vanished. I cried out. "No!"

"Stefan's spirit is safe in the realm of souls," Haldren said firmly. "You can do no more for his body." He disappeared.

A fresh wave of grief hit me. The fight left my body as I wailed, hands digging into the ice. Braidus picked me up, wincing at the force of my emotions. He tucked me close to his body and walked. My family and the soldiers followed

My eyes danced over the remnants of our battle. There were many patches of crimson, and small pieces of metal from weapons and armor peeking out of the snow. My gaze snagged on a bomb half buried under the ice. I opened my mouth to say something when Nathan unknowingly stepped on it. It exploded with a roaring boom.

Braidus dropped us to the ground. My ears rang. My head swam. Braidus's weight pressed on me as he covered me with his body. Shouts and agonized yells surrounded us. The Dregans cheered from their prison. Braidus groaned in my ear. I switched on my magic. A pained cry escaped my lips as I healed his burned and damaged flesh.

He rolled off me, breathing heavily. I sat up gingerly, touching my temple. A dizzying headache raged. Around me, green mages tended to others hit by the blast. Not trusting myself to stand, I crawled on my hands and knees to the nearest downed person. *Joshua.* My brother stared at me with a pain-filled grimace as I helped heal him with another mage.

"Thanks, sister," he whispered.

I squeezed his hand and moved to Nathan. I went to touch his still form, suspecting he had been knocked out.

A soldier stopped me. "I'm sorry, Lady Isabelle; he didn't make it."

What? I grabbed Nathan's hand. *Heal.* Boomer whined, tail tucked between legs, head down. Nothing happened. "Nathan!" I screamed.

Haldren appeared again, his expression somber. Nathan vanished along with him.

I clutched my chest. My heart thrashed against my ribs. Dark spots floated before my eyes. I couldn't get air into my lungs. Malsin touched my cheek and gave me breath. I choked on it.

Joshua held me. "Breathe, Isabelle. I know it hurts, but you'll get through it. You're strong."

I shoved at him and scrambled to my feet. I flew, rising until the air began to thin. I clawed at my throat, suffocating in sobs. *Stefan and Nathan are dead.* My agonized cry shook the sky. Hours, minutes, or seconds later, Braidus enfolded me in a hug, my back to his front. He pressed a chaste kiss to my temple. I turned and buried myself in his chest, shutting my eyes. He swept me up and descended.

I opened my eyes when Braidus deposited me on the couch in my living room. I sat still and silent while the men bustled about, speaking in low murmurs, preparing food, and washing the grime of the battle off. Malsin handed pink vials to my mage mates. They drank greedily to curb my emotions projected through our bond.

Henry approached with a steaming mug. "Hot cider?" When I did nothing, he set it on the end table beside me. "If you change your mind."

I didn't.

Sometime later, Andrew carried me to the bathroom and left. Malsin entered. In a blurred series of events, I found myself washed and clothed in a nightgown with his assistance. Andrew returned, lifted me into his arms, and went to my room. The glow of green magic sent me to sleep.

Nightmares of the battle with the Mazika held me in their icy grip. I watched in horror as Red thrust his fiery sword into Stefan's lower back. I shoved my hand out. *Kill.* Rainbow fire streamed out. It engulfed Red. He collapsed, becoming a charred pile of bones. The skeleton rose and formed into Stefan. Blood spurted from his wounds. "You killed me!"

I woke screaming at the top of my lungs.

The door burst open. Andrew, Braidus, Joshua, and Malsin rushed in. Andrew leapt onto the bed and pulled me into his arms as I cried and shook. My eyes faded to darkness. The dream repeated. I awakened again, a loud cry tearing out of my throat. Andrew and Braidus lay on either side of me. I trembled with tears running down my cheeks, barely registering their murmurs of assurance. When Andrew turned on his magic, I cringed with terror.

Braidus clutched me to him, leaning us away from Andrew. "Sleep isn't helping."

"I see that." Andrew turned off his magic.

Braidus stroked my hair. "The Gods have been especially cruel."

"Yes," Andrew agreed, his tone as equally dark as his brother's.

For the first time, I didn't feel his jealousy or frustration over Braidus holding me against him, treating me like his sweetheart. Andrew was changing. I didn't have the energy or heart to question it.

I held still and silent for the rest of the night. Liquid leaked from my eyes like a dripping faucet. I refused to close them except for occasional blinks. My mage mates remained by my side. Each kept a hand on me, offering silent comfort as they returned to slumber. Despite their presence, I could not be consoled. I wanted Stefan and Nathan alive so much that I physically ached.

As the sun peeked through the curtains, Joshua entered. Andrew and Braidus sat up, having been awake only a few minutes.

"How is she?" my brother asked quietly.

"She hasn't rested. She hurts," Braidus answered.

Malsin entered. Braidus moved off the bed to allow him to check me over. "Let's see if we can get her to the kitchen. She could use something to eat and drink."

"She should recharge her magic as well," Braidus said. "It's low."

Nobody asked what I wanted.

Andrew carried me down the stairs and sat me on a dining room chair like an invalid child. Falden and Dominic appeared to be trying their hand at cooking. They leaned over several pots and pans on the stove.

Henry approached, lifted the lid off something, and sniffed. "I think you're supposed to stir this."

Dominic cursed and grabbed a spoon. "Let's see you manage breakfast."

"No, thank you." Henry lifted his hands, backing off. "A Sorren is never expected to use a stove."

Falden shoved Henry. "Stupid royal."

A small squabble broke out between the three of them.

King Brian spoke in a firm tone from the other side of the table. "Boys."

All three immediately fell silent.

"Henry, assist your friends."

"Yes, Uncle," Henry replied dutifully.

Dominic grinned with satisfaction as he handed Henry a spoon covered in a tan glop. Henry made a face as he snatched it. Minutes later the two presented us with a slightly scorched meal of oatmeal, ham, and a kettle of tea.

Malsin set a bowl and mug in front of me. "Eat, Isabelle; we're not going to lose you too."

I couldn't bring myself to do anything.

Eight concerned faces focused on me. My eyes flicked from one person to the next, searching for the two people I knew I'd never see sit at this table again. Stefan and Nathan belonged in this rustic farm kitchen, not a crew of highborn nobility and royals. It wasn't right that Stefan and Nathan didn't get to be here. It wasn't fair that the Gods thought it fit to rob me of *two* precious loved ones. Why couldn't I have saved them? What good was all my power if I failed to keep Stefan and Nathan safe? Silent tears welled and spilled over. I hurt so Gods-forbidden much.

Andrew spoke in a strained voice. "She needs more time."

King Brian responded, his expression grim. "We can't give it. I need her well and able to help us against the Dregans. It's her magic alone keeping them at bay. I'm sorry, but her time to grieve will have to wait."

He met my eyes with sorrow. It occurred to me that he too had lost a friend in Nathan, and yet, as king, he had to soldier on for the benefit of Aberron. I thought of all the men in the First and Second Waves we'd lost already during this war and all those remaining who were forced to live on without a friend or brother. They too had to grieve later. The necessity of keeping the rest of Aberron safe demanded it.

With shaking hands, I reached out and grasped the hot mug. I brought it to my lips, sipped, and then grimaced. The boys couldn't even make apple tea properly. I stood, grabbed the kettle, and dumped it out in the sink. I replaced it with fresh water and spices and put it on the stove.

Dominic, Falden, and Henry wore shameful expressions. "Sorry," they said in unison.

I shrugged. When the kettle whistled, I swapped out everyone's tea with mine and returned to my seat. The men sipped with strong appreciation. I couldn't bring myself to eat anything, but I finished my drink.

As breakfast came to a close, Joshua vacated to gather reports for King Brian. Before he left, he stopped by me and pressed a kiss on the top of my head. "Love you, little sister."

I managed a brief, small smile.

King Brian tasked Dominic, Henry, and Falden with cleaning up.

Malsin took me in hand to ensure I got ready for the day. "I'm keeping a close eye on you, regardless of whether you want it or not."

Once we had dressed suitably for being outside, Malsin made me recharge all colors of magic. I used gold sundals for purple. Boomer woofed and danced excitedly with the newfound energy. I resented it.

Back inside, I sat on the couch in between my mage mates. Silence reigned for some minutes. Joshua returned. King Brian occupied Nathan's soft leather chair, and the boys took seats from the kitchen.

"What news?" King Brian asked.

Joshua sat in the remaining open seat. "The Dregans pounded on Isabelle's shields all night, even detonated a small Mazika bomb, but they have, obviously, been unsuccessful in breaking through. Her rainbow shields are the strongest magic I've ever seen. Our men have returned from Prastis after escorting two Dregans we held as prisoners to their ship with our message for King Cekaiden."

Braidus spoke. "With how many men Isabelle captured, we should expect a response in person. Cekaiden will want to meet the mage responsible to see what kind of deals he can make."

King Brian leaned back, his elbows resting on the arms of the chair, the tips of his fingers touching. "So we hold our position. Cekaiden has thus far ignored all our attempts at communication. He will have no choice now if he expects to get his brigades back."

Murmurs of agreement went out from the men.

"How long do you think it will take for Cekaiden to get here?" Joshua asked Braidus.

"He could reach Prastis as quickly as tomorrow," he said. "Cekaiden has a small keep in the heart of Dreskenar that he's rather fond of. I would not put it past him to have been staying there throughout our war—close enough to give orders but far enough away to keep him clean from battle. The man cannot abide any filth."

"The sooner he comes the better." King Brian centered his gaze on my brother. "Anything else?"

Joshua nodded. His emerald eyes flicked to me. "Our men are worried sick over Isabelle. She is their main topic of conversation. I could not go two paces without someone asking about her well-being. They wish to offer her comfort in any way they can."

"Not only has Isabelle captured the Dregans but my army as well," King Brian mused.

The men softly chuckled.

"Well, I will not ask her to do anything that is not absolutely necessary."

"I think a survey of her shields and perhaps a better heat dome would be prudent," Joshua said. "We may need a few tiny holes to shove things through to the Dregans. Food and such."

"Agreed. I'd like to keep the Dregans alive." King Brian rose and faced me. "Would you please accompany me?" He held out his hand.

I took it, allowing him to lift me. He placed my hand in the crook of his arm. Together we descended into the tunnels with the rest of my family following behind. Lounging soldiers jumped to their feet. They put their hands over their hearts and bowed. The hall became eerily quiet. King Brian paused to take it in.

"Your power abounds," he said in awe. "They show their respect to me." He inclined his head. "But this is for you." He put his hand over his heart. "They stand in solidarity with you."

Oh. I saw gratitude and devotion on the men's faces. With so much pain coursing through my heart, I didn't know how to feel about the soldiers' respect.

We began walking again. King Brian nodded at his men, acknowledging them. I shrank from the attention, no doubt appearing like a small and frightened child in the midst of battle-hardened warriors.

We climbed up the ladder into Mr. Layder's fields. Aberronians spaced about ten paces away from each other lined my shield that were keeping the Dregans contained. The prisoners roared and pounded on the walls when they caught sight of me. Anger and grief hardened me.

We stopped a good twenty paces away.

King Brian let me go. "All right, Isabelle, work your magic."

I caught sight of a thin red heat dome covering the top of my shield. I doubted that it did more than keep the temperature above freezing for the Dregans. I activated my power and lifted my hands, strengthening the heat dome and letting it pour down the sides of my shield. I increased the temperature to that experienced on a comfortable spring day. I saw fear and wonder on the Dregans' faces at the change.

Joshua used his hands to indicate how big he wanted the holes to be to send things through. The second I began to create one, a Dregan shot an arrow through at me. I decimated it before it could make contact. Closing the space, I turned to my family.

King Brian spoke. "Let's hold off on creating pockets. I suggest we use yellow mages to drop things in from above."

The Dregan archer moved to the forefront of the shield. "Braidus!" he shouted.

"Gavin." Braidus's voice was cool.

Gavin began speaking in rapid Gaitian, gesturing to his comrades as he did so. Braidus approached and listened. They appeared to have somewhat of a civil conversation.

Minutes later, Braidus returned to his father. "They ask to be released with a promise to concede to the better warrior." He nodded in my direction.

Joshua snorted. "The minute that shield is gone, they'll attack again."

"It is true they are taught to die before forfeiting," Braidus agreed, rubbing his bearded chin.

"We let them out and they'll run straight to Isabelle," Andrew said. "They know they could be formidable again with her gone."

Henry spoke. "Guys, this shouldn't even be a question. Let them sit in there until we can come to peace with Dregaitia."

King Brian spoke. "Of course, we're not going to let them go. This is casual speculation. King Cekaiden needs to understand Aberron's might before he thinks about sending his men here again. We're also still in the dark as to who wanted us to fight in the first place. I'm not letting anyone leave until those questions are answered."

"Gavin is insistent that we started the war with the attack on their Dreskenar port," Braidus said. "They were ordered to seek payment by acquiring the southeastern province by any means necessary."

"Izabel!" Danovic appeared at the front of the shield next to the archer.

He had survived our last battle. For a moment, my grief lessened. I was glad he had made it. I started walking over to him.

Braidus followed and raised his eyebrows in surprise at me. "You legitimately made friends with Danovic?"

I nodded.

Stopping in front of Danovic, I placed a hand on my shield and looked up at him. He pressed his hand on the other side as if to touch mine. He spoke to me in soft Gaitian.

Braidus translated. "He calls you a remarkable soldier and asks what you plan to do now that you have conquered."

"Make peace with Dregaitia," I said. "I do not want to fight anymore."

Braidus repeated what I said to Danovic in Gaitian. The Dregan archer beside him snorted as if he didn't believe me. I rolled my eyes, not caring what he thought. Danovic spoke.

Braidus said, "He asks why you attacked the Dreskenar port if you did not wish to fight."

I shook my head. "I do not know why that happened, nor does my king. I wish it didn't." I gestured to him. "I see a great and mighty warrior before me. You prove that Dregaitia is powerful. It is folly for Aberron to start a fight with you." I put a hand on my chest. "I am angry at whoever attacked your port and got us fighting."

Danovic grinned at me with evident delight as he heard Braidus translate my praise. He spoke rapidly, his eyes searching.

Braidus said, "He asks, if they promise not to fight you, can they be released."

Great. They wouldn't fight me, just everybody else. "My king must decide, not me."

Danovic frowned as he replied.

Braidus said, "He asks if you will talk to your king."

"I will." I dropped my hand from the shield and stepped back.

Braidus and I returned to King Brian and the rest of the family.

"What did you find out?" King Brian asked.

He repeated the conversation I had with Danovic and then said, "I've never seen a Dregan soldier more enamored with a woman." Braidus wore a bewildered expression.

"I want you to connect with Isabelle and search the Dregans' minds," King Brian said. "See if they are hiding something pertinent."

"As you wish." Braidus's hazel eyes met mine with gentleness.

I activated my magic and melded us together. I retreated my mental presence to a small corner and tucked myself into a ball. My magic was needed more than I was in this case. With Braidus's guidance, I tuned into Gavin's thoughts. A stream of strong Gaitian flowed. After a while, Braidus indicated that we should leave Gavin's mind and try someone else's.

We spent a good while riffling through Dregan minds, searching for anything useful. The rest of my family left to see to other matters, leaving Braidus and me alone with a few soldiers on guard. After some time, Braidus indicated he was finished. I ended our connection, and we returned to the tunnels to report to King Brian.

"Did you find anything?" King Brian asked as we arrived.

Braidus flipped his long hair over his shoulder. "No. Every Dregan I listened to fully believes we are the enemy who instigated this war. Many think we lured them here to be captured by Isabelle so we may invade Dregaitia with no opposition."

"I have no interest in conquering Dregaitia," King Brian said firmly. "Aberron is plentiful enough."

"Indeed," Braidus said, and others concurred.

"Plan?" Andrew asked.

King Brian spoke in a sure voice. "We wait for King Cekaiden of Dregaitia."

CHAPTER SEVENTEEN

NEAR EVENING, I SAT on my hands and knees viciously scrubbing the kitchen floor. My fingers cramped, my muscles ached, and exhaustion threatened to do me under. Despite the taxing pace on my body, I refused to relent. Malsin sat at the table, keeping an eye on me while writing in his journal. We'd returned to my house while the others remained in the tunnels managing things. I'd thrown myself into work, cleaning everything in sight, organizing, and cooking. I hadn't given my hands a second to rest.

Henry popped his head in. "Hey, I came to check on . . . how long has she been at this?"

"The floor, thirty-five minutes. Labor in general? Since we came in five-and-a-half hours ago," Malsin answered. "New plan is to work herself to death."

"And you haven't—" Henry started.

"No, she has been resistant," Malsin cut in. "Perhaps you can get one of her mage mates to calm her. Oh, and inform King Brian dinner is warming in the oven."

"Right." The cellar door opened and closed with Henry's exit.

I found a particularly stubborn dark stain. I rubbed mercilessly, becoming increasingly agitated when it wouldn't budge. It didn't occur to me until I'd put considerable effort into it that it would never come out. The memory came fast and sudden.

Nathan came into the house with his arm dripping crimson.

"I told Tobias that metal was second rate," he growled.

"Nathan!" Adel cried.

Blood slipped down his elbow and splattered onto the floor. It was a long scratch but not deep enough to need stitches. Adel and I hurried to patch him up. By the time we finished, the blood he'd lost had dried into the wood. Upon realizing this, he'd apologized profusely. "I'm sorry. I've gone and mucked up your nice kitchen."

"No matter. It's just a testament to living." Adel placed a soft kiss on his lips.

Nathan chuckled. "You're the Gods' gift to me, Adel. I love you."

I started at Andrew's touch, coming out of my memory. He crouched in front of me, hand on mine, lips set in a grim line. Liquid dripped down my chin. It took me a second to realize I'd been washing my face with tears. He took the rag from me and placed it in the bucket of soapy water. I got to my feet, wincing at the soreness I felt. Turning, I noticed the rest of my family had entered the kitchen. I went to the oven and pulled out dinner.

Andrew stopped me before I could do anything else. "Let someone else handle it."

He led me to a chair and made me sit. He sat beside me and wrapped his arm around my shoulder. I leaned against him, shut my eyes, and fell fast asleep.

I dreamed of the white courtyard with the magical tree. The moon and stars lighted the tree. Black lines oozed up the trunk and along the limbs. Many different colored leaves fell from the branches and turned black as they touched the ground.

It's dying.

Where was the Creator? Shouldn't he be doing something about this?

To the right of the tree, I discovered a large glass sphere. Something was inside it—frozen. A figure with golden hair, a beard, and bright-blue robes. A sense of familiarity overcame me. Oh Gods, the Creator.

I woke to morning light and Haldren standing beside my bed. He waved his hand. The world went black for a second. I stumbled as I regained my footing.

The cold wind bit into me. The two of us appeared near the maple tree by the creek: my favorite spot in all of Saren. Two headstones resided beside the tree. *Nathan and Stefan.*

Haldren spoke. "Their spirits are safe in the Realm of Souls, but here lie their bodies. Soothe your heart." He disappeared.

I dropped to my knees and put a hand on each marker.

I closed my eyes. "I'm sorry," I whispered. "I'm so sorry . . ." Even though a Mazika member had run his sword through Stefan and an undiscovered bomb had killed Nathan, I couldn't shake the belief that it wouldn't have happened if I had been more proactive. If I had just worked harder and figured things out quicker, I could have prevented their deaths.

A memory whispered through my mind.

"You worry too much, Iz."

I rested my head on Stefan's shoulder as we nestled against our maple tree on a warm summer night. Together, we watched the sun sink lower in the sky, shooting out rays of pink, orange, and yellow.

"And you don't worry enough," I answered.

He chuckled, flashing me his wry smile. "Guess we even each other out then."

A new recollection washed over me. Nathan crouched beside me as I stared at our ruined flower bed. The sunflowers I'd worked so hard to grow were shredded.

"Isabelle," Nathan said, "sometimes you have to accept that not everything goes the way you want it to. Sometimes things happen that are entirely out of our control."

"Like the weather," I said. It was the source of the destruction of my flowers.

"Exactly," Nathan agreed. "We pick up the pieces and start over." He handed me a new packet of seeds. "It'll take a bit of work and patience, but it'll be beautiful again, just like you."

Something inside me shifted as I came back to the present. A warmth seared my soul. At that moment, I knew without a shadow of a doubt I had the support of everyone I loved, whether mortal or spirit. I could get through this. I *would* get through this. No one was truly gone if I kept them in my heart.

As the sun beckoned, I rose, feeling lighter. I returned home.

Joshua stood on the front porch when I arrived. "Where have you been?"

Using purple magic, I relayed Haldren's appearance, where I'd been, and what had occurred.

Joshua swallowed me in a hug. "Whatever you need, I'm here for you too. I love you, little sister."

"Love you, brother," I answered quietly.

Henry popped his head out of the door. "Hey, is Isabelle up to making breakfast? Uncle Brian is ready to take on the task himself."

I nodded, giving him a tentative smile.

His eyes widened briefly, then he grinned. "Excellent."

I hurried to change and wash up and then tackled breakfast. The mood in the house drastically changed for the better as I moved about more like my old self. I still didn't speak much, but I was actively trying to be present.

As I handed King Brian a mug of hot chocolate, he put his hand on my arm and said, "You have my admiration for your efforts to overcome so much in such a short time."

I gave him a small smile. "Thank you."

One of Joshua's lockets glowed. He picked it up. "Report."

A man's voice floated out. "A Dregan ship has just been sighted docking at Prastis. It is different from the others we've seen. It bears red and gold sails."

Braidus spoke. "That is Cekaiden's ship. He had to be in Dreskenar to get here so quickly."

"Good. Perhaps we can put this mess behind us," King Brian said.

As breakfast ended, Joshua received another report. "A Dregan has ridden out of Prastis. He calls out for Aberronians."

"See what he wants," Joshua said.

While I washed dishes, the soldier contacted Joshua again. "They have brought King Brian's missive. The Dregans have written on the back of it." A pause, then, "King Cekaiden is requesting to meet with King Brian."

"Allow him passage to Saren," King Brian said.

Black emotions rolled through the bond. I sucked in a sharp breath. Braidus hated King Cekaiden something fierce. Considering that he had forced Braidus to marry Kiella and then murdered her, I could not blame him.

I dried my hands and touched Braidus's shoulder. He stiffened, clearly having not expected me. He tilted his head to see me.

"Support goes both ways," I said.

My chest eased as he released some of the darkness binding him. "Thank you, Isabelle."

I returned to the sink, distinctly aware that he would rather I stay at his side. While he had my friendship and, admittedly, a portion of my heart, I still did not wish to cultivate a romance with him. I had Andrew as my betrothed.

We received word that afternoon of a Dregan party approaching Saren. The men put on their armor before stepping out of the house. No one trusted King Cekaiden. My armor had been destroyed in the battle, but I had my magic to protect myself. My family and a large group of soldiers rode to the very edge of town and stopped at a cluster of trees. We could not see the approaching Dregans yet.

Tension nearly choked me. I spoke to my mage mates. "I'm not going to be able to breathe if you both don't relax."

"Sorry." They apologized and worked to dislodge some of the stress.

An Aberronian soldier cantered to us. "Five minutes."

King Brian spoke to me. "Isabelle, go hide among our soldiers. I don't want the Dregans to see you just yet."

I turned Nisha around. The men parted to allow me through. I stopped in the middle of the group, close enough to see everything but far enough away not to be noticed amongst the soldiers. Silence reigned apart from the occasional random cough, horse snort, or tail swish. The men around me sat alert, backs straight in the saddle. Their eyes darted to me more than I cared for. Within those brief flashes, I saw a fierce desire to protect me. I had the distinct impression these men would lay down their lives for me.

I inhaled sharply. My hand flew to my heart. Pure hatred rolled through the bond like a sudden hurricane. King Cekaiden of Dregaitia had arrived. I clenched my jaw, wanting to kick whomever thought bonding Braidus to me was a good idea.

"Lady Isabelle," a soldier beside me whispered. "Are you all right?"

I nodded stiffly.

"Greetings. I am King Brian Callen Sorren of Aberron."

I thought I would have to strain my ears to hear King Brian speak to the Dregan royals, but he spoke loudly. I assumed the Dregans had stopped some paces away.

"King Cekaiden Mikyle Zayne of Dregaitia," a deep but smooth voice answered with a thick Dregaitian accent. "Braidus, it is good to see you. I must say I am surprised to see you with your father. The execution block has not caught you yet."

"Old grievances have been put to rest," Braidus said curtly.

"So it would seem," King Cekaiden concurred. "Where is the woman mage? I want my people released."

I arched an eyebrow. Woman mage? Certainly he'd heard my name by now. The Dregans had captured me twice.

"You may have your men when peace is achieved," King Brian answered.

"Peace?" King Cekaiden scoffed. "You attacked my port. You wished for us to fight."

King Brian spoke sharply. "I am no fool. Your army is legendary. I have no wish to see Aberron or Dregaitia conquered. Someone is playing us."

King Cekaiden said, "Are you suggesting that *I* would attack my own port, kill *my* people, and blame it on Aberron so we could invade you? I want justice for the destruction your people caused!"

"I'm not accusing you," King Brian said calmly but firmly. "However, I am sure *someone* is orchestrating this. If we continue our attack on each other, we'll both lose to the real perpetrator."

There was a pause, and then King Cekaiden said, "I see no other perpetrator but you. You will give me my people and pay for your crimes with the southeastern province."

Braidus spoke in rapid Gaitian. Some sort of argument in that tongue broke out. His dark aggravation had me gasping for breath. An impression of Kiella laughing flowed through my mind, followed by an expression of total shock. I could only see her face, but I knew Braidus was remembering the way she'd looked after Cekaiden had plunged a knife into her heart. I could tell it had been totally unexpected by her and Braidus, who'd witnessed it.

The pain that came with these recollections felt as fresh and raw as my own for losing Stefan and Nathan. Braidus was going to make me lose it in front of everyone—and then I would be no good for King Brian when he needed me. Unable to take it any longer, I nudged Nisha forward. Aberronians moved to let me through, showing concern and interest.

Peeking through the men, I saw a host of Dregans sitting upon horses a good fifteen paces away. The sun glinted off a gold crown on the head of a man with coal-black hair. *King Cekaiden.* He cut an imposing figure, clad in white furs and gold spikes and sitting atop a massive horse that rivaled Nisha in size.

My heart boiled with Braidus's rage.

I rode into view. "Enough!" I yelled, voice dark and merciless. "It doesn't matter who started the war; this ends *now*!"

King Cekaiden's entire demeanor switched from anger to surprise. "What's this? Your woman mage is a child!"

The Dregans behind him wore complete disbelief as if they couldn't fathom losing to me.

"I'm not a child," I spat.

"Isabelle," King Brian cut in.

"Your age, child?" King Cekaiden asked.

"Seventeen," I answered.

Coal-black eyes bore into me with new interest. "I want to see the famed warrior. Show me your magic."

I didn't think twice. "I don't show my power to satisfy curiosity."

King Cekaiden raised an eyebrow. I doubted he'd ever been told no in his life. His eyes flicked to King Brian. "Are all Aberronian women so disrespectful?"

King Brian eyed me with something akin to cherished annoyance. "You'll have to forgive Lady Isabelle. This war between us cost her two precious lives, her father's and her best friend's. She harbors much anguish in her heart."

I felt a fresh wave of pain at the reminder of my losses and struggled not to show it.

"Hmm . . ." This seemed to mollify King Cekaiden.

King Brian reached over and put his hand on my arm. "Perhaps it would be best if you left the talking to kings."

I was too angry to feel embarrassed over the obvious setdown. "Fine, but if King Cekaiden isn't interested in working things out, I have no problem rounding them up like I did the others. One way or another, I will have peace."

"Don't worry; your determination matches mine," King Brian answered.

King Cekaiden spoke to King Brian. "You do not control her?"

"Isabelle has power like unto the Gods," he answered in a frank tone. "I am lucky she chose to come to my aid."

King Cekaiden frowned, clearly disconcerted. "We will talk, but first, I must see my people."

King Brian lifted his hand, palm up. "Allow me to escort you."

Joshua barked orders. Aberronians moved to the side to allow the Dregans passage, and then they brought up the rear, effectively keeping the enemy in our sights. I rode on King Brian's left. On King Cekaiden's right rode a young man who resembled him, a prince I suspected.

I sucked in a lungful of frigid air as I tried to keep my composure. Sharp stabs of pain accompanied every heartbeat. After trying hard all morning to keep my own monsters at bay, I had the sudden urge to dig my fingers into my flesh and rip my heart out to avoid the agony. I received strong impressions of different ways to shove a sword through King Cekaiden. I gripped the reins tightly to avoid giving in to Braidus's temptation.

Arriving at Mr. Layder's fields, King Cekaiden widened his eyes at the magic I had wrought. He spoke something to his son, his tone shocked. His son responded in an equal tone. They stared at me with wonder. I shivered at the attention. King Cekaiden dismounted, prompting the rest of us to follow suit. He and a small party of Dregans approached my shield. The rest of us stayed back.

King Cekaiden addressed his men. At first, they talked over each other while repeatedly pointing at me. He raised his hand. They shut their mouths. He spoke again. Gavin answered, speaking for the whole.

Malsin put his hand on my shoulder. Quietly, he said, "You're trembling."

"It's Braidus," Andrew explained, watching his brother translate for their father. "He struggles to see his father-in-law."

"You can feel your brother through the bond?" Malsin asked with a hint of surprise.

Andrew nodded. "When his emotions are this strong, yes, but I don't feel it as acutely as Isabelle."

"Interesting." Malsin then spoke with regret. "Alas, I am out of emotion suppressors."

I bit my lip as I experienced the intensity of volatile emotions coursing through my heart. Andrew and Malsin watched me carefully.

"You're his mage mate; calm him down," Malsin advised me.

"It's taking all my effort not to murder King Cekaiden myself," I responded tersely. "I don't know how Braidus is not doing it."

Andrew gave me a little nudge. "You'll think of something. Go."

I scrambled for a plan as I walked over to Braidus. Nothing immediate came to mind. No words or . . . I hesitated. "Gods, forgive me." Not thinking twice, I cupped Braidus's face, brought him down to my level, and kissed him. Pure shock consumed me head to toe, and then Braidus's soft, sensuous lips moved with mine in perfect symphony, a collaboration of two souls playing the same melody. His grip tightened around my waist.

My hands moved to wrap around his neck, fingers fisting his long silky hair. Passion ignited my soul like a blast of lightning.

Braidus pulled back; our breaths were rapid but soft.

Seeing the question in his eyes, I said, "A good memory to keep the demons at bay." I untangled myself from him, my heart on fire but for entirely different reasons from before.

Andrew appeared beside me, rubbing his chest. "Not exactly what I had in mind. Gods, that overwhelmed me."

I didn't detect much jealousy—which again brought me to the realization that Andrew had become more accepting of giving Braidus a chance to win me over. What I mostly sensed out of Andrew was him doing his best to adjust to the feelings Braidus brought out in me.

Seeing that Andrew wasn't too upset, I shrugged. "Well, it worked."

Braidus frowned at hearing about the setup. A bit of the heat cooled. I knew I should be ashamed for using him that way, but I wasn't in the slightest. That kiss had rocked me to the core. Panic had begun to set in over how good it had been.

"Too well," Andrew rumbled. I felt his sudden fear that Braidus would best him in laying claim to me.

King Brian spoke, his eyes on his son. "Andrew, I think you should reconsider your engagement with Isabelle in light of this bond. Braidus is as much Isabelle's soul mate as you are. He deserves a chance to claim her heart as you have. Learn to share her until she can make a fully informed decision between you two."

A pause, then, "A dual courtship until one comes out the winner?" Andrew asked.

"Not a bad idea," King Brian mused.

Wait what? "Hang on, I only kissed Braidus to calm him down."

Braidus spoke out of the corner of his mouth. "Your intentions might have been to distract me but it doesn't explain your strong desire to do so again."

I flushed. "I'm suffering from a momentary lack of judgement brought on by your encouragement. Don't read into it."

King Cekaiden approached and centered his coal-black eyes on me with an unreadable expression. "I hear you are impossible to kill. A one-woman army capable of world dominion."

I spoke firmly. "My only agenda is peace."

"And is the peace you are searching for to be found after you have conquered?" he asked.

I bristled. "I don't want to conquer anything. I hate power and attention."

King Cekaiden gave me a look that clearly said he thought I lied.

I gestured to the land around us. "Saren is my home, and I would like to return it to the solitude I'm used to. Speak with King Brian, come to a peace agreement, and then return to Dregaitia with your army. I have no plans to be a force unless Aberron is on the brink of destruction again."

He leaned forward. "If you think you can melt into the shadows after this, you are sorely mistaken." He straightened, eyes darting to King Brian. "I will not be coerced into an agreement. You are still the enemy in my eyes."

"Understandable," King Brian said briskly. "Isabelle, don't harry King Cekaiden. He has legitimate concerns."

I took a breath and exhaled. Braidus's darkness had started to creep up again. "I apologize. Emotion is clouding my words."

"As it is with females," King Cekaiden said.

"Bonded females," I muttered.

King Cekaiden heard me. Apparently, Dregans—or at least this one—had excellent hearing. "Bonded?"

King Brian gave me a sidelong glance that clearly said to be silent.

I looked at him apologetically. I hadn't meant my words to be heard.

"Isabelle shares an Amora bond with my sons, Braidus and Andrew."

"Is that so?" King Cekaiden's eyes narrowed, though his tone belied interest. "Two men to one woman. How is that possible?"

"We are unsure. It is a recent development and a shock to us all," King Brian answered.

King Cekaiden spoke frankly. "So much power now woven into your monarchy. I find this unsettling."

"As would I if I were in your place," King Brian responded. "Unfortunately, it is not reversible. Isabelle managed a consultation with the Goddess Amora to remove it. She inspected the bond and said there was nothing she could do." He shrugged. "It is permanent."

"Hmm." King Cekaiden wore a troubled expression. Honestly, I couldn't blame him.

King Brian turned to me. "Isabelle, would you be so kind as to prepare an area for King Cekaiden's men to rest for the night?"

"Of course."

I switched on my magic and shot into the sky. Next to the trapped Dregans, I created a heat dome and melted the compacted snow. I dropped down to the earth and sent out green tendrils of power, searching for dormant grass seed. Rich green strands sprouted and covered the ground like a soft blanket.

I returned to King Brian. "Anything else?"

"No, thank you, Isabelle," King Brian said.

Glancing at the position of the sun, I noted I needed to return home and check on dinner. My eyes darted to King Brian and King Cekaiden. "If you two feel safe enough with each other, may I please be excused to take my roasts out of the oven?"

King Cekaiden gave a small nod.

King Brian smiled good-naturedly. "Go ahead, Isabelle, and expect more for dinner."

I saw envy in King Cekaiden's eyes as I walked to Nisha and swung up. I couldn't wait to get the Dregans out of here.

CHAPTER EIGHTEEN

'D JUST TAKEN TWO loaves of bread out from the oven when King Brian entered through the back door with King Cekaiden, his son, and two other Dregans. The rest of my family piled in after them.

King Brian spoke. "Welcome to Lady Isabelle's home."

The Dregans observed the kitchen and dining area with mild interest. One showed outright disdain, as if he had become used to better accommodations. Saren *was* a farming community; he couldn't expect a castle.

I gestured to the table. "Please have a seat. Dinner will be ready momentarily."

I grabbed Braidus's arm, pulling him aside, and asked, "Who's who?"

Braidus quickly pointed out King Cekaiden's look-alike as Prince Kendar. "He is the second son, so he will only become king if his brother Timtric dies. He has the most casual attitude out of all of Cekaiden's children."

"Is that good or bad?" I asked.

Braidus shrugged. "It makes him unpredictable."

Next was General First Drekaris, a massively built Dregan with strong features. Everything from his forehead to his chin seemed prominent. "To claim this position means challenging the current general first to a fight to the death. Drekaris has fought off many men to keep his position and is the longest-standing general first in recent history. He is a favorite of the royals, which is why Cekaiden probably kept him out of the war. Rumor has it Drekaris is set to retire in the new year. It will be a first."

I fought not to shudder at the thought of killing someone for a job. "So barbaric."

Last was General Second Leeson, the man who showed repugnance for my home. I found his appearance in tones of brown unremarkable. After a second thought, I decided he reminded me of Muddy and shuddered. It appeared he too had escaped the execution block, considering Braidus told me he had started a rebellion with Kiella.

"Why is Leeson here?" I asked. "You said he was a part of Kiella's rebellion."

"He was." Braidus looked confused too. "I don't how he regained Cekaiden's favor, though I've never met a Dregan more persuasive than he is."

"He looks even less happy to see you than the others," I noted as I watched him glance our way and scowl.

Braidus nodded, clearly not surprised. "He has never liked me."

To accommodate everyone, Dominic, Falden, and Henry took a small table and chairs from the library and joined them with the kitchen table. Meanwhile, I sliced the bread and transferred it to a platter for easy grabbing, then set it on the loaded table.

I went around filling glasses with a cold cider, the last task on my to-do list before eating. I felt the Dregans' eyes on me wherever I went.

King Cekaiden commented, "One would think with so much power, the normal duties women take on would be beneath her."

King Brian answered, "On the contrary, Isabelle finds great comfort in it. In addition to protecting us in battle, she has ensured we are housed, well-fed, and sustained. I find her cooking particularly excellent."

I doubted the Dregans had ever discovered such a mystery as I.

Settled beside Joshua and Henry, I said, "Please eat."

The Dregans waited until my family delved in before tasting. Eyebrows subtly rose in what appeared to be pleasant surprise.

During dinner, King Brian and King Cekaiden kept up a casual conversation about industry. Prince Kendar's expressive coal eyes roved from my birthmark to my face. He had classically handsome features with thick black locks.

King Cekaiden leaned over and said something to his son in Gaitian, his eyes darting briefly to me. Kendar responded in a tone that sounded like agreement. Both of them turned their attention to me and watched silently. No doubt I had become the object of their study.

Drekaris focused on my brother. "You are Aberron's general first?"

Joshua nodded. "I am."

"I wish us to fight, general to general." Drekaris's face lit up with anticipation.

Joshua smiled as he shook his head. "Thank you, but I wish to live."

Drekaris laughed. "A wise general knows when to pick his battles."

Leeson remained silent, but his eyes were watchful. I got the impression he was memorizing every person and artifact within his sight. The only purpose I could think of for this was that perhaps he worried I had a trap set for them. Of course, that was the furthest thing from the truth, but I doubted there was anything I could say to ease him. I would probably feel wary too had I been in a foreign country, like Dregaitia. Occasionally, I caught Leeson glaring at Braidus as if he wished to squash him like an uninvited bug to the dinner table.

Braidus, on the other hand, kept visualizing stabbing his dinner fork into King Cekaiden's heart. I imagined confiscating Braidus's utensils and shoved that idea through the bond with as much force as I could muster. He loosened his grip on the fork. Catching my eye, he switched his focus from the Dregans to me.

I choked on my drink as his desire to kiss me consumed my heart.

Joshua pounded me on the back.

"Sorry," I gasped, cheeks flaming.

I waited until the conversation picked up again before I shot Braidus a steely glare. *Not going to happen again.* The single kiss we had shared scared me to death. It had confirmed my feelings of real attachment when I still desperately wanted to deny them.

Andrew patted Braidus's shoulder with a conspiratorial "tough luck" expression. Braidus frowned, but his amusement came through the bond. I had the sense he felt confident he could lower my defenses with some strategic planning. He knew he tempted me. He didn't doubt that he could eventually win me over. *I've got to get out of here.*

Unable to stomach another bite, I began gathering dishes to take to the sink.

This diverted King Cekaiden's attention back onto me. "Truly a woman that does all."

"Indeed," King Brian agreed.

King Cekaiden's eyes followed me about the room. "For too long we of the east have looked upon Aberron, noting its abundance of fertile lands, wealth, and magic. Perhaps a truce may be made if Aberron would be willing to share its resources.."

I sucked in a breath as my mage mates' possessiveness squeezed my heart.

King Brian followed King Cekaiden's gaze to me. "I would be delighted to open trade agreements between our people. I do not, however, speak for Isabelle. That right falls upon her brother Joshua, my commander, and my son Andrew as her betrothed." King Brian gestured to my brother and Andrew.

"Is that so?" King Cekaiden asked, his eyes flicking briefly to Joshua and Andrew then back to me. "As king, don't you have the power to intervene in an Aberronian's affairs?"

King Brian nodded. "Yes, but I prefer not to."

My stomach clenched at King Cekaiden's questions. What would he ask of me to ensure peace between Aberron and Dregaitia? My determination for peace outweighed my self-preservation. I was willing to be sacrificed if it meant saving Aberron. Andrew's and Braidus's unease wrapped around my heart. Both were paying close attention to the bond, gleaning impressions of my thoughts. I had the distinct impression that neither liked my steadfastness in preserving Aberron over myself. This wasn't something I would budge on though. One person did not matter more than a whole country.

Joshua spoke. "Isabelle dictates her life entirely. Her magic is strong enough to give her that power. She chooses to abide by mine and King Brian's guidelines solely out of respect."

I looked over my shoulder at the men as I put my hands in soapy water. "My brother is right. If you wish to do any business with me, ask me directly, please." Despite being willing to put Aberron above myself, I would do my best to avoid that scenario. I had no problem advocating for myself should I end up needing to negotiate.

Someone rapped at my back door. I quickly dried my hands to answer it. Nisha stood on the steps of the porch. He snuffled my face. *"Carrots please."*

I chuckled softly. "Sure, Nisha." I retrieved a handful from a basket on the counter. To the men, I said, "Please excuse me for a minute."

Most of the men nodded good-naturedly. Leeson wore a subtle frown that quickly changed to impassiveness when he realized I noticed. I mentally shook my head as I stepped out and shut the door behind me. Something about that man didn't sit right with me. Then again, most Dregans made me uneasy.

I tucked Nisha back into his stall and gave him his treat. Other horses poked their heads out. Some whinnied at the sight of food. Our cow Suzy mooed. I grabbed a tin of treats and fed the others.

My mind strayed to the Dregans, and my desire to find peace with them flared brightly. When I got back inside, I would ask them directly what I could do to see this accomplished. I hoped it would be something manageable and, if not, oh well. I had to see harmony achieved.

Assured the animals had all they required, I returned to the house.

Stepping through the door, I came face to face with Leeson. His arm swung toward me as I lurched to a stop to avoid running into him. I registered a flash of silver before my body went cold in shock. I looked down. Red bloomed through my clothes, surrounding a dagger in my chest.

Leeson sneered. "Not so powerful after all." He caught me as I started to fall. "You will die with the others. Kiella's revenge."

He lay me on the floor.

Boomer! I screamed. He flashed in front of me, barking wildly. *Knock out.* Leeson crumpled, landing over the lower half of me. I turned my head. The still forms of my family, along with King Cekaiden, Prince Kendar, and Drekaris, lay on the ground around the table. I felt nothing from the bond but the frantic beating of my own heart. *Gods, please don't let them be dead.*

I reached out and touched Dominic. With his breathing slow, his heartbeat irregular, he faded fast. *A toxin.* I sent tendrils of green magic to lock onto every person except Leeson. *Boomer, heal.*

He whined, wanting to fix me first.

No. Adrenaline surged, decreasing the pain as I filled the men with my power. The venom was hiding. I increased the power flow. I likened the poison to a snake with rows of razor-sharp teeth. As it slithered, I imagined grabbing onto its tail and tugging with force. It snapped back at me, sinking its fangs into my magic. I gritted my teeth but held tight, pinning the toxin in place. It fought back, striking my magic with sharp stabs. Boomer growled and barked ferociously. I flooded the men with green magic. *Out!* A faint hiss sounded in my ears. The toxin disintegrated. Boomer lay on his belly panting.

I didn't have a minute to lose. Similar to the time when fiery chains had tried burning my organs from the inside out back at the Sorrenian, I found damage everywhere in the men. *Repair them.*

Leeson stirred. I switched focus for a second to restrain him. *Shield.* I wrapped him in a full-body bind, making it impossible for him to move.

Groans and rustling filled the kitchen as I finished patching everyone, excluding myself. They might be weak, but they were alive. *Safe.*

Dominic sat up beside me. His eyes widened in alarm. "Isabelle!"

Panic slammed into my heart. Chairs scraped as people pushed them out of their way.

"Knife in her chest!" Dominic yelled.

Leeson's dark brown eyes popped open. He wiggled. I'd long lost feeling in my legs from his weight.

Awareness lit into him. He roared, his expression mottled with rage. "Release me!"

"No," I choked.

Dominic and Drekaris rolled Leeson off me. Andrew and Malsin pressed their hands on me. Andrew put my head in his lap.

"Stay with me, Isabelle," Malsin said.

I shut my eyes, too tired to fight anymore. Voices faded to indecipherable murmurs. The darkness of death appeared in my mind's eye. I found its presence warm and welcoming. I craved the respite death willingly offered. It wouldn't hurt anymore if I just let go.

Soft lips pressed against mine, sending a jolt of lightning to my heart. My eyes flew open. Braidus withdrew. Andrew slowly pulled the blade out of me. The adrenaline of green magic surged through my body as he and Malsin healed me. My heart tugged as Andrew used some of my stores.

I searched for Braidus's gaze. "Don't kiss me again."

"Don't try to join death," he countered, his hazel eyes alight and intense.

"Finished," Malsin said, lifting his hands.

Andrew helped me sit up. Wrapping his arms around my middle, he kissed me thoroughly.

I pulled back, a light protest on my lips. "Hey."

His blue eyes blazed. My pulse quickened as I nearly lost myself in their gorgeous depths. "You told Braidus no, not me."

I cursed.

Malsin chuckled. "I'd say she's all right now. Gods, that was close."

"When isn't it?" I asked rhetorically.

"If we had been a minute late, we would have lost you," Andrew said, his voice thick with emotion. My near-death experience bothered him more than his own. His expression grew stern. "Don't you dare try to welcome death again. I can't lose you—I just can't."

"Neither can I," Joshua said.

My heart flared hot with Andrew's and Braidus's censure and fear. I read the same feelings on my brother's face as well as on Malsin's.

"Sorry," I whispered.

I got to my feet, albeit a little unsteadily. The men stood with me. King Brian, Henry, King Cekaiden, and Prince Kendar had managed to get themselves back into their chairs. Drekaris stood over Leeson, both wearing matching expressions of anger and disgust. Falden and Dominic poured cups of red liquid on the ground outside the door. I noticed a new clay jug had been placed on the table, probably containing the poison that nearly murdered everyone.

I stared at the bloody mess I'd made on the floor. Not wanting another stain, I grabbed a bucket hiding in the corner and filled it with soapy water. I heated it with red magic, then got on the floor to wash it. Guilt ate at me for not trying to fight to live for my family's sake. I couldn't be so selfish. Yet I also held deep anger that I had been saved again when Stefan and Nathan hadn't. Tears pooled in the corners of my eyes. It wasn't fair. My knees hurt, my fingers cramped, and my heart ached. Still, I pressed on, not caring that I saw no traces of red anymore. In my mind, all I saw was a mess.

Henry crouched and stole the rag out of my hands. "Stop. It's clean." He put the rag in the bucket and helped me up.

King Cekaiden and King Brian questioned Leeson.

"I demand an explanation for your attempt to murder us," King Cekaiden said, his tone harsh.

I appreciated that he spoke in Fraison so that everyone could understand. Leeson only glared.

I took that as a sign to speak up. "He said to me that our deaths would be Kiella's revenge."

King Cekaiden looked at me sharply. "You are certain?"

"Yes," I said with conviction. "Perhaps he meant to restart the rebellion?" It was the only thing I could think of that might explain this.

King Cekaiden turned back to Leeson. "Is that what your intentions were?"

Again, Leeson remained silent.

"Speak the truth and I'll make your death quick," King Cekaiden said.

After a moment, Leeson answered. "Yes."

"Did you commandeer an Aberronian ship and attack the Dreskenar port to start this fighting?" King Brian asked.

Leeson nodded. "Yes."

"Why?" King Cekaiden and King Brian asked simultaneously.

"For revenge and honor for Kiella." Leeson's tone darkened to venom as he eyed his king. "She should have been mine. Instead, you gave her to a weak Aberronian who refused to support her in her plans for Dregaitia. Braidus did not wish to see Kiella's new Dregaitia come to fruition. He never intervened on her behalf and let you kill her for treason. I vowed I would see Aberron and Dregaitia pay for her life. You were all meant to die so I could take over both countries and rule in Kiella's honor. Dregaitia and Aberron would be no more and New Kiella would rise to take its rightful place."

Braidus's anguish squeezed my heart like a vice. Silent tears flooded down my cheeks as his grief made mine all the stronger. My hand went to my heart, fingers digging into my cotton shirt. I fought against the urge to run—to find an escape from this agony through whatever means possible.

Andrew wrapped his arms around me from behind. Gently, he pried my hand away from my chest. "I've got you," he murmured.

I didn't have the words to speak, so I leaned into him, needing his support.

King Brian had his hand on Braidus's shoulder, and I was grateful he had someone to rely on too. The sadness of losing a loved one was difficult to manage alone.

"Do you think I wanted to execute Kiella?" King Cekaiden asked Leeson rhetorically. "I did not. I grieve every day for the loss of my daughter." He pounded his chest. "She had the world and my heart at her disposal, and she chose to commit treason. The law decrees that the punishment for that is death. I had no choice. A king must uphold all the laws, even if it pains him."

King Brian winced, and I suspected this conversation brought up memories of Braidus's treason. The law for that crime in Aberron was death as well. Unlike King Cekaiden, King Brian had made an exception for

Braidus. It was a good thing he did, too, considering Braidus was innocent and a Fate over Fates had pulled the strings. I imagined that decision had plagued King Brian for many years. How many people, or even himself, saw him as a weak king for not upholding the law like King Cekaiden had? How many times had King Brian wished Braidus's treason had never happened and that he wouldn't have had to banish him?

I admired King Brian's benevolence. He had pardoned me for my crimes of robbing the royal treasury. He could have stuck to the letter of the law and executed me, not caring that I had stolen to save Henry. Yet I also saw little reason to fault Cekaiden for upholding the law. There were rules for a reason, and if no one paid the consequences for breaking them, then no one would follow the laws in the first place, and chaos would run rampant. I mentally shook my head. What a difficult position to be in as king.

"Have you done anything to hurt my other children, Timtric and Sarkyah?" King Cekaiden asked Leeson.

"Not yet," Leeson said. "I planned to dispose of them after you."

King Cekaiden turned to Drekaris. "See that Timtric and Sarkyah are accounted for and safe."

"Of course." He pulled a locket from under his shirt and walked to the other side of the room. Lifting the locket up to his face, he spoke in rapid Gaitian.

King Cekaiden turned to Braidus and stated, "You truly had no part in Kiella's treason."

Braidus's voice rang clear. "I did not."

"I have misjudged you," King Cekaiden said. "I offer my apology."

Braidus inclined his head in acknowledgment. Through the bond, I felt his surprise. This must be a first.

Drekaris returned. "Timtric and Sarkyah are safe. I have increased their guard."

King Cekaiden nodded with relief. Prince Kendar also appeared reassured.

King Cekaiden announced to King Brian, "It is time we end this war."

"I agree." King Brian smiled.

"I must address my people about this." King Cekaiden's eyes flicked to me. "Please remove the shield around Leeson, but keep his hands bound."

With a flick of my fingers, I did as he ordered. Drekaris lifted Leeson to his feet and shoved him out the back door. King Cekaiden, Prince Kendar, and my family followed. King Brian held out his arm. I slipped mine through his and exited.

King Brian spoke, his tone mild. "While at times you can be a handful, in moments like this, I am reminded of what great courage and strength you possess. I thank the Gods for the extended magic they blessed you with and for your willingness to use it selflessly. I wish to thank you from the depths of my heart for saving our lives this night."

My heart warmed. "You're welcome."

We went to Mr. Layder's fields. King Cekaiden addressed his men in Gaitian. Those trapped in my shield pressed against it to hear. Braidus said, "He's explaining Leeson's treachery."

Mixed feelings of disgust, anger, and sadness came through the bond. I took Braidus's hand, entwining it with mine. He smiled softly, grateful for the comfort.

King Cekaiden turned to me and said, "Lady Isabelle, would you join me?" I stepped forward. Braidus came along too, refusing to let go. King Cekaiden gestured to me while he spoke in rapid Gaitian.

Braidus quietly explained. "He's showing them the evidence, your bloodied shirt."

The Dregans looked upon me with wonder.

Danovic cheered. "Izabel!"

I couldn't help but grin back. King Cekaiden raised an eyebrow as he looked at me and Danovic.

Drekaris then shoved Leeson to his knees. King Cekaiden reached for a blade.

Leeson looked to Braidus and spoke in our native tongue. "You were a disgrace to Kiella. She never loved you. I go now to be reunited as her true lover and protector."

Braidus's pain lashed through my heart. I buried my face into his chest and wrapped my arms around him. I didn't care to witness Leeson's execution, and Braidus needed my support. I knew Leeson's words could not be true. When Braidus opened up, I found it impossible not to fall in love with him. With startling clarity, I realized it was time to own up to the truth. I was in love with Braidus too. I couldn't try to make myself deny it any longer. A small amount of panic set in as I accepted my feelings. *Oh Gods, what have I done?*

King Brian spoke. "Remove the shield, Isabelle."

I jumped out of Braidus's arms, grateful for something to do. I dismantled the shield over Leeson's fallen form. Joshua threw a fireball, incinerating his body.

King Cekaiden spoke to his men again.

Braidus said, "He calls for a truce with us."

King Cekaiden then faced us. "There will not be any more fighting. Peace will be achieved." He held out his hand to King Brian. They shook.

Joshua took his locket out and relayed the information, asking it to be distributed amongst the First and Second Waves.

King Cekaiden addressed me. "If you would please release my people."

"You swear on the Gods, no more fighting?" I asked, hands on hips.

King Cekaiden's lips curled in amusement. "Not unless there is suitable cause. Currently, I see none."

"All right." I lifted my hands.

The shield vanished. The Dregans cheered. "Cekaiden! Cekaiden!"

I rolled my eyes as I smiled. Clearly, his efforts mattered more than mine. I didn't mind though. The less attention on me the better.

"Thank you, Lady Isabelle," King Cekaiden acknowledged me before stepping forward to converse with his people.

Henry, Dominic, and Falden joined me.

Henry grinned. "Congratulations, Isabelle; you saved Aberron."

Falden said, "Aberron's Lady Champion."

Dominic yelled. "Cheers for our Lady Champion!"

Surrounding Aberronians answered Dominic's call, fists raised in the air. Their excitement was infectious, and a surprised laugh escaped my lips. I wished Stefan and Nathan were here to see this—to celebrate with us.

I put my hand on Henry's arm. "I'll meet you guys at the house. I've got somewhere I need to be." At his nod, I shot into the sky and directed the wind to carry me to my maple tree.

I sat beside Nathan's and Stefan's resting places. I brought my knees up and wrapped my arms around them. "We did it. No more fighting." Shutting my eyes, I rested my head on my arms, grieving and gathering strength. I could almost feel Nathan's bear hugs, Stefan's laughter . . .

I sprang to my feet at the touch of a hand on my shoulder. My head spun as I searched for the threat.

Andrew grabbed hold of me. "Whoa, Isabelle, it's just us."

I blinked back tears to see Braidus beside Andrew and me. "Sorry," I mumbled.

Braidus asked, "Are you ready to come home?"

I nodded. With seemingly no second thought, they positioned themselves on either side of me and each grabbed one of my hands. I sensed complete ease between them as we walked. I knew they had become more comfortable with each other in my life after the losses of Stefan and Nathan, but I had the distinct impression something more had changed. I discovered a harmony between them I hadn't sensed before, as if they'd solved some conflict and become stronger. A conversation between them must have happened while I had been at the maple tree.

We descended into the tunnels. Soldiers scrambled to a standing position. They bowed, then straightened, wide eyes on me as I passed.

Whispers broke out. "The rumors are true; look at all the blood on her."

"Singlehandedly saved two monarchies. She's a legend."

"I heard the Dregan prince wants to put in a bid to court her."

"Dregans don't have a chance. I heard she shares an Amora bond with both princes."

"That's impossible—two men to one woman?" Multiple men appeared to be equally skeptical.

A man replied, "I happened to be walking by the commander when I heard him ask both princes to check their bond with Lady Isabelle."

"You're lying."

"Swear it on the Gods," the man protested.

"Has the Dregan prince been added to the pool?" one man asked.

"Yes, but no one's wanting to bet on him," another answered.

I stopped. Andrew grabbed my shoulders to stop himself from running into me. I swiveled around, searching for the men belonging to the voices I heard, but all had become silent. So I addressed Andrew. "I've become a bet?"

He shrugged. "It's just a bit of entertainment."

"Who's in the lead?" I asked.

He grinned. "Me."

Braidus spoke. "Confirm our bond and my odds will go up."

I rounded on him. "Seriously?"

"Betting is best when you have all the facts," he said, his tone reasoning. "Andrew's winning simply because he's crown prince. They should know you share an Amora bond with both of us to even things out."

Andrew conceded. "I'll give him that."

"What of our engagement?" I asked Andrew.

Andrew and Braidus shared a look.

"How would you feel about a dual courtship until one comes out the winner?" Andrew asked.

I stiffened. "Gods, no."

"Why not?" Braidus asked.

I spoke firmly. "It's out of the question. You two can't share me and be happy about it." I rubbed my chest. "I get enough jealousy from you as it is. I'm not going to increase it by kissing you both consecutively." Glancing away from my mage mates, it occurred to me that I was still standing in the middle of the tunnel with soldiers hardly breathing in order to catch every word. I started moving again, eager to get home and out of sight.

"Isabelle," Braidus started to petition.

I quelled him with a look. "No."

Andrew said, "Give her a minute. She'll come around."

Not likely, I thought as I pulled the knob on my cellar door.

I went to the bathroom to wash up, grateful for the separation the task would provide me. Andrew and Braidus's proposal rattled me all through the bath and dressing. How in the Gods could they have agreed? The whole thing was preposterous.

I entered the kitchen. The men sat at the table in casual conversation. Moving to join them, I stopped short at a bright flash. Haldren appeared by the stove. Talk halted.

"Haldren," I greeted.

He turned to face me. A small smile graced his lips. "Congratulations on saving Aberron."

"Thank you," I said, then added, "Perhaps thanks to you is warranted as well, considering you awarded me the power to save Aberron."

Haldren's smile grew. He inclined his head in acknowledgment. "You're welcome."

"So what brings you here?" I asked.

His expression darkened. "I came to offer a warning. My feud with Isaac grows, as does his interest in you. No, I won't tell you what our quarrel is about yet, but suffice it to say, my association with you makes you a target in our war."

I frowned. I appreciated the warning, but I didn't want to be a target, especially in a war where I was sorely outmatched and had no idea what the fighting was about.

"Isaac is testing how much he can affect me by causing pain and chaos in my dealings with the world," Haldren said. "Expect him to come after you."

"There's nothing I can do about this, is there?" I asked him.

"No," he answered with frankness in his tone. "Isaac is my superior. Once his curiosity takes hold, there is little I can do to stop him."

I sighed. Just great. Isaac had unimaginable power. I just hoped he didn't do anything to hurt my family.

Haldren stepped back so he could view the princes and me. "Now I understand you're giving your mage mates trouble."

That shifted my attention. "I don't want what they do."

He surveyed me. "That's not true."

Andrew and Braidus perked up.

Haldren smiled. "I read your reservations, but deep down your interest grows."

I didn't protest. How could I against a God who could look into my very soul?

"Embrace your bond, Isabelle," he ordered, his blue eyes flashing. "Allow Andrew and Braidus to court you. You will be better for it."

I'd barely thrown together a thought before he answered it.

"Yes, think of the dual courtship as temporary with the goal of choosing whom to marry. Both should be given ample opportunity to win your heart and experience love with their soulmate before you decide between them. It will ensure you've made the right choice for your future happiness." His lips curved upward as he turned his eyes to my mage mates. I had the distinct impression they thanked him for putting in a word, no, a command. With a nod at me, Haldren said, "I'll take my leave. Take care." He vanished with a bright flash.

I turned to my mage mates. They sat together, wearing matching serious expressions. Andrew's blue eyes blazed and Braidus's hazel eyes held an intensity strong enough to steal my breath. I read their desire and unity. Love them both. Could I do it?

Braidus spoke. "You already do."

CHAPTER NINETEEN

I STOOD ON THE SHORE of Prastis watching the Dregans board their ships. The early afternoon sun shined through a break in the clouds. I enjoyed the rays on my back. Once the Dregan army had settled in their home country, King Cekaiden planned to return with a small delegation to officially open talks between our people. I suspected I would have a heavy hand in this involvement.

I had yet to give my agreement to Braidus and Andrew about the dual courtship. They often gave me sidelong, wishful glances but knew to give me space to fully think it over. Although with Haldren backing them, I doubted I had much choice. Still, I would resist until I felt invested. I couldn't go into something like this half-heartedly.

Prince Kendar approached me. He inclined his head in acknowledgment. "I look forward to seeing you again under better circumstances."

I managed a small smile. "Yes."

He smiled softly, picked up my hand, and bestowed a chaste kiss upon it. "Until we meet again, Lady Isabelle."

"Until then, Prince Kendar," I murmured.

He grinned as he retreated to stand beside his father.

Someone placed a hand on my shoulder. I blinked, realizing I had been in a fog. I looked up into King Brian's blazing blue eyes. "Give the Dregans a little wind to push them out to sea."

I let Boomer out and relayed the instructions. I lifted my hands into the air, calling for my yellow magic to give me wind. It started slow, then gradually grew stronger. Strands of my hair whipped around my face. The waves slapped against the shoreline and the boats. Black sails filled, pushing the ships into the channel. *Guide them home quickly.*

I paid very little attention to our return journey to Saren. Andrew and Braidus rode close, heads cocked toward each other, deep in conversation. Multiple times they tugged on my heart, assessing my mood, no doubt conversing about it. Their brotherly bond seemed to be getting stronger by the minute.

At home, I sat by the fireplace in Nathan's favorite chair, sipping hot chocolate, when they pounced. They brought chairs from the kitchen and positioned them beside me. "We need to talk," Andrew said.

I read the tension in the two men and tried to steel myself against it. "Talk, then."

Surrounding conversations between other family members ceased. Braidus nodded at Andrew to proceed.

Andrew spoke. "Peace has been achieved for Aberron and Dregaitia *and* between me and Braidus." He gestured to his brother.

Braidus nodded.

I put a hand to my forehead and groaned. *Not the dual courtship again.*

Andrew plunged on, unfazed by my reaction. "You know this, feel it, even, but you're refusing to acknowledge it. You're still tense, as if expecting to go into battle any second. You have been steadfast in our engagement, and I'm grateful beyond words." He raked a hand through his hair. "I've given this a lot of thought, and I think we should put a pause on our betrothal so you can see what Braidus has to offer. I worry we'll marry and you'll second guess whether you should've chosen Braidus instead."

I scowled. "You don't think I can be faithful."

Braidus leaned forward and spoke passionately. "We are bonded, Isabelle. This isn't you forming a random dalliance."

"Exactly," Andrew agreed, glancing at his brother. "Braidus is as much your soulmate as you are mine. He has a right to stake a claim." At my lifted eyebrow, he raised his hands. "Yes, I've struggled with this, but I've come to peace with it. My heart knows you don't love me any less even though you've grown to love Braidus too."

I rubbed a temple. "I don't know."

Andrew pressed me. "Since Stefan and Nathan died and I've experienced your pain, it has become clear to me that I value your happiness above all else. To that end, I believe it is only right to see if Braidus is the better choice for you—that you may be happy till the end of your days with no regrets over whom you chose to be your husband."

I sighed. "Embrace the bond, court you both, make a decision, and then live happily for the rest of my life."

"Yes," my mage mates agreed.

Braidus tucked his long hair behind his ear. "Our feelings for each other are too strong to ignore. Agreeing to the dual courtship is simply putting a name to what is already happening within our hearts. It ensures no hard feelings when you choose to show affection to either of us."

"And us to you," Andrew added.

The earnestness wafting off the princes was hard to combat. Andrew took my hand in his and rubbed his thumb over my palm. I interlaced Braidus's fingers with mine as I read his desire to touch me. He had better restraint than Andrew.

"You both find this acceptable?"

"Until you make a decision between us and proceed to marry," Braidus said. "Any advancement afterward would be considered a serious offense."

"Agreed," Andrew said.

I bit my lip, mulling it over. Love without censure held an appeal. My pulse quickened at the thought of warm embraces and heated kisses. As much as I initially didn't want to admit it, I could easily lose myself in either prince's affection. It would be pleasurable, even painless at first . . .

Shaking my head, I pulled my hands free and wrapped them around my stomach. "You make it sound so simple, but I know it won't work that way. You saw how hard it was to maintain a friendship with Stefan after I turned him down. We both hurt, even if it was the right thing to do. H—" I choked on sudden grief. "Hearts will be shattered."

Braidus didn't hesitate. "I'm willing to accept that for a chance with you."

Andrew straightened. "As am I."

I read sincerity in their eyes and felt it through the bond. They were serious about this. Their pleading pulled on my heart. I sighed, not entirely sure I was making the right decision. "All right, I'll do it."

Andrew smiled. Braidus grinned. I jumped as their excitement sent a thrill of adrenaline through me.

"Finally," King Brian said with an exasperated smile in our direction.

"Indeed," Malsin agreed sagely.

Falden, wearing a gleeful expression, held out his hand to Dominic. He grudgingly reached into his pocket and paid Falden a sundal. I held back an eye roll. It figured.

Henry shrugged as if this was of no consequence. "It's not like it wasn't already happening. She's kissed them both already."

Joshua said, "It's an improvement for her to acknowledge it."

"Yes," all the men agreed.

"What about embracing the bond as well?" Braidus asked.

I made a face. Hadn't I already agreed to enough? "How connected do you think it will make us be?"

Andrew shrugged. "I believe it's only supposed to improve your impressions. Nothing more."

"You're sure?" I asked. "No other hidden surprises?"

"Not that I know of," Andrew said, resonating with sincerity.

"Me either," Braidus said.

Gods help me. "Fine, we'll try it."

"Let's do it now while Isabelle's in an agreeing mood," Braidus said to his brother.

"Definitely," Andrew agreed.

Both turned eager, expectant gazes on me. I rolled my eyes, but my mouth twitched with a smile. "What do I need to do?"

Malsin spoke. "Try turning on your magic, think of your bond, and express your desire. I don't know if it will improve your impressions. It could just be a false rumor, but it's worth discovering."

"All right." Turning on my magic, I stood and tugged on my mage mates' hands until they rose. My gaze flitted between the two of them. "Braidus Alexander Sorren, Andrew Brian Jason Sorren, my princes of Aberron." I took a deep breath and then exhaled, letting go of my resistance and filling myself with compliance. I turned my thoughts to our bond. "I embrace you both as mage mates to me."

My powers sparked. The cords that bound my heart to the princes' materialized with vibrant brilliancy. Silver nautical rope interlaced with ruby, sapphire, and gold, glittering in an ethereal glow, wrapped snugly around our chests. Smoky ribbons of all colors of magic swirled around us, above our heads and down to our feet. Our hearts pounded against our ribcages as three singularly erratic beats melded into one.

My eyes burned from the radiance as the magic faded. I blinked rapidly, seeing spots. My hands cramped under Braidus's and Andrew's tight grips. I shifted uncomfortably and they immediately loosened. Braidus's and Andrew's eyes gleamed. Their joy stole my breath for a few seconds. I felt them acutely.

"It worked."

Braidus's lips curved into a smile. "We are wholly united."

I blanched. "Gods forbid, I've practically just married myself to you both, haven't I?"

The room erupted in laughter.

"Only emotionally," King Brian said, grinning like a proud father. His blue eyes turned severe. "Sons, don't get any brilliant ideas like I had with Hannah until one of you is standing in front of the high priest with her."

"Same goes for you, Isabelle," Joshua warned.

"Seriously?" I raised an eyebrow. "I don't think I'm going to be a problem."

Braidus snickered.

I turned on him. "What?"

"Sometimes your desire for Andrew overwhelms me." He turned his snickering into a cough as I shot him a dark look.

"Her passion is my favorite thing about her." Andrew's blazing blue eyes danced. "Especially when it's directed at me."

Braidus patted his brother on the back with a wolfish grin. "Enjoy your time living on the other side of that passion, brother."

I spoke loudly, cutting through whatever Andrew had planned to retort. "I think I've heard enough. Good night, all." I grabbed my now cold cup of hot chocolate and exited.

I woke an hour or two before sunrise. The Dregan battles and Stefan and Nathan's deaths had haunted me all night. Exhaustion settled in the marrow of my bones. The tears I'd cried in my sleep had stained paths down my cheeks. Knowing I'd return to the nightmares, I found it pointless to try to rest. I picked out some clothes and descended to the bathroom. I washed and dressed quickly, then went to the kitchen to get a start on the day. Braidus entered as I pulled ingredients out to make bread.

"Good morning," I greeted with a tired smile.

"Is it morning?" He made a show of looking out the window to the dark sky. "I was under the impression it is still night."

I rolled my eyes. "It will be soon enough."

He moved to my side. "You have no respect for your body. You should be resting, not working."

I placed the jar of yeast on the counter. "I couldn't sleep."

"I can feel your exhaustion," he said, pointedly.

"I'm not going back to bed," I told him, jaw set.

His frustration bit at me, as did his need to see me taking care of myself. I pleaded with my eyes. No amount of sleep could fix me. I couldn't go back to the horrors of the dream world.

He sighed, relenting. "Then allow me to keep you company." He wrapped his arms around my waist, pulling my back snugly to his chest.

"Thank you," I murmured, relieved.

"You're welcome." He kissed the top of my head. "Gods, you smell good." He buried his face in my hair.

I laughed softly. His delight warmed me from the inside out. "Happy, are we?"

"Immensely," he said.

While measuring out the ingredients, I said, "I fail to see how I can bring you or anyone happiness, since my dominant trait is getting into trouble."

"You do attract trouble," he agreed, his tone musing. "But I think my favorite trait about you is your ability to make people feel alive. You bring fresh air to a stagnant room. Every part of you, from your appearance to your personality, rivets people's attention. Men grow taller in your company."

I turned to meet his eyes. "You think so?"

"I know it."

The conviction in his eyes caught my breath. My skin tingled. My stomach fluttered. I quickly turned around to focus on the bread.

"I make you nervous even after your declared feelings. Why?"

I sprinkled flour on the counter and dumped my dough onto it. "Have you looked at yourself? You're a force to be reckoned with." I dug my hands into the sticky mixture. "You're cunning, with years of world experience. You're a skilled mage and fighter. I seriously think you can accomplish anything, and if that isn't enough, you're also exceedingly handsome. With all that you are, how am I not supposed to be intimidated?"

"You put too much importance on my abilities," Braidus answered. "I am just a man, an imperfect one."

"No, you're more than that."

"You see Andrew as a man over a prince; why can't you do the same for me?" he asked.

"I still struggle with Andrew's importance to Aberron," I countered, kneading the dough. "You're harder because I keep thinking of you as a mountain lion and me as prey. A helpless bunny or something."

Braidus laughed, his voice rich and melodic. "You are by no means a helpless bunny. You should think of yourself as a majestic eagle soaring over Aberron with sharp eyes and talons—a power in the sky and on land."

"An eagle, huh?" I left the dough to rise and grabbed the kettle.

"For certain," he replied. While waiting for the water to boil, he enfolded me in a hug.

I breathed deeply, inhaling his exotic citrus cologne. He brought his hand up and tucked my hair behind my ear. I shivered.

Leaning down, he whispered, "Don't be intimidated. I am a simple man, falling in love with you."

Braidus opened his heart to show me the depth of his feelings. I gasped as my chest flooded with love—a fiery warmth that would have knocked me to the floor had he not been holding me. His lips brushed against my earlobe and trailed across my cheek, finding my mouth. He kissed me with a feather touch until I responded, bringing my hands to cup his face and tug him closer. His mouth claimed mine with the ease and conviction of a man in love. It resonated down to my very soul.

The kettle whistled. Braidus pulled back, reached over with one hand, and pulled it off the heat. He kept his other arm securely wrapped around my waist, holding me upright. My legs had become mush, and my breathing was unsteady.

"I've overwhelmed you," he murmured.

"It's fine," I rasped.

He chuckled. "Sit. I'll make tea." He lifted my feet off the floor and set me in a chair.

A minute later, Andrew entered the kitchen. I sensed mild annoyance. Abruptly, I regained my faculties and stiffened.

"Andrew." Braidus nodded at his brother.

"Braidus." Andrew returned the gesture.

"Tea?" Braidus asked.

"Please," Andrew responded, coming to the table.

Braidus set three cups down.

Andrew reached over and grabbed my hand. "Isabelle, will you calm down? I'm not here to rip into you."

"But—"

He cut me off. "Braidus should've been convincing you to go back to sleep, not romancing you at an absurd hour. You need the rest. We *all* need the rest."

I spoke adamantly. "I'm not going back to sleep."

Andrew's displeasure intensified.

Braidus spoke. "Short of knocking her unconscious, I couldn't think how to make her go. It is better for someone to watch her when she is awake, lest she finds herself in a scrape."

"Granted." Andrew raked a hand through his hair.

I knew a good portion of his irritation stemmed from lack of sleep, which I had caused. I switched on my magic and washed away his tiredness with a boost of energy. Then I did the same for Braidus. Andrew's mood shifted slightly for the better. I went to check on the bread.

Andrew spoke to his brother. "The sooner we return to Carasmille, the better. This place is not doing Isabelle or us any favors."

"Agreed. Perhaps she would sleep better in a different environment."

"What do we have left to do before we can go?" Andrew asked.

My heart clenched, drowning out Braidus's response. *Leave Saren?* I knew I would be made to go eventually, but so soon? I was hoping for a little more time. I couldn't leave Nathan and Stefan yet.

"Love." Andrew stood behind me. He wrapped his arms around me and pulled my hands down, making me aware that I'd been gripping my chest, digging my fingernails into the flesh. "I know it's hard, but we've got to get you better. You're not doing well here."

"Out of sight, out of mind," I whispered.

"No," Andrew gently disagreed. "I'm not telling you to forget them. I'm simply hoping a change of pace might help." When I said nothing, he added, "Stefan and Nathan would want you to remember them but not drown in grief. They'd want to see you living and taking care of yourself. I don't see you doing that here."

I bit my lip, understanding his reasons, but unable to fully commit. Andrew pressed a kiss to my cheek. "Trust me, please."

"All right," I agreed softly.

My heart leapt with his relief. "Thank you, Isabelle."

Andrew and Braidus sat at the table and planned our departure. I began preparing food to take with us. When King Brian and Joshua arrived, the princes laid everything out. Admittedly, I didn't listen to a word of their plans. I did, however, hear King Brian's response, posing little to no objection. Joshua gave orders to his men through his lockets.

Over breakfast, Braidus said, "News of Isabelle's powers will surely spread. We must turn some of our attention to what is to come."

"Agreed," King Brian said, setting his teacup down. "The people will want to see Aberron's Lady Champion."

"We must be careful. Many may seek her out," Andrew said, buttering a slice of bread.

I frowned. Every fiber of my being scorned their considerations. Braidus reached under the table and took my hand in his.

Joshua spoke. "I suggest we assign guards to Isabelle."

I objected. "I don't need guards. I can take care of myself."

All eight men looked at me with complete disbelief. Not a single one believed me.

Henry said, "When has leaving you alone ever worked out in the past?"

I set my jaw. "I don't want guards."

"What if they were people you know?" my brother asked.

"Who?" I had a limited social circle.

The corners of my brother's lips turned up. He jerked his thumb at Dominic and Falden. They raised their eyebrows.

"I assume you're not going to want to break up 'the family' upon our return. They've proven themselves to be capable soldiers and seem to be good friends with you. Let's offer them jobs and rooms at the castle."

"They are high-ranking nobles," I argued. "I'm sure their families would consider those roles beneath them."

"Not necessarily," King Brian said. "They would receive a handsome wage and be able to sit in on any major proceedings you're involved with, along with joining us for family meals, activities, and such. Their families could consider it an apprenticeship at the table of the king."

Falden spoke, wearing a good-natured smile. "That would be very appealing to my parents. I'm not due to inherit much as the youngest of four sons. I have to forge my own path if I want to meet my usual standard of living."

Dominic grimaced. "My mother would balk if I told her I was a guard, but she'd jump at an apprenticeship with the royal family. She's always trying to figure out how to elevate our status. Sometimes she complains I wasn't born a girl so I could secure Prince Andrew's hand."

Pure disgust showed on Andrew's face.

"Then consider this arrangement to be apprenticeships with a heavy investment in keeping Isabelle safe," King Brian said.

Dominic and Falden nodded. "I accept," they said.

It still didn't sit well with me. "But they'd really be my guards. Don't you think that's a bit deceiving?" I asked.

Joshua spoke. "All I want is a few pairs of eyes on you when I or your mage mates can't be there. Someone to alert help if something goes wrong. If or when nothing crazy is happening, they'll get a real education like you and Henry were meant to have before the Dregan war started."

Henry grinned. "We'll stick together like in the Sorrenian days. It'll be great."

His enthusiasm made an impact on me. "Fine," I agreed.

"Excellent." Joshua smiled. "I will be assigning extra men to guard you outside of the castle grounds." His face grew stern. "No objections."

I frowned but said nothing, knowing it would be pointless to argue. I was the most powerful mage alive, trained in defense, and they treated me like a breakable ornament. It grated my nerves.

Braidus murmured in my ear. "Do not fret. We have your best interests at heart."

"I know," I responded softly, working hard to dislodge my irritation. I pulled my hand free and stood. "If you'll excuse me, I've got somewhere I need to be." I didn't wait for a response as I walked out the door.

Snow fell heavily as I took to the sky, making it hard to see. I'd never seen so many snowstorms one after another in my life. What an unnatural winter. Pure muscle memory got me to my maple tree. I descended and rested my back against the tree, gathering strength beside Nathan and Stefan's resting place.

A few tears escaped as grief threatened to drag me under. I knew it would be some time before I returned. Perhaps never. I shut my eyes and searched through my memory for the warmth of their love, reminding myself that their souls lived on. A sliver of warmth flickered and went out, leaving a cold ache to linger in my heart.

I jolted at the touch on my shoulder. A soldier stood in front of me. "My lady?"

It took me a second to recognize the man. *King Brian's messenger.* "James?"

"You've remembered." He wore a soft smile. "Your brother sent me to fetch you. We're prepared to head out once you're ready."

"Oh." I blinked, trying to regain my bearings. A good finger length of snow coated me.

James held out his gloved hand. "Allow me to offer some assistance." I let him pull me up.

"Thank you," I murmured.

Joshua waited for me on the front porch. He helped me pat off the snow on my clothes before I went inside.

"Who's going to take care of the animals?" I asked quietly.

"A regiment of soldiers will be remaining in Saren for a bit," he said. "They will see to the livestock."

"All right."

I tried not to think as I packed a small bag. My family waited on their mounts as I led Nisha out of the barn. I quietly settled into place between my mage mates. Their eyes centered on me, showing concern. As we began our trek, I let my love for home burn to ash and blow away with the wind. That part of me would never be recovered.

We arrived at the camping ground in the Trivail forest well after dark. Snow had fallen the entire ride and still continued to come down. It made our travel slow and arduous. I had done my best to protect the men and their mounts from the elements with a red ribbon of heat above their heads to keep them warm. Now hovering over the camp, I dried out the ground and made a heat dome. The falling snow evaporated against it. It would keep us warm and dry for a night.

The soldiers cheered. "Lady Champion!"

I shouted back, "It's just Isabelle! I'm nothing special!"

The men laughed good-naturedly. Every person I passed on my way to my shack bowed with deep respect on their faces. "Lady Isabelle."

I acknowledged them with a nod and a small smile.

Andrew said, "I'm putting you in a deep sleep tonight. No dreams. I want to ensure you get a good night's rest."

"Fine," I agreed.

As everyone settled in for the night, Andrew held my hand. My eyes faded to darkness. I dreamed I stood in a stone room where a single torch was lit. I could hear the flames dance. I sensed a realness to the room, like the dreams I experienced with Haldren. Searching for him, I turned, then froze.

Isaac stood before me. Haldren's warning that he would interfere played in the back of my mind. I braced myself for something unpleasant.

Isaac walked from behind me to face me. "Calm yourself, Little Champion. I am no crueler than Haldren."

I beg to differ, I thought, raising an eyebrow. *Haldren didn't murder my parents or get Braidus banished for a crime he was innocent of.*

"No, his disruptions are subtle, woven through with logic and need. Mine are not," Isaac said, no doubt reading my thoughts. "However, Haldren's machinations have and will alter you far more than anything I do to you."

"Are you saying Haldren is a greater threat to me?" I asked with some hesitancy.

The conviction in his voice rang clear. "Yes."

My stomach twisted with unease, confusion, and concern. "But you have greater power. You are a Fate. Haldren is not."

Isaac smiled. "Indeed, but it is not I who set you on the path to become Aberron's Lady Champion."

I shrugged. Sure, I didn't enjoy the amount of attention my extended magic gave me, but it had saved Aberron from Dregaitia, so I did feel a measure of gratitude for it.

"Granted." Isaac inclined his head, still reading my thoughts. "You are mistaken if you think Haldren extended your power for the purpose of saving Aberron though. He cares little for its survival."

Dread curled low in my belly at his statement, and yet, I believed Isaac enjoyed baiting me. I tried for nonchalance. "Whether he does or not, I am still grateful he afforded me the power to save Aberron."

Isaac tilted his head a smidge, his sea-green eyes assessing. "Would your gratitude to Haldren change if you knew he is the reason you have two Amora bonds?"

I stilled. "Haldren bonded me to Andrew and Braidus?"

Isaac nodded. "He narrowly escaped death's grasp to do it—but enough talk of Haldren. I brought you here to show you something." He cupped his hands together and then opened them, revealing a large bead of water. "Take it." He dropped it into my palms.

I brought it up to my face. A scene formed. I saw my house in Saren under a clear blue sky. In the practice area behind the garden, Nathan and Stefan fenced together. They appeared healthy and unscathed. Blades swinging, they laughed heartily. An unexpected smile graced my lips. A memory?

Isaac spoke. "No, this is happening right now in the Realm of Souls."

Surprise flitted through me. The Realm of Souls?

"It is patterned after our living world," Isaac explained. "Souls judged worthy are free to do what they enjoyed in their mortal life in a familiar setting."

Abruptly, Nathan and Stefan dropped their arms, letting their swords hang at their sides. They turned as if to greet someone. Except no one came. Their gazes seemed to lock on to mine. My breath caught. Did they know I could see them? They both smiled in welcome, and I knew they felt my presence whether they could see me or not.

Pain lashed through my heart that I couldn't have them with me. Their expressions dimmed as understanding seemed to cross their faces. I read a touch of wistfulness and regret in both. Exhaling, I pushed my heartache away, not wanting to dwell on what couldn't be changed. My chest burned with my love for them. Their smiles grew into grins, and I could've sworn I felt their reciprocating affection. With a subtle nod to me, they lifted their weapons and returned to practice.

The bead of water vanished. I dropped my hands and met Isaac's gaze. Curiosity took hold. Why had he shown me this?

Isaac answered my thought. "Haldren paints me as a villain and warns you of me. I wish to show something different."

He wanted me to think better of him just as Haldren desired me to believe his meddling was to my benefit—to make me stronger to survive what the world threw at me. "Why do you and Haldren involve me in your feud?" I couldn't understand why two beings of immeasurable power would care to involve a mortal like me.

"Because we both seek to recruit you as our weapon," Isaac said. "The Gods are going to war."

THE END

Note to the Reader

I really appreciate the time you took to read Fate Challenged; I am thrilled you chose to add it to your home library. If you enjoyed reading this book, it would mean the world to me if you would do two things for me.

1. Share on social media or tell your friends about my books.

2. Leave an honest review by simply visiting my website:

www.ScribbledReads.com
click on the series,
click on the book you read, and
click the "Write a review" button,
or email me your review Tara@ScribbledReads.com

Thank you. Your reviews, and support help me to write more new worlds scribbled in ink!

Tara Lytle

ABOUT THE AUTHOR

    Tara Lytle is the talented author behind the captivating Fate Series, and enthralling Matching Series. She draws inspiration from her love of clean young adult fantasy and paranormal romance. With a steaming cup of hot chocolate, her Spotify playlist, and an open word document, she embarks on crafting worlds where love, adventure, and epic fantasy intertwine. Tara Lytle's passion for the genre fuels her creativity, resulting in two completed series in the last three years and more novels on the horizon. If you're seeking enchanting tales that transport you to new realms, her books are a delightful choice! Visit: www.ScribbledReads.com

OTHER NOVELS BY AUTHOR TARA LYTLE

THE FATE SERIES

FATE NOT CHOSEN
FATE CHALLENGED
FATE CONQUERED

THE MATCHING SERIES

MATCHING FEATHERS
MATCHING FOXES
MATCHING FIRE